MURDER:
THE MUSICAL

T ♭

ANNETTE MEYERS

MURDER: THE MUSICAL

PERFECT
CRIME

A PERFECT CRIME BOOK

DOUBLEDAY
NEW YORK LONDON TORONTO SYDNEY AUCKLAND

A PERFECT CRIME BOOK
PUBLISHED BY DOUBLEDAY
a division of Bantam Doubleday Dell Publishing Group, Inc.
1540 Broadway, New York, New York 10036

DOUBLEDAY is a trademark of Doubleday,
a division of Bantam Doubleday Dell
Publishing Group, Inc.

Grateful acknowledgment is made for permission to reprint an excerpt from "Recuerdo" by
Edna St. Vincent Millay. From *Collected Poems,* HarperCollins. Copyright 1922, 1950 by
Edna St. Vincent Millay. Reprinted by permission of Elizabeth Barnett, literary executor.

Library of Congress Cataloging-in-Publication Data

Meyers, Annette.
    Murder : the musical / Annette Meyers. — 1st ed.
       p.   cm.
    "A Perfect crime book."
    1. Wetzon, Leslie (Fictitious character)—Fiction.
    2. Smith, Xenia (Fictitious character)—Fiction.
    3. Women detectives—New York (N.Y.)—Fiction.
    I. Title.
    PS3563.E889M87   1993
813'.54—dc20   93-3244
                                                  CIP

Book Design by Patrice Fodero

ISBN 0-385-42592-9
Copyright © 1993 by Annette Brafman Meyers
All Rights Reserved
Printed in the United States of America
September 1993

First Edition
1   3   5   7   9   10   8   6   4   2

10/98

FOR MY FRIEND FRANK PRINCE,
WITHOUT WHOM THERE WOULD BE NO CARLOS.

IN LOVING MEMORY.

A U T H O R ' S N O T E

I appreciate the time and input from a bountiful group of theatre friends who helped with sources and advice and memories.

Stephen Finn and David Colfer of the Colonial Theatre in Boston; producer Elizabeth I. McCann and Jeff Bieganek; Mary Bryant, Shirley Herz and Philip Rinaldi, publicists; Ann Ledley of Actors Equity; lighting designer Richard Winkler, Steve Terry of Production Arts; Joan Fisher; and Fran Lewin.

And my thanks go to the many who preferred to remain anonymous. But let me hasten to add that despite all the help I received for this novel, there are no real-life counterparts lurking behind my fictional cast of characters, all of whom are, in every way, purely the product of my imagination. For the purposes of verisimilitude, however, I have occasionally referred to well-known Theatre people, and, with some minor physical changes, I have borrowed the Imperial Theatre, where *Les Miserables* is currently playing, as the home for my fictional *Hotshot: The Musical.*

Further thanks to Josip Novakovich; Cathi Rosso; Linda Ray; Gail Shapiro; Detective George Lotti, Boston Police Department; Michael Levy, M.D., of Mt. Sinai; Russell Perreault of Doubleday; my agent, Chris Tomasino; Marty, who keeps me honest; and my wonderful editor, Kate Miciak, who encouraged me to go back.

I have taken a liberty by making Leslie Wetzon a graduate of Douglass College, Class of 1975. And further liberty in giving her my memories of the Class of 1955.

It's not enough that I succeed, my friends must also fail.
—Theatre saying (apocryphal,
but sometimes attributed to Gore Vidal)

There are two end products when one produces a musical for Broadway: the production and money. If you believe the play is the thing, you should get the hell out of the commercial theatre. On the other hand, if you think money is the only product, get into another business. It's easier to make money on Wall Street.
—Leslie Wetzon, partner
Smith and Wetzon

THE LIMITED PARTNERSHIP INTERESTS BEING OFFERED ARE SPECULATIVE SECURITIES WHICH INVOLVE A HIGH DEGREE OF RISK. ACCORDINGLY, THE OFFERING IS SUITABLE ONLY FOR PERSONS WHO CAN AFFORD TOTAL LOSS OF THEIR INVESTMENT.
—From the offering circular of
Hotshot: The Musical, a new
Broadway musical

MURDER:
THE MUSICAL

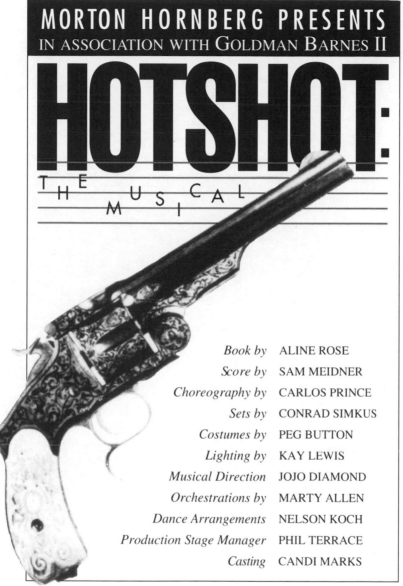

MORTON HORNBERG PRESENTS

IN ASSOCIATION WITH GOLDMAN BARNES II

HOTSHOT:
THE MUSICAL

Book by	ALINE ROSE
Score by	SAM MEIDNER
Choreography by	CARLOS PRINCE
Sets by	CONRAD SIMKUS
Costumes by	PEG BUTTON
Lighting by	KAY LEWIS
Musical Direction	JOJO DIAMOND
Orchestrations by	MARTY ALLEN
Dance Arrangements	NELSON KOCH
Production Stage Manager	PHIL TERRACE
Casting	CANDI MARKS

ORIGINAL CAST ALBUM BY COLONADE RECORDS

MUSIC PUBLISHER • HANS GREENSPAN

ASSOCIATE PRODUCER • DILLA CROSBY

PRODUCTION DIRECTED BY MORTON HORNBERG

C H A P T E R

The alley behind the theatre was dank and eerily quiet. Generations of urine, cat and human, had infused the brick and concrete with a permanent acrid stench. Hardly noticeable during the run of a hit show, the odor became all the more pronounced when the theatre was dark and infinitely worse when it rained. Above them, the fire escape climbed the outside wall like a skeletal iron vine.

The stage door was locked. A nor'easter complete with driving rain and fierce winds had been whipping the city all night. It had now calmed to an icy February drizzle verging on sleet.

Carlos kicked the steel door. "Damn!" He was tense, wired tighter than a spring.

The rain thumped on her umbrella. Wetzon shifted it to her right hand and put her arm around Carlos's shoulder. Conspicuously absent was the production stage manager, Dilla Crosby, not quite affectionately known as Killa Dilla, who should have been there to open the stage door. "It's early—"

"I told Dilla I wanted her here early—and look—no doorman—and Walt's not here to turn on lights!" Carlos stamped his booted foot in a filthy puddle. "It's all so thankless. Why do I bother—?"

"Because you love it and you know it. And you know that Killa Dilla never fails. Whatever her shortcomings, she always comes through—"

"For Mort. She comes through for Mort. And me only when it suits her. Or when it suits Mort."

Wetzon tilted her head. "My, my. Who is this paranoid person? Certainly not my best friend Carlos."

Carlos was taken aback for a moment, then gave her a great bear hug, umbrella and all. "I love you, Birdie, darling. Do you know that?"

"Hey!" The figure coming toward them was nearly hidden behind a huge black umbrella.

"Well, see, there she is." As soon as she spoke, Wetzon realized her error; she knew Dilla from the old days, and the figure under the umbrella wasn't Dilla.

"That's not the Killa, you dope. That's Phil Terrace. The ASM and utility gofer. And him you don't know." Carlos stepped out from under Wetzon's umbrella to join the assistant stage manager under his more generous one. Another figure was splashing toward them through the slush. "Oh, good. Here comes Walt. Bless us, we won't be in union violation."

"Hey, look who's here."

Walt Greenow was huge, built like a linebacker. Over the years, his shoulders had softened; protruding from his waistline was an old-fashioned spare tire. "Leslie, right?" His brown hair had crept all the way to the back of his head and was now liberally salted with gray. In spite of his size, Wetzon remembered Walt as a sweet pushover. He'd done it all over the years: props, electrics, carpentry. His face was lit by a big smile. "Have you seen the Killa? I was here earlier, but she wasn't around." He held up a huge ring of keys. "I had to get the spare from the Shuberts. They said she never returned the keys last night."

Phil looked worried. "I don't know." Phil Terrace was a serious young man with moist eyes and a dark wispy beard. The damp black fisherman's cap hid his hair. "We were supposed to meet here at eleven so we could tape the stage. She must have overslept. . . ."

Wetzon shook her head. "Killa Dilla? I don't think so. Unless, of course, she's changed radically."

"She hasn't," Carlos assured her. "More likely Mort gave her something urgent to do, like get him a milk shake, for Chrissakes."

"Hi, darling!"

"Morning all."

"Lovely day, guys!"

Three lithe young women straggled down the alley balancing stuffed-past-bulging shoulder bags and umbrellas. That they were dancers was hard to miss, for they wore their tights and leg warmers and soft low boots with a certain casual air, their legs splayed, their walk, ducky. Watching them, Wetzon felt a sharp twinge of envy.

One demanded, "Why are we standing out here in the rain?"

"That sounds like a lead-in to me," Carlos said, twirling Phil's umbrella from him and splashing a soft shoe à la Gene Kelly.

"Shit! Some asshole jammed something in here." Walt pulled a mini tool kit from the inside pocket of his shabby tan raincoat and bent over the lock. "Christalmighty, these old locks—"

"I'm going to try the front of the house," Phil announced, dashing off.

"I *needed* this?" Carlos raised a dramatic plea to the dreary sky and let the rain come down on him. "What's going on, Walt?"

"Come on! It's open!" They all looked toward the mouth of the alley, where Phil was beckoning to them.

Behind Phil, the three boy dancers who completed Carlos's chorus stood waiting, and together they all slogged through the pelting rain to Forty-fifth Street to the front of house. An unlit marquee, still heralding the last show, which had closed eight weeks before, a flop, hung like a bleak warning over the entrance.

Wetzon shivered. It was always creepy seeing the remnants of the departed . . . almost as if the funeral were over, but the closets of the dead would have to be gone through. The box office was dark, although there was probably a treasurer assigned. Previews would begin in just over a month. Box office personnel on Broadway usually consisted of a treasurer, an assistant treasurer, and one or two others, depending on the success of the show. The treasurer's particular responsibility was for the count but everyone sold tickets and answered phone inquiries.

Across the street, readying themselves for the matinee, the lights on the marquees of the Golden for *Falsettos* and the Plymouth for *The Song of Jacob Zulu* bled streamy neon raves in the rain, and if she squinted, she could just barely see the Martin Beck where the hit revival of *Guys and Dolls* was playing. Sam's, next door to the Imperial and the Broadway gypsies' favorite burger spot, thrived in the center of all this activity.

Phil was holding the center door open. Trailing wet umbrellas, they all trooped into the dark house.

"Walt, get the lights. I'm going to kill Mort, I am," Carlos muttered to Wetzon. "We're supposed to be sharing everything, and he *monopolizes* Dilla. I have to claw for every second I get."

They walked into the orchestra and the stage lights came on. The theatre secreted a musty odor, laced with ancient mold.

Inside, Carlos became considerably more cheerful. "Come on, boys and girls. I just want to go over one tiny change." He vaulted to the stage, a slim, elegant man in a black silk turtleneck under a black leather trench-coat.

Wetzon, watching him, decided he hadn't changed much since they'd been gypsies together, and dancing partners. Maybe a little line here and there on his handsome face. A little gray at the temples. He was a dear man, and they had been close for over fifteen years. She had seen him become a choreographer and he had seen her leave dancing entirely, and to his dismay, go into the Wall Street headhunting business with Xenia Smith. "I'll just wait here . . ." Wetzon stopped in front of the orchestra pit.

"You could come on stage, Birdie. I won't be long."

"Naa." If she put her feet on the stage, Wetzon thought, she might want to be twinkle toes over Broadway again. She laughed out loud, and Carlos shot her his sardonic look over one leathered shoulder.

Phil took off his wet cap and slapped the moisture out against his jeans. The assistant stage manager had a high forehead, showing the beginning of premature baldness, and a crown of kinky hair. Self-consciously, he smoothed his hair and replaced his cap. "I'd better do the tape," he said, looking around for permission.

"Sure . . . sure . . . go ahead, Phil." Carlos's attention was on the dancers and his work.

Wetzon stood for a moment looking into the desolate orchestra crypt—Oops, she thought, where was her mind? Orchestra pit. A brown paper bag lay crumpled on the seat of a chair with a broken leg, three other chairs were upended every which way. A lone metal music stand, bent out of shape, and a page or two of sheet music were all that remained of the doomed last show. The lingering smell of the sweat of orchestras past was palpable. If this were a movie, she thought, the orchestra pit would suddenly be full of musicians in tuxedos, tuning up.

Gawd, Wetzon, she told herself. It must be the rain. And Carlos was a wreck. In a couple of hours the gypsy run-through would end rehearsals in New York. Then everyone would load out for Boston. The scenery was already en route.

A faint noise brought her eyes back to the pit in time to catch a glimpse of a brown creature with bright eyes and a long tail taking flight. Yuk. Yes, when a theatre was dark, there were problems with rats. Hell, even when they weren't dark.

She walked slowly up the inclining aisle. Some of the red velvet seats were up, others down. Scraps of candy wrappers lay on the grimy floor, along with a few abandoned programs. Running her hand over a seat in the center orchestra, not quite under the shelf of the mezzanine, Wetzon sat. Walt hadn't bothered with all the lights in the house, so where she sat was dusky. The tip of her boot touched the side of an empty soda can, making a hollow sound. She bent to pick it up, but it was already on its roll down the incline toward the orchestra pit. No one seemed to have bothered cleaning the theatre after the last show folded.

The familiar ". . . five—six—*seven*—eight . . ." came with fingers snapping rhythm. Dust motes beaded around the arc of light from the stage as Carlos worked with the dancers, changing a motion, a nuance, fussing.

Phil rolled an upright rehearsal piano on stage, its innards and bare wood facing Wetzon. The nap of the seat's upholstery crunched under Wetzon's tan Burberry raincoat. The theatre was cold. A chilling draft leaching up from the floor. Walt was fiddling with the lights. On. Off. On. Off.

"Five—six—*seven*—eight . . ."

Wetzon was weary. The sun hadn't come out in over a week and the constant gloom depressed her. Her recruiting business was active, but she felt burned out, tired all the time. Smith was acting as she had in the early days of their partnership, making all kinds of decisions on her own, as if Wetzon were not her partner but an employee. And then there was her love life.

A squeaky noise, like a giggle, came from somewhere in the dark.

You may laugh, rat, she thought, swinging her legs up from the floor to the seat next to her. That was odd. She touched the seat. Damp. She rolled her head back to look at the ceiling, a concave dome containing a huge chandelier—covered with cobwebs, no doubt. Rain was coming through from somewhere. She forgot the rat and stood, her back to the stage. As she stepped out into the aisle, she noticed someone in standing room behind the last orchestra row.

At that moment, Walt turned the house lights up. Whoever had been there was gone.

The mezzanine had a sweet curve to it, trimmed with plaster cupids, nosegays, and garlands in goldleaf. A brass rail gleamed dully. And dangling from the rail was an arm encased in a cream-colored jacket.

"Walt!" Wetzon's knees buckled. She couldn't take her eyes from the dark red rivulet running down the arm and splashing on the seat next to where she'd been sitting.

"What the fuck?"

Wetzon spun around. Walt had come to the edge of the stage, shading his eyes as he peered upward. Carlos and the dancers seemed frozen in mid-gambol. All stared over Wetzon's head.

"What the fuck?" Walt said again.

Wetzon looked back at the mezzanine.

Hanging over the brass rail was the upper portion of a body, the head a bloody pulp.

CHAPTER

Phil was the first to break. The ASM bolted up the aisle veering past Wetzon. On stage, no one had moved. The horror of what they were seeing was not processing.

Wetzon started down the aisle toward the stage, then stopped. Phil's thumping footsteps echoed through the musty house like phantom knocking. "Phil, wait," she shouted, regaining her voice. "Someone—Carlos—Walt, call 911—Get the police here." She swayed, nearly lost her balance, caught herself and scrambled after Phil, then, up the aisle, past standing room. "Phil, don't touch anything!"

At the top of the mez stairs, she skidded to a stop. The light here was spare. The place stank of death and all that went with it. And Phil had disappeared. She heard voices from the stage. Someone was sobbing. "Phil!" Her voice sounded thin, but this old theatre had superb acoustics, and her call carried through the empty house.

Stomach heaving, her whole body began to quiver. She went back to the stairs and sat, bending her head to her knees.

"Oh, God!" Phil's voice. Then sounds of retching.

So much, Wetzon thought miserably, for an uncontaminated murder scene. She heard stumbling behind her and, rousing, asked, "Is it Dilla?"

Even in the poor light, Phil's face was parchment. He'd lost his cap; perspiration mottled his forehead and upper lip. There was blood on his hands, and he reeked of vomit. "Christ," he choked. "Christ, Christ, Christ. Somebody's bashed her head in." He staggered down the stairs, babbling incoherently.

"Phil? Is it Dilla?" But Wetzon was talking to the air. Phil had disappeared once again. She rose and instead of heading down, edged slowly toward the center aisle.

Blood tinged the rose-patterned carpet black all around the top of the stairs. It soaked through a stack of old Playbills that had been left behind the first seat. The carpeting on the steps down to the edge of the mezzanine showed a trail of black roses leading to a crumpled mass at the foot of the stairs. Shit, Phil had moved her.

Wetzon pressed her lips together. There was so much blood up here, how could Dilla have gotten all the way down to the edge of the mez and half over the ledge? Unless she'd still been alive. . . . She bowed her head and backed away.

"Birdie!"

Turning abruptly, she almost lost her balance again, tottered over the top step and clutched at the wall; her hand was sticky and left a red smudge. Carlos was coming up the stairs. "Don't," she gasped. "It's . . . bad." She went to meet him and together they walked down holding on to each other. Phil was crouched on the bottom step, his head in his hands. She had the dippy thought: *He'd have blood on his head.*

"It's Dilla, isn't it?" Carlos had trouble getting the words out.

"Who else would it be?" Wetzon brushed her hair out of her face, almost angrily. It was over a year since she'd had to cut her hair off after what she referred to as the let's-take-a-shot-at-Wetzon affair, and it was taking forever to grow long enough to put back in her old dancer's knot.

"And I was cursing her out—God!" Carlos looked down at Phil and patted his shoulder. "Walt's going to keep watch on the stage door."

"Is it open?"

"Yeah. Someone broke a key in the lock and jammed it." Carlos knelt in front of Phil and touched the hands still masking his face. "Come on, Phil," he said very gently. "Come with us."

Phil rubbed his eyes with his fists and hiccuped back a sob. He stood, his eyes ringed with blood like some kind of vampire fiend, and mutely followed Carlos and Wetzon.

"Mort's going to go crazy when—"

Carlos never got to finish his statement. Mort Hornberg, the esteemed director of *Hotshot: The Musical,* stomped on stage from the wings with a woman Wetzon didn't know. They were followed by Sam Meidner, composer-lyricist, and JoJo Diamond, the musical director, even more slovenly than Wetzon had remembered and now sporting a short gray beard. Aline

Rose, book writer, with the latest in her long line of precious boy assistants, brought up the rear.

Mort was agitation in motion.

Wetzon and Carlos, Phil in their wake, drifted down the aisle toward the stage. Wetzon could see Carlos's dancers sitting in the first row, whispering and rustling, heads bobbing up and down. Twitching bundles of nervous energy.

Waves of hysteria, led by a high-pitched wail, rolled off the stage and careered through the house. The keening reverberated downward from the dome, fluttered the crystals of the chandelier, then ceased. Silence dropped a chill blanket over all.

Wetzon took an aisle seat, third row, and waited. Carlos had mentioned something about talking to Mort. . . . She lost time somewhere. Now blue uniforms and other strangers filled the stage to overflow—or seemed to—spilling over the sides. She could hear voices coming from the mez above, but she didn't look up.

Someone settled down behind her. She could feel his breath on the back of her neck. "Detective Sergeant Bernstein, Miss. Walter . . . um." She heard him thumb over a page in his notebook. "Greenow. Walter Greenow says you were the first to see the deceased."

She nodded, her heart sinking. There was no mistaking that voice. Turning in her seat, she recognized the bushy eyebrows that crossed the line between his eyes. She lowered her gaze. Maybe he wouldn't recognize her.

"Okay. Stay right here. I'll be back." The detective heaved himself out of his seat and joined the stream up the aisle toward the mez staircase.

It was the disagreeable Detective Bernstein she remembered from Manhattan North. Paunchy, gray curly hair, and she knew there was a yarmulke pinned to his head under his brown fedora. Three years ago he'd accused her of murder.

She shifted in her seat and looked up toward the mez, catching a flash of Phil in the last row of the orchestra talking earnestly to someone, a thick-waisted woman, whose back was to Wetzon. The mez was filled with blue activity and yellow tape. Now they were contaminating the crime scene, too.

When she turned front again, she saw Gerry Schoenfeld, chairman of the Shubert Organization, had arrived. He came into the orchestra and quickly up the aisle. There he was met by the woman Phil had been huddling with. She was standing near the last row, a faceless silhouette in the deep shadows cast by the mez overhang. Wetzon heard Schoenfeld say, "There's a room off the box office you can use. What do you think, Edna?" It was a statement rather than a question. "We'll set up some chairs and I'll send over some coffee. This is a terrible tragedy, terrible. We want to do everything we can—"

"Fine, sir. We appreciate that." Bernstein was back. He squeezed Wetzon's shoulder and whispered *sotto voce* in her ear, "Now don't go away, ya hear?"

She stole a glance at him and he gave her a wink. Or was it an eye twitch? Charming, she thought glumly. Just charming. She wondered if the woman detective he'd worked with when she last met him was still working with him. He was such a sexist pig.

With a flurry of purple cashmere, Aline Rose flounced into the seat behind Wetzon after Bernstein left. The seat protested with a loud creak, to no avail. The voluminous folds of Aline's cape didn't conceal a stump-shaped body. "Bad stuff, huh?" Her red-framed glasses were missing one temple bar and sat crookedly on her nose, giving her the appearance of a pug with glasses. "Do I know you?"

"I'm Leslie Wetzon, Aline." Wetzon offered her hand. "I used to—"

"I remember you. Carlos's friend." The book writer ignored Wetzon's hand. "Over here, Edward!" An androgynous young man, whose leather motorcycle jacket didn't hide bulging muscles, sat down behind Aline and began kneading the back of her neck. "There's a dear good boy." Aline nodded to Wetzon. "My assistant, Edward Gray." It seemed she'd already forgotten Wetzon's name.

Edward had little gold hoops in each dear little earlobe. He rolled his eyes over Wetzon. She saw him conclude she wasn't important to him, which was fine with her.

"Ah, ah, don't stop, Edward." Aline's head lolled. Her black eyeliner was a loop-the-loop on her lids, as if applied by Ray Charles. "They think it's Dilla. Mugged or something. I guess when you deck yourself out with all that flashy jewelry, you become a target."

"Yeah." Edward kept kneading. His expression didn't change.

"Of course, Dilla was still Dilla. She made a lot of enemies—Ouch! Not so hard, Edward."

"Enemies?" Wetzon smiled. "Not our Dilla."

"Anyway, she was all right last night when we left . . ."

"Huh? You mean you were here last night?"

"We all were. Well, almost all. Mort, Sam, JoJo, Edward and I. And

Sunny Browning, Mort's assistant. We were going over last minute staging
. . . changes . . ." Aline's voice trailed off.

"You forgot to mention Carlos."

"Oh." Aline looked blank. "Carlos? Of course." She shifted in her seat to
take full advantage of Edward's hands. Her cashmere cloak separated and a
bit of white gauze showed for an instant, then was gone.

There was a bandage on Aline's right wrist.

C H A P T E R

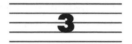

The cold was acid creeping into bones, mixing with fear, horror, and speculation. Up in the mezzanine the police activity inevitably created by a murder progressed in full view of those on the stage and in the first few rows of the orchestra. A theatrical performance in reverse.

Wetzon could feel her back stiffening from the endless sitting. Cold locked her fingers and her knees. She rubbed her hands together. Her gloves were in her pocket, but her fingers were crusty with a pale film of dried blood. She dug a Wash'n Dri from her cosmetic bag and surreptitiously scrubbed the blood from her hands. When she finished, she folded up the square and stuffed it back in its envelope and the envelope into her coat pocket. And out came her leather gloves, lined in cashmere. Immediate relief. The washup was something she probably shouldn't have done, but she hadn't killed Dilla, so why should she sit here suffering in the cold?

Bernstein hadn't come back. She caught glimpses of the detective in the mez, moving back and forth, talking to people. Rising, she stretched her spine. Aline was still getting her massage from Edward, whose gaze seemed riveted not on the object of his ministrations but stageward, where Carlos, eyes closed, was dancing a slow dirge oblivious to everyone.

On the stage, Mort was leaning on the piano talking to Sam Meidner while Sam compulsively ran his hands over the keys without making a sound. The tenor of their conversation could only be assumed. Mort's body language was rigid.

The piano exploded with sound!

Sam was playing the score for *Hotshot* at a furious pace, beating the rhythms with the foot that was not on the pedal. Everyone's eyes were drawn to the stage by the shock of the music. With Dilla lying murdered in the mez, there was something inappropriate about the rocking rhythms. But, Wetzon thought, it was also typical of the self-absorption of people in show business, wasn't it?

When Wetzon turned away from the stage, Phil was no longer in his seat in the rear of the orchestra. Now where had he gone? Had he seized just this moment to disappear? Or had he gone to the men's room? The assistant stage manager'd been the only one of them to see Dilla's body up close. And he'd moved it. Wetzon shook herself. Forget it. Phil was a kid and violent death had a way of—

"Darling—"

She spun around. On the stage, Mort was beckoning to someone. She looked behind her, and sideways, then hand on breast, mouthed, *Me?*

"Yes," the producer-director said. "Come up here. I want to talk to you." It was an order, and she obeyed.

She walked up the pass stairs and came on stage from the wings. Immediately she felt that peculiar, joyous lurch in her midsection, followed by the tingling anticipation she'd always felt when her feet touched the stage. She looked out at the rows of seats, fantasizing all the faces eagerly awaiting the dance number . . .

"Darling!" Mort threw his arm around her as if not a day had passed and nothing was different. Yet more than a dozen years had elapsed since she'd worked in one of his shows. "Listen, Leslie, you know all these moneybags now." Mort was giving her his most charming toothpaste-ad smile, walking her a little to the side. He'd had some dental work done, bonding maybe, for the gap between his two prominent front teeth was gone. He was wearing a blue sweater that set off his eyes, and jeans, his *auteur* costume when he went into his director's mode. Producers—*business* people—wore suits and ties. A brown suede jacket covered Mort's shoulders, and a semipermanent tweed cap covered his balding crown. He looked fairly trim, less paunchy than last year when she'd run into him at Lincoln Center.

"Overture ends," Sam said. "Ah, the beauteous Leslie."

"Hi, Sam." She was astonished the composer remembered her. She'd only worked in one of his shows early in her career, and he'd been very nice. In New Haven he'd bought her a drink at Kaysey's after the show and told her funny show business stories. And he'd been charming when she'd rejected him.

But he wasn't charming now. "Not particular about the company you keep." Sam's hostility was venomous. He gave it off in great waves, and it shook her.

Mort moved her away from the piano, not happy to share her attention, even with Sam. "He's pissed about Dilla," Mort whispered loud enough for Sam to hear. "Afraid it'll hurt the show."

Wetzon stifled her response, which would have been, "And you're not?" Sam hadn't written the score for a musical in over five years. Something about writer's block. He'd had two breakdowns and then a stay at the Betty Ford Clinic for substance abuse. His career had been a geographic map of dips and peaks, two hit shows—mega hits—and three flops, then years of not being able to get arrested. *Hotshot* was to mark his triumphant return to the Broadway stage.

". . . moneybags," Mort repeated in a half-seductive, half-teasing tone.

Wetzon was utterly confused. "What are you talking about, Mort?"

"Darling, all these financial types you know. Isn't one of them interested in the Theatre?" You could hear the capital *T*.

"Some, of course." Mort smelled of stale gin and Obsession for Men. She tried to ease herself out of his grasp. "What's this about?"

Two spots of pink hit Mort's cheeks just above the gray of his beard. "The truth is, Leslie, and I know you'll keep this under your hat—?" He paused. The question hung between them.

"First act ballad," Sam announced, and drove into the music. The sound was deafening.

"Give me a break, Mort," Wetzon protested. "I'm out of the loop. Who would I tell except maybe Carlos, and I presume he's clued in on whatever this is—?" It was her turn to hang a statement with a question.

Mort shrugged and looked down at his Bally loafers. Still the unreconstructed shitkicker, she thought. God, he's not wearing socks. It's freezing and he's not wearing socks.

"The truth is, we're short three-quarters of a mil."

"You're *what?*" Wetzon's voice rose over Sam's musical recital.

"Shsh! Keep your voice down." Mort sneaked a look around over each shoulder, then adjusted the contents of his jockeys in full view of everyone. That, too, hadn't changed. It was like a nervous tic. "You see, Dilla had a guy who was giving her the check today after the run-through."

" 'Show Her Your Hot .45,' " Sam sang, pounding away. There was nothing melodic about the comedy patter song, at least not the way Sam was playing it. The spot over Wetzon's right eye began to hammer. A raging migraine was in the offing.

"Why wouldn't you still be able to get the money from him? Just talk to him—"

Mort was looking at her with actual pity in his eyes for her stupidity. "He was Dilla's investor."

"So? Spell it out for me, Mort. I'm not too bright."

"She was keeping his name to herself. You know Dilla. Someone who owed her, she said."

"Jesus, Dilla was a piece of work." Wetzon shivered and hugged herself, rubbing her arms to keep warm. "Maybe he'll make himself known."

"Not bloody likely. And we can't wait. We've got only enough left to get us to Boston. We have a decent advance for the first two weeks, but if the reviews aren't good and business falls off the last week, we're dead. You must know somebody."

Wetzon thought, I do know somebody, and I'll go straight to hell for this, bringing poor old Twoey into the theatre. On the other hand, I may be doing everyone a favor, and then I'll get to heaven. So she said, "I may know somebody, Mort. He's been a partner with a big Wall Street firm, and he's going through a midlife crisis. The poor fool wants to be a Broadway producer." In reality, Twoey's crisis had been triggered by Smith's dumping him the year before for the notorious and flamboyant criminal attorney, Richard Hartmann. Devastated, Twoey had taken a leave of absence from Rosenkind Luwisher and was determined to change his life.

"Leslie, darling!" Mort grabbed her elbows and lifted her off her feet. "You're a sweetheart! Who is he? When can I meet him?"

The guiding principle of her partner Xenia Smith flashed in front of Wetzon's eyes in bright red neon: NO FREEBEES.

Well, maybe in this instance Smith was right. While Dilla was already getting billing as associate producer, Wetzon knew damn well Dilla would also have demanded points—percentage points—of the producer's share of the profits of the show. George Abbott, the legendary Broadway director, had maintained actors would always go for billing over money. Give 'em billing, he'd advised. And he was right. Because it's fame they're after. But, Dilla had given up acting long ago. No doubt she would have preferred the money.

Leslie Wetzon, ex-actor and Wall Street headhunter, didn't give a hoot about billing; she, too, would rather have the money. And as producers were extremely protective about points because points always came out of their piece of the profits, she would have to pry points out of Mort. She would do it with relish.

"Reprise!" Sam shouted.

"You'd better put me down, Mort," Wetzon said to the top of his suede cap. "We have to talk seriously."

"Sure, darling." He set her on her feet and straightened her clothing for her, fussing. "What?"

She squelched a giggle. "I'm going to introduce you to someone who will put up the money you need . . . on the condition that you let him hang around and learn."

"Done! You're—"

"*And* I want a finder's fee."

"Leslie—" Mort put his hand on his breast and looked pained.

"Come on, Mort. You were giving Dilla points, weren't you?"

"That was different."

"Why?"

"She was working on the show. But okay. We'll work it out. Set up a meeting." He looked at his watch.

"First act finale. Everyone on stage," Sam called to a void. He'd lost it.

"Two percent, Mort. I want two percent of the gross from day one."

"Leslie, goddammit—"

"Deal, Mort?"

He shook his head in disbelief. She'd obviously wounded him to the quick. "You've gotten hard, Leslie. . . . Two percent of the net, after payback."

"One percent of the gross from day one."

"You're holding me up." She was silent. He sighed. "Very well. One percent of the gross."

"From day one." He nodded. "Deal," she said, extending her hand. Peripherally, she could see Carlos was still dancing a morose funereal ballet.

"Second act opening!" Sam yelled.

"Okay, vampire. Dilla's not even cold yet."

"Did *I* start this, Mort?" She was pissed and moved away.

He came after her. "Okay, okay, that was unfair of me . . ."

"Lunch tomorrow, twelve-thirty at the Four Seasons."

"Christ, the Four Seasons—"

"Be a sport, Mort." She grinned at him, emphasizing the cheap rhyme. Then, she saw Aline in the wings about to bear down on them, and Wetzon faded back. She dropped her bag at the rear wall and fell into step with Carlos as if they were still dancing together. Slowly, she began to tease him into the old Fosse combinations, splayed fingers, small soft steps, moving long from the hipbones. He was wearing a gorgeous new watch. She caught his hand and inspected it. Carlos lifted his head and smiled at her, one of her Carlos's dazzling smiles. "Present from Arthur. Cartier Panthere."

"Snazzy."

"Birdie, what would I do without you?"

"What would I do without you?"

They held each other for a long moment. Then she pulled back and looked at him. "Aline mentioned there was a meeting here last night."

"Yeah." His smile faded.

"You didn't tell me."

"I went ballistic, that's why. I left early." He put his hand on her shoulders. His eyes glinted. "If I'd stayed here I might have been tempted to kill her."

"Aline?"

"No," Carlos said, his face grim. "Dilla."

C H A P T E R

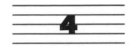

"Can we cut down on the noise, please! We're going to start our interviews. Please be patient and we'll get you out of here as quickly as possible." Bernstein was out front leaning over the orchestra pit.

With five crashing chords, Sam concluded his bizarre recital and slumped on the keys, arms akimbo. He looked like some great damaged bird, downed.

The interruption drew Wetzon's eyes from Carlos momentarily, then back. "What do you mean, you would have killed Dilla?"

Carlos looked wretched. "That's the way I felt when I left here last night, Birdie. I wanted to put my hands around that scheming throat of hers and squeeze—" He grabbed Wetzon's hand and pulled her into the wings, stage right. The stale, almost fruity smell of the closed theatre was more pervasive here. "The late great Killa Dilla was working on getting me fired. And my dear friends and collaborators were not exactly rushing to my defense. It seems her big secret investor was insisting on Gideon Winkler for choreographer. The bitch told Mort my work was totally derivative and was dragging down the show." He turned his head away from her and blinked rapidly.

"Oh, baby." Wetzon took him in her arms, her cheek against his. He had been her best friend since they'd first danced together. When he was hurting, she felt the pain. "And what, may I ask, did your dear collaborators say to that?"

"They hedged."

"The wusses. And you say Wall Street is sleazy."

"I told them to do whatever they pleased and, may I tell you, I breezed out of here. When I got home, I called Arthur—he's been in Virginia since

Thursday doing up a complicated trust thing—and we went over my contract carefully. Shit, I'm in good shape financially—they have to pay me or buy me out—but the creative part of me was taking a beating."

"Show business!" Wetzon almost spat the words. She surprised herself with how bitter she sounded.

"Yeah, well, then Mort called me at twelve-thirty and said not to worry, that he loved me, that they all did, and they wouldn't think of doing the show without me."

"You're kidding? What about Dilla and the phantom money guy?"

"Mort said he'd taken care of Dilla."

"Huh?"

"Those were his very words."

"Dear Mort always had a way with words, don't you think?" Wetzon and Carlos smiled at each other.

"Mort would never have killed her."

"How can you say that, Carlos? If I've learned one thing over these last few years, it's that we are all capable of killing . . . and if there's a lot of pressure—"

"Not Mort, darling. He doesn't have the balls."

"Then what is he always shifting and stroking in his pants?" She couldn't control the laughter that bubbled up and out. Nor, it seemed, could Carlos. It was suddenly unspeakably hilarious. But in the back of Wetzon's mind she knew it wasn't that funny. Four hundred feet from where they stood the police were combing the bloodstained mezzanine for any evidence that might reveal Dilla's murderer.

And with Arthur away, Carlos had no alibi for last night.

"Where's Miss Wesson? We'll start with her." Bernstein again.

Wetzon swallowed her laughter and choked, coughing. Carlos clapped her on the back. Laughter streamed through hands clasped over mouths. "Oh, God." She was a whimpering wreck. "We'd better get straight."

Carlos lowered one eyelid halfway. "Maybe you, Birdie, but not me."

That was enough to set them off again.

"Miss Wesson?" A detective. A woman, but obviously a detective. How did she know? It was something Wetzon couldn't quantify. Stance? Tone? Gestures?

"They want you, Miss Mazola, darling." Carlos tittered. They locked eyes and fell on each other again in a fit of laughter.

"Get a grip, son," she gasped, using her friend Laura Lee Day's favorite phrase.

The detective was looking at them curiously. "Miss Wesson?"

Wetzon giggled. "Sorry. Oh God. I'm sorry. Nerves."

Carlos turned his back on her. His shoulders shook. She couldn't look at him. Rather, she focused on the detective: stolidly built, broad-assed, short brown hair, prominent nose, pale skin devoid of makeup. She wore loose fitting brown gabardine pants and an open, down jacket in an electric shade of blue.

"Detective Bernstein would like to start with you, Miss Wesson."

"That's Wetzon." Wetzon spelled it out, "W-e-t-z-o-n," and another giggle burbled up in her throat. Carlos was howling now, leaning over the stage manager's desk, which was really just a small table with a drawer, set in the wings under a computer. On the desk were a large black pocketbook, an umbrella, and a battered Burberry.

"I'm Detective Renee Gross," the woman said. "If you'll come with me, please." She spoke in the clipped speech of the New York streets, and she clearly found nothing amusing in Wetzon's amusement. In fact, she looked disgusted. Her expression brought Wetzon up short.

"Carlos, doll, I'll talk to you later."

"How about dinner?" He'd gotten control again, but tears spotted his face.

"Can't. I'm having dinner with Smith."

"Well! If you'd rather dine with the Barracuda—"

"Oh, please. You're an impossible creature." Carlos loathed her partner Xenia Smith and the feeling was mutual. They were constantly taking jabs at one another through Wetzon. "But adorable." She planted a kiss on his cheek, then followed Detective Gross across the stage.

Sam was straddling the piano bench, head tilted, talking to Aline and JoJo. He caught Wetzon's hand when she went by. "Oh, beauteous Leslie, that we should meet again like this. Later?" He kissed her palm.

"Sure, Sam." He'd fallen right back into the corny routine he'd tried on her years back. And what was more, he knew it.

She did not see the woman who had arrived on stage with Mort earlier, but Mort, who was immersed in conversation with Gerry Schoenfeld, gave her thumbs-up and a broad wink, as if they were in some sort of conspiracy together. She felt Schoenfeld's eyes following her, and she wondered what Mort would tell the theatre owner.

When Wetzon and Detective Gross descended the side stairs, Wetzon saw that the six dancers were gone. And except for a couple of cops, the orchestra section of the theatre was now empty. Still no sign of Phil. What could have happened to him? A light flashed from above, then another.

Someone called a question; shadow voices answered. The members of the Crime Scene Unit of the NYPD were still at work.

She followed Gross up the aisle into the rear of the orchestra, beyond the seats. A uniformed cop stood at the closed door to the house manager's office that Schoenfeld had appropriated for the inquiry. He had a little red metal apple pinned to the collar of his coat. Light seeped from under the door to the box office, the next room over.

Gross knocked, then opened the door and stuck her head in. "Ready for us?" A waft of caustic cigarette fumes drifted out.

"You first, Gross."

Shrugging somewhat apologetically, the detective slipped into the room and shut the door, leaving Wetzon in the lurch. She could hear the rumble of Bernstein's and Gross's voices through the closed door. The uniformed cop ignored her. She wandered a few feet to the lighted box office. This door, too, was closed, but the catch had sprung.

Inside, a woman said, "This has nothing to do with us."

"But I should tell them—" The voice that answered was Phil's.

"No! I'm—"

"Come on in," Gross said in a loud voice.

Wetzon turned and headed for the house manager's office. Behind her she heard the door open and close. Looking back, she caught a glimpse of Phil emerging from the box office.

Bernstein hung up the phone and waved her in. "Grab a seat."

Bernstein was ensconced behind a desk that looked as if it had been through the Peloponesian Wars. Its Leatherette top was stained and scarred; ancient gouges marked its varnished oak exterior. Bernstein had a cardboard cup and a notebook in front of him. The room was cold and airless.

Wetzon sat in a straight-back chair. The leather padding was worn thin, dry and cracked, patched with black electrical tape. On the floor was a carpet so thin, pieces had worn away, and disintegrating backing surfaced in large areas, like mold. Someone had set up a coffee urn on a table, with a stack of cardboard cups, a container of milk, and a paper plate of sugar and Sweet'n Low envelopes. Coffee dripped from the spout into a cup, *plop, plop, plop.*

Unnecessarily, Gross announced, "Detective Morgan Bernstein, Ms. Wesson."

Bernstein seemed almost affable. He shunted his coffee to the side, shook a cigarette from a pack of Marlboros and lit it. His bushy mustache was new, at least she hadn't remembered a mustache. "Coffee, Miss Wesson?"

"No, thank you. And my name is Wetzon."

"That's what I said, didn't I? Sit down, Gross. You're making me nervous."

Detective Gross pulled another dilapidated chair around to the side of the desk so that she faced Wetzon. Her face was impassive. She took a pad and a pen from the pocket of her coat.

"What happened to Irma?" At least Wetzon thought that had been the name of Bernstein's partner three years before, when she'd first encountered him.

Bernstein took a long pull on his cigarette and squinted at her, then let out a puffy stream of smoke. He'd taken off his hat; his blue crocheted yarmulke was pinned to his curly hair with a bobby pin. He needed a haircut, and he looked as if he'd put on some weight. In fact, he was downright beefy.

"Detective Ignacio is downtown with the Homicide Bureau. I train them good." He smirked at Gross. "Isn't that right, Gross?"

Gross nodded solemnly, but Wetzon saw an eyebrow rise ever so slightly. Her eyes met Wetzon's for a fraction of a second, then Gross looked down at her pad.

"I just talked to your boyfriend." Bernstein grinned at her. His blue eyes were ice under bushy brows.

"I'm sorry?" Was he talking to her, or Detective Gross? No, he was talking to her. He meant Silvestri. "Oh," she said, noncommittally. *Shit,* she finished silently.

"Yeah. I told him you were in trouble again." He leered at her.

"Why the hell did you do that?" Her anger drove her to her feet. She and Silvestri had split up eight months ago. They had agreed to take time out.

"Sit down, Miss Wesson. I didn't want him getting in my face when he found out."

She didn't want Silvestri in her face either, charging in here on his white horse to save her from the dragon.

Damnation! She was seething, and her body temperature went through the ceiling. She broke out in a sweat. Silvestri would think she was incapable of taking care of herself. That was one of the things they had fought about. *Leave off, Wetzon,* she told herself. *What do you care what Silvestri thinks?* She suddenly felt queasy and light-headed. She'd missed lunch. She sank back into the chair.

"He thanked me nicely for letting him know," Bernstein continued. He seemed to be trying to fathom her reaction.

She thought: That's it? That's all he said? She said firmly, "I am not a suspect here."

"You're not?" Bernstein inhaled smoke and breathed it out with elaborate aplomb. He was all dragon. "How do you figure that?"

"I was not alone last night. Or this morning—"

Bernstein cocked his head at her and scratched under his yarmulke. "So?" His eyes were mocking.

"So, Dilla was murdered last night."

"How can you be so sure?" He stabbed out the cigarette against the Leatherette of the desk, scattering ash and adding a new scar to the multitude already there.

"She wasn't?" What was he getting at? "When then? The theatre was locked up tight when we got here."

"What time was that?"

"About eleven-thirty."

Bernstein nodded. He was savoring her indignation. "Yeah. But she was still warm when we got here."

C H A P T E R

"Tell me everything," Smith commanded. "And I mean *everything.*" Her hazel eyes were alive with curiosity and a kind of joy. The weirdest things turned her on.

Coco Pazzo on a Sunday night. Actually, it was only six-thirty, but Wetzon could have sworn she'd just spent two weeks locked in a cold, filthy nightmare. She sighed. "Oh, Smith, give me a break. I've been over and over it with that awful detective—"

"Dilla Crosby was in a layout last month in *Mirabella.* She was up-and-coming—"

"Not anymore." It came out flip, flipper than she'd meant it.

"Oh, for pitysakes, jokes. All you do is joke, Wetzon. You never share."

"We're sharing right now." What they were sharing was a Tuscan antipasto of grilled vegetables and linguine with sea food, family style, which was the way Coco Pazzo served dinner on informal Sunday nights. The restaurant was so in that reservations had to be made weeks ahead. All the right people dined there. But aside from all that, the food was delicious, and the setting, which had once been the Volney Hotel's dining room, was serene cream color walls, simple white tablecloths, and murals of bottles and carafes.

Smith rolled her eyes heavenward as if dealing with Wetzon were a great burden. She fluffed her dark curls. Her fingernails were an immaculate deep rose. "You are the most difficult person, and you're getting worse as you get older."

"Thanks a heap. You're a pal. You wouldn't exactly win an award for amiability yourself." Wetzon studied her partner. The woman was beautiful. Smooth olive skin, high cheekbones, and almond-shaped eyes. And permanently thin to boot, which Smith maintained without so much as lifting her little finger to exercise. And tall. What more could anyone want? But Smith was never satisfied—at least not for very long. She was narcissistic. She changed lovers the way she changed her wardrobe, and she approached life as if it were a grand seduction. Seduce, and control.

That Wetzon should know enough after all these years not to be hurt was understood, but it didn't always work that way.

Smith took a sip of her red wine, and replenished the dark green olive oil from a beaker onto the small flat plate, then dipped her wedge of focaccia into the oil. "Why are you acting so whipped?" She took a dainty bite and practically purred. "This is *wonderful.*"

Wetzon looked down at her plate and moved the roasted red peppers closer to the eggplant, and the eggplant closer to the zucchini. "You know, Smith, sometimes I think of us as an old married couple. We came together in a whirlwind romance and have practically nothing in common. And now that the dew is off the rose, our different ways of looking at life are a source of conflict." She looked across the table and was astonished to see Smith's eyes swimming in tears. "Oh, dear, now don't do that."

"What do you mean, don't do that? You have hurt me terribly. Are you trying to tell me you want to dissolve our partnership?"

Wetzon was dismayed. How had she gotten into this? "No! My God, no! We're good together, aren't we?"

"I always thought so." Smith blotted the tears away with a tissue and sniffed. "And you're my best friend, sweetie pie. I love you." She reached across the table for Wetzon's hand.

Wetzon felt like a shit. "Me, too. I was just talking off the top of my head." She let Smith take her hand.

"But you're so careless about my feelings. . . ."

"Okay. Enough. I didn't mean it. What do you want to know about Dilla?" There she was back in Smith's clutches again. How had it happened?

"Why would anyone want to bash her head in?" Smith was savoring the picture her words conjured up. Ordinary murder didn't thrill her, but a glamorous, publicity-filled celebrity murder was quite another thing.

"I don't know. I haven't seen Dilla in years. She was a gypsy with Carlos and me, but she was ambitious. And greedy. She never did anything unless there was a payoff. Money and/or power. I mean, relationships and stuff. Men were always showering her with jewelry, clothes, and furs. God, I remember she paraded around with a gorgeous Blackglama mink coat while we were auditioning for *Chorus Line.* She flaunted it. You knew she always had some sex-for-money thing going on . . ." Yikes, she thought, I'm describing Smith.

Fingering the pavé diamond clip on the gold mesh chain that Richard Hartmann, Smith's current lover, had given her for her fortieth birthday, Smith said, "I really *hate* women like that." She turned to get the waiter's attention.

Wetzon smirked. She couldn't help it.

Smith was frowning when she turned back. "Still, why would anyone kill her?"

"The only things Dilla was attracted to were money and power. She cozied up with a lot of people, and she had a nasty habit of collecting things about them."

"Things?"

"Information. You know, gossip. Stuff people wouldn't want to get out."

"Oh, then she was a blackmailer." The waiter arrived at their table. Smith announced: "We're finished."

Wetzon shook her head. "I wouldn't go that far." To the waiter she said, "No, wait. I'll take our leftovers home." While the waiter removed the plates, Wetzon added, "But Dilla managed to build herself a whole other career rather quickly as a stage manager and associate producer. She knew people who would give her money."

"We'll have some biscotti," Smith told the waiter. "And two double espressos."

"Make one of them decaf, please," Wetzon interjected.

"Maybe she was just a smart businesswoman, sugar."

"I'm sure she was." Wetzon grinned at her. Smith had finally realized she and Dilla had something in common. "What do you want with those scraps?" Smith pointed to the foil package of leftovers the waiter deposited on the table.

"Tomorrow night's dinner."

"I can't believe you and Alton are going to eat those scraps of food."

"Alton's in Caracas this week."

Smith nodded sagely. "I might have guessed. You've gone back to being a church mouse." The biscotti arrived with the espresso.

Wetzon dipped the tip of one of the biscotti into the espresso, and nibbled it. "Sublime."

Sudden inspiration shone on Smith's face. "You know, she could have been mugged. This city is being overwhelmed by derelicts. Lord, I wish Pat Buchanan would run for mayor of New York."

"Oh yuk. Now you've really gone off the deep end. And what does Patrick Buchanan have to do with Dilla's murder, may I ask?"

"Why are you being so difficult? I only meant that some derelicts could be sleeping in empty theatres."

"Possibly."

"So what's going to happen with the show?"

"I don't know. They're supposed to open in Boston next Saturday."

"Will the cops let them?"

"We're talking about a Mort Hornberg show, darling," Wetzon drawled. "Mort's an institution. He has but to pick up the phone and call his senator, the mayor, the attorney general, the district attorney. It'll be tricky, but mark me, they'll go to Boston. The only thing that could stop them really is the three-quarters of a mil they need to cover road costs, and I may have taken care of that." Should she tell Smith about Twoey?

"You?" Smith burbled, "We'll have the check, dear," to the waiter when he asked if they wanted anything else.

"Mort asked me to see if I could come up with an investor, and I may have. I've arranged for them to have lunch tomorrow at the Four Seasons with me as chaperone and agent."

After a brief moment of hesitation, Smith said, with dangerous calm, "I can't believe it."

"Believe it. You would have been proud if you'd heard me negotiate my share."

"Your share?" Smith looked as if the marvelous biscotti had turned to ashes in her mouth.

"Yes." It was hard for Wetzon not to feel smug, and finally she gave up trying.

"When did this happen?"

"While we were waiting to be interviewed by the police. I had a good teacher, partner," she quipped.

Smith smiled, pleased. "Who did you get? I didn't know you knew people who invest in the theatre. Every fool knows it's like throwing your money into a bottomless pit."

"Yes. Maybe. But the person I set up with Mort is much more interested in learning the business, and he's willing to pay three-quarters of a mil for the privilege." She'd called Twoey, Smith's previous lover, from the theatre before coming uptown to meet Smith for dinner. "And then, of course, losses in the theatre can be offset against ordinary income."

"Well, very nice," Smith said grudgingly. "What did you work out for yourself?"

"One percent of the box office gross from day one."

"That's not such a big deal."

"It is if the show grosses $600,000 a week, which is what it can do at capacity."

"Humpf. Who's your investor?"

Wetzon paused. Smith would have a fit. Smith always felt that even if she ended an affair, all of her ex-lovers still belonged to her. "Goldman Barnes Two."

"Twoey?" Smith's voice rose. "You can't mean that!"

"Oh, but I can."

"Well," Smith said ungraciously. "*I* should get a piece of that. After all, Twoey was—"

Putting as much starch in her voice as she could muster on short notice, Wetzon said, "I'll pretend I didn't hear that, Smith."

"I was only kidding, sweetie."

Wetzon watched her cautiously. What was she up to? Then she thought: *This is wrong. We're partners, and I have no right to act alone.* "I was kidding. We'll go fifty-fifty on this."

Smith smiled her cheshire cat smile. "Imagine, Twoey a Broadway producer." Her smile became radiant. "Mark will be thrilled. He just loves the Theatre. Maybe we can arrange an internship for him."

"Maybe. I'll talk to Mort." Wetzon was particularly fond of Smith's seventeen-year-old son, Mark, and knew the boy was enamoured of the Theatre. She would see what she could do.

"No," Smith said. "I will."

"You?"

"Yes." She nodded emphatically. "I may be interested in making a little investment myself."

"But—"

"So I'll just be joining you three for lunch tomorrow."

C H A P T E R

6

When Wetzon unlocked the door to her apartment and pushed it open, she had the strange sensation that she had opened the wrong door. *Chez* Wetzon was still *chez* Wetzon, but the environment was radically different, thanks to Louise Armstrong, contractor extraordinaire.

It had been Louie who had persuaded Wetzon to knock down instead of replaster the wall between the living and dining rooms. Now, the foyer extended, even swelled, into the living-dining room. The whole area had a decided loftlike personality. Sweeping, open space.

Her barre had been restored, along with the mirrored wall between the dining area and her bedroom, and although Louie had found her a wonderful old coromandel screen, all red lacquer and long-legged cranes, Wetzon used it for decoration behind a love seat rather than as a space divider. She had no desire to cut into the exultation she felt whenever she realized this was her home.

It was like coming to terms with being grown up.

The antique Muller Freres chandelier with the blue and yellow globes was still hanging from the ceiling in the foyer, and the centennial sunburst quilt was still mounted behind her sofa. But the drunkard's path quilt had lost its wall in the foyer and had been moved to the space between the living room windows and the former dining room windows.

Wetzon had splurged on a Stickley dining table and six chairs, thanks to the placement late last year of a broker whose gross came to two and a half million dollars, the biggest placement she had ever made. In fact, she had gone overboard on mission furniture, adding a rocker, side tables, and a love seat with lots of slats, and three different sizes of footstools.

She switched on all the table lamps and let the ambiance creep into her pores. Earth colors. Nothing sharp or alien. She hung her coat from the doorknob, spreading its skirt out on the floor to dry. The rain had changed to sleet, back to rain and back again to sleet. There was a chill in the apartment, and she turned the radiator on to bring up the heat.

Ambiance or no, she still felt edgy as she toured her apartment, turning on radiators in each room. Dilla's murder, then dealing with Smith, had taken their toll. Her nerves were raw.

Oh, hell, she thought. She stripped down to her leggings and bodysuit and kicked off her low boots. The barre beckoned and she responded, first putting the *Goldberg Variations* cassette in the boom box. She began with *battements tendus,* going from *simples* to *grandes jetés,* until she felt her equilibrium returning. It was so lovely that her body still responded to the movements.

Gathering up her sweater and boots from where she'd dropped them, she went down the short hall to her bedroom and put everything away.

Her bedroom had also been totally renovated and redecorated so that it looked as if it had been lifted from an English country house. She had taken Alton with her when she bought everything, but he had never seen the final version. For whatever reason she was not quite able to give words to, she spent their weekends together at Alton's apartment in the Beresford on Eighty-first Street and weekdays solo in her very private space.

She had been seeing Alton Pinkus exclusively for the last eight months, and he seemed satisfied with their relationship, now that Silvestri was out of the picture. At least, he wasn't pushing her to make any further commitment, which was fine.

Mirrors told her that time was marching on, but she pretended not to hear. Let Smith worry for the two of them. Alton was twenty years older than Wetzon. He had three grown children and had been a widower for five years. Although retired, he had a hefty pension and investments and because of his expertise in the American labor movement, he was constantly called on to consult, particularly since the breakup of the Soviet Union. His celebrity had even spilled over onto her, and she'd found she liked it.

After a hot shower and a cold rinse, Wetzon wrapped her head in a hand towel, her body in a huge bath sheet, and went into the kitchen to check her phone messages. Two. She played them back. Carlos. Detective Morgan Bernstein.

Carlos answered on the first ring.

"God, were you sitting on the phone?"

"Close. Birdie—"

"How are you—" They'd spoken at the same time and both stopped. "I'm sorry—"

Carlos said, "In answer to your question, I don't know. I needed to talk. I went up with Bernstein and his shadow to talk to Susan Orkin—"

"Susan Orkin? What does she have to do with this? The only Susan Orkin I know is the one that's married to our handsome, somewhat retarded Congressman Greg Orkin."

"Was."

"Was?"

"Was married. Remember when Greg came out of the closet six or seven years ago?"

"Yes."

"Well, it turned out that Susan and Dilla had been lovers since high school."

"You're kidding!"

"Nope. They've been living together almost six years."

"I don't know why that should surprise me. I always knew Dilla was gay— or at the very least, AC/DC."

"Let me tell you, she wasn't anything but gay," Carlos said. "Everything else was for profit. She fucked men only to get ahead."

Wetzon giggled. "I'm certainly glad I didn't say that."

"And you say I'm bad." But the spark was missing. Carlos sounded so depressed.

"I'm sorry, Carlos. My reaction to Dilla's murder has been weird, even for me. My mind keeps making jokes."

Carlos sighed. "No, you're all right. It's me. I'm bone weary."

"When does Arthur get home?"

"Tomorrow."

"Do you want me to come over and give you a big hug and spend the night?"

"Yes, but no. It's just the reaction to the shock, I guess. Susan took it very hard. She's sort of fragile, I think, or maybe it's just that she looks fragile, you know. She's got that kind of transparent skin you can see blue veins through. All I could think was, if anything happened to Arthur—"

"Oh, Carlos. I'm coming over right now."

"No! Get some sleep. I love you. I'll talk to you tomorrow." He hung up before she could say another word.

Wetzon stared at the receiver in her hand, then cradled it. She padded back to the bathroom and hung up the wet towels. Deep sadness enveloped her, and she tried only half-heartedly to shake it off. She slathered herself in moisturizers and combed her hair, peering into the mirror, fingertips seeking and finding the tiny indentation just above her hairline. Her hair had grown back around it, but she would never comb her hair again without remembering the searing light, the explosion, the smell of cordite. Her shudder was involuntary. She was freezing.

In the bedroom she began opening drawers, looking for a nightgown and came up with an old T-shirt, this one with a V-neck—one of Silvestri's that she'd appropriated. She pulled it on and got into bed. A minute later she was back in the living room turning all the lights out. She double-locked the door and got back into bed. Her clock said ten-thirty. She was exhausted. Reaching up, she turned out the light, and lay in the soft darkness, easing herself into sleep.

The phone rang, jerking her out of that sliding-into-feather-bed sensation, and her hand shook as she reached out and picked up the receiver. "Hello?"

"Ms. Wesson," Bernstein said, almost jovially. "Hope I'm not disturbing you."

"You're not." She'd be damned if she'd let him know he'd caught her just as she was drifting off. "What do you want?"

"Don't you believe in returning phone calls?"

"Don't start with me, Bernstein."

"That's what I like about you, lady. You get right to the point."

"What is the point, Detective?" She hated this cat-and-mouse thing he instigated.

"We found Dilla Crosby's raincoat and umbrella on a table on the side of the stage where you and Carlos Prince were standing."

"We were standing in the wings, Detective, stage right."

"Yeah. But we know she always carried a big handbag, and that we haven't found. You didn't by any chance see it?"

Wetzon closed her eyes and saw the area where she and Carlos had stood talking.

"Hello? Are you there?"

"One second, Detective. I'm trying to remember. On the stage manager's table, I remember seeing a raincoat—a Burberry, I think—and an umbrella —it was wet—and . . ." She opened her eyes and stared into the darkness.

"And what, Ms. Wesson?"

"And a large, black leather bag."

"So maybe you know what happened to it," Bernstein said amiably.

"How would I? Detective Gross came for me and I never saw it again. Are you sure it wasn't just put away for safekeeping?"

"Hardly. Are *you* sure you saw it?"

"Yes." She was emphatic. "I'm sure Carlos saw it, too. We were both right there."

"He didn't see it."

"What?"

"I just got finished talking to him, and he says he didn't see it."

"He must—" *Shut your mouth, Wetzon.* "I guess I could have been mistaken. We were both very upset."

"That's not what I heard."

"Excuse me?"

"Detective Gross tells me you were laughing up a storm."

"We were under a lot of stress." Wetzon measured her words. "Detective Gross misunderstood."

"Did she really? Then I'll say good night to you, Ms. Wesson." He leaned on the *Ms.*

Wetzon lay still for what seemed like a long time after her conversation with Bernstein, replaying her stream of memory. Dilla's bag had been on the desk when Detective Gross had come for her. She was sure of that. And there weren't that many people on stage and in the wings. Mort Hornberg, Gerry Schoenfeld. The woman with Mort, whom she didn't know. Aline Rose and body-beautiful Edward, probably. Sam Meidner. JoJo Diamond.

Walt Greenow had to be somewhere in the wings or backstage even though Wetzon hadn't seen him. The illusive Phil, possibly. And Carlos.

She switched on the light and called Carlos. His answering machine proclaimed: "What a stroke of good fortune. You've reached the residence of Prince Margolies. Neither of us royals can come to the phone right now, but we want to talk to you. So leave a message." *Beep.*

"Carlos? Hello? It's me. Carlos? Pick up. Carlos?" He wasn't picking up. How strange. She hung up the phone, uneasy. Was something going on with Carlos? He'd been firm about her not coming over. Oh, dear. Her wild imagination was leading her down uncertain paths. She looked at her digital clock-radio. Eleven. She groped for the remote and turned on the television set and listened to CBS's local news coverage.

". . . a brutal murder in a Broadway theatre. Sounds like the stuff for a play, but reality hit with the force of a sledgehammer when production coordinator—associate producer—Dilla Crosby was bludgeoned to death in the mezzanine of the Imperial Theatre. No suspects, the police admit, but plenty of leads." They flashed a photo of Dilla from the *Mirabella* article, looking coy and hoydenish in glisteny silver leggings and a long tailored jacket, swinging one leg and one arm from a ladder. "The police have asked that anyone with information about the circumstances of Dilla Crosby's death call oh four seven, six seven oh oh. All calls will be kept confidential."

Enough! Off with the TV. Lights out. She was roasting. She got out of bed and opened the window wider, turned off the radiator, then crawled back into bed, thoroughly wiped out.

The dream came again as it had before, and she fought it. Sucked into its vortex of terror, she saw the flash of flame, smelled the cordite, felt the sting. Then something new: intense pain. The pain stabbed her awake, and she lay in the darkness gasping for breath. A heart attack. She was having a heart attack. No. She was too young. There was nothing wrong with her heart. It was indigestion.

Sharp needles of rain attacked her windows, pinging on the air-conditioner. Her heart was racing. Sitting up, she broke into a soaking sweat. She couldn't breathe. She swung her feet to the floor and stood, terrified, but her legs wouldn't hold her. She crumpled to the floor. The pain. Call 911. No, she couldn't. She'd die of embarrassment. It was just indigestion, a stupid virus. She got to her knees, to her feet, and holding the walls, she staggered into the bathroom and turned on the cold water, thrusting her wrists under the faucet, then splashing her face with cold water.

Oppressively, the pain displaced itself and settled in her stomach. She bent over in agony. It might be indigestion, but she was dying of it. Who would even know if she were to die here? Alton was in South America. She wouldn't show up for work tomorrow, and maybe Smith would investigate if it didn't conflict with something more important. If she weren't so frightened, she could laugh at that. Another stab of pain came, and another. She clutched the edge of the sink. She wasn't going to make it.

When she caught her breath, she thought: *It's an ovarian cyst.* She'd had one once years ago. *Get Dr. Hirsch's number.* Sweat ran down her forehead, the back of her neck. Fever. She was blazing with fever. Her address book was in her bag. With trembling hands she found the number and crawled into the kitchen, reached for the phone and brought it down on the floor with her.

It rang. Jangling in her hand. Insistently. Four times. She grabbed it. Gasped, a hoarse gasp, into it. She would never have recognized her own voice.

There was a pause as if the person on the other end were trying to decide if he had the right number, then, "Les? What's the matter?"

"Help—" was all she could choke out as the pain swept over her. The receiver slipped from her hands and bounced once on the floor before coming to a rest. Great chunks of time fell away. A noise at her service door yanked her back, almost fainting with terror. She crawled, panting, into the living room before it came to her that the sound was merely night collection of garbage.

Freezing cold, she found refuge under her dining room table, head on knees, hugging her knees tightly, trying to confine the shaking. Her teeth chattered to their own rhythm. Slowly, she felt herself begin to disappear. . . .

"Les?" She heard his voice. The lights came on. "Where are you? Les?" She tried to call him, but nothing came out. He went into the kitchen; she heard him hang up the phone she'd left off the hook. "Les?"

Fear. She heard it in his voice. His footsteps raced down the hall, into her bedroom, back out in the hall. She wanted to shout, "Here I am!"

"Les." His voice softened. "Les. What are you doing there?" He was on his knees, pulling her from her hiding place.

She thought: *I must look like hell.*

"Come on, come here, it's okay. Everything'll be okay." Gently, he pulled her hands from her knees, and checked her out. "Are you hurt? Where? Show me." If she weren't dying, she might be turned on, she thought.

Then he was lifting her, carrying her, and she felt the shoulder harness against her breast through his sportjacket. He put her in bed and covered her with the quilt and the red, white, and blue afghan that she and Carlos had crocheted when they were in Bob Fosse's *Chicago* during the Bicentennial. But she couldn't stop shaking.

"Cold," she moaned. "Hurts. S'matter with me?"

He stroked her hair and bent over her. His eyes were deep turquoise, and she tried to thank him for coming but couldn't get the words formed.

"Les, listen to me. Can you hear me?"

"Y-y-yes. So . . . cold." She closed her eyes and gave herself up to the trembling. He was moving around the bedroom. Then he was in bed beside her, holding her against him.

"Les." His warm breath made her skin tingle. He radiated heat. "Breathe very slowly." He held her tight. "I'm here. Don't be afraid."

She shuddered, then rested her forehead against his chest. The trembling slowed. The wild heartbeats began to subside. His heat brought warmth back to her. The tightness in her chest eased. "Oh, Silvestri," she murmured. She put her arms around him and held on for dear life.

C H A P T E R

Shortly before six-thirty, when her alarm would go off, Wetzon awoke with a sensation of euphoria that seemed so alien that she was filled with the wonder of it. It was similar to the aftermath of a migraine, when the pain is gone and the muscles are relaxed and the sense of peace and joy are heightened. Was it possible that only a few short hours ago she was sure she was dying?

Lying in Silvestri's arms, her head on his chest rising and falling to his even breathing, she thought: *This is where I belong.* They had made love twice during the night with an intensity that had amazed and perhaps even frightened her.

She tilted her head and kissed his chin with its familiar dark stubble. He stirred and opened his eyes. A brief flicker of puzzlement about where he was, and then his arms tightened around her.

"What are you feeling?" His voice was gruff and scratchy.

"Peace," she said. She eased herself on top of him. "And love."

His hands found the small of her back and ambled up her spine. "Les—"

His beeper went off, and before they could react, her alarm. "Damn," she said.

They looked at each other. It *was* funny. Wetzon rolled over on her back, stretched out her hand, and turned off the alarm. Silvestri reached for the telephone and called in.

The T-shirt she'd been wearing was on the floor near the bed. She pulled it over her head, aware of Silvestri's eyes following her, and suddenly she felt shy. Her feet in her moccasins, she danced into the kitchen and got the coffee going, opened her front door and brought in the *Times* and *The Wall Street Journal* from her doormat. She wondered what the *Times* would have on Dilla's murder.

Silvestri was still talking on the phone in a hushed voice when she stuck her head into the bedroom, so she brushed her teeth and got into a steaming shower. She did some bends and stretches. Well, all right! So what *had* happened to her last night? But that's as far as she got because Silvestri joined her, and it wasn't until they were having coffee that he brought it up.

He put down his mug. "Les, have you talked to anybody about last year?" His eyes demanded she look at him.

"What about last year?" She folded her napkin, folded it again.

"Don't hide," he said gently. "About getting shot. I'm talking about a shrink."

"Oh, Silvestri—" She dismissed him with a wave of her hand. She wanted to stop herself, but she couldn't. It was as if he pressed the buttons and off she went.

"Don't 'Oh, Silvestri' me." He grabbed her floating hand. "What you had last night was a full-blown, classic anxiety attack."

She stared at him, shocked. An anxiety attack? She felt foolish. "How do *you* know?" It came out unintentionally belligerent. Or maybe it was intentional. She pulled her hand away from his.

"I've had a couple myself in my time. The shrinks call it post-traumatic stress syndrome. They're particularly likely to follow a life-threatening situation."

"But that was last year, Silvestri." She unwound the turban of towel from her head, dropped it on her shoulders, and ran her fingers through her damp hair. Her fingers sought the tiny ridge in her scalp; she shuddered.

He took her hand away from her head, where it seemed to have frozen. "It doesn't matter when. You haven't dealt with it. You have—"

"I think I've dealt okay with it."

"Don't get on your high horse, Les. Okay?" He sounded exasperated. "I know you. I can bet you parked it away in your mind somewhere and left it there. And now you're up to your ass in this new thing."

She tugged at her hand. She was furious. "You *know* me? You don't know me at all, Silvestri. I haven't seen you in eight months, and you still think you can tell me what to do."

"Nine."

"Nine? Is it really?"

"Yup."

"Oh, God, nine months . . ."

"And I'll bet you have that dream at least once a week."

"What dream?"

"The dream about getting shot."

"How do you—"

"I told you, Les. I've seen big brave cops and soldiers have panic attacks."

"It felt real to me. It's not psychosomatic."

"It was real."

"Silvestri." Her voice was so tiny, she could barely hear herself. "I dream I see the flash of the flame from the gun. I can smell the cordite, feel the sting. But I've never had an anxiety attack before."

"Then you're lucky, Les. What happened yesterday did it."

"What do you mean?"

"I mean the Dilla Crosby murder."

"Dilla."

"Your subconscious is trying to tell you something, Les. You're in overdrive. Listen to it. You're not going to be okay till you learn how to ask for help."

She sighed. "You've changed, Silvestri."

He looked confused, frowned. "This is not about me, Les. Stick to the subject."

She ignored him. Refolded the napkin the other way. "Are you doing one of your psych profiles on me?"

"Maybe I should. I might figure out why I—" He stopped short, rose and left the room.

She was stricken. She pushed away the coffee mugs, put her head on her arms on the table. When he returned, he was dressed, except for his jacket. He was adjusting the shoulder harness.

"I'm sorry," she murmured without lifting her head. "Thank you for last night."

He put his palm on her head. "Oh, Les, you're such hard work."

She bristled—she couldn't help herself—and stood up to him, all sixty-two inches of her. "Thanks a heap, Silvestri."

"Tell me you're not."

She shook her head.

"Are you still seeing Pinkus?"

She nodded.

"He's too old for you." Then he added, "And you probably have him wound around your little finger. He never says no to you, does he? Poor slob."

"Get out of here, Silvestri. Stop telling me what to do." She was burning; her hands were fists.

But Silvestri only seemed amused, which made her even more furious. And Alton never did say no to her. That was true.

"Must be a little boring." He put on his jacket.

"Huh?"

"Like having a Big Daddy—"

She flew at him, pelting him with punches, and he laughed, catching her hands, and kissed her, and they were back to square one again.

"Get out of my life, Silvestri," she whispered into his shirt.

"I wouldn't dream of it," he said. "Besides, I'll be working with Bernstein on the Crosby case."

C H A P T E R

"Chump change, Wetzon. That's what he offered me. He wants me to fucking relocate to New York and take a pay cut."

"Let me get this straight, David. He offered you ten K a month for six months versus a sixty percent payout? That's not chicken feed."

"Wetzon, he offered me a draw, a goddamn draw, of ten K a month with a payback if I don't make it. I want fifteen or I'm not coming. You tell him if he fucking thinks he's such hot stuff and can make me a million-dollar producer, he can fucking take a risk, too. He wants me to take all the risk. Do you know what it costs to live in New York?"

Do I ever, she thought. "I'll see what I can work out, David."

"Wetzon, listen to me. All he has to do is make it fifteen a month for six months versus sixty percent and I'll be there tomorrow."

She hung up. This wasn't going to work. There were very few surprises for her left in the business after almost seven years. She'd developed a sixth sense for which situations were going to work and which would not. In this case, two gigantic egos were dueling and both would lose.

The phones bleated, blinking lights. It was busy. It had been for the past year since the brokerage industry had burst out of the recession while the recession continued to hold the rest of the country in a death grip.

"I'm not going to kill myself over this," she told Smith, who had just arrived, bringing a cold breeze in with her.

Their office was in the ground floor of a townhouse on East Forty-ninth Street between First and Second avenues. It had been an apartment once, and where the kitchen had been was now their reception area. B.B., whose birth certificate read Bailey Hinson Balaban, had a tiny cubbyhole of an office in a corner of the room. The big room Smith and Wetzon shared, and their rear windows looked out on their own private garden. After renting for years, they had bought the building for a bargain price in 1992, when real estate had bottomed in New York. Now they were landlords.

Smith was all gussied up this morning in a copper knit suit. Her slim skirt came only to mid-thigh and her hose and shoes were a perfect match with her outfit. Now how had she managed that, Wetzon wondered.

"What did you say, sweetie pie?" Smith sat down at her desk and crossed one fabulous leg over the other, posing.

"I said, how nice you look, Smith." Wetzon grinned at her partner. They were both such phonies.

"Well, we do have a lunch appointment, don't we?" Smith lowered her lids to slits and peered at Wetzon. "What's the matter with you? You have no color in your face. And I don't like the foundation you're using. It makes your skin sallow."

"Gosh, I love spending time with you, Smith. You always make me feel so good."

"I see. You miss Alton."

"Let's not discuss Alton." *No, I don't miss Alton. I like being with him, but I don't miss him when he's not here.* He'd been gone three days and she'd been glad to be alone in her apartment—at least until last night. "And for your information, I don't miss him."

"There is a God." Smith gave Wetzon a smug nod of approval. "Just remember what I told you, sweetie. A relationship is only good if he loves you more than you love him."

Give me a break, Wetzon thought. She looked down at her suspect sheets, shuffling the most likely candidates to the top of the pile.

"How are we doing with David Dwyer?" Smith demanded.

"Yeah, well, what looked like an easy slam-dunk placement, isn't working. I don't think David is asking too much—fifteen a month for six months, but Ron has dug his heels in and won't budge."

"Set him up somewhere else."

"He isn't interested in any other firm."

Smith sent Wetzon a you're-not-trying-hard-enough look and turned her back. "I can't believe all these messages." She flipped through the pink slips, folded the lot in half and dropped them into her waste basket. Smith made a fetish of never returning phone calls. It drove Wetzon crazy.

"How do you know there wasn't something important in one of those?" Wetzon demanded.

"Oh puh-*lease*. If it's important, they'll call back. Anything new?"

"B.B. had a start this morning." Their young associate B.B. had come a long way since Smith and Wetzon had hired him right out of college. He had joined them, a preppy cold caller. In those days their associate had been the duplicitous Harold Alpert, who had subsequently betrayed them and gone to work for their major competition, Tom Keegen and Associates.

Last year they had added Max Orchard, a retired accountant, as a part-time cold caller, over Smith's loud objections, and he had turned out to be a gem, reliable and efficient. Net-net, they both agreed now, Max was a winner.

"B.B. did? Where? How much? Who?"

"Larry Cooper. Three hundred thou. We'll see fifteen on him. Rivington Ellis."

"Larry Cooper? The guy the Stock Exchange censured for laundering money?"

"The very one. He's a bundle of charm. I hate to work with these guys. They make me want to wash my hands after a simple phone call."

"Well, I'm certainly glad you put him at Rivington Ellis. At least they pay us on trailing twelve."

"Do you think I'm a fool, partner? Who knows how long he'll be around?"

"Let's light a few candles. You should probably hold his hand until the ninety days are up."

"I fully intend to, but it's a toss-up. His past will catch up to him, or he'll do something terrible at Rivington Ellis. These guys can't stop themselves before they kill again." Yikes, Wetzon thought. She had murder on the brain.

Smith tapped her mauve fingernails together and looked up at the Andy Warhol pencil drawing of a roll of dollar bills on the wall. They had purchased it years earlier to celebrate their first fee, both thinking it wonderfully symbolic. "Well, they didn't buy a pig in a poke."

"They know what he is. They wanted him anyway. Laura Lee claims Larry had a moral bypass at birth."

"Humpf. That Laura Lee Day thinks she's so clever. When are you going to understand that you can't be friends with these scum?"

"Smith, you know very well that Laura Lee has been a good friend to me. So keep your opinions to yourself."

"Oh, for pitysakes." Smith threw up her hands. "What time is lunch?"

"Twelve-thirty. I think maybe I should war—tell Twoey you're coming, don't you?"

"If you do, I'll never speak to you again."

Wetzon shook her finger at Smith. "You're going to torture him. He's still in love with you."

Smith's only rejoinder was her slow feline smile. She wrinkled her repouse nose.

Now it was Wetzon's turn to throw up her hands.

"Enter," Smith called imperiously in response to the knock on their door. "Ah, Max, sweetie pie." She winked at Wetzon. "You are such a fashion plate today."

Max was wearing his usual shiny brown suit, white socks, and brown gum-soled shoes. His pants were pulled up to his lower chest and held in place by suspenders. Today he had added a jaunty red-and-white polka-dot tie. A matching handkerchief drooped from the upper left pocket of his coat.

"Thank you." Max always treated Smith indulgently as if she were an errant daughter. "Your son is on line two."

Smith blew Max a kiss and scooped up the phone, purring, "How's my baby boy?" She made kissy-poo noises into the receiver.

"Oh, Smith," Wetzon groaned. "He's seventeen years old, for godsakes."

Smith glared at her. Mark was finishing his final term at Choate and would enter Harvard in the fall, yet Smith still referred to him as her baby boy. It was a wonder he'd managed to grow up at all.

Wetzon picked out Carlos's number, listened to the phone ring. When the answering machine came on, she said succinctly, "Please call me," and hung up. He was probably at rehearsal. But still, a little spot of apprehension niggled at her.

The phone rang. Three lines were lit and the in-coming call was on four. Wetzon answered, "Smith and Wetzon. Leslie Wetzon speaking."

"Oh, hi, Leslie. This is Sunny Browning, Mort Hornberg's assistant."

"Right. Are we still on for lunch today?"

"Yes, we are. I just wanted to confirm twelve-thirty at the Four Seasons. I've made a reservation for four."

"Okay, babycakes," Smith said into her phone.

"Four? Oh, you heard my partner is coming?"

Smith hung up with a clatter and turned her chair ostentatiously to listen to Wetzon's conversation.

"No. I guess it should be for five then," Sunny said. "I'm the fourth because I'm in charge of capitalizing Mort's shows."

"Okay, make it for five then. My partner, Xenia Smith, is very interested in investing in the show."

Smith began applauding in slow motion and Wetzon ended the conversation.

"Who was that?" Smith's expression was pure Eloise.

"Mort Hornberg's assistant, Sunny Browning. She raises the money for the shows. You'll meet her at lunch." But lunch, Wetzon was sure, would be a trial. Smith was in her troublemaking mode.

Inspecting her manicure, Smith said, "I'm sure." She rose and threw open the bathroom door and smiled at her image in the full-length mirror. "What kind of people name a child Sunny? Is she black?"

"No, she isn't. And what difference would it make anyway? Her real name is Sunshine."

"Sunshine! Unbelievable!" Smith began fussing with her makeup, putting blush on her face.

My kingdom for a Valium, Wetzon thought.

The phone rang, rang again, then stopped. Max knocked and opened the door. "Mrs. Orkin for you, Wetzon."

"For me?" Mrs. Orkin? Susan Orkin?

"Yes." Max closed the door.

She picked up the phone and said, "Leslie Wetzon."

"Leslie, this is Susan Orkin." A soft voice with a kind of sexy croak. There was something vaguely familiar about it.

"Yes?" Wetzon stayed noncommittal.

"You don't remember me, do you?"

"I'm sorry?"

"I was Susan Cohen when we were at Douglass together."

"Susan Cohen? From Douglass? I can't believe it." How astonishing. All this time Susan Orkin had been Susan Cohen, and Wetzon hadn't known it. She saw the girl who was Susan Cohen as clear as yesterday. Slim, tiny, honey-blond hair, an attractive angle to her nose, dimples. They'd had more than a few classes together throughout their four years of college.

"I'm Susan Cohen Orkin. Dilla and I—"

"I know. I just didn't know you were the Susan I knew. God, that sounds so convoluted. I'm so sorry about Dilla. Is there anything I can do?"

This time, Susan's voice broke. "Please, can we talk privately? I need your help."

C H A P T E R

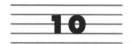

They checked their coats in the street-level coatroom and walked slowly up the blue-and-rust diamond carpeted steps. As always, Smith turned heads in her wake. They were late. Wetzon obsessed about being on time to the point where she was always early, but they were always late when Smith was involved.

For Wetzon, the Four Seasons was a magical place. Eighteen steps led to the most dramatic restaurant setting in New York. Ceilings soared at least twenty feet. This season being winter, the pottings contained the stark straight-arrow stalks of white birches. The staff uniforms were brown. All year round the restaurant was the home of the let's-do-business drink, the power lunch—in the Grill Room—and the reward dinner in the Pool Room. Actually, Wetzon could never really take the Pool Room seriously. It was just on the line of precious with a dash of pretension, and you were more likely to see tourists there than in the Grill Room, which was her favorite spot, and lunch was her favorite time.

She and Smith had been introduced at the Four Seasons by the man who was then their mutual attorney. They had formed their company over drinks in the Grill Room. Wetzon interviewed brokers there. One—Barry Stark—had been murdered in the phone booth just off the ground floor anteroom. The detective who caught the case had been Silvestri.

Although she still interviewed brokers at the Four Seasons, Wetzon could never erase the rush of jitters that passed over her whenever she climbed those stairs.

Without a sense of haste, Smith was engaged in exchanging pleasantries with Paul Kovi, one of the owners, who today stood behind the reservations desk. Wetzon surveyed the room. Wouldn't you know, they were all there, even Mort, who was as conscientiously tardy as Smith. They were sitting at one of the rectangular tables along the rosewood-paneled backdrop below the balcony.

The men leapt to their feet with a sight more energy than Wetzon thought necessary. Mort, the bags under his bloodshot eyes pronounced today, was well into his role of creative genius, wearing jeans and a red cashmere pullover—to match his eyes no doubt—a tweed jacket and a flashy silk tie. His tortoiseshell glasses were parked on top of his bald pate. He was focused on Smith.

Twoey Barnes, dear Twoey, wore his heart on his face. Goldman Barnes II was a gangly, red-haired, myopic softy, all six feet plus of him. A killer on the trading floor, maybe, but a pushover where Smith was concerned.

"Mort, my partner Xenia Smith," Wetzon said. She felt as if she were not part of the scene at all.

"Mort Hornberg," Mort said, riding over her, practically falling on Smith's extended hand, his eyes on her legs. He was notoriously ambivalent about women. Still, he'd always liked attractive ones around. Legs were his thing. And Smith had fabulous legs.

"Charmed," Smith said.

"And this is Sunny Browning." Mort motioned to Sunny Browning to change her chair so that Smith could sit next to him. He was drinking some sort of evil brown liquid in a glass.

Smith's eyes flicked over Sunny Browning in her Armani jacket and stark white shirt and loosely knotted purple silk tie, and then moved on to Twoey. "Sweetie pie, I've missed you desperately." Her voice was husky. She gave him a dazzling smile and turned back to Mort.

Wetzon caught Sunny's eye. The woman didn't miss much. You could almost see her totaling things up. Wetzon gave Twoey a peck on the cheek and sat between him and Sunny. Smith was up to her usual tricks: seduction and manipulation, and once again Wetzon had an aisle seat.

The baked salmon won out. A waiter in a brown toreador jacket took their food and drink orders, and Mort added a bottle of champagne. Smith beamed. Mort was doing all the right things.

"I'm sorry we kept you—" Wetzon was stopped in her tracks by Smith's glare. Smith's motto was *never apologize,* along with *if they give, you take and if they take, you scream.*

Smith smiled sweetly at Mort and patted his hand. "Do go on. We'll just sit here like quiet little mice and listen."

"I was just telling Mr. Barnes—"

"Twoey, please." Twoey's eyes crinkled behind gold-rimmed glasses.

"Twoey it is," Mort said with another burst of heartiness and brushed imaginary dandruff from one shoulder, then the other. "I was just telling Twoey that *Hotshot* is a ten-character musical, six dancers and four actors, but of course, everyone will be equally important to the whole." He took a sip of the evil liquid and smiled at Smith. "Each actor is a principal on a white contract. Of course, Carlos Prince, our choreographer, has his work cut out for him. Getting actors to do review pieces is my job; getting them to dance is his." He gave Wetzon an exaggerated wink. "And he's done his usual amazing sleight-of-hand."

A waiter arrived with their platters and another brought a bottle of champagne in a bucket of ice. Tulip glasses were filled halfway. Wetzon and champagne did not agree so she left it sparkling in the glass, and whispered to the waiter, "Amstel Light."

"We've capitalized *Hotshot* at five million, taking into consideration our three-week tryout in Boston . . . ah, Twoey." Mort rolled Twoey's name around on his tongue, registered it, then tucked it into one of the little compartments in his mind. "Sunny can give you the budget. We have an ensemble company—no stars—so we can keep costs down."

"No stars?" Smith asked innocently, then moved in for the kill. "How do you expect to pay back your investors?"

Mort looked nonplussed. Had he thought Smith was stupid? Well, surprise, surprise.

"On the strength of the book and music." It was the first time Sunny had spoken. She'd pulled some papers from a zippered, hand-held Louis Vuitton portfolio and now she efficiently passed a set around to Twoey, Smith, and Wetzon. "The top page is the budget. The second page is a breakdown of our royalty schedule, estimated break-even at the Colonial in Boston and here in New York."

Mort smiled benevolently at Twoey, who was running his eyes down the budget. "I understand from Leslie that you're serious about becoming a producer."

"Mort, old chum." A tall man in a two-thousand-dollar suit, dark hair showing just the right touch of white at the temples, clasped Mort's shoulder. They shook hands solemnly. "How's it going? Terribly sad about Dilla. Such a tragedy."

"Yes, we'll miss her," Mort said, with just the right amount of studied melancholy, "but she would have wanted us to go on."

Sure, Wetzon thought. The show had to go on, didn't it?

She recognized the man in the two-thousand-dollar suit. Joel Kidde was the eccentric head of the top talent agency in the world. He had the appetite of a goat. Once at Sardi's Wetzon had seen him eat a contract.

Kidde glanced at Smith and hung in there until Mort made the introductions. "Well . . ." Kidde said, giving Smith an aural caress. "I'll see you in Boston, Mort." He moved on to the next table, where he bestowed more greetings.

Smith purred, "What an interesting man."

What have I done, Wetzon thought.

In the meantime, Mort had resumed his commentary on the budget. "What we didn't figure on, Twoey, is that we wouldn't get subscription for the full three weeks in Boston. We're okay for the first two, which means we could go into the hole in the third week if the reviews are boring, or mixed."

"How much do you suppose you'll need?" Twoey asked.

"Safely, a million should cover us and give us a sinking fund."

Twoey studied the budget figures. "That's do-able."

Sunny said, "If there's anything you don't understand, please ask." Her shoulder-length hair was the color of sand with streaks of bottled sun. She wore it pulled back from her slightly horsey face with a black velvet headband.

Twoey grinned at her; she smiled at him. That Sunny liked him was obvious.

Lowering her eyelids halfway, Smith contemplated Twoey, then Sunny and Twoey again. Danger, Wetzon thought. Danger-danger-danger.

"We estimate our break-even—that's the weekly operating budget—at approximately four hundred ninety-two thousand. Based on gross weekly box office receipts at capacity at a Broadway theatre of six hundred fifty thousand, the weekly operating profit would be one fifty-eight. With full houses it should take us about thirty-one weeks to pay back the investment. And the road is another story. There are built-in costs, higher salaries, travel expenses, and load-in and load-out costs. We never expect to make money on the road, but we don't want to lose money either."

"Must you go to Boston?" Smith inquired. "Why not preview in New York? Wouldn't you save a lot of money?"

Mort shook his head, his smile on the edge of patronizing. "Yes, but I know you can't fix a show in New York with all the goddam know-it-alls coming in every night and second-guessing you, telling you what you're doing wrong."

"Besides," Sunny said, "we're committed to the Colonial. They've sold subscription in good faith. We have to go."

"What about the murder?" Twoey was making notes on the budget with a gold Mont Blanc pen.

"It shouldn't affect us at all," Sunny said. "Although in a perverse way it may sell tickets to the usual ghouls who love this kind of thing."

"Dilla was a dear friend," Mort intoned, "but we have a lot on the line here."

"The show must go on," Wetzon murmured.

"Of course, Leslie is absolutely right. She was one of us not so long ago, and as far as we are concerned, she still is."

"Well, thank you, Mort," Wetzon said. "I think." She looked over at Smith, who was being uncharacteristically silent. Smith was smiling like the Cheshire Cat.

Mort settled his glasses back on his nose and fondled his baldness. "Look, if you're interested, Twoey, I'd be willing to take you on as associate producer and teach you what I know. Sunny here is my numbers cruncher so she can sit down with you and—"

At this point Smith pounced. "The Smith and Wetzon pension fund," she pronounced cheerily, "will invest fifty thousand dollars in *Hotshot.*"

"I can't believe you did that!" Wetzon had worked herself into such a fury that it was propelling her several paces ahead of Smith. "And with our pension money." She ended up having to wait, steaming, on the corner of Forty-ninth and Lexington until Smith caught up.

"You know, there's no pleasing you, Wetzon. Did you or did you not tell me that this musical Mort Hornberg and Your Gay Person are working on was going to make theatre history?"

Smith had stopped referring to Carlos as the Degenerate after he became a celebrity choreographer. "Your Gay Person" was his new designation. And never to be outdone, Carlos loathed Smith. He blamed Smith for luring Wetzon from the Theatre and for trying to impose her values on Wetzon. That his darling Birdie should be partners with someone so bigoted and greedy was a constant source of irritation. Carlos and Smith fought out their battle, around and through Wetzon, usually leaving her quivering in the middle.

This was one of those times. " 'My Gay Person' has a name, Smith. Read my lips. Carlos Prince." She found herself stamping her foot on the sidewalk to punctuate her words, to the great entertainment of a multilayered bag lady whose top layer was a moth-eaten mouton coat.

The woman cackled and seemed about to join in the fray when Smith snarled at her. "On your way, or I'll have you put in a shelter."

The woman froze. Her face showed abject terror, as if Smith had condemned her to death.

"I mean it." Smith shook a leather-clad finger at her.

"You are an evil person!" the bag lady shouted. "I put a curse on you." She pointed two fingers at Smith, spitting at them, then, muttering under her breath, grabbed her shopping cart loaded with bursting plastic garbage bags and a dilapidated broom, whiskered ends up, and pushed off up Lexington.

"Oh, my God." Smith clutched Wetzon's arm. "Did you hear her? She put a *curse* on me." Her face had a yellowish tinge.

"Don't be ridiculous. She's disturbed, and you shouldn't have gotten into it with her. It didn't mean anything."

Smith looked slightly relieved, but still seemed to be rattled. She shuddered. "Let's get out of here."

Wetzon locked arms with her. "You've been hanging around with these psychics too long. Come on, she was just blathering." Wetzon would have loved to recapture her anger, but, alas, most of it had dissipated. "Of course, I did see a broom in her shopping cart. . . ."

"No!" Smith turned miserable eyes back to look for the bag lady, but she had disappeared up the avenue.

Wetzon groaned. "I was kidding!"

"You were?"

"Cross my heart." She made the motion. "Can we get back to *Hotshot?*"

"You are the limit," Smith said, recovering. "Well, did you or did you not say this would be a landmark musical?"

"I did, but—" Wetzon shoved her gloved hands into her pockets and grouched all the way to Third Avenue.

"Well, then." Smith had entirely retrieved her equilibrium. "It was a business decision. Last year was the best year we've ever had. We have to diversify where we put our money."

"But fifty thousand? Jesus, Smith, no one makes money investing in the Theatre anymore."

"*We* will. The Tarot says turmoil, then buckets of money, and the Tarot never lies."

"I might have guessed." Wetzon stretched the *s*'s out into a hiss.

"Trust me."

Wetzon would have felt a shade better if Smith had not said those last two words. Years earlier a broker had warned Wetzon that *trust me* is code for *fuck you.* "Oh, hell," she muttered.

"Angels!" Smith said with relish. "We're angels. Isn't that wonderful?"

The question was rhetorical. Smith had never before expressed any interest in the Theatre, only went to mega hit shows like *Miss Saigon* and *Phantom* because one did, and the last thing she would ever have done was invest money in it. And she would have been right. Investment in the Theatre was notoriously risky. Wetzon came to a stop in front of Steve Sondheim's house.

"What are you doing?"

"Paying homage." She tipped her beret to Sondheim and then did the same to Kate Hepburn, whose house was next door, and who had, it was said, complained vigorously about the noise from the legendary composer's piano. "You should join me now that you're going through the blood rite of investing in a musical."

"Oh, puh-*lease.*" Smith tugged at her arm. "You're making a fool of yourself, and of me. What if he came out and saw you?"

"He'd love it."

"Well, if you don't mind, I don't want to be here to find out." She steered Wetzon across Second Avenue and back to their office.

It was two-thirty. Max had worked his half-day and was gone. Three neat stacks of suspect sheets sat on his desk. Wetzon hung up her coat and collected the stack labeled *Wetzon—Priority.*

B.B., who was on the phone, waved. The blinking button indicated someone was on hold. Wetzon went into the office she and Smith shared and set Max's priorities on her desk next to the four phone messages on pink slips. One was from Laura Lee. And Alton. He'd be home Saturday morning and would call her then. If things went as planned, she would be in Boston on Saturday for Carlos's opening. She had told Alton weeks ago and he'd forgotten.

Wetzon picked up the phone and released the hold button. "Hi, this is Leslie Wetzon. May I help you?"

"I . . . oh . . . Leslie? Oh, Birdie?" It was not Carlos but the voice was familiar.

"Yes?" She straightened out her date book and plucked a pen from the pressed-glass spooner she kept pens and pencils in.

"Hi, this is Phil? You know, Phil Terrace? From *Hotshot?*" Everything he said ended with a question. It was disconcerting. "Carlos wanted me to find out if you can meet him at five?"

"Where?" She had told Susan Cohen, or Susan Orkin, as she called herself now, they could meet at six o'clock. That didn't leave her much time.

"The Polish Tea Room."

The Polish Tea Room was really the coffee shop of the Edison Hotel on Forty-seventh Street in the Theatre District. It had, over a decade ago, been dubbed the Polish Tea Room because the chef was Polish. "I've got a six o'clock, Phil. Do you think he can make it four-thirty? Is he rehearsing?"

"We loaded out this morning. Carlos just wanted a couple of hours with the company and they're finishing up now. I think four-thirty will be all right. I'll call back if it's not."

"Are you taking over as production stage manager, Phil?"

"Temporarily, at least. I don't know what Mort's plans are." Phil seemed slightly less tentative. He'd stopped ending sentences with questions. "I know the show backward and forward."

"Well, good luck then, and I'll see you in Boston. I'm coming up for Friday's preview and will stay through the opening on Saturday. Unless that's changed."

"No. We're right on schedule. I'll tell Carlos four-thirty. *Ciao.*" He definitely sounded more confident. Knowing Mort, Phil would become production stage manager, and life, for *Hotshot,* would go on without a ripple.

Wetzon sat down at her desk. Dilla's death had left her on the verge of melancholy, and she had not even liked Dilla. A frisson of her pain and fear of the previous night intruded. She pushed it away.

"I can't get over Twoey," Smith said casually to Wetzon's back.

Now what was Smith up to? "I give up. Tell me."

"Well, he just doesn't seem like the same person."

Wetzon turned and looked at her partner. "There *is* life after Xenia Smith, you know."

"Very funny. That's not what I meant at all."

"I'm sorry. What did you mean?" Wetzon's voice dripped with sweetness.

"Humpf." Smith lowered her lids partway to see if Wetzon was mocking her, but Wetzon gave good cipher. "I just never knew he wanted to be a Broadway producer, or even that he had any interest in the arts."

"If you weren't so wrapped up in yourself and the wonderful Richard Hartmann, mouth piece for the Mob, and money launderer *par excellence,* you might have seen that Mark and Twoey both are interested in the Theatre." One day soon, Wetzon thought, Smith will get tired of Hartmann and I'll take what's sitting in my safe deposit box to the district attorney's office.

"Oh, spare me one of your goody-two-shoes lectures," Smith said waspishly.

"Twoey is a love, and you've let him slip through your fingers. Did you happen to notice how Sunny Browning was with him?"

"That slut?"

"Smith! You don't even know her."

"He would never look at her twice."

"Whatever." Wetzon turned away and took the budget material on *Hot-*

shot out of her purse and dropped it on her desk. Absentmindedly, she flipped over the page to the breakdown on royalties and the weekly costs to run the show.

It is estimated that the gross weekly box office receipts at a theatre with 1500 seats, with an average price ticket of $45 would be $600,000.

Ha! So what if orchestra tickets cost upward of $65? No wonder the Theatre was dying.

Her eyes wandered down the first six names and numbers on the list:

Morton Hornberg, director:	4%
Aline Rose, librettist:	4%
Sam Meidner, composer-lyrist:	4%
Carlos Prince, choreographer:	3%
Dilla Crosby, assoc. producer:	2%
Morton Hornberg, producer:	2.5%

When she got to the seventh name on the royalty list, she blinked and looked again. Vaguely, she heard Smith talking behind her, saying something about Mort Hornberg, but it didn't penetrate.

The last name on the royalty list was Susan Orkin.

Fran Burke, even if you didn't know better, would never be mistaken for a woman. He'd been christened Francis Xavier, but everyone called him Fran at least as long as he'd been in the Theatre. He was a road manager who specialized in taking out touring companies and tryouts. Although gnarled with arthritis and dependent on a cane, at seventy, Fran was still sharp as a steel blade. It was said that Fran controlled the ice on the street.

Not for the first time Wetzon marveled at the fact that her two careers both were referred to as The Street—one Broadway, the other, Wall. And the similarities didn't stop there. Both contained producers and managers—stars with tremendous egos. The stalwart reliable Equity actor-dancer could find his like on Wall Street in the honest responsible broker. And Wetzon well knew there were almost as many ways to commit fraud on Broadway as there were on the other Street. Skimming, kickbacks, and padding all came under the heading of "ice."

Wetzon, lost in her puzzlement about Susan Orkin being on the *Hotshot* Company's royalty list, didn't see the man with the cane until she walked right into him. "Oh—excuse—I'm so sorry," she stammered, and then she realized it was Fran Burke, and he was smiling a big, broad smile, showing receding gums and nicotine-stained teeth.

"Leslie Wetzon! Where you been, girl? Off raising some young ones?" He clasped her hand and chucked her under the chin. Fran wore a rumpled blue suit under his black Aquascutum and no hat covered his thick yellowish white hair, which he combed straight back. Once long ago, when *Company* was in Chicago, he had not docked Wetzon for missing a performance. She'd sprained her ankle when a wagon was off its mark. "You're family," he'd said when she thanked him.

"Nope," she said now. "I'm still single, Fran, just making a lot of money running a business."

"Come on and walk with me to Shubert Alley." He didn't wait for her to make up her mind, but took a firm hold of her elbow. "Yeah, your buddy Carlos said something about it." Wetzon knew Fran was of the generation that didn't approve of career women. Oh, it was all right for a young girl to be stagestruck, but once that had worn off, women should marry and have children. Fran had outlived two wives that Wetzon remembered. His third was in a nursing home in Spring Lake, and he was living, last she'd heard, with a woman who had been amanuensis to a Broadway producing team in the 1960s. Now he gave her a thorough once-over. "You don't look a day older, Leslie." He walked her along at a fairly brisk pace, considering his condition.

"Fran, you're a peach. You always were. I loved it when you took us out. A road tour with you as company manager was like being part of a well-oiled machine. There were never any screwups."

His beefy hand, all dotted with liver spots, clutched the head of the cane. Through his thick fingers she saw a carved wooden skull. "You're a good girl."

She found she didn't mind being called a good girl by Fran, because that's the way it was. As they turned off Broadway onto Forty-fifth Street, one neon marquee after another testified to the fact that Broadway was enduring, with the active, and hyped, participation of the English, and spectacle musicals like *Cats, Phantom, Miss Saigon,* and *Les Mis.*

"Hey, Fran!" Fran was hailed by two hefty stagehands. Both looked familiar to Wetzon.

A bus was loading up in Shubert Alley. Battered suitcases of every variety, color, and condition, from grubby duffels to Louis Vuitton, were piled in a huge mound at the open side of the bus, and the driver, wearing a blue cap with an *X* and a sleeveless down vest over an itchy-looking navy-issue sweater, was arguing with a dancer who had a champagne-colored poodle on a leash. The poodle kept yapping. He was answered by a particularly feisty Yorkie on the bus, who thrust its minuscule nose out of a barely open window.

Fran Burke took charge immediately. Within minutes everything was sorted out and made right. Peace and order descended.

Wetzon watched as cast members and wardrobe people got on the bus, off, then on again, some carrying covered cardboard containers of coffee or tea. She drew a soupçon of nostalgia into her lungs with each breath. The *Hotshot* Company was loading out for Boston, and Fran was taking them. But Leslie Wetzon, girl dancer, was not one of them.

"Fran, listen, Avery wants to take up two seats—" Wetzon recognized one of the actresses who had been with Carlos on Saturday at the theatre. She stopped and stared at Wetzon, and Wetzon thought: *Does she think I'm replacing someone?* She remembered those feelings, too. It was not a part of show biz that she missed.

"Let him." Fran winked at Wetzon. The actress shrugged, tossed her ponytail, and got back on the bus.

A limousine pulled into Shubert Alley. It edged around the bus, stopping near the door to the Shubert Organization offices. Three men emerged, one of whom Wetzon recognized as Cameron MacIntosh, the English producer. They were greeted almost immediately by Bernie Jacobs, president of the Shubert Organization, and headed in the direction of the Shubert Theatre, where *Crazy for You* was still singing and dancing.

"Awful about Dilla," Wetzon said. She was shivering. Fran took her arm and led her out of the wind and into the outside lobby of the Booth, conveniently on the Forty-fifth Street corner of Shubert Alley.

Fran grunted. He shifted the cigarette to the other side of his mouth with a clench of his lips. Neither sorrow nor joy registered on his florid face. "It's a wonder it didn't happen sooner."

Wetzon's ears prickled. She couldn't help it. She kept her tone casual. "Why do you say that?"

A distant look passed over Fran's watery blue eyes. "She was always playing one against the other." He shrugged, keeping a wary eye on the activity around the bus. "Oh, what the hell. Dilla always got what she wanted . . . until Saturday. Listen, I warned Lenny about her, not to trust her—"

"Lenny?" Who the hell was Lenny? She flipped through her mental Rolodex. Lenny Bernstein?

"Forget it. It was a long time ago. We've brought Phil along and he's a good boy. It'll be okay now."

Okay, at least she knew he was talking about Phil Terrace. "Yes, he seems like a nice kid. Do you think he'll be able to handle the show?"

Fran gave her a grim smile. "We're all going to help him, you can bet on it." He patted her on the back and opened the lobby door. "I gotta get the show on the road."

"I'll be up for the opening, Fran."

"Good." His attention was on the business at hand, getting his company moved out. He opened the lobby door, admitting a piercing gust of wind and a woman in a mink coat and humongous gold earrings, who thanked him and moved on to the box office to buy tickets for *Someone Who'll Watch Over Me.*

The temperature was falling rapidly. Tucking her hands in her pockets, Wetzon followed Fran out into Shubert Alley, watched him do his rolling walk over to the bus. He reached inside his coat and pulled out a notepad. Its pages snapped in the wind. "Anyone missing?" His voice barely carried back to Wetzon.

The driver closed the luggage compartment with a thump and got on the bus. The engine turned over, then filled the Alley with exhaust fumes. Lights came on. Fran climbed the bus steps with some effort, stopped, peered out, and waved at her. The door closed. The bus crawled out of Shubert Alley onto Forty-fourth Street toward Broadway.

Wetzon watched until she lost sight of it. The wind was making her eyes water. Or was it good old *déjà vu?* Get a grip, she told herself. It had been fun, maybe more in retrospect because we were all young and talented and each show was going to be The Big One. Had she forgotten the injuries, the tears when a show folded immediately after the *New York Times* pan? Why was it that memories tended to get mushy around the edges with time?

Eager to be indoors, she made haste to Forty-seventh Street and the Edison Hotel, smack in the middle of the block between Broadway and Eighth. The coffee shop had become very popular, particularly with the producers, theatre owners, directors, and choreographers, since the old Gaiety Deli, a longtime Broadway favorite on West Forty-seventh Street, had closed in the late 1970s, reopened, closed, reopened, and closed again. The very uncertainty of its existence proved too hard for the regulars to handle.

On the corner of Forty-seventh Street a derelict picked through a trash basket, opening plastic food cartons and tossing the detritus on the sidewalk. People hurried past, dodging his missiles, ignoring him when a carton sprayed its contents on their shoes or boots, afraid to confront the possibility of deranged violence. Wetzon caught herself— What was the matter with her? She wasn't usually so cynical. Maybe Silvestri was right. Maybe she ought to talk to someone. Maybe she should just pick up the phone and call Sonya Mosholu. Sonya's specialty had been bioenergetics, but she was also a shrink, working body and mind. Yes, she would call Sonya when she got home tonight.

She quickened her pace. She wanted to see Carlos before he left town.

The awning over the entrance to the Polish Tea Room said *Café,* which always made Wetzon laugh, but then, everyone on Broadway was reaching for the stars, including hotels and restaurants.

A curtain of steam decorated the windows facing the street. Only visible was the notice of the special on a cream-colored signboard:

Cabbage soup
Beef goulash with noodles
$9.95

A bargain, for sure. Wetzon pushed the door open and looked around, shading her tearing eyes. On the right was a cordoned-off area, reserved for theatre notables. The Shuberts, producer Manny Azenberg, and others who were part of the private theatre community, often lunched there on Polish specialties not featured on the menu.

A counter and a smoking section were in the back of the restaurant. On Wetzon's immediate left were about a dozen tables. Only a sparse few were occupied. Carlos sat at the last table next to the foggy windows. He had a decidedly unhappy expression on his face, and he was not alone.

Silvestri was with him.

C H A P T E R

Neither Carlos nor Silvestri noticed her; they were leaning toward one another, Silvestri talking intently, Carlos listening, nodding. Like two conspira-
tors. That was an odd switch. She stared up at the arched ceilings that
towered over the tacky, greasy-spoon layout. Everything was decorated in
uninspired dark browns and beiges. Show posters were scattered without
method about the available walls. Sam Meidner was sitting at the counter
alone over a bowl of soup, working the London *Observer* crossword puzzle.
Hotshot's composer saw her and pursed his lips into a kiss at her. If she ever
accepted his overtures, she was sure he would run like the wind.

As Wetzon neared them, she saw the table was a swamp of spilled coffee
and soaked and discarded Sweet'n Low packages, in the midst of which sat
two grungy mugs. Silvestri was wearing a new tweed jacket over a dark blue
turtleneck. Carlos was in black, head to toe. The two were so involved in
whatever they were talking about that neither saw her until she stood over
them.

"My, my, you boys sure do leave a messy table."

"Birdie!" Carlos shot out of his seat. Guilt stuck out all over him as he
gave her an effusive hug, held her away from him, searching for something
on her face, then hugged her again.

She pulled away from Carlos, angry with both of them. "You told him,"
she accused Silvestri.

Silvestri had pushed back his chair and was standing, so she had to look
up at him. All kinds of emotions churned, tumbled, and bled inside her. She
felt as if she'd forgotten to separate the whites from the colors. "It's not

fair, you guys. You have no right." She was so close to tears she shocked herself.

"Les," Silvestri said, probably with more gentleness than she deserved, "we weren't talking about you." He shoved his hands in his pockets and sat down.

"That's right." Carlos's dark eyes took on some of their old sparkle. He pulled over a chair from an empty table. "Sit, dear heart, and tell Carlos just what it is he's not supposed to know."

He sounded so sincere that Wetzon felt bratty and acquiesced. She chewed her lips, conscious that they were already chapped, and began going through her purse for lip cream, getting increasingly agitated and unable to control it. When she found the tube and looked up, she caught Silvestri and Carlos exchanging glances. "Gotcha," she said. They weren't talking about her? Sure. Well, she could take care of herself.

"We were talking about Dilla, Birdie." Carlos glanced at his watch. Parked behind his chair were a buttery black leather carryon and a matching shoulder tote.

"What did the M.E. say?" She caught Silvestri's annoyance in the stiff tilt of his shoulders. "I'm in this, Silvestri, up to my ears. You can't keep me out. I know all the players better than you. And I was there when Dilla's body was found."

"What damn good will it do if you know? All this stuff only adds more pressure to your problems."

"I don't have any problems," she said haughtily. "And I might be able to help."

"Oh, yeah? And when did you get your gold shield?"

"Please, children, play nice. Poppa is leaving town for a little while—he has to dance for a living—and he would like to know that his babies aren't going to kill each other while he's gone."

Silvestri gave in first and Wetzon felt a thrill of triumph. "The vic was covered with vomit—"

"Phil Terrace barfed when he saw her. I heard him."

"Yeah, well, so far we have murder by repeated blows from a blunt, cylindrical-shaped instrument."

"Then she was beaten to death with a stick or a pipe?"

"Maybe."

"Sometimes," Wetzon mused out loud, "the treasurer kept a billy club in the box office."

"My Birdie is so smart!"

Wetzon curled her lip at Carlos. He was being altogether too complimentary, as if he wanted to prop her up. She flashed him what she hoped was a withering look, but he only lowered one mocking eyelid at her.

"Okay." Silvestri jotted a note in his book.

"You said blows?" Carlos frowned.

"Her head was beaten in and she was left for dead."

"A crime of passion?" Wetzon waved to a waitress, a tall, fleshy woman in tight pants and cowboy boots. A crimson scarf was tied loosely around her neck. She was suddenly famished. "Can I have a chocolate milk shake?"

"She knew her murderer," Silvestri said.

"Everyone who made Dilla's acquaintance at sometime or other wanted to kill her. Even Susan," Carlos said.

"You mean Susan Orkin?" Silvestri asked, pen poised.

"Susan? Really?" Wetzon asked. In college, Susan had always been a gentle person, always looking for a fourth for bridge. Actually, Susan had been an aggressive player with a compulsion to win. But then, Wetzon thought, most people played bridge that way. Bridge was an especially popular sport among the moguls on Wall Street.

"I'm not telling tales out of school, but Dilla was a bit of a slut. She was all over the place and sexual persuasion hardly mattered." Carlos looked down at his nearly empty mug. "To know Dilla was to loathe her. She was trying to get me off the show." He spread his palm on his chest and lisped, "So even *I* have a motive."

"What about Sam Meidner?" Silvestri rose and brought the pot of coffee from the counter to the table. He refilled the mugs, returning the pot.

He was looking very fit and trim, Wetzon was thinking, and then he caught her eye and read her mind. She resented his grin. "Sam's sitting at the counter," she said. "So keep it down."

"He's going up with us," Carlos said.

"Go on," Silvestri prompted.

"He's a bit of a masochist," Carlos said with just the right amount of reluctance.

"Aren't we all?" There was a pause during which Wetzon studied Carlos and he avoided making eye contact.

"Is that so unusual?" Silvestri persisted.

"Only if you like being tied up and beaten by nubile maidens."

"So all those stories about him are true?" Wetzon wasn't surprised. The stories about Sam had been around for years.

"Add to that, Sam has sticky fingers."

"He's a klepto." Silvestri rubbed his nose as if he were trying to remember something.

"Let's just say Sam's attracted to bright, expensive objects. I bet he has a rap sheet a mile long," Carlos said.

"Okay," Silvestri said, making another note. "Let me run some people by both of you."

"Carlos, baby!"

Carlos jumped to his feet and practically disappeared into Daisy Robera's voluminous red velvet shawl as she hugged him. "When do you leave?" Daisy was wearing a dancer's garb of leggings and leg warmers under a short pleated skirt. An aging gypsy, last year she had played Desiree Armfeldt in the City Opera's revival of *A Little Night Music.*

"Momentarily. This is Silvestri and—"

"Leslie! I can't believe it's you. I have to run now but call me and we'll have lunch. I can fill you in on how I'm getting all of Angie Lansbury's old roles."

Wetzon smiled. "I will."

"Break a leg, you beautiful boy," Daisy told Carlos and was off in an energized flurry of frantic blond hair, floating past the waitress carrying Wetzon's milk shake.

The chocolate turned her mellow with her first thick strawful. Better than Valium any day. She sighed happily and looked up. Carlos and Silvestri were watching her like two goddam mother hens. "You two—" she began, then remembering she was mellow— "Okay, Silvestri, ask away." She unbuttoned her coat.

"Aline Rose." He moved on to a clean page.

"Didn't she and Dilla have something together once?" Wetzon looked at Carlos.

"Aline was married to a garmento with tons of money. She dumped him and moved in with Dilla, the husband divorced her and got custody of the kids—I think there were three or four. Aline got nothing, not even what she left behind in her closet. That was before she had her first show. Dilla dumped her for a big agent, someone who was going to make her a movie star."

"Hey, I remember now. That was Dilla's big dream. She would have killed to be a movie star." Wetzon clamped her hand over her mouth. "Sorry." She'd only drunk half the shake but felt stuffed and a little high. She pushed it aside. "But I don't remember any liaison with an agent."

"You were on your way out of the business, Birdie."

"I guess she didn't make it in the movies?" Silvestri looked at the milk shake. "You finished?"

"Yes."

He dumped the straw on the table and drank what was left in the glass in one elephant swallow.

"The camera hated her," Carlos said. "And with good reason. The agent moved on. Dilla came back to Broadway and hooked up with Mort, and the rest is history."

"Who was the agent?" Wetzon wondered out loud.

"The sultan of BAM."

"What's BAM?" Silvestri asked.

"Best Artists Management," Carlos and Wetzon said in unison.

Then Wetzon said, "Wait a minute, Carlos, you don't mean—"

"You got it, darling. The sunburnt kid himself. Joel Kidde."

C H A P T E R

"Carlos! I've been looking all over for you. I was afraid you'd left and I want
to show you my new design for the finale—"

A string bean of a woman with orange Brillo hair and dead white
makeup, her hollow cheekbones unwisely accented by deep blusher, was
standing near the door to the Edison lobby, propping up a huge black
portfolio with her knee.

Carlos rolled his eyes. "Design number five. I still like the first one. I
keep telling her I like the first one. Mort likes the first one. Everyone likes
the first one. We've made up the first one. We're opening on Saturday, for
Chrissakes. It's an exercise in masturbation." He rose and went to meet her.
"Darling," he drawled, and they cheek-kissed elaborately.

"Who's that?" Silvestri asked Wetzon.

"Costumes. Peg Button." Wetzon looked at her watch. Twenty after five.
She needed to be out on the street looking for a cab in another fifteen
minutes.

"Button? Costumes?" He gave her a suspicious look.

"Honest." She grinned at him and folded her hands in her lap because
they wanted to reach out and touch him.

"I suppose she also has a motive?" He jotted Peg's name in his notepad.

"Probably."

"Les, how's it going?" The intensity of his tone forced her to meet his
eyes.

She shrugged. She wanted to lay her head in the hollow of his chest.

He shifted in his chair so that their knees touched. "You're so goddam
spiky. You won't let anyone help you."

"I promise you I'll talk to someone. I even know who."

"First thing tomorrow?"

"Tonight, if she can fit me in." Their fingers grazed near their knees. "Oh, God." She closed her eyes.

"Is he still away?"

She opened her eyes. "Yes." There was so much heat between them they were almost melting down together.

Silvestri put his palm on her knee briefly, then stood and walked to where Carlos was talking to Peg Button. Wetzon watched as introductions were made. On an impulse, she rose and sat down at the counter next to Sam. A bowl of ruddy cabbage soup to his immediate right was hardly touched.

He looked at her through bloodshot eyes. "How's the world treating you, beauteous Leslie?"

"I have no complaints, Sam. Your score is lovely."

"Thanks, dear." He scratched his chin.

"The beard is very attractive."

That caught him by surprise. "Do you really think so? If the show is a hit, I was thinking of shaving it off." Moving his eyes away from her, he said, "I need this show, Leslie, or I'm dead."

She felt an overwhelming sadness. Sam had been so sweet, funny, so nice to her so long ago. "Sam, the show will be a big hit." She smiled at him. "And Carlos says I'm a witch, so you'd better believe it. I'm even coming up to Boston to make sure." His writing block, his failure, had become a comfortable companion, even a security blanket. How would he handle success this time around?

"We'll have our reunion drink then, dear?"

"That we will." She saw that Silvestri was leaving with Peg Button. He did not look back.

Patting Sam's hand, she returned to the table, where Carlos was already ensconced. "Everyone's a suspect," she said.

"Listen, dear heart, we're practically the whole world of the theatre now. Mort, Sam, Aline, and me. Same with Peg. How many of us are left? And where is the next generation? Where are the Cole Porters, the Jerry Robbinses, the Hammersteins, the Rodgerses, the Loessers, the Fosses?" He took her hand in his.

"I know." She leaned over and kissed his cheek. "Did you like what Peg showed you?"

"No. At the very least, I want costumes that move. It's bad enough I've got to work with actors who can't."

"What's going on with you, Carlos? Talk to me straight."

He raised one supercilious eyebrow and tilted his head to look at her. "Darling, that's hardly possible." The big diamond stud in his right earlobe caught the light and winked at her.

"Don't try to weasel out. I know something is wrong, and it's not just Dilla. Are you and Arthur okay?" She stopped, thinking the worst. "It's not—"

Carlos reached around and hugged her. "Birdie, I love you for this. I've got to work it out. And no, it's not HIV or AIDS or anything like it." He sighed. "There's this beautiful young man . . . Smitty . . . he's been turning up at rehearsals, hanging around. Now Mort and Mrs. Mort—Poppy, to you—have adopted him."

"Uh oh—"

"They're competing for him. You know how they are. Mort is making Smitty all kinds of promises about jobs and Poppy took him up to Boston with her today. By limousine, no less."

"How old is he?"

"Twenty-two, he says. But he's a young twenty-two. He's a senior at Wesleyan."

"Don't worry about him. He probably knows what he's doing." She looked at Carlos and saw something. . . . "There's more, isn't there? You like him, too."

Carlos nodded, not turning away from her.

"You *know* he's gay?"

"Unmistakable, dear heart."

"Oh, Carlos." She put her head on his shoulder.

"Aren't we the pair?" He smiled down at her.

Wetzon shifted gears. "Silvestri told you, didn't he?"

"He loves you."

"Sure."

"And you love him. So get it together, will ya?"

"Dearest Abby, I didn't ask you."

"Dearest heart, see a shrink about your anxiety attacks. Now."

"I knew he told you."

"Fess up. There's been this funny whine in your voice that's not the Birdie I know and love. And you've turned into Irritable Irma."

"Thanks, you're a pal."

"Of course, if I had to work with the Barracuda every day, I would be much worse. . . ."

"Don't start."

He sighed. "I've got to get going." He put a ten dollar bill on the table.

"I ran into Fran Burke on the way over. It was like old times—almost. He thought I should be married with lots of children."

"He's good people. He's taking the company out."

"I'll be up on Friday. Okay?"

"God!" Carlos whacked his head with the heel of his hand. "I almost forgot. I got you a ride up on a corporate jet Thursday night. Can you cut your body-snatching on Friday?"

"In a flash!" She'd have to rework her schedule and break it to Smith, who would be absolutely green with envy.

He pulled a scrap of paper from his pocket. "All you have to do is call Janice and set it up."

"Yum."

"And you're at the Ritz?"

"Yup. I requested the same floor as the famous choreographer, Carlos Prince. I told them I was your sister."

"You are. I'll book you in for Thursday night when I get there." He gave her a hard look. "Now I want you to tell me what you're going to do about these attacks."

"I'm calling Sonya Mosholu the minute I get home. You remember her, don't you?"

"Yeah, big girl. Very into the moderns—Merce for a while. I heard she left the business a long time ago." Merce was Merce Cunningham, perhaps the leading exponent of modern dance after Martha Graham.

"Sonya's a therapist now. She worked at the Pilates Studio and with Carola Trier, doing physical therapy, then she went back to school and became a shrink." She looked at her watch. Five-forty. "Ouch, I'm going to be late."

"Me, too. Phil said he'd have a car pick up Sam and me here at five-thirty. What do you have? A broker?"

"No. Promise you won't say anything to anyone and I'll tell you."

"Oh, man." Carlos licked his lips and leered. "Delicious gossip. Wonderful! Send me off with something *really* disgusting."

She wagged her finger at him. "You're bad. I'm going to see Susan Orkin. And at her invitation."

Carlos looked stunned. "How come?"

"She called me. It turns out we were in college together. Only I knew her then as Susan Cohen."

"My, my what a coincidence."

"Well, don't you always say there are only fifteen people in the world?"

"I do indeed. What does Susan Cohen Orkin want?"

"I haven't the foggiest."

"Hmmmm, scrumptious. That ought to be good for a dinner or two in Boston."

"Oh, listen, before I forget—"

Phil Terrace entered the café from the street door, jumping like a hyper-jack, looking around.

Carlos waved. "There's Phil."

"Hey, Phil," someone called. "Going to have a team in the league this year?"

"Count on it." He smacked his fist into his palm as if into a catcher's mitt.

"And I suppose you think you can beat us."

"Count on that, too."

Carlos got up and reached around for his bags. "What did you start to tell me, Birdie?"

"Forget it. Go on. I'll catch up with you in Boston." Wetzon rose.

"Hi, Birdie." Phil wore a big smile and a cap just like Mort's. It didn't take long, Wetzon thought, greeting him, for everyone in the theatre to imitate Mort. Pretty soon, there'd be nothing but beards and caps. Phil took Carlos's carryon outside to the car. He seemed fully recovered from the trauma on Saturday.

"I take it he's into the Broadway Show League," she said to Carlos.

"A real fanatic. He's lined me up for center field."

"You? Oh, my God, that I have to see."

"You mock me. Just you wait." He patted her on the rear. "Bye, pet. Give us a big kiss and wish us *merde.*"

"*Merde,* my love." She gave Carlos a big hug and a kiss. Then another. She felt chilled. "Be careful."

She received one of his sardonic winks, but it didn't make her feel any better. She was scared for him, for herself.

After Carlos left, Wetzon stared at the paper in her hand without focusing on the numbers. Maybe she ought to try to reach Sonya now. She went into the Edison from the coffee shop and found a pay phone. Sonya's number was in her address book. She put a quarter in the slot and picked out the digits. She would leave a message on Sonya's answering machine and perhaps there'd be a message from Sonya when Wetzon got home later. She listened to the ring, waiting for the machine to pick up.

"Sonya Mosholu."

"Sonya! I'm glad I caught you."

"Leslie?"

"Yes. Is this a bad time?"

"No, you caught me between patients. How are you?"

"Not my usual sparkly self. I need a consultation."

Sonya's voice became instantly professional. "When can you come?"

"How about tonight?"

"Oh. Mmmm. Okay. How about eight o'clock?"

"You're on."

There, she'd done it. She hung up the phone feeling proud of herself. The phone box chung and clunked, and damned if her quarter wasn't returned to her in the change well. It had to be an omen. She made a gun of her right hand and shot herself in the side of the head. She was getting more and more like Smith.

When she dropped the quarter in her coat pocket, her fingers touched the paper with the phone number. She might as well try it while she was still here and get Thursday squared away. She picked out the number and listened to the phone ring, once, twice, three, four, and was about to hang up when a voice said: "Joel Kidde's office."

CHAPTER

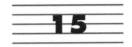

The cab she'd just gotten out of was captured by the doorman of Susan Orkin's building for an older couple in evening clothes. The woman had a mink cape loosely over her shoulders, revealing her skeletal frame. Her face had the frozen look of one too many lifts. Her companion was one of those androgynously handsome white-haired men of the flashy tans and fine gold jewelry who often escorted rich widows and divorcees about town.

This was so typical of the East Side that Wetzon had to smile. Her Upper West Side with its actor-musician-dancer-writer and young upwardly mobile professional Zabar-dependent inhabitants was more to her taste.

She paused for a moment listening to the wind *snap-slap* at the awning overhead, then she pushed hard on the heavy lobby door and crossed a marbled vestibule bigger than the office she and Smith shared. Down two steps was another lobby the size of her whole apartment. The decor was chocolate brown leather sofas and good reproduction walnut tables. Waxy leaved plants filled fat, pebbled brass pots. Floor-to-ceiling windows on the far wall looked out into a winter-blighted garden of brown manicured hedges and walkways.

A second, older, doorman, his face a treasury of broken blood vessels, stood at a telephone board. He waited for her to approach him, blinking faded brown eyes.

"Mrs. Orkin," she told him.

"Your name, Miss?" His Irish brogue was downright plush.

"Ms. Wetzon."

He plugged a cord into his tenant intercom box and announced her, actually pronouncing her name properly but giving it a romantic lilt. "Ms. Wetzon here for you, Mrs. Orkin." He disconnected and nodded to Wetzon. "Go right up. Eighteen C. Elevator's to your right."

This building on Fifth Avenue was a full square block, half facing Madison, half facing Fifth. It was legendary for the size and layouts of its apartments. You couldn't buy in without being connected, and its co-op board was notoriously rigid. Even with the recession, which had severely hurt high-flying New York real estate prices, Wetzon knew prices here had not dropped. People were willing to wait for years for apartments in this building to come on the market.

The elevator was wood-paneled, its brass trim polished to the nth degree. The elevator man was young and rolled curious eyes over Wetzon when she told him the eighteenth floor. Whose apartment had it been, she wondered. Dilla's or Susan's? The reactionary board of this building would not look kindly on a lesbian couple, that was for sure. They consistently refused to accept entertainers, even classical musicians.

There were only two apartments on the eighteenth floor, C and D. The little foyer was embellished by rust ceramic floor tiles and taupe-striped wallpaper with tiny rust flowers. Four old floral prints in plain black frames were lined up on the wall opposite the elevator. A photocopied letter to all tenants was taped to each door informing that negotiations with the Building Employees Union had broken off and that there would be a strike. She had seen a similar notice taped to the inside wall of the elevator in her own building that morning.

Wetzon rang C's bell and, fully expecting soft chimes, heard instead a rasping ring followed hard on by barking, the kind made by a small dog.

The woman who opened the door was not someone Wetzon would have recognized as the Susan Cohen she'd known in college. This woman's hair was spun-sugar white, absolutely devoid of color, parted on the side and puffed around her small face, making it look even smaller. All that hair made Susan's head seem too big for her body, which was as tiny as it had been almost twenty years ago. Susan was actually a woman in miniature, shorter than Wetzon and nicely rounded without being fat.

They stared at one another for a brief moment, then clasped hands, and Susan drew her into the apartment and closed the door. The sound of barking increased in volume. Susan ignored it.

"I would never ever have known you," Wetzon said. "Your hair . . . it's so beautiful." There were so many things that were different about Susan, but the hair was probably the safest to mention.

Susan's smile was perfect. In college she'd had a snaggled front tooth. "New nose, silicone chin, collagen cheeks and lips. I was so ugly in college."

"No, you weren't," Wetzon protested, and meant it.

Susan led Wetzon through a foyer filled with antiques and into the kitchen. The dog's barking became frenzied. "I hope you don't mind. It's easier to talk here. Dilla's mother and sister and brother-in-law are in the back."

The kitchen was huge: a work island in the center, and off to the right an old cherry wood table, French country chairs with pretty paisley cushions. Hexigons of brown quarry tile covered the floors, and on the walls were framed posters of Dilla's shows. Wetzon pulled out one of the chairs and sat down, laying her coat, briefcase, and purse on another chair. She watched Susan fill a copper kettle with water and turn the burner up so high on the massive Garland stove that the flame licked the edge of the kettle and crept up the side. The room was cold; she could hear the wind whipping against the windows, which were not curtained, and rattling the service door.

"What a great apartment."

"It is, isn't it? We were lucky to get into the building."

"I thought you couldn't without connections."

"That never stopped Dilla." Susan smiled. "Actually, it was Fran Burke who had the connection. He has friends in the building. You know Fran, don't you?"

"Yes. He company managed a few of the shows I did."

"Tea? Or something stronger?" Susan's eyes were dark ringed and spidery lines ran from the outside corners. She wore little to no makeup, not even lipstick. "Do you want to hang your coat?" She nodded toward the rack of Shaker-style pegs where several coats and mufflers and two black felt borsalino hats were already hanging.

"Tea is fine. With lemon, please." Wetzon took her coat from the chair and hung it from the only free peg. The kettle began to shrill.

A muffled howl came from the dog, and somewhere in the apartment, quarreling voices were raised. A door opened and a woman shrieked in frustration. A hard slam followed. Then the sound of scurrying, nails on bare wood floors, and a round bit of white fluff exactly the color of Susan's hair streaked into the kitchen and hurled itself into Susan's outstretched arms. Susan laughed and buried her face in the little dog's fur, letting the animal give her a face wash. Presenting the Maltese to Wetzon, she said, "This is Izz. Izz, behave."

"Izz?" The dog flapped her ears and peered at Wetzon with jet, glass-button eyes. She wore a wide red collar and dangling from a brass loop, her license. "Such a pretty collar."

"Short for Isabella. The collar has this little pocket for my key. Isn't that ingenious? You can't even see it. And it's useful, too, because I am always losing my key." Susan set the dog on the floor and poured a splash of hot water into a porcelain teapot, swirled it around, then poured it out. She filled a mesh ball with tea leaves and dropped it into the pot, covered it with boiling water, and put the lid on the pot, letting it steep. Izz danced on the tiles, slipping and tumbling, begging to get picked up again. "She misses Dilla. She keeps wandering around the apartment looking for her or running to the door. Oh, God. . . . They're taking her to Pennsylvania today, to the family plot." Susan removed some scones from a tin box and arranged them on a plate. She set the plate on the table in front of Wetzon.

"Is that where Dilla's from?" Izz jumped on Wetzon's lap and nuzzled the plate of scones with her coal black nose. Wetzon cuddled the squirming animal and got a nose and chin wash in quick succession.

"Yes. King of Prussia, Pennsylvania." Susan took a lemon from the fridge and sliced half of it, put the slices on another plate and returned the remainder to the fridge. "We met at camp . . . when we were kids."

Loud voices again. The dog growled, jumped off Wetzon's lap, and ran to the doorway, barked furiously, came back and jumped at Susan's legs. Susan scooped her up. "I wish they were out of here."

"What is that about?"

"They're fighting about what to take. The sister wants all her clothes and so does the mother. I said go ahead and take them. Dilla had so much stuff—designers were always sending her samples. And I—" she looked down at herself, "wear nothing but jeans." Still holding the dog, she set out lemon slices and cups.

"You are planning to have a memorial service here?"

"Oh, yes. Mort's arranging it. It'll be after *Hotshot* opens." She poured tea into the cups, then sat down with Izz in her lap.

"I guess Dilla and Mort were very close."

"Too close sometimes." There was just a feather of resentment in Susan's voice and then it was gone. Izz jumped off her lap and left the kitchen, her nails clicking on the tile.

"Oh? It's been so many years for me—"

"Oh, Leslie, I'm sure you know Mort—how he uses people, soaks everything good out of them and then takes all the credit."

"I guess he hasn't changed much."

"He's gotten worse, if anything. And he's such a bully. The tantrums are worse—everything—oh, damn it all." Tears began running down Susan's cheeks and she brushed them away impatiently with her fingertips. "He was making Dilla crazy. Calls all hours of the day and night. He wouldn't leave us alone. I kept telling her to stand up to him and she was just starting to—"

"Funny, I always thought Dilla was the tough one and that she had Mort wrapped around her little finger."

"Oh, Leslie, how little you know. People misjudged her. She wasn't that strong. And she made emotional decisions that often got her into trouble." She swirled sugar into her tea. "Dilla and Mort had a screaming fight in the theatre Friday night." There was satisfaction in her voice.

"How do you know?"

Susan stared at her. "Dilla called me. She was frightened. I could hear it in her voice. She hadn't been herself the past week, sort of edgy and nervous. I thought it was because the show was undercapitalized. I wanted to get in a cab and come right down there, but she said no. She'd get it settled once and for all and would be home later. But she didn't come home."

"God, Susan, weren't you worried?"

"Worried? I was furious. It's so funny." She wasn't laughing.

"Furious?"

"I thought she made it up with Mort by spending the night with him. He demands total loyalty. He hates—*hated*—me because Dilla always put me first. She was my lover. There'll never be anyone else for me." Her eyes were magnetic, fixed on Wetzon's. "Does my being a lesbian make you uncomfortable?"

"Not at all."

"I didn't think it would, but I wasn't sure."

"I always thought Mort was ambivalent about women."

"Mort's ambivalent about a lot of things, especially about coming out of the closet. That's what makes him so mean. He and Poppy . . . well, you know . . ."

Wetzon squeezed a slice of lemon into her tea, wincing when the acid juice touched a paper cut on her finger. She dropped the slice into the tea and licked her wound. "Why am I here, Susan?"

"I've read about you, Leslie. You and your partner. I know you've been involved in things like this before."

"Not exactly." *Oh, shit,* Wetzon thought. *She's going to ask me to find out who killed Dilla.* Nevertheless, a ripple of excitement ran through her.

"Well, I hope you'll do it for me, then. I can pay you. Oh, Izz." The dog scampered into the room, a straw hat in her mouth. She dropped the hat at Wetzon's feet and wagged her tail, looking up at Wetzon for approval. "She likes you."

Wetzon laughed. "Oh, sure."

"Don't laugh. Izz has a sixth sense about people."

Voices rose again in the other room along with sounds of thumping.

"It's not a question of money . . ."

"What then?"

"I'm not a detective."

"But you know how to do it. Even though we haven't seen each other in a lot of years, I trust you. I think you'll tell me the truth." Susan's face was bleak. Wetzon found herself responding to the desperate appeal in Susan's teary eyes.

She asked slowly, "What do you think the truth is, Susan?"

"That Mort killed Dilla."

"Mort? Good God, Susan, not Mort. Never! He's a bully and a coward, but he's not a killer."

"Leslie, have you ever wanted to kill someone?"

Wetzon picked up her cup; her hand trembled and she set it down. Smith's latest lover, Richard Hartmann, would be at the top of Wetzon's death list. "Yes, but I wouldn't. What about you?"

The commotion on the other side of the apartment commenced again, only louder this time, along with more thumping. Glass shattered. Izz sailed off Susan's lap and raced out of the room yelping, tail down.

"Oh, damn them to hell! Excuse me." She left Wetzon in the kitchen. The volume of shouting increased.

Wetzon poured herself another cup of tea and took a scone. A single bite told her it was slightly stale. She rose, looking around. No garbage can or bag in evidence. Look under the sink, dummy, she chided herself. *You* may leave your garbage bags for all to see, but this is the Fifth Avenue crowd. They *hide* their garbage. She opened the door to the sink cabinet and saw cleansers, bottles and crockery, and a brown plastic garbage bag into which she dropped the partially eaten scone. The kitchen windows looked out on a street of beautiful old townhouses and mansions. Night had come on quickly. Below, in the townhouses, light was diffused behind blinds and draperies. She wished she were home, or at the very least, with Sonya.

When Susan didn't return, Wetzon wandered into the foyer. A huge Welsh cupboard sat against the wall opposite the door. The sun-bleached skull of a steer hung nearby. On the floor was a vivid Native American rug. It was all very Santa Fe. Dilla and Susan lived well, no doubt about it.

The solidly closed doors of the cupboard invited her to open them. She never passed up an invitation like that. The shouting confrontation in other parts of the apartment continued unabated, as did the sound of heavy furniture being displaced. Wetzon opened the cupboard doors. The shelves held an amazing collection of blue-and-white old Canton china, platters, teapots, serving dishes, plates, cups and saucers, pitchers, bowls, and an elegant, long-necked vase. Very nice. Very valuable. Whose was it, she wondered. She wouldn't mind owning a piece or two of Canton.

She became aware all at once of the quiet. A door slammed. She was sitting at the cherry wood table again when Izz scampered into the kitchen making right for Wetzon with something in her mouth. "What do you have there, Izz?"

Wagging her tail, Izz dropped her bounty on Wetzon's feet. Wetzon picked it up. It was a needlepoint pouch full of—she opened it—jewelry. Diamonds, rings and more, and gold bracelets, rings. God! Her fingers sifted through the glittering treasure trove. Embroidered on the inside lining of the flap closure were the words: *Lenny/Celia.* Lenny again. And who, pray tell, was Celia? Wetzon closed the bag, keeping it on her lap while Izz danced around begging to be picked up.

"Where did you get that?"

Suddenly, Susan swooped down on her. She snatched up the bag, turning it in her hands, checking the zipper clasp, frightened.

"Izz brought it to me. I'm sorry it upset you."

"Oh, Izz, go away, bad girl." Susan smiled. "Forgive me, Leslie. I am at my wit's end with Dilla gone. I just can't seem to tell the difference between friend and foe."

"I'm not your foe, Susan."

"I know that." Susan sighed, opened the compartment under the sink and tucked away the bag. *What a peculiar place to put all that valuable jewelry,* Wetzon thought.

"Susan, I have an appointment—"

"Don't think you'll get away with this, bitch!" a woman's voice screeched. Susan turned, her face mottled with fury.

Wetzon stood up to get a better view of the enormously fat woman in a several-sizes-too-small mink coat who was standing in the foyer. Her hair was so black it had blue highlights. She was banging on the floor with a cane, enunciating each furious syllable.

"I think I've been very reasonable, Ruth." Susan's voice was iced steel. "I don't have to put up with this. This is my home. You are not my mother. You made Dilla's life miserable, but you have no hold on me. Get your things and your family and be gone."

The fat woman's face contorted. "Dilla owned this palace."

Who would have guessed chic old Dilla even had a mother, Wetzon thought, let alone someone like that.

Susan's lips moved but she wasn't smiling. "Ah, but you're wrong. This apartment is in my name."

"It can't be. You're lying," Ruth shrieked. "Dilla told me all about you. Dilla paid for everything. We're going to take you to court."

"Mother!" An apparition closely resembling the mother tottered into view. She looked like someone had filled Dilla with helium.

"Shirley, please take what you're taking and get the hell out of here." Susan began to cry. Izz howled.

Shirley shouted, "Rudy, bring the bags!"

This order produced more thumping and bumping as if things were being dragged across the floor, and then there was Rudy. He was definitely in the right family. Big as Shirley, but a head shorter, he was dragging two humongous suitcases and a black plastic bag stuffed to the gills. Izz ran at him and began nipping at his heels and whining, scratching at the bags, tail wagging, as if she knew what they contained.

"Oh, God," Susan moaned. "She knows they're Dilla's."

It was another five minutes before Dilla's Munster Family finally left.

Susan returned to the kitchen, her face streaked with tears. "Aren't they awful? They don't give a hoot. Not one iota. All they care about is getting theirs. Poor Dilla." She wiped her eyes with a tissue, then ran cold water in the sink and rinsed her face, drying it with a paper towel. "The only time Dilla had any happiness was with me. That's why I want to find out who did it. For her." She sat down opposite Wetzon. "So will you help me? I have money."

"Susan, as I said, I'm not a licensed detective, and I couldn't take a fee from you."

"Please, Leslie. I'm begging you. I can't ask a stranger to do this. No one would talk to him. You know everybody. Mort is bound to slip up and say something. All I want is for you to tell me, and I'll deal with it."

"What if it's not Mort?"

"I can live with whatever you find. If it wasn't Mort, it was one of them. They all hated her."

"And what will you do with the information?"

Susan and Wetzon locked eyes. "I don't know," Susan said softly.

"I would have to tell the police, Susan."

"Okay." She said it too fast, and Wetzon tucked that away for later thought.

"I'm going up to Boston Thursday night. How about if I just keep my eyes and ears open while I'm there and if I come up with anything, we can donate the fee to the Gay Men's Health Crisis in Dilla's name?"

Susan's face brightened. "Okay. That's a deal."

Wetzon got her coat from the hook and put it on. "Before I go, Susan . . ."

The intercom buzzer blared. "Oh, please don't tell me they've come back." When Susan didn't respond, it blared again. "Excuse me, Leslie." She left the room.

The intercom snarled, then Wetzon heard Susan say, "Who?" The snarl came again. "No! I'm not here. Tell her I'm *not* here."

When Wetzon came into the foyer, Susan was staring bleakly at the intercom, her shoulders slumped with misery. "Um, Susan?"

Susan whirled around. "Oh, Leslie, I'm sorry. You were asking me something. . . ."

"I happened to see the royalty list on *Hotshot,* and I saw your name was on it."

Susan didn't seem surprised. "Lord, it's going to get out. I told Dilla it would."

"What is?"

"Sam needed help with the lyrics. I've been a published poet for years."

"I didn't know that."

Susan nodded. "Under the name S. C. Orkin. Sam was in trouble, so I was helping him out with the lyrics, sending them in with Dilla. He's become so weird."

"I noticed."

"He didn't want anyone to know he needed help."

"But there are never any secrets in the Theatre, at least not for very long. I'm surprised it's not out already."

Susan shrugged. "I didn't care. I don't have that kind of ego." She squelched a sob. "I can't believe Dilla's never coming home again."

She walked Wetzon to the door, so forlorn that Wetzon put her arms around her.

The doorbell rang.

Susan looked angry. "He sent her up." She pulled away from Wetzon and yanked the door open. Standing in front of them was a bald man in tan slacks and a bright red cardigan sweater. His eyes were apoplectic in a fiery red face. Hands clenched at his sides, he screeched, "This has gone far enough! I've got a sick wife!" His accent was essence of Vienna, but the *schlag* was missing.

Behind him the elevator door was open and the elevator man's mouth was agape.

Wetzon stepped around the enraged man carefully. "Bye, Susan."

"What are you doing up here, killing each other?" the man demanded of Susan, ignoring Wetzon entirely.

"I'm sorry, Mr. Nadelman. It's over now. They're—"

Mr. Nadelman interrupted, his voice taut with anger. "First Friday, now today. Next time I call the police!"

The cold was crinkly, so dry that Wetzon felt the skin on her face pull taut. Good. She needed the cold to clear her mind. Susan was so sure Mort had killed Dilla, yet Susan and Dilla had had a dreadful fight on Friday, or someone in that apartment had, according to their downstairs neighbor.

On Fifth Avenue, car and bus traffic swept steadily downtown, a trail of headlights all rolling in one direction. Cabs still disgorged passengers, but rush hour was over, and except for a few isolated stragglers heading homeward, pedestrians were scarce. Only the dog walkers came out consistently day or night, summer or winter.

A woman in a black cloth coat was getting into a cab in front of the building. The street light reflected off her glasses as the doorman closed the cab door. Over his shoulder he called to Wetzon, "Cab, miss?"

"No, thank you."

Across the street, Central Park was an oasis between the east and west sides of Manhattan. Mercury vapor lights bathed the park the pinkish hue of a magical kingdom within the nighttime of the city.

The indomitable Metropolitan Museum, closed on Mondays, was lit up like the White House. Wetzon plucked at the collar of her raccoon coat and loosened the gray cashmere scarf around her throat, drawing it upward to cover her mouth and chin. Monday evenings were always quiet in New York, as if everyone was recovering from the shock of returning to work after the weekend.

Just as she reached the shelter, the Seventy-ninth Street crosstown bus pulled up. She put her token in the slot, and having a rare choice of seats, chose one next to a window. Four teenage girls in an array of coats—down, suede, and wool—but with matching jumpers, were sitting across the back seat of the bus, howling with laughter. They would grow quiet for a second, then one would start and the others joined in.

The years were passing so swiftly, Wetzon thought. In another year she'd be forty, and . . .

When the light changed, the bus crossed into the park. But Wetzon had tuned out of her surroundings.

There was really a simple explanation for Joel Kidde and the corporate jet going to Boston. Joel must be Mort's agent. He might even represent every one of the creators on the show. It happened; small agencies had merged into big agencies, just the same as Wall Street firms had. That was it.

When Carlos had said corporate jet, she'd somehow assumed it would be the record company's. Don't assume, Wetzon. Never assume.

All right, that took care of Joel Kidde. On to the next curiosity. Why was Susan so upset about Wetzon seeing the little bag of jewelry? And why did she then put it under the sink? Had safe deposit boxes gone out of style? And who was Lenny? Who was Celia? The only show biz Lenny Wetzon knew was Leonard Bernstein, whom everyone called Lenny, and while he probably knew Dilla, there would be no reason for her, or Susan for that matter, to have jewelry that belonged to him. Besides, he was dead. And Lenny Bernstein's wife had been Felicia. And she, too, was dead.

A bronchial cough close by jolted Wetzon back to the real world. Flu was rampant this winter. Sitting beside her was a distinguished woman in a ranch mink coat and matching hat. She was coughing into a tissue. "Oh, dear," she gasped. "I'm so sorry." She snapped the book she was reading shut—*Female Sexual Perversions*—and rose. The bus ground its winding course through the park and came out on Eighty-first Street and Central Park West, where the coughing woman, the four teenage girls, and most of the other riders got off.

The Museum of Natural History and the Planetarium, also closed on Mondays, stood like dark sentinels guarding the entrance to the West Side.

Wetzon took the bus to Seventy-ninth and Broadway. Then she got off and walked toward Seventy-third Street, where Sonya had her office in a shabby brownstone near West End Avenue.

Unlike Fifth Avenue, Broadway was crowded with people. It was the main thoroughfare of the open-twenty-four-hours-a-day Upper West Side. People were en route to and from aerobics classes, step classes—the latest craze of the exercise obsessed—dinner. Shoppers carried heaping bags from the Fairway Market, which had the best-priced quality selection of produce on the Upper West Side, or perhaps anywhere in the city, with the possible exception of the farmers' market on Union Square.

Wetzon spun into the Fairway, dodged a white-haired lady with a speeding shopping cart, and managed to get stepped on and pushed by an ancient woman wielding a walker like a battering ram. The stack of Granny Smith apples was at least six feet high. Although the temptation to try to slip out one at eye level was overwhelming, the vision of a landslide of apples in this crowded market was too much for her. Instead she stood on the tips of her toes—after all, she was a dancer—and took one from the top. Her next stop was the dairy case, where she reached over for a Dannon coffee yogurt. The tiny amount of caffeine in the yogurt would give her the extra buzz to get through the session with Sonya. When she straightened, yogurt in hand, she was poked sharply in the calf by a cane in the gnarled hands of a tiny old man with patchy white whiskers, who was trying to take Wetzon's place at the dairy case.

"I'm very sorry," Wetzon told him. "Can I help you get something?"

"Just get out of my way, girlie," the man snarled.

Shocked, Wetzon stepped aside. She'd forgotten how aggressive the elderly were in Fairway. She walked to the checkout lines, keeping a wary eye out for any other aging marauders, and was about to get on line when she was rudely butted aside by a shopping cart propelled by a little old lady in a storm coat and dirty white Reeboks. "Wait a minute," Wetzon protested.

"I saw that," the old lady yelled. "You tried to push me out of line! Did everybody see that? Miss Piss Elegant here tried to push me!"

"I didn't do anything of the kind," Wetzon said indignantly. "You pushed me."

"Who cares? You're holding up the line," someone shouted. Stretched out behind Wetzon was a stream of impatient shoppers.

"It's not you." A woman in a hot pink coat carrying a plastic shopping basket full of groceries stood behind Wetzon. "I shop here all the time and I never fail to get run down or told off by one of these crazy seniors."

"Thanks." Wetzon breathed a fervent prayer that she would never become an elderly curmudgeon. She paid for the apple and the yogurt and walked the short distance to Sonya's building, climbing the chipped and cracked stone steps to the front door. In the tiny vestibule she rang the bell marked *4* and waited, looking out at Seventy-third Street through the glass panel. Two women coming from different directions stopped to talk in front of the brownstone while their dogs, a leashed dachshund and an unleashed Weimaraner, sniffed each other.

Wetzon pressed *4* again. Finally, the intercom crackled, "Yes?"

"Leslie." Wetzon put her hand on the door and waited for the buzzer, then pushed the door open.

It was immediately obvious to Wetzon that the old brownstone had a new owner. The place had been so run down last time Wetzon had been there that Sonya had told her that the only reason she stayed was because the rent was so cheap. Now the hallway looked almost elegant with new cabbage rose carpeting and an upholstered Victorian sofa. In the corner near the staircase was an old maple rocker. Antique costume prints in beautiful frames hung on the walls. The cabbage rose runner went right up the stairs under rubber tread guards on each step.

Sonya's two-room office was on the second floor in the rear. The place was still seedy, but it was now a good-quality seedy compared with what it had been.

Tall, broad-shouldered, Sonya Mosholu wore a black leotard, slim black pants, a long, loosely cut red blazer, and low snakeskin cowboy boots. Her short dark hair was in a side flip, her dark eyes accented with mascara and a taupey shadow. Artwear earrings framed her face.

"God, Sonya," Wetzon said, "instead of aging like the rest of us, you look younger every time I see you. Now you have the nerve to look girlish."

"Girlish? Me?" Sonya laughed. She had one of those rare throaty laughs that made you want to join in.

The room had twenty-foot ceilings, a ceiling fan, and wonderful old moldings. Small exercise equipment—balls and weights—lay in every corner and on the mantle of a Wetzon-high fireplace. Two exercise mats were rolled and set upright in one corner.

Wetzon hung her coat and hat on the standing coatrack next to Sonya's black shearling, sat down on the low, striped sofa with metal legs. She took the apple and the yogurt from the paper bag. Setting the apple aside on the bamboo table, she opened the yogurt. "Oops, I forgot a spoon."

Sonya went into the next room and returned with a plastic spoon, handed it to her, then sat in one of the two Bauhaus-style metal-and-leather chairs facing Wetzon. She studied Wetzon for a moment. "You've cut your hair."

Wetzon's fingers went involuntarily to the tiny line in her scalp. She tore her fingers away and got busy with the yogurt.

"So . . ." Sonya smiled, after a while. "Do you want to tell me?"

"It's stupid." Her hands were squeezing the empty yogurt container out of shape.

"Why do you say that?"

"Well, isn't it stupid to know why you're scared, but also know you're okay, now that the danger has passed? You have to get on with your life, don't you?"

"Leslie." Sonya's voice was soft, almost hypnotic. Wetzon had to strain to hear her. Or might it be that she didn't *want* to hear her? "Tell me about the danger," she urged. "Why are you scared?"

Wetzon sighed. She dropped the savaged yogurt container on the table. "Last year. It happened last year." Her fingers touched the tiny scar. She started to speak again and couldn't for the lump in her throat.

Sonya waited. Wetzon kept her eyes on the bamboo table and the yellow box of tissues for patients who cried. She was certainly not going to be one of them. "I got shot. Here." She inclined her head to show Sonya. "It was hardly anything."

"Being shot is hardly hardly anything, Leslie. How did it happen? Was it an accident?"

"Someone was trying to kill me." She saw the flicker of a reaction push through Sonya's enormous self-control. "I was okay, though, Sonya. I was lucky. I got over it. Then I started having these dreams. Before this happened I used to have the most wonderful dreams. Smith said they were psychic."

"You're still in the headhunting business?"

"Yes."

"Go on, Leslie."

"Well, at first I had no dreams at all, and then I started waking up every hour or so, and then the dream started coming."

"Tell me about them. Are they always the same?"

"Yes. First there's a flash of fire and I'm terrified but I can't move, then the smell of gunpowder, then a burning pain in my head and I wake up soaked to the skin, shaking. I hear it even has a name: post-traumatic stress syndrome."

Sonya's expression didn't change. "How long has this been going on?"

"Four months."

"Oh, Leslie—"

"But Sonya, I was handling it fine until Saturday night."

"What changed?"

"I went to the gypsy run-through of *Hotshot*—Carlos's new musical.

They're setting up in Boston as we speak. Anyway, when we got to the theatre we found Dilla Crosby. She'd been beaten to death." She told Sonya about finding Dilla and the events immediately following.

"Most of these people are familiar to me," Sonya said, when Wetzon had finished.

"Did you know Dilla?"

"Slightly. We had a jazz class together a long time ago. How did finding Dilla affect you?"

"I was upset, but the way anybody would be if they'd found a body, and I didn't like Dilla and hadn't seen her in years. But God, Sonya, I had the dream that night and I woke up with terrible chest pains. I couldn't breathe. I couldn't even stand up. And sweats and chills and absolute terror. I thought I was going to die. I thought people were coming to kill me. It was crazy. If Silvestri hadn't called when he did . . ." Wetzon shrugged. "But I guess I would have been all right. It would have gone away without him."

The carillon in the old Rutgers Dutch Reform Church behind Sonya's brownstone began to play a hymn that Wetzon recognized but couldn't name. A Thanksgiving hymn. Something about gathering together to ask the Lord's blessing. For no reason at all, her eyes got teary. She pressed her lips together and shook her head at Sonya.

Sonya waited patiently. After several minutes, she prompted, "But Silvestri came and helped you?"

"Yes." Wetzon's hands wouldn't stop fretting. "I'm not seeing him anymore, Sonya. It's over. At least, I'm trying for it to be over. I'm seeing someone else. It's a much better relationship."

"Why do you say that?"

"Because Alton is nice and doesn't fight with me about everything I do."

"You like that?"

"Well, of course." Wetzon couldn't keep the irritation out of her voice. "Isn't it easier to be around people who—oh, never mind. I don't want to get into the differences between Alton Pinkus and Silvestri and why one is better for me than the other."

"Alton Pinkus? The labor leader?"

"Yes. And don't say it, please. I know. He's twenty years older than I am."

"All right. What happened Saturday night, or was it Sunday morning by that time?"

"Silvestri eased me down and then made me promise I would talk to someone. . . . Which is why I'm here."

"Well, chalk one up for him." Sonya smiled. "Is there anything else that's bothering you?"

Wetzon sent Sonya a suspicious look. "Why do you ask?"

"Think about it. Don't be in such a hurry. We still have some time. How are you and your partner getting along?"

"As well as we ever will, I guess. Smith's shallow and drives me to distraction, but we have some history together. And we work well in business. From my point of view, except for her son, Mark, her personal life is a disaster, but she would say the same about me, minus the child."

"Her personal life?"

"She dumped a wonderful man for that sleaze lawyer, Richard Hartmann."

"Oh?" For a fraction of a second Sonya gave herself away. Feminists hated Richard Hartmann. When he defended a rapist or murderer, he always tried the victim, who couldn't speak for herself, and got his client off. And Sonya was a feminist.

"Yes. I've always wondered what kind of woman would be attracted to a creep like that—" Wetzon remembered his body against hers, his hands on her throat, his threat. Her hands curled into fists.

"Leslie." Sonya's soothing voice penetrated the intense memory. "Did something happen between you and Richard Hartmann?"

"How could you think that?" Wetzon glared at Sonya, then lowered her eyes to her lap, clasping her hands together.

Sonya didn't react. "Why don't you tell me about it?"

Minutes went by. Someone began moving furniture in the upstairs apartment. The floorboards protested with a humanlike groan.

Wetzon cleared her throat. "I found some papers that could prove Richard Hartmann is laundering money. Smith was just getting involved with him, so I warned her not to. I was going to take what I found to an assistant D.A. I'd gotten to know. But Smith told him—"

"She *told* him?" Sonya's voice crackled and Wetzon looked up.

"I know how that sounds, but Smith's in love with him. I couldn't go to the D.A. with it while she was part of his life."

"Why not, Leslie?"

"Sonya, she has so little and, believe it or not, she's fragile. I care about her." She bit her lip. "And I'm afraid of Hartmann. He threatened me— physically—and coward that I am, I have done nothing about it. So the evidence against him sits in my safe deposit box, aging. How's that for your highly ethical friend, Leslie Wetzon?"

"Don't be so hard on yourself, Leslie. You're not Superwoman."

"I'm not? Here all this time I've been thinking I was." Wetzon sighed.

"Do you want to come back and talk to me next week at this time?"

"Oh. You want to see me again? I thought once was enough."

"Leslie, this is serious. None of this is going to go away overnight simply because you told a therapist about it. Do you want to help yourself or not?"

"Oh, okay. If you think so. I don't want Saturday night to happen again."

"Good. Then we'll see each other next week?"

Wetzon stood. "Thanks, Sonya." Fifty minutes had gone by faster than she would have believed. She put on her coat and shoved the uneaten apple in her pocket. Sonya was standing at the door to show her out. Wetzon asked, "Am I your last patient?"

Sonya nodded; a slight flush colored her cheeks.

"Well, have a good night then."

Wetzon went down the stairs feeling as if a small weight had been lifted from her shoulders, but she couldn't say why. She was thinking about her life again and doing so somewhat critically, so she didn't see the man at first. She popped out the front door of the brownstone and almost fell over him. He was sitting on the stone railing smoking. All one could see was the pinpoint of light the tip of his cigarette made in the darkness. When he saw her, he stood up, looming over her, forcing her back against the door.

CHAPTER

The door gave under her weight and swung in, sending Wetzon sprawling backward in a tangle of fur, purse, and briefcase. She landed ungracefully on her backside.

"Here now," she heard a man say. "I'm sorry I frightened you." He reached down and helped her up and back outside, then gathered up her briefcase. Embarrassed by her almost irrational fear, she straightened her clothing and found she was clutching her purse in a death grip.

"Are you okay? I guess you didn't see me sitting there."

Wetzon peered up at him in the dingy light. Way up. He had a nice smile, yellowed teeth under a wiry mustache, deep lines around his eyes. He flipped his cigarette butt into the street and frowned down at her.

"O'Melvany," Wetzon said.

He squinted, then snapped his fingers. "Yeah, Silvestri," O'Melvany said. She saw he didn't remember her name.

"Leslie Wetzon."

"Yeah," he said, pointing his finger at her. Eddie O'Melvany was a detective with the Nineteenth Precinct and one of Silvestri's sometime poker buddies. Wetzon had met him three years earlier when her friend Hazel's school chum had been murdered. And she hadn't seen him since. What the hell was he doing here?

"I didn't see you," Wetzon said. "And you cast a long shadow. Are you with the Twentieth now?" The Twentieth was her precinct and probably covered Seventy-third Street as well.

"Nah. Still with the One-Nine." He lit another cigarette and the light flared on his orangy mustache. "Ah, here she is." He was smiling and looking behind her.

Wetzon turned. Sonya had just opened the inside door.

"You two don't need to be introduced, do you?" Sonya spoke evenly, but Wetzon was sure she looked flustered.

Wetzon grinned. "Not at all. It was nice seeing you again, Detective O'Melvany. Good night." She practically skipped down the steps and over to Broadway. How absolutely amazing. How long had this been going on? Silvestri had brought her to the Nineteenth to talk to O'Melvany about Peepsie Cunningham's murder. O'Melvany had been in a vile mood that day; his back was out and a blizzard had left his detective squad decimated. Wetzon had handed him one of Sonya's cards and suggested O'Melvany try Sonya's bioenergetic therapy.

The fun of it carried her smiling all the way up Broadway. Did Silvestri know?

At Ollie's on Eighty-fourth Street, she stopped and bought an order of hot-and-sour soup. She still had leftovers to nibble on and with a little luck she might be able to sleep through the night.

A scraggly haired man in a filthy down jacket, torn pants, and shoes without laces or socks approached her on the corner of Eighty-sixth and Amsterdam with a cardboard cup, shaking it at her so she could hear coins against coins. "I need a hundred and fifty thou for the down payment on a co-op," he said. He sounded like a stockbroker pitching a client.

Taken aback, she made the mistake of looking directly at him. He shoved the cup in her face.

"If you're hungry, this is hot soup," she said, offering him her package.

He pushed it away with such force she almost lost hold of it. "Soup! Don't want no soup." He was outraged.

Wetzon didn't wait around to see what he'd do. She made tracks. What was this now? Food wasn't good enough. Now they only wanted money—and a lot of it. Well, why was she so surprised? He was a New York derelict, and everyone knew New Yorkers reached for the stars.

She was going over her meeting with Susan Orkin in her mind when she reached her building. The outside door was locked and Rafe, the night doorman, was nowhere in sight. She began searching her purse for her key case, found it, pulled it out. A hand closed over hers and took the keys.

"It's not smart to stand on the street fumbling for a key. Which one is it?"

She pointed to the longest one on the chain. "Is there anything I do that you like, Silvestri?"

He smirked at her and unlocked the door, letting her precede him inside. Silvestri held the elevator while she picked up her mail, then rode up with her. When they got to her door she pulled off her beret and raised an eyebrow at him.

"Do you want company tonight?" he asked.

Her heart did a shuffle step. "God, I hate this," she whispered.

"Yes or no." His breath tickled her forehead. He unlocked her door and followed her in.

"Do I get a choice?" She set the bag containing the soup on the table with her briefcase and purse.

"Sure." Nudging the door shut with his heel, Silvestri kissed her. He tasted of garlic and olive oil, her favorites. His words had been joking, but the kiss was no joke.

"Some choice," she said when he let her go. "Have you had dinner? I've got some soup and leftovers."

"Had a couple of slices at Vinnie's. I'll have a beer."

Wetzon hung up her coat in the hall closet and he hooked his leather jacket over the back of a chair, slipped off his shoulder harness and gun and rolled it up next to her purse.

"Did you know Eddie O'Melvany is seeing my friend, the therapist—Sonya Mosholu—romantically, I mean?"

"Oh, yeah? Maybe he said something about it. I forget."

"The great detective Silvestri forgets? I can't believe it."

She took two bottles of Beck's Light from the fridge and the leftover veggies in their plastic container, piled napkins and the hot-and-sour soup on a tray and brought everything into the living room. Silvestri had taken off his shoes and was lying on the sofa inspecting the room. "Shove over," she said.

"I like what you did with the place." He gave her some space and took a swig of the beer.

"Thanks." The soup was wonderful. She did in the soup while Silvestri picked at the vegetables with his fingers. "I saw Sonya tonight about the dream."

"Okay." He looked pleased and took another swig from the bottle.

"And Susan Orkin earlier tonight."

"Oh, yeah?" He looked less pleased.

"I went to college with Susan. She wants to hire me to find out who murdered Dilla." She closed her eyes and waited for the explosion.

He didn't say anything for a while and she opened her eyes.

"Surprise, surprise," he said sarcastically. "Trust you to find a way to get into it."

She gave him a nasty look. "You're going to need me on this, smart ass."

He laughed, then he lay back and pulled her down on him.

The phone rang.

"Is your machine on?" She nodded, her chin on his chest. "Don't answer it." He kissed her forehead, her nose. The answering machine picked up and began clicking. She put her arms around his neck. The machine took its message.

"Leslie, this is Alton. It's after eleven here, and one of those incredibly beautiful nights. I miss you very much. . . . In a way I'm glad you're not there. There are things I want you to think about. . . . We can talk when I get home."

Wetzon put her hands over her ears. She could hear the undercurrent of excitement in Alton's voice.

Silvestri held onto her tightly, aiming warm, sweet kisses around her face. She didn't want to hear what Alton had to say but she heard it. They both heard it.

"I love you very much," Alton went on. *"I want you to marry me, Leslie. I want to know you'll be there, that we'll be together for the rest of our lives. I'll see you Saturday, and we can talk about it. Good night, baby."*

The connection was broken. The machine clicked off.

"Oh, no, no, no," Wetzon howled. "I can't stand it. I'm going to become a hermit."

Silvestri's laugh started like a rumble in his stomach. She pulled away from him and sat up, her head in her hands. "What the hell am I going to do?"

"You could marry him." He was laughing out loud.

"I don't want to marry him or you or anybody." She jumped up and began prowling around the living room.

"Well, you're lucky there, Les."

She stopped dead. "Huh?"

"I'm not asking you to marry me."

She stood frozen for a minute, then fell on her knees. "Thank you, God," she said fervently.

He picked her up and took her to bed. Neither heard the second call come in.

The roof of the brownstone below Wetzon's kitchen window was a fuzzy blanket of snow embroidered with thousands of sparkly ice diamonds that glinted in the brilliance of the morning sunlight. She turned away and poured coffee into the mugs, waiting for Silvestri to get his head out of her refrigerator.

"Jeeze, Les, there's not one goddam thing to eat in here."

She looked at her watch. "I'll buy you bacon and eggs at E.J.'s. I didn't know I was going to have a guest for breakfast."

He looked at his watch. "I don't have time."

"Are you still working on Dilla's murder?"

"Yeah, among other things." He took the mug from her, gulped coffee, set the half-empty mug down on the marble counter and pulled his notepad from his inside pocket. "What did Susan Orkin have to tell you?"

"Why do I feel suddenly as if I'm being interrogated? There's no need to turn into a cop. Oh, excuse me. I forgot. You're always a cop. I'll be happy to share information." She stepped around him, opened the fridge and rummaged around in the vegetable bin. Plastic bags filled with rotting lettuce, a lemon gone to mold. She tossed them in the garbage and came up with an Ida Red apple, washed it, dried it, and cut it into quarters. "Julia Child's favorite apple. I share food, too." Grinning, she handed Silvestri one of the quarters and put the rest on a plate.

He looked at the chunk of apple in his hand and laughed. "Okay, share."

"She told me very little. And I said I'd keep my eyes and ears open while I'm in Boston."

"You're going to Boston?"

"I always go to Carlos's out-of-town openings. You know that. I'm going Thursday night. I'm staying through the opening Saturday and I'll be back Sunday night."

"And just what are you supposed to hear and see in Boston?"

"Susan thinks Mort killed Dilla—" She held up her hand before he could say anything. "Let me finish, Silvestri. Because Dilla was standing up to him."

"Great motive."

"I do think Dilla had something on Mort, and maybe he had something on her. It was a weird relationship. Symbiotic almost. But he certainly picked himself up and dusted himself off quickly after she was murdered."

"All of which leads us nowhere."

"But I did find out two things." She was very pleased with herself. She held out the plate of apple quarters to him.

"Bird food," he complained, but he took another quarter. "What are these great things you found out?"

"First, Susan is really frightened about something. And second, Dilla and Susan had a big fight sometime on Friday. Check with their downstairs neighbor, a Mr. Nadelman. He came up in a state about the noise Dilla's mother and sister were making and happened to mention it."

Silvestri grunted.

"That's all you're going to say?" She felt deflated. "You just hate when I find out things you don't."

"Bernstein or his partner would probably have come up with it sooner or later."

"Oh, please." She finished the apple and put the plate in the dishwasher. "Have you done a profile of her killer?"

He gave her a hard look and wrote something in his notepad.

"If you have, I'd love to see it."

She could see him get all bristly. "What for?"

"Be a good sport, Silvestri."

"Good sport? Amateurs always fuck up investigations. And get themselves hurt in the process."

She took her coffee and walked out of the kitchen. Opening her door, she picked up the *Times* and the *Journal* from the mat, closed the door, and sat down in the living room. She set her mug on the coffee table. The business section became particularly interesting to her. She began to read.

Silvestri followed her. "I don't want you hurt. I can't stand to see you hurt." His voice cracked.

That almost did her in, but she couldn't let it. "You think what you do is man's work and women should stay out of it. Right?"

"Not all women. Most. You in particular."

She got to her feet. "Oh, God, Silvestri, you are so Italian." Folding the newspaper, she thrust it into her briefcase, put the mug into the dishwasher, then padded into the bedroom, ignoring him.

"I hate the idea that you're with him." Silvestri looked around. He was leaning against the door frame. "Here."

"He never comes here." Wetzon inserted the earring posts in her ear-lobes and stuck her feet into her pumps.

"Why not?"

"I don't know. I guess I haven't encouraged it. Him. I don't know." When she looked up at Silvestri, he was grinning at her. "Stop that. You're making me crazy." She tried to push by but he caught her and held her close.

She thought she heard him say into her hair, "Les, what am I going to do with you?"

Pulling away, she said, "Why do you have to do anything with me?"

He threw his hands up and walked away down the hall and this time it was she who followed him, watching while he took his leather jacket from the chair. "I don't get it," he said abruptly, turning to face her. "What do you see in him?"

Wetzon sighed. "He's a very nice man. Must we do this to each other, Silvestri?"

"And?"

"And what?" She didn't bother to hide her testiness.

"What else? There must be something else."

"Okay." He'd asked for it. "He's a sensitive, caring lover."

"And I'm not?"

"Now who's getting spiky?" This made her tired, and sad.

He stared down at her for a long moment, then planted a kiss on her nose. "Keep it clean in Boston."

He was gone before she had a chance to respond.

"Damn him," she said to the door. If he wasn't around, she wondered, would she accept Alton's proposal? God, if Silvestri wasn't around, her emotions wouldn't be in such a turmoil; life would be so much easier. The proposal was still sitting on her answering machine. And the little light was still blinking. She was not yet ready to erase it. She walked over to the machine and was surprised to see the number of messages said "2." When had the second come in? She fast-forwarded Alton and stopped to listen to the second message.

The voice was such a low, tremulous whisper, Wetzon could hardly discern it. "This is Susan. Something dreadful has happened. Please call me as soon as possible. Please."

C H A P T E R

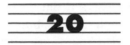

Wetzon stood in front of her building waiting for Tony, her doorman, to rustle up a cab. The sun was dazzling but deceptive. Every building seemed etched against the chill blue sky in sharp detail. People moved briskly—not because of the cold but because people always moved briskly in New York— the joggers in their sweats, mothers with young children, dark-skinned nannies with pale-skinned babies, and those like Wetzon, going to offices.

The light snowfall of the previous evening still decorated car roofs and trees, but the sidewalks were clear. Ordinarily, she would revel in a day like this, but today she was preoccupied. Each time she'd tried to reach Susan, she'd gotten a busy signal.

A cab made a U-turn in response to Tony's whistle, and Wetzon climbed in. "Forty-ninth Street, between Second and First," she said, and sat back. The driver had an embroidered pillbox on his head, and his I.D. noted that his name was Mohammad Mohammad and he was a probationary driver, which didn't stop him from taking her to her destination at breakneck speed.

Opening the outside door to her office, she called, "Good morning, Max," to the figure at Max's desk. Only it wasn't Max. Max wasn't due in until one today.

"Good morning, Wetzon." The man sitting at Max's desk was holding a mug of coffee. He gave her a charming, if sheepish, grin.

"Rich McMartin. What are you doing here?" Wetzon hadn't seen Rich in more than three years, not since she'd placed him at Loeb Dawkins. It had been a lovely fee. She hung her coat in the closet between B.B.'s all-weather and what was evidently Rich's Burberry. Another Burberry? Good God.

That did it. She was going to have to break with tradition next time she bought a raincoat.

B.B., who was out of Rich's line of sight, was pointing to McMartin and miming exaggerated shrugs. "What's up, Rich?" Wetzon asked.

"I have a little problem . . ." He let the words trail off.

"Uh-huh," she said, stretching it out. "Come on in here and tell me about it. Smith will probably interrupt us, but you sit down here, Rich." She put him in her chair and pulled Smith's over next to him, then went to the door and called, "B.B., please get me Rich McMartin's suspect sheet. You'll find him under placements. And if you could get me a cup of coffee, we'll be in business." She closed the door and sat down in Smith's chair. "Okay, what's up?"

"I got fired yesterday."

"You got fired?" Rich was a gorilla, producing close to a mil last she'd heard. "Excuse me if I'm repeating what you say. I'm in shock. Why were you fired?"

"Actually," he said glumly, "they asked me to resign, but they wouldn't give me a reason why."

"That's crazy. They have to. Do you have a compliance problem? Is anything going to be written on your U4?"

"Nothing. I'm clean. You've got to find me something. I have some megaclients and I don't want to lose them. Skip has probably already given out my book."

"Look, I have to call Skip and see what I can find out before we send you anywhere. We have to know what we're up against and we don't want any surprises." Sending Rich out to sit at Max's desk again, she closed the door and called Skip Beck at Loeb Dawkins on his private line. She'd intended to call him today about a broker anyway, so she'd be doing double-duty now.

"Skip Beck."

It never failed to amaze her: men, particularly men in power positions, who continued to use their little boy names. "Good morning, Skip, it's Wetzon. How are you?"

"Terrific. What do you have for me?"

"I do have someone to introduce, but first, I came in this morning and found a very unhappy broker waiting for me. Rich McMartin."

"Oh."

"Yes, oh. What's going on, Skip? Why would you let a producer of his size go?"

"I don't know how to answer that, Wetzon."

"What do you mean, Skip? It's a fairly simple question."

"No, it's not, Wetzon."

"Then what is it? Did he do something illegal? Is there anything I should know about that will keep him from getting hired elsewhere?"

"No. Everybody liked him. He's a popular guy. I would hire him again in a minute . . . if I didn't know him."

"Then why ask him to resign?" Skip wasn't going to commit himself, Wetzon realized, even as she asked the question. He was afraid of being sued. But stockbrokers rarely sued their companies because they were afraid they'd be blackballed on the Street. And they were right to be afraid.

"Wetzon, let me just say this, and I'll probably regret it—I can just hear my words coming back at me from another direction—"

"Not from me, Skip."

He hesitated. "Let's just say Rich is a great guy, but he's hard to manage."

"Umm?"

"And he's a compliance nightmare."

"Ah. But you say there's nothing on his U4 and you're not going to write any surprises on his U5?"

"I'm not. Is that good enough for you, Wetzon?"

"I can run with it. Thank you, Skip." She looked down at the suspect sheet in front of her. "I have an individual who's been with Faulkner and Sons on Madison for ten years. The bulk of his business is muni bonds, some governments, some mortgaged backs. He grossed three hundred and fifty thou last year, and has over three hundred in to date."

"Sounds like my kind of guy."

"They moved his manager up to region and brought in a woman manager to run the office, which ordinarily would be okay, but this one's a stiff. I know her. No sense of humor. She's a contest runner. The latest prize is dinner for two at her house. That was the last straw for Steve Zuckerman. Are you in at eight in the morning?"

"If I weren't, I'd be out of a job. Set it up. Eight is fine with me, but have him meet me at the Edwardian Room of the Plaza. I'm okay for tomorrow or Thursday this week."

"Well, great, Skip. I'll call you back to confirm and send you a thumbnail bio on Steve."

"Listen, any time I can eat out on the company I'm happy."

She hung up and made some notes on Steve Zuckerman's suspect sheet, then rose and opened the door, just as B.B. was about to knock. B.B. handed her McMartin's suspect sheet and a mug of coffee.

McMartin looked up at her from Max's desk, a total package of misery. There were actually tears in his eyes. "Did you get him? What did he say?"

"Thanks, B.B. Come on back, Rich." She held the door for him. He was a great-looking guy, clean-shaven, clear blue eyes, beautifully dressed, with the broad shoulders and the slim hips of an athlete. He looked directly at you when he spoke, seemed sincere and kind, had perfect manners and a magnetic smile. So what was there about him that made her uneasy? Then she knew. It was all surface. Rich was an eight-by-ten glossy, as they used to say in show biz.

"Did you talk to Skip?" he asked. "Did he tell you why?"

"I did and he didn't. All he said was there would be nothing on your U5 when it was transferred."

"I can't understand it. I was doing great. I was going to have the best year I ever had. . . ."

"I think maybe you stepped down hard on someone with power."

"Well, I did tell that govie trader where he could get off."

"Maybe he complained. Maybe it was a him-or-me proposition."

"I wonder if it had anything to do with the newspaper story."

Daylight was beginning to dawn. "What newspaper story?"

"Uh, I did this interview with *Newsday.* It came out on Saturday. I'm sure no one saw it."

Famous last words, Wetzon thought. "What did you say, Rich?"

"I said anyone who bought any firm's proprietary products was a chump. I really said schmuck, but they printed chump."

"Thank you very much. At least that explains it. Chump or schmuck, no firm wants its brokers to hint that the public is being defrauded."

"Okay, I get it." Rich didn't look the least bit fazed. "But now, Wetzon, you've got to help me. I've got to set up somewhere and fast."

They went over a list of firms and settled on Rosenkind Luwisher as first choice and Simson, Milgram and Quinn—known on the Street as SMQ—as second, and while Rich repaired once more to Max's desk, Wetzon set up the appointments. She told both managers exactly what Skip Beck had said about Rich and gave them Skip's phone number so they could check for themselves. Both managers were eager to meet Rich, so she set up the Rosenkind Luwisher meeting for eleven and SMQ for two-thirty that day. She knew that if they liked Rich, Rosenkind Luwisher would pull out all stops and have Rich up to the executive dining room in the tower for lunch. They were aggressive recruiters and a pleasure to work with. She admired their style.

Wetzon was showing Rich out when Smith emerged from a cab, long slim legs first, then the glamorous rest of her. She looked at Rich, then at Wetzon.

Like pressing a light switch, Rich's charm got the go signal. His glow enveloped Smith. "Well, hello there."

And Smith bloomed at him.

Wetzon broke in. "This is my partner, Xenia Smith. Smith, this is Rich McMartin. We placed him at Loeb Dawkins almost four years ago. Remember?"

The bloom came off Smith like a movie wipe. Smith hated brokers, called them dirtballs and lying scuz. She preferred dealing with their clients, the heads of brokerage firms. Wetzon, on the other hand, felt that their clients were no different from their candidates—the brokers. In fact, she liked stockbrokers. She, too, was a salesperson, almost one of them. She recognized their insecurities and vulnerabilities; she usually understood their arrogance. They reminded her of her people, the actors, singers, and dancers of her previous life in the Theatre.

"What was that about?" Smith demanded, when they were inside. She frowned at seeing her chair near Wetzon's desk and rolled it back to hers.

"Skip asked him to resign."

"How much production?"

"Maybe six hundred for his trailing twelve."

"Ah." Smith's frown receded. "And where are we presenting him?"

"Rosenkind and SMQ."

"Any problems?"

"Nope." She could see Smith mentally totaling up the fees. Wetzon had already done the same. They grinned at each other and slapped palms.

"All right!" Smith sang.

"Do we have anything important on for Friday?" Wetzon sat down at her desk and looked over her schedule. She had to try Susan Orkin again.

"No, sweetpea."

Wetzon looked over at her partner. Smith was smiling her Cheshire Cat smile. What was she up to?

"At least not in New York, sweetpea."

Wetzon was annoyed. She hated Smith's games. "And what is that supposed to mean, sweetpea?"

"You know exactly what it means, and you're mad because you hate to share with me," Smith said, almost wallowing in smugness. "You just like to keep your theatrical connections and your murders to yourself."

"Smith! Dammit." Wetzon stamped her feet. Why was she letting Smith get to her? Count to ten. Breathe slowly.

"Well, you don't have to get so hysterical, sugar. I was hoping you would be more grown-up about it, not to mention generous . . ." When Wetzon looked daggers at her, Smith continued serenely, "Joel Kidde called me. I'll be flying up to Boston with you Thursday night for our opening."

CHAPTER

"And I'm going to surprise Mark." Smith just kept right on talking, ignoring Wetzon's stupefaction. "My sweet baby is attending classes at Harvard on his spring break. Isn't that lovely?"

"Isn't that lovely?" Wetzon repeated. "Isn't that lovely, Wetzon? Oh yes, indeed, it's absolutely lovely. Now we can all have a pajama party at the Ritz."

"The Ritz? Oh, no, sweetie pie. You theatricals can have the Ritz. I always stay at the Four Seasons."

Wetzon flipped her palms up and rolled her eyes. "But of course you do."

Smith looked at her sharply and strolled over, placing her hands on Wetzon's shoulders. "Just as I thought. You're tense. I can always tell when something is wrong." She squeezed Wetzon's shoulders.

"Go away, Smith."

"And you look peak-ed. What's the matter? Is it Alton? I think it's time for a new man in your life." Smith began kneading Wetzon's shoulders.

"Sure. The more the merrier." In fact, that was almost funny. Wetzon would have laughed if she weren't feeling so low. She shook her head. "No, it's not that."

"Then what is it? You know you can tell me." Smith kept kneading.

"Ouch!" God, Smith was right. She was wound up tight, so tight she didn't even hear the beginning of what Smith said next.

". . . a massage. And I know just the person."

"What about a massage?"

"It would help." Smith stopped kneading and patted Wetzon's head.

"I'm seeing a shrink," Wetzon said. She'd meant to drop it in casually, but now it sounded like something momentous.

"A shrink? About what, for pitysakes? Your life is so uncomplicated—" As if to emphasize her words, their phones began ringing, all lines at once.

"Excuse me?"

"Do go on, sweetie." Smith smiled at her indulgently.

"Oh, why bother?" It didn't take much these days for Smith to wear her down. Wetzon picked up one line. "Smith and Wetzon, good morning."

"Hi, is B.B. there?"

"Hold on, please. Who's calling?"

"Wendy."

Wetzon put Wendy on hold. "Wendy, huh. B.B. has a girlfriend."

Smith scowled. "Personal calls during business hours?"

"Oh, come on, Smith. Lighten up. He doesn't abuse—" She went to their door, opened it and called, "B.B., Wendy on two for you." She closed the door and grinned at Smith.

"Humpf," Smith said. "Why are you seeing a shrink, then?" Like a dog with a bone, Wetzon thought. She should never have given Smith an opening. Smith had stopped her own therapy shortly after she got involved with Richard Hartmann, which was too bad. It might have helped her see what a genuine reptile Hartmann was. "You know you can tell me."

Do I? Wetzon sighed. "I have something called post-traumatic stress syndrome."

"What's that? It sounds awful."

"I'm not sleeping and I have a recurrent dream about being shot."

"Well, sugar, people do get shot. You are not the first, you know. You just have to get over it." Smith was examining her fingernails.

"Sure people get shot, Smith. Soldiers, cops, drug dealers, innocent by-standers in slums. Not people like us."

"Oh, for pitysakes. Here I am trying to empathize."

"Smith, you wouldn't know empathy if you fell over it in broad daylight."

"Sweetie pie, you just don't know how to accept help."

"You've been talking to Silvestri."

"Oh, I don't believe it. If you're seeing that loser again, you really do need help. Are you?"

"I'm not telling." Why did Smith have a way of saying things that were true and then twisting them? "I'm going for help now."

"You don't need a shrink. You should talk to me. I won't even charge you."

Wetzon stared at her partner. Smith was dead serious. In spite of everything, Wetzon began to laugh.

Smith was indignant. "You are the limit. I try to be your friend and you reject me and laugh at me."

"No, no, honest." Wetzon was laughing so she could hardly talk. "No, really. Love you for caring."

"Humpf." Smith returned to her desk and pawed through her messages. "This one's for you." She started to hand it to Wetzon, then pulled it back and read it.

"Who's it from?" Eyes wet with laughter, Wetzon caught the moisture with a tissue, gently, else—waterproof or not—her mascara would run.

"Susan Orkin. Isn't she married to the senator?"

"Not anymore."

"How do you know her?" Smith sounded peeved.

"She was Dilla Crosby's lover—"

"Must you? I hate that expression."

"Try to get over it, dearie."

"Lord, I knew I'd regret letting you drag us into the Theatre."

"May I remind you that you bought us into it?"

Smith said, "I guess I deserve that." She looked hurt.

And Wetzon, taking pity on her, said, "Susan and I were at Douglass together."

"Oh."

"Are you hatching that message?" She stood up to take the pink slip from Smith.

"There is no message. Just that she called . . . at nine o'clock this morning. Are you taking up with her again now that she's unattached?"

"What do you mean by that?"

"It was a joke. Don't get so crazy. It was just a joke. I know you're *normal.*"

"Normal! God, Smith, you have no idea what normal is."

"Well . . ." She was defensive. "I know you're not one of them."

"How do you know, Smith?" Wetzon asked wickedly. "I might just be in the closet. How would you ever know?" She leaned toward Smith and in her most intimate voice purred, "I'm really a very good actress."

Smith stared at Wetzon, aghast.

"So you should never judge." She ran her fingers lightly over Smith's cheek. Smith flinched. "And now you'll never be certain." She said it with glee.

"You are the absolute limit. I *know* you're okay."

"What's okay? Is it like normal? Don't you know the view depends on the point of view?" Wetzon gave up. There was really no point in trying to raise Smith's consciousness. She had none.

"What about Alton?" Smith was really distressed.

"What about Alton?"

"Well, you've been with him." Suspicion made her eyes glaze. "It's that Laura Lee Day, isn't it? I knew it. She's led you astray." Smith's face was getting a funny pinched look. She reached into her handbag and removed her tarot cards, holding them to her breast as if to ward off a vampire.

"Oh God, Smith, Laura Lee is not gay, and neither am I. Alton asked me to marry him last night."

Smith let out a shriek and after a moment of hesitation when Wetzon could see her wondering whether she should, pounced on Wetzon and hugged her. "I'm so happy for you, sweetie. He's so perfect."

"Since when do you think he's perfect?"

"Well, look." Smith began counting on her fingers. "He's got money, he's a wealth of good business contacts, he's old enough and secure enough not to have ego problems with your career." She finished triumphantly with, "And he loves you more than you love him."

"Very good, Smith. I like the way you boil it down to the nitty-gritty."

"What did you tell him?"

"I'm thinking about it."

"That's a giant step in the right direction. It'll be so good for business."

"Listen, Smith, can I change the subject here for a minute?"

"Of course, sweetie pie. Leslie Wetzon-Pinkus."

Wetzon shook her head. Smith was more excited than she was. "I took on a little investigating job yesterday. For Susan Orkin."

"Without me?"

"For an old friend. No money will be exchanged. She'll contribute the fee to a charity. The Gay Men's Health Crisis." Wetzon gave Smith slow-motion eyelash flutter. "I'll have her do it in *both* of our names, shall I?"

"You love to torture me, don't you?" Smith said, but she was smiling. "You think you're the only one here with a sense of humor. What kind of investigation?"

"She wants me to sniff around a little in Boston. She's certain that Mort killed Dilla and that, in the stress of the tryout he's going to give himself away."

"Mort Hornberg? That nice man? She's wrong of course, but we can certainly give her an overview while we're in Boston."

Wetzon smiled at Smith. Smith was funny when she thought she might be playing detective. "We certainly can, partner."

"This is so wonderful," Smith said. "We're back in action again."

"I'd better get Susan on the phone and see what she wants." Wetzon punched out the phone number on the pink message slip.

After two rings, Susan answered.

"Susan, this is Leslie. I'm sorry I kept missing you."

"I have someone here with me." There was caution—or was it fear?—in Susan's whispered voice. "Excuse me," she said louder, to someone else. "I'll be right with you." She lowered her voice again. "Leslie, please listen. Someone tried to break in here this morning. He didn't get in because Rhoda, my housekeeper, scared him off. Whoever murdered Dilla is coming after me."

"Susan, my God, you still can't believe it's Mort. That's hardly his style. What did the police say?"

"I didn't call them—I can't—you don't understand. It's just too complicated. . . ."

"Call the police, Susan, right away."

"Leslie, I didn't tell you everything . . ."

"For godsakes, Susan!"

"The day before she was murdered, Dilla got a threatening letter."

C H A P T E R

"I'm not walking tonight," Wetzon told Laura Lee Day. "It's too cold." They were in Rockefeller Center, under the NBC Building, standing at one of the little espresso bars—this one was called Main Caffe—that now dotted the city, sipping espresso and sharing a carrot muffin.

Laura Lee had been a young stockbroker with a small business when Wetzon placed her at Oppenheimer five years before. They'd become instant friends; they shared a passion for the arts: Wetzon had been a dancer, Laura Lee had been a violinist and still played with an amateur string quartet.

Whenever Laura Lee had a client to visit or a presentation to make in midtown, she would schedule it for midafternoon, then would arrange to meet Wetzon for a drink or an espresso and they'd walk home together. In cool or inclement weather, Wetzon would part with Laura Lee in front of Laura Lee's high-rise opposite Lincoln Center, but in the summer they sometimes bought frozen yogurts and sat at the fountain in Lincoln Center Plaza in the afternoon sun, catching up on each other's lives.

"Not only are you a wuss but you're a cranky wuss." The words may have been sharp, but the tones were mellifluous and southern. Laura Lee's roots were Mississippi, and the soft Delta drawl was an integral part of her persona.

Wetzon felt a surge of love for her friend. Laura Lee's brown eyes were brimming over with warmth. Her short chestnut hair was swept back from her face and she didn't look a day older than when they'd met. If anything, she was prettier, thinner, and had much more self-confidence. For the past year, she'd been having a steamy affair with a sculptor who showed at a top

SoHo gallery. "Not husband material," she'd told Wetzon happily. She and Laura Lee shared the same ambivalence about marriage. "After all," Laura Lee was fond of saying, "once you've been married, you can't ever again say you've never been married." Which made perfect sense to Wetzon.

"I called Francesca for you," Laura Lee went on. "Actually, I wanted to talk to her anyway. She knows everythin' about Provence. She's not interested in leavin' Smith Barney. She has such a good deal. They let her go off on her food trips; someone always covers her book. Why should she leave?"

"It was a lead, and I wasn't sure it was a good one. Francesca's so hard to get on the phone. Thanks."

"She proceeded to tell me all about where she'd eaten lately and what she'd eaten and what she'd cooked. Good Lord, I thought, when I hung up the phone, one day we're goin' to see Francesca walkin' down Park Avenue and she'll be an eggplant."

Wetzon laughed. "How was Provence?"

"Fabulous. Unbelievable. I ordered us a case of olive oil directly from a mill, and wouldn't you know, when I told Francesca about it, she said, 'But my dear Laura Lee, I much prefer the olive oil from the mill outside Mougins.' "

Wetzon giggled.

"Wait, you haven't even heard the best part. She tells me, 'We had a blind tastin' and we think ours is better.' Can you imagine, they sat around dippin' bread into various olive oils? A blind tastin' of olive oils? Give me a break."

"Oh, I don't know. I wouldn't mind dipping some really good semolina bread in different olive oils."

"But you certainly wouldn't *talk* about it."

"Probably not." She laughed again, and Laura Lee smiled at her. "This is amazing coffee."

"It's Starbucks', all the way from Seattle. The best coffee in the world. And, I'm delighted to see your disposition is improvin'."

Wetzon drained her espresso. "I've had a couple of traumatic things happen to me this week, and it's only Tuesday. I can't wait to see what the rest of the week will bring."

Laura Lee signaled for a refill and managed to accomplish a tiny flirt with the counterman, a sleekly attractive man with a dense Mastroianni accent. "Such a nice bod." She grinned at Wetzon. "I'm dyin' to hear all about it, darlin'."

"I'm dying to tell you, if you can pull yourself away from the espresso man, although I don't know why I should judge you, I've got one in my life."

"An espresso man?"

"An Italian."

"Uh oh." Laura Lee shook her head. "Wetzon, darlin', life is way too short to take everythin' as seriously as you do. What's the story?"

"First, Dilla Crosby gets clobbered to death just before Carlos's run-through and we find the body. Then the detective on the case recognizes me from when we met three years ago—"

"And doesn't know you and Silvestri have split—"

"You got it. So he picks up the phone and tells Silvestri I'm involved in a homicide. And then guess what?"

"Silvestri rides in on his white stallion. Yum."

"More or less."

"And where is the grand Alton Pinkus while all this is happenin'?"

"In Caracus at some labor convention. That's the other thing, Laura Lee. Picture this: While Silvestri and I are making out on my sofa, Alton calls and leaves a message on my machine for all the world to hear, asking me to marry him."

"Ooooo," Laura Lee intoned.

"Laura Lee, behave."

"What a delicious situation. Don't you love it?"

"Well . . ."

"Come on now, Wetzon, think about it."

"But Laura Lee, if I married Alton I would have to give up my apartment."

"Listen to yourself, darlin'. Did you hear what you just said?"

Wetzon laughed. "I guess I don't want to get married. At least, not if I have to move. Seriously, how would I ever find another apartment like mine for what I paid for it?"

"Wetzon, you and I know that square footage is the secret to a perfect relationship in New York."

"Ah, the pure, sweet sound of truth." Wetzon reached for her wallet.

"Put that away, darlin'. I've already taken care of it."

"I didn't see any money change hands."

"Marcello thinks I'm cute." She looked over at the counterman and he flashed her a sexy smile.

"You are cute. Come on, I'll walk you uptown. We'll be two furry animals chugging up Broadway."

"I thought you might change your mind about walkin' once I jollied you up. And besides, we both can use the exercise."

They walked up Sixth Avenue to Central Park South at a good pace, a damp, chilly wind at their backs, urging them along. Cabs were lined up in front of hotels. New York night life was about to begin.

"How's it going with you and Eduardo?" Eduardo was Laura Lee Day's SoHo artist.

"Oh, fine, I guess, but I'm gettin' a little tired of livin' in a Gabriel Garcia Marquez novel."

Office workers and professional women were homeward-bound to the Upper West Side in their dark pantyhose and white socks; the obligatory white Reeboks crowded the sidewalks. Whenever the MTA raised bus and subway fares, more and more decided to walk. And there were many more women than men. Wetzon wondered what that meant.

"I had another New York Moment this mornin'," Laura Lee said. "Do you want to hear it?" Laura Lee had started calling absurd things that could only happen in New York "New York Moments" and now she and Wetzon were always trading can-you-top-this stories.

"I know you're going to tell me anyway."

Laura Lee chortled. "This is better than anythin' you've had lately. This mornin' I got a seat on the subway and opened my *Journal*. I went right through the third section first, just to make sure about where all my stocks closed, then I started on the front page. Suddenly it came to me that someone was breathin' major halitosis down on me, standin' awfully close. I looked up and this homeless person is practically in my face. He was grubby beyond words. He looked as if he'd rolled in the mud last November and it had dried on him. He was talkin' to me, and I swear, I almost stopped breathin'. 'Excuse me,' I said, 'but would you mind'—and what do you think he says?"

"I haven't the slightest idea."

"He says, 'Can I read your newspaper?' Like a fool, I say, 'But it's the *Journal*.' He just stares at me and won't go away, so I gave him the section I finished, you know, with the stock quotes and all, and what do you think, Wetzon? He starts readin' it. And just as we're rollin' into the World Trade Center, he folds it up and gives it back to me and says, 'Market's overbought —due for a correction.'"

"You made that up."

"Cross my heart and hope to die."

"Then I'd probably recognize him."

"How come?"

"Easy. He's an ex-stockbroker."

Their laughter got them to Laura Lee's building.

"By the way," Laura Lee said. "His daughter is havin' a big dinner party."

"Whose daughter? The derelict stockbroker?"

"Get a grip, Wetzon. Alton Pinkus's daughter."

"How do you know?"

"I told you, Sandra Semple is my client."

"I forgot. Alton's going to be fifty-seven in March. Maybe it's a birthday party."

"She invited me, so I'll see you there."

"Don't be so sure. I don't think Alton's kids like me."

"Well, they're hardly kids. Sandra is thirty-one and the other two are in their late twenties and don't even live around here. And Alton likes you, so what does it matter? You're not marryin' *them.*"

"I'm not marrying *him* either."

With a wave, Wetzon continued up Columbus. Laura Lee always made her see the humor in their lives. And this was good. She was a buoyant spirit and wrung more enjoyment out of life than any ten people Wetzon knew.

Wetzon was feeling so good that she didn't at first recognize Detective Bernstein and his partner getting out of an unmarked and going into her lobby.

"Shit!" she said out loud, and a kid on a bike echoed her, "Shit, lady, shit, shit, shit." She stopped in her tracks. She had half a mind to turn on her heels and have dinner out. But she was tired. She didn't want to eat out. She wanted to be home.

Bernstein emerged from her building and looked up and down the street. And up again. He'd caught sight of her, and now stood waiting under the navy blue canopy.

"Ms. Wetzon." Well, at least he had dropped his sarcastic Miss Wesson routine.

"Detective Bernstein. Good evening. To what do I owe the pleasure of your visit?" He held the door for her, and they entered her lobby, where his partner Gross was distracting Wetzon's doorman.

"It would be easier if we talked upstairs." Bernstein followed her to her mailbox and watched as she collected her mail.

"You mean you want to come up?" Wetzon pressed the elevator button. The car was on the ninth floor and not moving. An alarm bell began to ring. The elevator was obviously stuck again. So much for the six thousand dollar assessment she'd had to pay for her share of the new elevator.

"Come, I take you up, then I get the super," Julio said. He motioned them to the service car, then went to the front door and locked it.

The service elevator, an antique even for the West Side, was on its last legs. A ripe smell seeped from the stacks of filled plastic garbage bags in the rear of the car. It was not a pleasurable ride, but it was better than walking up twelve flights.

When she unlocked her door and preceded them, she lit the chandelier in the foyer and then went on to the living room turning on the lights.

"Boy, this is great," Gross said.

"Yeah." Bernstein scratched his head under his yarmulke and sat down on the sofa.

"Is it a co-op?" Gross was checking out the quilt hanging on the nearest wall.

"Yes." Wetzon hung her coat in the closet. Gross walked around the living room looking at everything.

Bernstein took out his grubby notepad. "Just wanted to go over a coupla things with you."

"Okay." Wetzon sat down in the Shaker armchair and waited. He was actually pleasant, well, as pleasant as he was capable of being. Gross was now studying the titles on Wetzon's floor-to-ceiling wall of bookshelves.

"You said the box office attendant used to keep a club under the ticket window."

"You mean the treasurer. The treasurer bears the responsibility for what comes in—money—and what goes out—tickets—on a day-to-day basis."

"Okay, yeah. What about the club?"

"Some treasurers did keep one, but it's been a long time since I was in a show. Maybe they don't anymore. Maybe now it's an Uzi. You should talk to whoever is treasurer of the Imperial. I don't even know if he was there that afternoon."

"She." Bernstein sounded smug.

"Oh, a woman. There weren't many women in that union, as I remember. Things have changed."

"Did you see her?"

"How would I know her if she wasn't introduced to me? There were so many people milling around—detectives mostly— What does she look like?"

Bernstein nodded to Gross, who reluctantly stopped her peregrinations and stood beside Wetzon's chair. She took out her notepad, flipped over some pages, and read, " 'Heavy woman. Midforties. Maybe five eight, five nine. Wearing a black suit. Light brown hair to her shoulders, held back with a headband. Big glasses.' " Closing the notepad, she added, "Her name is Edna."

Wetzon wrinkled her brow. "She sounds vaguely familiar. I must have seen her. Otherwise . . ."

"Do you know her?"

"No. How would I know her? I don't know anyone named Edna."

"But you know her son."

Wetzon sat up. "Is this a trick question? Yes, union jobs were often handed down from father to son. But who's Edna's son?"

"Phil Terrace."

CHAPTER

Wetzon put Anita Shreve's new novel aside and turned out the light. Thick, cottony darkness immediately enveloped her. She lay motionless a long time, listening to her heart thumping.

But this is foolish, she chided herself. You've talked with Sonya, not to mention Silvestri, so it's been dealt with and you're not going to have the dream again.

Think about other things. Okay. What was Susan Orkin so frightened about? And did the attempted break-in have anything to do with Dilla's murder? Why hadn't Susan gone to the police? What had happened to the threatening letter? Did Susan know who the killer was? Was she, for some reason, protecting him . . . or her? Lord. She turned over on her side.

And then there was the surprise information about Edna Terrace being the treasurer at the Imperial. Had Edna been in the box office when the creative contingent had the stormy meeting the night before Dilla's death? Had she been there on Saturday when Dilla's body was discovered? It must be Edna Terrace, then, whom Phil was talking to that afternoon in the box office.

And Bernstein had actually been less obnoxious, thanking her for her help, asking her to keep an eye out in Boston. He'd even given her his card and written his home number on the back so she could call him.

On her back again—it was going to be a long night—she put her body in the sponge position. *Begin deep, slow breathing, relax the toes first.* Silvestri hadn't called. *Relax the arch of the foot. Breathe into it.* Just as well. Alton would be back in four days and she was going to have to deal with that. *Relax ankles. Feel all the tension flowing out.* She hoped Smith wouldn't be a true pain in Boston. *Relax shins and calves . . .*

She knew even in her sleep that it was starting, and implored, no, no no. Fighting it, she was losing. She felt herself being sucked inexorably into a giant vacuum.

The light exploded in her face hot as a flame, and her nostrils were burning with acrid fumes. Her head, her eyes—"No, no, stop!" Her cries thrust her thrashing out of the dream. She woke locked in a fetal position, trembling and sweating, her heart pounding.

Her digital clock said 3:35.

"It's all right, it's all right," she told herself aloud. "It's a dream. Deal with it. You don't need Silvestri. You don't need anybody." She talked herself down and lay again in the sponge, cold sweat chilling her even under the quilt.

When she finally stopped shaking, she got up, slipped on her robe and padded down the hall to the kitchen. There she made herself a cup of hot chocolate with Dutch-process cocoa and skim milk. Sipping a reasonable facsimile of soothing maternal nostalgia, she returned to her bedroom. She took a few small sips, then set the mug on the antique washstand next to her bed, got back into bed. One more swallow of cocoa. The yawn was unexpected; she lay back against her pillow.

Her clock radio woke her at six-thirty. About a third of the chocolate remained in the mug; the bedside lamp was still on. But she'd gotten through the night in fairly reasonable shape. By herself.

As a reward, Wetzon stopped at Mangia on Forty-eighth Street on the way to the office and bought a whole wheat scone for breakfast and a mozzarella and sun-dried tomato sandwich for lunch.

She squared her shoulders and strode purposefully east on Forty-ninth Street toward her office. A scrap of melody from a song Gwen Verdon had sung in *New Girl in Town* kept going through her head. "It's good to be alive," Wetzon hummed. Coming toward her was a young woman in a shiny black raincoat with yellow flannel trim and yellow rubber boots. A golden retriever charged yards ahead of her on one of those extension leashes. Wetzon had just stopped to pet the friendly dog when she heard a terrifying shriek. The dog owner's face was scrunched into a grimace. Always on the alert for the seriously disturbed who could pass for acceptable—a bit of necessary armor in New York—Wetzon immediately stepped into the gutter between a black BMW and a red hatchback and started across the street.

"Do you know how many animals bled to death so that you can wear that coat?" the young woman was screaming at her. The golden started barking and raced back to its owner.

Furious, Wetzon got back on the sidewalk. "Do you know what your precious synthetics have done to our ozone layer?" she responded. "Look at yourself and weep. You're a walking advertisement for ozone depletion."

The woman looked stunned, which was good enough for Wetzon. She was sick and tired of the trendy wealthy who set themselves up as judges, condemning meat eaters and fur wearers, when there were children who went hungry and guns were readily available.

Mentally brushing her hands together with satisfaction, Wetzon waved cheerfully to Steve Sondheim who was coming out of his house.

All in all, she thought, crossing Second Avenue to their office, a very good start to the day.

"Rich McMartin is sitting at SMQ," Max announced when Wetzon sailed through the door. The rich smell of coffee filled the office.

"Well, that's the kind of news I like."

"Do you mind, Max?" Smith appeared in the doorway. Her eyes flared a warning at Max. "It's not your job to report on hires," she said severely.

Wetzon shook her finger at Smith. Surreptitiously she mouthed, *none of that.*

Smith paid no attention. "We're going to have to wait a few weeks until he gets clearance before we bill."

"Really? Why? Rich said he was clean."

"A little computer check turned up three glitches on his U4."

"Damn. What kind of glitches?" Wetzon hung up her coat and poured herself a mug of coffee.

"Minor things—like unauthorized trading. Reprimands, but no lawsuits."

"Unauthorized trading is a minor thing?" Max was aghast. He had been a strictly-by-the-book accountant in his previous life, and still thought like one, which made him, as Smith was fond of saying, anal-obsessive.

"Trust me, Max sweetie." Smith gave him a patronizing pat on his slumping shoulder. "In a world where money laundering, insider trading, and stock parking go on as always, a tiny bit of unauthorized trading is a *minor* offense. Especially when nobody sued."

Max frowned. He was wearing a blue-striped shirt with white collar and cuffs and a crimson bow tie. When he frowned, his tie bobbled. "Then why wouldn't McMartin get clearance?"

"If a broker with a clean record moves," Wetzon explained, "the New

York Stock Exchange transfers his license electronically within twenty-four hours, and the new manager gets verbal clearance on the broker even sooner. But if there's anything at all on his U4, everything has to be hand carried, looked into with a magnifying glass. It can take weeks, sometimes months."

"Then what does the broker do without his license?"

Smith threw up her hands and went into their office, slamming the door.

Wetzon raised an eyebrow at the closed door. "Most firms let the broker work on the manager's or the branch's number. Not particularly legal, but everyone looks the other way. Max, is something going on I should know about?"

"She's in a bad mood," Max said.

"I would never have guessed."

Max eyed the closed door sympathetically. Since he'd joined them two years before, he had always treated Smith with indulgence. "Something to do with Mr. Hartmann, I think."

"Oh, dear. Thanks, Max. You're a sweetheart." Wetzon caught herself about to blow him a kiss and stopped. What the hell was wrong with her? Was she becoming Smith? She opened the door to their office, stepped in, and closed the door. In truth, she would be downright delighted if Smith broke up with Hartmann. She dumped her briefcase on the chair, set the mug on top of her desk calendar.

"You are altogether too chummy with the help." Smith was half-sitting on her desk, swinging one long leg back and forth angrily. Her face was dark as thunder.

"Come off it, Smith. What's really bugging you?"

The phone rang, was answered, and another line began ringing. The little hold lights were blinking.

"Well?" Wetzon asked.

Smith's face crumpled and she burst into tears.

"Oh, my God, what is it?"

Wetzon rushed to her. Smith sobbed on her shoulder. "It's awful. Awful."

"What's awful?"

"Dickie's been arrested."

"Aw, Richard Hartmann, Esquire, arrested? For what, pray tell? Did they finally find out he was laundering money?"

Smith pulled away, dried her eyes with a tissue, and blew her nose. "You don't have to look so pleased. And I'll have you know it wasn't for laundering money, it was for contempt." She blew her nose again and dropped the crumpled tissue in her waste basket. "I wanted to fly down to Miami to be with him, but he wouldn't hear of it."

"Contempt, huh? That's perfect. Contempt for the law, the jury system, judges, human beings. You know something, that man's not worth shedding a single tear over. He doesn't give two hoots for anybody. I warned you about getting involved with him. You deserve better."

"You are heartless, you know that? Absolutely heartless." Smith took out her compact and began to powder her nose. "I know you mean well, but—"

"Now Twoey, that's quite another story."

"Twoey!" The gold compact closed with a snap. "I'm so sick of hearing you sing Twoey's praises. If you like him so much, you can have him."

"Don't start that, Smith. Besides, I have more than enough on my plate right now. But Twoey Barnes is platinum, all the way. Don't be so quick to toss him aside."

Smith ran her fingers through her short, dark curls and smiled. The storm was over. "We'll see. I have my eye on Joel Kidde. He appears to be unattached at the moment."

Max knocked on the door, interrupting Wetzon's groan.

"Come, Max sweetie," Smith commanded.

"Carlos on three for you, Wetzon."

"Ah, dear Carlos," Smith said. She smoothed her stockings around her ankles and gave Wetzon an utterly guileless smile. "Please send him my best wishes."

Wetzon picked up the phone. What was this with Smith's sudden change in weather? "Hi. How's it going?"

"Birdie, it's the worst of the worst." Carlos's voice was so hoarse he croaked. "Everyone's fighting with everyone. Mort's carrying on like a lunatic. You know, no one ever realized how Dilla used to keep him in line. Your friend Twoey Barnes is walking around looking shell-shocked, and Mort just keeps ordering more scenery, and who needs it? We all agreed early on that less was more—"

"I thought there was barely enough money left to open in Boston?"

"His new partner seems to have deep pockets."

"Oh, God, Twoey . . ."

"I can't wait till you get here. Mort used to listen to you."

"That was a long time ago, Carlos."

"Darling, I can tell you right now this is the last show I'll do with Mort. You have no idea how awful it is. He called Sam an untalented hack. Then he had a screaming fit about the orchestrations because Poppy didn't like them."

"What does Poppy know about orchestrations?"

" 'What does Poppy know about orchestrations?' she asks. What does Poppy Hornberg have to know about anything? She just makes these pronouncements and everyone listens to her, especially Mort. Poppy thinks the lighting is too dark, so Mort told Kay she couldn't light her way out of a paper bag."

"Original."

"Then he called Phil a retard in front of the whole company and crew because he miscalled a cue."

"That certainly leads to trust all around."

"And when Aline came to Phil's defense, Mort called her a fat dyke masquerading as a woman."

"Well, la di dah. The usual Mort Hornberg tantrum. How did *you* escape?"

"But I didn't, darling. He told me he'd sent for someone who knows how to choreograph a Broadway show."

"Jesus." This was serious. "What did you say?"

"I said if he did that I'd cheerfully kill him."

"I'll be glad to help you if you'll wait till I get there."

"Too late, darling. Someone else may have gotten there ahead of us."

CHAPTER

At thirty-six thousand feet, somewhere above Bridgeport, a steward served champagne, Tattinger's no less, and pâté on little wedges of dark bread.

Wetzon was sitting on the wing, her legs stretched out in front of her. It was a magical February night. The sky seemed endlessly concave and the twinkling lights from the Grumman G-2 jet mingled happily with the stars. Raising her glass, she toasted them. The club soda had lost its fizz. Ah well. Even so, this was the good life.

Smith had arranged for a limo to pick them up at the office and drive them out to Westchester County Airport in White Plains. The limo had been one of Joel Kidde's, complete with a bar and a television. Oh, Smith was in top form.

In this brief, peaceful interlude on the plane, Wetzon felt quite alone, and it was a wonderful feeling. She had left a note for Alton. *Dearest Alton,* she had written, choosing her words carefully. *I'm sure you forgot I was going to be in Boston—at the Ritz—this weekend for Carlos's opening. I'll be back Sunday night.* She'd signed it, *Love, L.* and then read it over and added a P.S.: *Your message was received and is being digested.* She hadn't known what else to say, so she folded the note in an envelope and left it with Alton's doorman.

She hadn't heard from Silvestri again and, thinking about it, was suddenly pissed. Who did he think she was? Just someone to screw around with when he felt like it? A slow burn started in the pit of her chest. Damn it all, why did he make her care so much? Alton was better for her. . . .

A bubble of phony laughter pierced her reverie. Around her, which she had almost succeeded in tuning out, was the irritating hum of people who were trying to impress one another. Smith was really on a roll. It made Wetzon more impatient than it usually did. On the other hand, everything made her more impatient lately.

In spite of the depth of her feelings for Carlos, she almost dreaded what she would get caught up in when she reached Boston. Out-of-town tryouts were trying in more ways than one. Everyone was on edge, people would say unforgivable things to each other and then expect to be forgiven. Costumes wouldn't fit right, cues would go wrong, follow spots wouldn't follow. The performers would be physically and mentally exhausted. When she'd talked with Carlos late last night, he'd been agitated and brusque. Mort was back in action, his arm in a sling, his neck in a collar. Whoever had attacked him, for whatever reason, had not succeeded in killing him, Carlos had reported. This time. The police were classifying the attack as a mugging, because Mort's Cartier watch and his wallet were missing. At that point Carlos had laughed diabolically and told her, "So, darling, we still have our shot at him."

Wetzon felt rather like the Tennyson poem, as if she were riding, half a mile, half a mile, half a mile onward, into the valley of Death—

"Mystery spread."

"Huh?"

"I wouldn't eat it, if I were you." Sunshine Browning was pointing to the wedge of black bread Wetzon hadn't even realized she still held.

"I hadn't intended to. Frankly, I don't even remember taking it."

"Dump it in here." Sunny held out one of the barf bags and Wetzon obediently dropped the wedge into it. "I never eat the food on these things. Amazing, isn't it, that private flights are even worse than the majors." Sunny had a wide, toothy grin and a mane of streaked blond hair. Park Avenue natural. Her skin was pale, its pallor exaggerated by the all-black ensemble of skirt, sweater, jacket, hose, and boots. She stared intently at Wetzon. "I remember you. I was just out of Radcliffe and Mort hired me as his assistant."

"I doubt it. I was only a gypsy." Wetzon certainly did not remember her. Mort Hornberg always hired women from the top schools, and Sunny Browning was just one of a long line. They usually didn't last. But Sunny had. For one very important reason. Sunny was connected. She could raise money.

"You're the one he used to fight with."

Wetzon felt herself flush. "Fight? No. I'm sure you have me confused with—"

"Mort used to say he could look at Leslie Wetzon's face and read what she was thinking. Am I right?" Sunny had a way of engaging that was making Wetzon uncomfortable.

"He used to say something like that. . . ."

"Ha! There, you see. I have total recall." Sunny tilted her champagne glass and drained it. "I never forget anything."

"Never forget what, chum?"

Joel Kidde leaned over them, tall, sleek-haired, slightly bulging eyes looking out of a Vegas-tanned face. His scent was good cigar, and he looked like what he was, a mogul, cut from the same cloth as Time Warner's late chairman, Steve Ross. Joel Kidde was almost rancid with power. No wonder Smith was attracted to him.

"Leslie Wetzon," Sunny said.

Kidde looked blank. He gestured to the steward for more champagne and sat down in front of Wetzon. He was wearing a red cashmere turtleneck under a gray suit.

"This is Leslie Wetzon, Joel," Sunny repeated, winking at Wetzon.

How wonderful, Wetzon thought, to have made such an impression. They'd been introduced when Wetzon and Smith had lunch with Mort and Twoey at the Four Seasons, and again when they'd boarded the plane. But Joel had been straightaway mesmerized by Smith. So what else was new?

"Oh, Joel." Audrey Cassidy smoothed her honey beige chignon. She was as tall as Joel and so thin her hipbones protruded from her slim purple knit. Her large head seemed balanced precariously on her gaunt frame. She worked for one of those new fashion magazines, doing bitchy stories on celebrities. She and Joel were half-sister and brother. Very close. Incredibly close. They were known in the business as Butch Cassidy and the Sunburnt Kidde. "What did you say you do, Leslie?"

"I'm a headhunter. You might say I hunt top guns for Wall Street's most prestigious firms." She nodded toward Smith, who was holding forth several seats back. "Xenia Smith and I are partners."

Audrey's eyes settled on Wetzon, inventorying her Donna Karan suit, her black suede boots, her mabe pearl earrings, even her raccoon coat, which Wetzon had tossed on one of the seats near the bulkhead. Gee, it was just like being with Smith.

"Oh, I see." Audrey nodded, bored. "I understand that the show is a trifle rough."

Sunny's response was swift. "You know, opening on the road . . . things don't always come together right away. But that's what the road is for." She smiled brightly.

"And of course," Audrey persisted, "they haven't found Dilla's murderer yet." For a second, there was a catch in her voice and something like pain behind her eyes.

"What the hell is that supposed to mean, Audrey?" A white line of fury appeared around Sunny's lips.

"My dear, you don't have to be a brain surgeon to know it was one of *them.*" Audrey patted her chignon, seemingly recovered from whatever had upset her.

Smith's brittle laugh floated from the back of the plane and Wetzon, sensing it was a good time to excuse herself, got up to join Smith, but the pilot's voice crackled over the intercom announcing they should take their seats and fasten their seat belts. Wetzon looked back to where Smith sat with Gideon Winkler. Smith had appropriated Gideon the minute they were introduced. Gideon, with his golden boy looks and yellow hair to his shoulders, had been a gypsy once-upon-a-time, the same time as Carlos and Wetzon. He'd been in a slew of hits, including *On the Twentieth Century, Side by Side by Sondheim,* and *Evita.* Then he'd become a movie star, a director, had written an Oscar-winning screenplay, and now was an almost legendary play doctor. His presence on the plane had been casually explained by Joel Kidde. It was, Kidde said, a lift to Boston for a speaking engagement at Harvard.

A bit too pat. Too convenient, Wetzon thought, as they all piled their luggage into a waiting cart and headed out to the stretch limo for the short trip from Logan to the Ritz-Carlton.

"Hssst." Wetzon finally caught up to Smith as the latter checked herself out in the glass of the windows that looked out on the snow-flecked street. "What were you and the golden boy talking about? Did Gideon tell you why he's here?"

Smith looked down at her partner and pulled her cashmere coat around her. She, too, had adopted the no-fur zeal, and now she stood shivering in the Boston cold. Wetzon smiled. Her fur felt good, and she'd worked very hard to pay for it. And furthermore, the golden boy was wearing Blackglama to his ankles.

"If you want to freeze like Jane Fonda," Wetzon whispered.

"Well, if she's okay for Ted Turner, then—"

"Oh, Smith, give me a break."

Smith tugged up her collar and stepped out of the building. "I thought you wanted to know why Gideon is here."

Wetzon followed. "I do. Tell."

"He said *Hotshot* is moritose."

"That's comatose. Or moribund."

"Whatever. Joke all you want. There's a good chance that we're going to lose every penny of our money on your precious show and that doesn't make me very happy."

"How dare he say that? He hasn't even seen it yet." Wetzon was outraged. It negated Carlos, Mort, all the creative people, and the play didn't even open until Saturday night.

Smith patted her cheek. "Gideon will fix it, sweetie pie. Gideon said we're lucky he's available. Without him, *Hotshot*'s dead in the water."

C H A P T E R

25

The Boston Ritz-Carlton, with its top-hatted doormen in their electric blue jackets and black-and-gray trousers, was Wetzon's all-time favorite hotel. As a gypsy, she'd never been able to afford a stay there, and she and Carlos had bunked in dumps like the Avery and the Bradford that catered to touring actors and musicians and sometimes hookers. Once, years earlier—before Poppy—Mort, who always stayed at the Ritz—had taken Wetzon upstairs to show her his suite. To Wetzon it had seemed *fin de siecle* splendid, with rococo furniture and soaring ceilings. Mort had asked her to make him a martini while he changed his clothes, and she hadn't known how. He'd laughed at her, patted her ass, and showed her. In his early days as a director, Mort had tried to make everyone his friend. Too soon after his success, however, he no longer cared.

Wetzon was shown to a room on the seventh floor, overlooking the Public Garden, the bellman said, but the draperies were closed against the cold so there was nothing to see. She gave him a dollar for her small bag, which she could have carried herself, closed the door behind him, and leaned against it. The immaculate room was filled with furniture, yet had an uncluttered feel to it. There were two beds instead of the usual double bed in a single room. It was just this side of elegant. Let Smith have elegance; Wetzon would take the warm, nurturing comfort of the Ritz-Carlton.

She dropped her coat and Lucas bag on the bed nearest to the door. Good. A spare bed was perfect for laying out one's clothing. On the night table, along with the telephone, was a cache of gold-wrapped chocolates. Slipping out of her shoes, she plunked herself on the other bed and folded her legs yoga-fashion. Her watch said six forty-five. She was starving.

Tomorrow night would be the first—and only—preview of *Hotshot,* so Wetzon was pretty sure that everyone would be at the theatre for the tech/ final dress till late tonight. In her experience no one ever got through the technical rehearsal before the first preview, but by some theatrical miracle, things would fall into place anyway.

She could run over to the theatre and see when they were breaking for nourishment. Otherwise, she was on her own for dinner. Wetzon had assumed Smith would be dining with her son, Mark, but Smith had been unusually reticent about her dinner plans, which was fine with Wetzon. This was Wetzon's world: great chunks of her past, her soul, her youth, her deepest friendships, joys and sorrows, were interwoven in it like an old overshot coverlet.

Enough, she thought, getting off the bed. She unpacked the bag, dumped it on the floor of the closet, and hung up her new little basic black next to a thick, white terry bathrobe—courtesy of the Ritz, of course—then set up her toiletries in the bathroom on the shelf over the sink.

Did she need to redo her makeup? The face that looked back at her was still strange after one year. Somehow she always expected to see the old Leslie Wetzon with her ash blond hair up in the dancer's smooth topknot. The aftermath of the shooting had left her with a crew cut, and the growth had been excruciatingly slow, so that even now her hair barely came to her jaw, and thanks to her long neck, had quite a way to go to her shoulders. Not to mention the suggestive little sprays of white that had made an appearance at her temple around the tiny scar.

She blotted her nose and forehead with toner on a cotton ball. Actually, this hairstyle made her look younger and less programmed than the other Leslie with the topknot. But she missed the security, albeit imaginary, that she had felt. Maybe once her hair was back in its knot, her nightmare would go away.

On second thought, she rolled her gray eyes at herself. She could never wait that long. A bit of sheer powder to cover the sheen, fingers through hair, controlled disarray, add a touch of lipstick, and voilà: Leslie Wetzon, successful businesswoman.

Parting the draperies, she looked down at the snow-covered Public Garden. The street lamps bathed it in a glazy glow. Her mind danced from Alton to Silvestri and then settled on Carlos. He would be very upset about Gideon Winkler.

Mort bought into the Sturm und Drang style of directing. He was notorious for keeping everyone on the edge of hysteria with him. Just so long as he got it together first. Which meant ulcers, rashes, diarrhea, migraines, and tears for everyone around him. He was part of a whole slew of theatre people who actually believed creativity came out of mean, nasty turmoil.

Lordy, lordy, fess up, Wetzon. You don't miss one minute of that.

She put on her boots and her coat, gathered gloves and beret, slung her purse over her shoulder, and left the room with all the lights blazing. A warm den to come back to. These days she put a lot of faith in lights.

In the lobby she joined the line at the front desk to leave a message for Carlos, just in case he called. Two women stood ahead of her asking the clerk to recommend a restaurant. When it was Wetzon's turn, she gave the clerk her room number and asked him to tell Carlos Prince, if he called, that she was heading over to the theatre.

"Oh, Ms. Wetzon," the desk clerk said, his voice low and discreet. "Someone was asking for you. He's in the bar."

"Oh, good. Then never mind the message for Mr. Prince."

"It's not Mr. Prince," the clerk said, "It's—" A low cry came from behind her; the desk clerk's eyes left Wetzon's and focused on something over her shoulder.

Wetzon turned. An elderly woman lay on the carpet in front of one of the elevator cars, her walker toppled beside her.

"Oh, dear, Mrs. Kennedy." All of the clerks were suddenly distracted.

A man in a chauffeur's uniform and a tall middle-aged woman were helping Mrs. Kennedy up on her feet. Mrs. Kennedy adjusted her black cloche hat, which was tilting precariously over one ear. She was smiling and seemed unhurt.

Wetzon walked into the bar. What a splendid way to distract attention. She would have to remember that.

The lights in the bar were dim, dimmer than anywhere else in the hotel, the lighting enhanced by the flaring flames in the fireplace. Several of the small tables were occupied. The bartender was pouring manhattans into two glasses. Manhattans? Who drank manhattans anymore?

She did a quick look-around, seeing no one she recognized. Maybe the clerk had misunderstood. Her stomach emitted a low rumble; she'd better eat soon.

Near the entrance to the bar on a glossy walnut table was a gigantic bowl of fresh flowers, so colorful and springlike that Wetzon stopped to touch a rosy tulip. It was real all right.

Someone was staring at her. She could feel eyes boring into her back. Turning quickly, she saw a grotesque figure sitting in the shadows. He was beckoning to her with his cane.

CHAPTER

"What the hell?" Wetzon pushed the cane out of her way and glared down at the man who'd used it. "Mort, goddammit, couldn't you just say, 'Hey, Leslie,' like a normal person?"

Mort's right arm was in a sling and he wore a cervical collar around his neck. An ugly scrape covered the right side of his face from his forehead to where his beard began; his eyes had the glaze of too many painkillers. Under his cable-knit cashmere a bandage of some sort made his shoulder a bulky mound. He looked like Quasimoto in a cap, and he was drinking double martinis.

Wetzon immediately felt remorseful. "Good God, Mort, I'm sorry."

With the cane, he pointed to the empty chair next to him, then waved to the waiter with his good hand. Still shocked by his battered condition, Wetzon sat.

"Amstel Light," Wetzon said, surprised at how fast the waiter had appeared, but then, Mort was a celebrity. She couldn't take her eyes off him. "And some munchies, like cheese or crackers, please."

Mort made a refill gesture to his own glass. Was he unable to talk? Had the attack damaged his vocal cords?

"Carlos told me you were mugged, but I had no idea—"

"Mugged—" It was a derisive croak, and Wetzon realized he could only open his mouth fractionally, because of the swelling. He took her hand and squeezed it so hard she winced. "You'f gotha help me, Leshlie."

"Me?" She stared at the line of foam rising in the glass as the waiter poured. "What can I do?"

"Ish wash one of dem. Firsh Dilla. Now me."

Mort's ego was such that he would want to believe he was a potential murder victim rather than the victim of a random mugging. Wetzon took a sip of beer and sliced off a small chunk of stilton cheese. "Ah, Mort, maybe you're just being a wee bit melodramatic?" Then, because she couldn't resist, "You're such a nice guy, why would anyone want to kill you?"

The good side of Mort's face reddened. He looked at Wetzon suspiciously. She smiled her sweetest smile at him. "Gideon Winkler?" she prompted, knowing that the play doctor had to have been invited up to see the show by Mort. It was not something that just happened casually. There was a protocol to all this.

"Leshlie, you could nefer hide what you think from me. I trush you. Now I shee you're like the resh." Tears actually welled up in his eyes; Wetzon felt terrible. "Dey're all againsh me."

"Oh, now, Mort. Don't do that." He was such a shit; he hurt so many people, and here she was feeling sorry for him.

"And now Poppy'sh dook Shmitty away from me." Tears were rolling down his cheeks into his beard. He tried to put his head in his hands, but it wasn't easy with the collar.

Oh, dear God, Wetzon thought, how in heaven's name do I get out of this? Was this Shmitty, the young man Carlos was interested in, the one that Mrs. Mort—Poppy—had taken up to Boston with her in the limo?

"Mort, why aren't you at the tech? Where is everybody? You can't just sit here drinking gin and feeling sorry for yourself. You've got a show to get on. There are a lot of people depending on you." She rose and did a shuffle step. "Come on, boyo. Get your act together." She grabbed the navy duffle coat, which was lying on an empty chair, holding it for him while he laboriously signed the check, then when he stood, placing it over his shoulders. Her long scarf went twice around her neck, and she pulled the lavender beret down over forehead and ears. Boston winters were no joke.

Outside, the doorman offered them a cab, but Mort waved him away, and they walked the short distance to Boylston Street and the Colonial Theatre. She saw at once that Mort didn't really need the cane. He was using it as a prop to kindle sympathy and misplaced guilt in the people he verbally abused.

She almost walked past the theatre. Where was the old marquee? Gone, replaced by what seemed a ledge. "How would anybody know it was a theatre without the marquee?" she asked Mort, who grunted.

But obviously, people did. There was a line of eight at the box office window. The sight made Mort brighten considerably.

A tall man in a plaid sport jacket held the door for them. Mort gestured at Wetzon. "Thish ish Bob."

"Bob Foley," the man said. "House manager." He offered his hand to Wetzon.

She took it. "Leslie Wetzon. What happened to the old square marquee?"

"A truck backed in under it and pulled it down."

"What a pity."

"Under the old one, though, was a fabulous antique marquee with scallops, but it was replaced because it was fragile and could have been a hazard."

Wetzon saw Mort's eyes cross; without a word he went inside. She shrugged at Foley and followed Mort.

Almost a century old, the Colonial Theatre was a beauty. Wetzon remembered hearing that Ziegfeld had originated his *Follies* here years ago. Like the Imperial in New York, the mezzanine of the Colonial had an exquisite—but even more lyrical—curve. The first boxes were lush and at stage level. The Colonial was an aging beauty, a courtesan, still sumptuous from her boxes to her proscenium. It was rococo splendor: satinwood paneling, gold-leafed carving, a painted frieze in the dome of the house, murals. It was by far, Wetzon thought, the most beautiful old theatre in the United States.

Inside, the house was dark except for the small orchestra lights, the light from the technical board set up on wooden planks, huge across a couple of rows center-front orchestra, and, of course, the stage lights. The atmosphere was chaotic.

Wetzon waited to let her eyes acclimate to the darkness. Even after all these years she felt the same thrilling tingle on seeing the set on stage for the first time, seeing a show begin to breathe. And on the stage was a particularly beautiful, painted and constructed set with walkways and struts, a fractionalized stage floor, each raked at different angles. Horrible to dance on, but a joy to look at.

At the planked table on which two computers were spinning magic, several figures wearing earphones sat with clipboards and pages of script. They were calling cues. The table was a riot of coffee containers, half-eaten food, crumpled paper bags, and napkins. Lighting equipment and cables lay strewn in the aisles.

Carlos was standing near the orchestra pit, watching the actors in full costume sing and dance their way through a number Wetzon remembered from the demo Carlos had played for her as the first act finale.

Mort thrust his cane at her and she took it. He went right down the aisle, gestured to the people at the computer and joined Carlos gazing up at the stage from front orchestra. From where Wetzon stood in the back of the house, she saw Mort pat Carlos on the back, and Carlos nod.

Somewhere down front, a flashbulb went off, then another. Dress rehearsal—called "the dress" by theatre people everywhere—was always the best time to get scene shots to use for publicity. Wetzon scanned the front rows looking for the photographer, wondering if Irwin Rodgers was still Broadway's photographer of choice. Irwin would be in his sixties now, and was probably still wearing the bad toupee, which never lay flat, always tilting at an off-angle over one ear.

JoJo stopped the orchestra in mid-strings. It took several more seconds for the company on stage to come to a halt, sort of like a clock alarm winding down. Calling out something about not listening and coming in too soon, JoJo turned and spoke to Carlos and Mort. Carlos veered left of the orchestra and came to the apron of the stage. Talking with his hands, he made some indication about combinations that Wetzon couldn't hear. Then JoJo raised his arm and the orchestra and the actors began again. JoJo had grown a spacious rump and rolls of fat, which crept out from under his short T-shirt, as well as a Mort-inspired gray beard.

Wetzon sighed. It would be a long night. This was a tech and a dress combined. She looked down at the cane in her hand. Dammit, Mort had parked the cane with her as if she still worked for him. She was hooking the cane on the handle of the door to the lobby when a woman in shapeless brown pants and a man's beige safari shirt with thousands of pockets came down the stairs from the mezzanine, followed by a younger woman in jeans carrying a lighted clipboard. Kay Lewis, legendary lighting designer. Kay had worked with all the great musical directors: Jerry Robbins, Hal Prince, Michael Bennett, Bob Fosse, Gower Champion.

"Hi, Kay."

Kay squinted bleary eyes at Wetzon. Her face was an intricate system of lines, beautiful in their symmetry; her hair was short and chopped straight around her cheekbones.

"Christ, you look like that little dancer, Leslie something or other." Her voice was deep and scratchy.

"Wetzon. And no, I'm not back in show biz, Kay. I'm here as Carlos's buddy."

"Well, aren't you the lucky one."

"I guess Mort has been—"

"Mort!" Kay spat the name. "For beginnings, I've got a boil on my ass and I can't sit down, and Mort has outdone himself. This is my last show with him. I'm finished. I don't care if he's the only director left. I'll die before I work with him again." She motioned to her assistant. "Come on, Nomi."

The two women headed down the aisle, expertly sidestepping the tangle of cables to the computer board, when a loud whooshing noise stopped them in their tracks. The stage was suddenly bathed in an eerie blue light. "Those goddam, fucking color changers!" Kay flung her clipboard down in disgust.

Mort started screaming. *"Sixty* color changers! *Sixty,* for Chrissakes."

"You got what you asked for," Kay snapped.

Wetzon leaned her arms on the standing room ledge behind the side orchestra seats and looked around. Two stagehands came from the wings and were looking upward.

She caught sight then of Twoey sitting with Sunny Browning on the left aisle, midsection. A few rows behind Carlos and Mort were Aline and her young man, Edward. And Sam Meidner, in a cap similar to Mort's, was off to the right, leaning against a column.

"Okay, let's go," JoJo ordered. "Once through, then we'll break for twenty minutes." JoJo raised his baton and the light caught the conch belt on his low-lung jeans.

Whispering was coming from somewhere near Wetzon, and then an odd sound, like water slushing, almost like that of a dog slurping. The orchestra started playing and drowned out whatever it was. Curious, Wetzon walked along to where the side aisle dipped inward two rows.

An ample woman with a mass of wild red hair sat in the last seat, all the way left, her back to Wetzon. Poppy Hornberg's hair was unmistakable. As Wetzon came closer, she saw Poppy was holding the face of someone squatting on the floor in the side aisle, and lathering it with kisses. Smitty, for it had to be Smitty, moved his head a fraction.

Wetzon gasped and clutched at the ledge. She could almost feel the floor rocking under her feet.

The man—only it wasn't a man, it was a boy—looked up. His eyes met Wetzon's and registered horror. Poppy continued to devour him, covering his face with sloppy wet kisses.

Wetzon fled. Smitty was Mark, Smith's son.

C H A P T E R

"Whoa, there, girl—"

She'd run smack into Fran Burke for the second time in two days, this time almost knocking the wind out of both of them. His falling cane slammed into the wall with an explosive crack, filling the sudden void left by the silence from the orchestra pit.

"Oh God, I'm sorry, Fran." She felt sick to her stomach. All she could hear was her heart pounding in her ears.

"Overpaid!" Mort shrieked, behind them. "You're all over*paid!* If I stop directing, *none* of you will ever work again!" He was having a major tantrum, which was over the top, even for him.

"What's going on?" Under scraggly white brows, Fran looked serious. He paid no attention whatever to Mort's ravings, and Wetzon was too overwhelmed by the realization that Smitty was Mark Smith. In the sum total of what was important in her life, Mort and his posturings had no ranking. She picked up Fran's cane with its ornately carved death's head, surprised by its weight, and handed it to him.

She threw a look back along the path she'd just come, then pressed a hand to her mouth. Shaking her head at Fran, she made a dash for the ladies' room and upchucked the beer and what little else she'd had in her stomach, all the while thinking, *This is stupid. Stupid!* She dried her eyes with toilet paper and rinsed her mouth with cold water from the sink.

Someone was hammering on the door. Fran? If he was doing it with his cane, he'd break the door down. What had Bernstein said about the murder weapon? A blunt cylindrical object? She tucked that thought away for future rumination.

"Birdie! Are you all right?"

"Barely."

"What? Oh, forget it." Carlos opened the door and came in, concern making his face mushy.

"Carlos! You can't come in here." Another wave of nausea hit her.

"Oh, please!"

"Okay then, change with me." She shrugged out of her coat and thrust it at him. "I don't want to barf on my fur."

"Oh, I get it." He grinned at her. "Barf is okay on my leather. Mmmmmm." He stroked the fur. "Just try and get this back."

Shivering, she wrapped herself in Carlos's leather coat and gave him a wan smile. "Thanks. I'm okay now. It was from drinking beer on an empty stomach."

"Really, darling? Do tell. Fran said, rather quaintly I thought, that you were running as if the devil himself was chasing you."

"Moi? Oh, no." She became engrossed in the buttons on his coat. Anything to avoid meeting his shrewd eyes. "It was just an accident in the dark. I tripped over his cane. . . ."

"Birdie, I know you're hiding something, and I won't have it." He jumped up and down with both feet doing a dancer's version of Rumplemortskin. A clever gypsy had once dubbed Mort in mid-tantrum Rumplemortskin, and it had stuck. "Tell Carlos at once."

Wetzon laughed and hugged him. "Hanging around Mort is contagious."

"Don't breathe on me, please."

"God, I love you," she said, "but you're not going to be any happier about this than I am. And for totally different reasons."

"Birdie—"

"It's Mark Smith."

"Mark Smith? Who's that? Oh, wait, don't tell me. The Barracuda's kid. What does Mark Smith have to do with anything?"

"He's your Smitty."

"Smitty. Smitty?" The implications of it began to sink in. "Oh shit! I thought he looked like someone I knew . . ."

"Carlos, he's barely seventeen, and—"

"Trouble." Carlos looked as green as Wetzon felt. "I can't believe the Barracuda could produce such a nice kid."

"I just saw Poppy trying to—"

"Don't tell me, I know. She's been at him for weeks, torturing Mort. Mort is crazy about him."

"Oh, come on, Carlos."

"Birdie, believe me, Smitty is gay."

"God, Carlos, Smith will *die.*" Wetzon had a sudden, terrible thought. "Did anything happen between you?"

"No. But it could have. Shit, he's told everyone he's twenty-two."

"You all right in there?" Fran called, thumping on the door.

"Yes." Wetzon groped in her purse for her lipstick and made her lips pink again.

"Come on, Birdie." Carlos bumped shoulders with her gently. "We decided to break for dinner. Let's get you some tea. Personally, I need something a whole lot stronger."

They exited the ladies' room to find the stage lights dimmed. The theatre was almost deserted, except for some activity near the orchestra pit. Wetzon could make out JoJo's profile because he was such a lump of lard.

Kay Lewis's assistant Nomi sat with her feet up on the tech table. She was watching one of the computers and eating out of a cardboard container. The aroma of Chinese food surrounded her.

Wetzon's stomach gurgled. How could she be hungry now? But she was.

They came out through the front of the house because it was easier. Sunny Browning stood in the lobby with Twoey, examining the picture boards holding photographs of the actors. Later they would be replaced by scenes from the play the photographer was shooting at the dress.

"We're going around the corner to Remington's," Sunny announced. She kept a proprietary eye on Twoey.

"Birdie?"

"Let's go with them. You can get a drink and I can have ginger ale and saltines." She was thinking: *Smith is going to need someone who loves her very much once she finds out about Mark. Someone like Twoey.* It's a pity Smith was so hardheaded. Wetzon had the uneasy feeling that Smith would lose Twoey to Sunny Browning.

"You're looking a little pale." Twoey planted a kiss on Wetzon's cheek. He was flushed. Well, at least Twoey was enjoying himself.

"And you look as if you're having a wonderful time."

Twoey laughed. "I am. Sunny's been filling in the gaps for me. I'm going to be an expert in out-of-town tryouts. Would you believe it cost $150 thou to load the scenery into the theatre?"

"Going out of town may cost a bloody fortune," Sunny said, "but it's better than staying in New York and trying to fix a show with the theatre mavens second-guessing you all the way. It's vicious. And with a little luck we'll cover salaries, at the very least, out of box office receipts."

Boylston Street at night. This part of Boston had changed little from Wetzon's road experience. Derelicts and panhandlers sized them up on the sucker quotient. Twoey emptied his pocket change into the cardboard cup a bedraggled woman held out to them.

"Now every vagrant in a three-mile radius will have your number," Sunny warned.

"Listen, Sunny darling." Carlos grabbed Sunny's arm and walked ahead with her. "I'm a little worried about Phil. He's not up on the cues. The changes are consistently late. I hate to say it but Dilla would have . . . ."

Wetzon and Twoey fell in behind Carlos and Sunny.

"Twoey, Mark's here."

"I know. Xenie told me. He's sitting in on some classes at Harvard. Maybe we'll get to see him." Twoey held the door for her, and they followed their companions into Remington's, which Wetzon remembered as having been a bank in an earlier incarnation. They had to wait for a table.

"I don't mean in Boston. I mean Mark's on the show. He's got some sort of gofer job. And he's calling himself Smitty."

"Good for him!" Twoey said heartily. Then he frowned. "Xenie's not going to be happy about it." He shrugged. "Hell, I don't know that that's true. Xenie may surprise us. There's no telling what she'll do."

"That's true."

"You say he's working on the show now?"

"Yup."

"I've been here since Tuesday. How has he managed to stay out of my way?"

"Twoey, he's been hanging around rehearsals in New York telling everyone he's twenty-two and in college. Mark's got a vivid imagination, and he's inventive, but he must have had a jolt when he saw you, and then me."

Twoey chucked her under the chin. "Don't worry about him, Wetzon. He'll be all right."

"I'm worried about him, and I'm worried about Smith, too. She's especially vulnerable where Mark is concerned. You know that, Twoey."

The bar was packed with serious drinkers. More people lined up behind Wetzon and Twoey. Still, it was only ten minutes before they were seated in the crowded dining room opposite the bar.

Obscene things were ordered, by Wetzon's taste, like knockwurst and baked beans, fish and chips, New England clam chowder—"Fridays only," and beer. Wetzon stuck with ginger ale and a crock of French onion soup.

". . . have to give the devil her due," Carlos said, seemingly continuing on a subject he and Sunny had discussed on the walk over.

"She could cajole the crew to do anything for her. I don't know how she did it," Sunny agreed. She was absently stirring her Bloody Mary.

"Dilla?" Wetzon, sitting opposite Carlos, was weary and a bit light-headed. She felt her eyelids droop.

"Yes." Sunny looked at her intently. "Leslie, you know these detectives. Do they have a clue who killed her?"

"I'm not piped in, Sunny, if that's what you mean, and they wouldn't tell me if they did."

"I'm sure it was a robbery. Her purse was missing—and—did anyone notice? I'll bet anything she wasn't wearing the ring when they found her."

"What ring?" Wetzon snapped quickly alert.

Sunny frowned. "Someone gave it to her, I would think. It was not the kind of thing you give yourself. Probably that mysterious investor she was bringing in. It was hard to miss it. She wore it all that week."

"Did you see it, Carlos?"

"What is this, Birdie darling, the third degree?" He was chomping on fries with such pure abandon that Wetzon was jealous.

Her foot nudged his under the table. "Come on, give."

"Yeah, I saw it. Who could miss it? It had a stone as big as . . . the Ritz."

Sunny closed her eyes for a brief moment, then opened them. "It was this wide yellow gold band, right, Carlos?"

He nodded. "And set flat into it was a humongous yellow diamond."

Wetzon *comme* Holmes felt a tingle of pleasure. It was elementary. A crack addict could turn that little item into a number of hits. Why hadn't anyone mentioned the ring earlier?

Another thought struck her. Could the diamond ring have anything to do with the pouch of jewelry Izz had brought Wetzon in Dilla's apartment? She hadn't gotten a good look at the contents of the pouch. The question was, had Dilla been wearing the ring when she died?

The names embroidered in the pouch were *Lenny* and *Celia*. Susan had called Dilla's mother Ruth. Sunny could be right. Dilla might have been murdered for her ring. Unless Susan . . . , no, that couldn't possibly be. . . . But Wetzon well knew that given certain circumstances even she herself was capable of . . . What if Dilla was leaving Susan for someone else? The mystery investor in *Hotshot* who had never come forward. Maybe the ring was Susan's. If Susan had done it, she could have taken the ring and . . . God, no. Not Susan. Enough of that, she scolded herself. Close it down, put it away, think about the show.

They got back to the theatre at seven and the tech/dress for the second act began. The company was in "ten out of twelves," which meant the unions would allow producers to rehearse ten out of a consecutive twelve hours until the opening without an overtime penalty. Theatrical union contracts were based on an eight-and-a-half-consecutive-hour day, of which seven hours could be spent on rehearsal. But in the few days before an out-of-town opening, everything changed. Producers were given more leeway. Rehearsals ran eight to noon, one to six, and seven to midnight—when everything stopped dead. After midnight was "golden time," when stagehands received double their rate—fifty, sixty, or seventy dollars an hour—although they were already getting overtime.

Wetzon chose an aisle seat three rows behind the computer board, which was even denser with crumpled napkins, coffee, and food containers, keeping half an eye out for Mark. The theatre was cold and stale.

The light cue was late again.

"Stop!"

Mort came blasting out of the shadows front of house right screaming for Kay. But when he turned, Wetzon saw it was not Mort, but Sam Meidner, wearing that Mort-sort of cap. With his gray beard, at first glance in the dim light, the composer looked remarkably like Mort. But there was Mort sitting in the third row with Carlos.

Fran shuffled down the aisle and sat in the row behind Wetzon. His cane rattled against the arm of the seat. He pressed her shoulder firmly. "How're you feeling?" He spoke conversationally, making no stab at a whisper.

Wetzon nodded and smiled at him.

"From the top," JoJo ordered.

Sam retreated and the actors started the number from the beginning. When they finally got to the first ending without interruption, everyone breathed a sigh of relief. The encore went smoothly until the last note. Then a backdrop designed for a speedy transition came down way too fast, crashing to the stage. The actors scattered. There was a moment of stunned silence. Like an eruption, minus his sling and cervical collar, Mort rose out of his seat behind JoJo.

"Phil! Where the *fuck* is he? *Phil!* Goddammit. I'll *kill* him."

"Everyone okay?" JoJo called.

Everyone was.

Behind Wetzon, Fran was emanating angry vibes, muttering under his breath.

When Phil finally appeared, stricken, Mort screamed, "What the fuck is wrong with you? Can't you get *anything* right?"

The stage manager hung his head. "I'm sorry, Mort. I don't know what happened."

"Bastard," Fran mumbled.

"Go easy on the kid, Mort. We're all feeling a little stressed out," Carlos interjected.

Mort turned on Carlos, but thought better of it. He stamped his foot and shook both fists. Rumplemortskin was having a fit. "Get this cleared!" he roared.

Walt Greenow and a stagehand came out on the stage. They looked up into the flies, pointing. Walt spoke to Phil, who went back to the wings. "It's okay," Walt called to Mort. Then, "Take it up." The backdrop jerked. A groan rose from the orchestra pit. "Slowly!" Walt urged.

The drop went up again, tilted briefly, came down, then went up like a breeze.

The relief was audible. Wetzon turned to say something to Fran, but he was gone.

"All right, let's take it from the end of the encore." Mort seemed to have cooled off. He put an arm around Carlos's shoulders and whispered something. Carlos laughed.

This time the drop came in as it was supposed to. A spattering of applause from different parts of the house greeted it.

JoJo raised his hand and the dress continued. Flash bulbs flared. The photographer was indeed Irwin Rodgers. Wetzon recognized him when he turned to reload. His toupee was askew.

Wetzon skimmed the dark house. She saw Fran move laboriously through the side curtain to the wings.

Poppy Hornberg stood in the aisle near the back, hands on her broad hips, talking to Peg Button, who held a large swatch of shiny material.

Where was Mark? Even as she wondered, Wetzon saw him come out the pass door backstage right carrying a cardboard box with just enough care to let Wetzon know it was a liquid delivery. Coffee, Diet Cokes. The responsibility of the gofer.

Wetzon edged across the row of seats to the other aisle. Maybe she could catch Mark. She saw him stop near Mort and Carlos. Mort passed a container to Carlos and took the next one from Mark, setting it on the arm of the seat. He reached up and caressed Mark's neck, and Mark nestled into the caress as if Mort were his own true love. Oh, shit, Wetzon thought. Smith will die.

"Hold it!"

This time it was Carlos who stopped the show. He strode to the apron, clapping his hands. "Five, six, seven, *eight*. Stay on the beat. JoJo, help us out here. The beat, guys. You'll kill the number. You'll kill the applause." He grabbed his chest. "You'll kill *me*. Okay, JoJo—"

Mark stopped at the computer table and delivered three more containers, then headed up the aisle toward Poppy. The producer's wife had parked herself in the last row of the orchestra. She patted the seat next to her. "Sit with me, Smitty," Wetzon heard her say.

"I'll be right back," Mark told Poppy. "I have to give Kay hers."

Wetzon, blending into the shadows, followed Mark. "Kay's in the ladies' room," she called.

Mark started and dropped the cardboard box. The last coffee container sloshed black coffee from the pinhole in its plastic cover, and seeped through the cardboard into the carpet. He looked as if he'd seen a ghost. "Oh, God. Wetzon. Don't tell Mom, please." He bent and picked up the box, his hands shaking.

"Mark, what is this Smitty business and telling people you're twenty-two years old?"

"I want to be in the Theatre, Wetzon. I'll do anything. I don't want to go to college." His voice was a plaintive whisper.

"You can be in the Theatre—no one will stop you if that's what you want —but finish school first. Your mother is going to be very upset when she finds out."

"Please don't tell her." The boy was so miserable she wanted to hold him, but he was too old for that and too many people were entirely too anxious to hold him at the moment. "I never expected to see you here," Mark said.

"But you knew Carlos was my friend."

"He's been really nice to me. So have Mort and Poppy. Mort's going to help me get work in the Theatre."

"Mark, you can trust Carlos, but Mort and Poppy will cut you in two rather than let the other . . ." She paused. ". . . have you. Do you understand? Poppy is using you."

He bowed his head. "Wetzon, it's not what you think. . . . I'm . . . not . . . Poppy is . . ." His lips pressed together.

"What, Mark? You know you can tell me anything."

He looked at her then, almost defiantly. "Wetzon—I'm—" His voice cracked. He swallowed. "I'm gay."

Wetzon's first anguishing thought was of Smith. But Mark's need was greater. She touched the boy's cheek, then stood on tiptoe, took his face in her hands, and looked into his eyes. "Honey, you know me well enough to know I don't care what your sexual preference is. I want you to be happy. But your mother—"

Kay came out of the ladies' room; awkwardly, Mark and Wetzon separated. The lighting designer looked from one to the other, amused.

"Here's your coffee, Kay," Mark said.

"Christ, Smitty, you're really something." There was admiration in Kay's voice. She took the coffee.

"It's not what you think, Kay," Wetzon said.

"What *am* I thinking, Leslie?"

They watched Kay march down the side aisle. Wetzon looked around. "Come in here, Mark."

"But it's the ladies' room."

She smiled. "This is show biz." Opening the door, she called, "Anyone here?" When no one replied, she pulled Mark in and shut the door. She took the empty cardboard box from him and dropped it on the floor near the waste bin. "How long have you known?"

"I felt different, but I didn't know why. When I went away to school, I knew. . . ."

"Oh, baby, it's not going to be easy for you. You know that?"

"I know."

He didn't know, but she let it pass. "How did you get into this Theatre stuff?"

"Dilla. She caught me sneaking in and hanging around rehearsals."

Wetzon sighed. "And what about school?"

"I told them Mom wasn't feeling well and I took the train in the afternoon about three or four times a week—whenever I could get away."

"Where did you stay?"

"At Dilla's and Susan's. They sort of adopted me. I told them I was an orphan."

"Oh, Mark." Smith would absolutely die. "Your mother is here, you know, and she'll see you, so you're going to have to tell her—"

"God, Wetzon, I can't tell her I'm gay."

"No, I guess you can't, but you can tell her you're working on the show. Promise me you'll do it."

"Okay."

"How did you get on the show anyway?"

"Dilla introduced me to Mort. And Carlos, too, of course."

My God, Wetzon thought. Dilla was pimping for Mort. "Were you hanging around the theatre at the meeting the night before Dilla was murdered?"

He nodded. "I'd just gotten there. It was raining so hard, I got soaked. I don't think anyone really noticed me. They were arguing about something and then Carlos left. He was really mad. I hung around for a while, until Sam and Aline left. But then Mort and Dilla had a big fight."

"About what?"

"I don't know. Something about how she always covered for him, and when she needed him, he turned her down. I didn't know what to do so I went outside. It was sleeting and raining, and I was freezing, but I'd closed the stage door and couldn't get back in because it was locked. And I didn't have an umbrella. Mort was supposed to take me to dinner—we'd had this plan—but I guess he forgot."

"Where did you stay that night?"

"I called Carlos. He let me stay with him."

"For just that night?"

"For the weekend."

Wetzon sighed, disheartened. "Was the front of the theatre dark? Was anyone around?"

"You mean when I got locked out?"

She nodded.

"I ran around the block to Forty-fifth Street to the front, but that was locked, too," Mark said. "I could see someone inside, in the box office, but she wouldn't let me in."

C H A P T E R

"I broke the news about Smitty to Mort," Carlos announced.

"And?" She was really angry with Mort, but she was probably wrong to be. How would he have known Mark was only seventeen?

Wetzon and Carlos were stretched out, shoes cast off, side by side on Carlos's king-size bed. A bottle of a French cabernet sauvignon and a double order of scrambled eggs and bacon were history.

The company had broken at midnight, and everyone was ravenous. Carlos and Wetzon had rushed back to Carlos's room and ordered room service.

"If he wasn't such a nice kid, I'd be only too happy to see the Barracuda suffer."

"He is a nice kid. Carlos, he told me he's gay."

"Didn't I tell you, darling Birdie? Carlos is never wrong about that."

She kicked him. "Oh, go on. You always say everybody is gay."

"But darling," Carlos drawled, "everybody *is.*"

"Well, I'm not."

"You say." Carlos chortled diabolically, and she kicked him again.

"Let's get serious here," she said sternly.

"Okay." He laughed and threw his arms around her. "We're getting old together."

"Speak for yourself."

"Birdie, I worry about you."

"Carlos—" She pushed him away. "What's this?"

"What if something happened to me?"

She felt a stab of fear. "Is anything wrong?" She sat up. "Are you okay?"

"No. I mean, yes. I'm fine." He raised himself on his elbow and leaned his head on his hand. "It's not that."

"Swear"—she traced a cross over his heart with her finger—"and hope to die." He shivered an exaggerated sensual shiver. "I'm not kidding," she said sternly.

"I *swear,* dear heart."

"Well, fine then." She flopped down on the bed beside him again, facing him, elbow on bed, head in hand. Now they were bookends.

He laughed at her. Then he got serious again. "I'd like to see you settled."

"You're just jealous 'cause I'm still playing the field."

"Ha!"

"You are not my father, you know."

"Forgive me." He fluttered his long dark lashes. "I just care. I want you to have someone steady—like Arthur. He's my rock."

"I could marry Alton. He's a rock. What do you think? Is he too old for me?"

"I think if you love him—fine." Carlos looked at her, his eyes bright.

"I love him. But—"

"But what?"

"He's so easy to be with."

"That's a but?"

"Don't start." Wetzon closed her eyes and rolled over on her back. She'd had too much wine. "It's too smooth."

"What is?"

"The relationship."

"Oho. The earth doesn't move."

"You got it."

"And with Silvestri?"

"A veritable earthquake."

He took her hand. "Well, la di dah, darling. I guess there's your answer."

They lay side by side for awhile, silent.

"I ought to go. Otherwise I'll fall asleep here."

He grinned. "And ruin your reputation."

She reached over and tickled his side along his ribs, and he coiled up like a satisfied snake. "You're in great shape," she said enviously.

He poked her and she rolled off the bed gracefully, landing on her feet. "You're not so bad yourself, Birdie."

"Mark said someone was in the box office Friday night after you left in a huff."

"Yeah? I guess the treasurer could have been there that late."

"The treasurer is Phil's mother. She must have gotten Phil the job as Dilla's assistant."

"No, I don't think so. I think it was Fran, but I'm not sure."

"Fran?"

"Well, you know Fran and Dilla had this cautiously adversarial relationship." He patted the bed next to him. "Come on back."

"Cautiously adversarial. Interesting way of saying they hated each other. They had to work together, though. Maybe Dilla wanted a piece of the ice. Carlos, do you think Fran could have killed her? He could have bludgeoned her with his cane. Do you know how heavy it is? It must be weighted."

"I don't think Fran has the strength in his arms to lift that cane over his head." He patted the bed again.

Wetzon lay down. "My skirt is getting wrinkled."

"Take it off."

"Going straight, darling?"

"Au contraire."

"Gideon Winkler was on the plane with Joel."

"Oh?" Carlos shot upright.

"He told Smith he was coming up to fix the show."

"How does he know the show needs fixing? We haven't even had an audience. The long knives are out."

"It's not enough that I succeed, my friends must also fail."

Carlos fell back against his pillow. "I'll think about it tomorrow."

Neither spoke. Wetzon listened to their breathing.

"If Smith finds out Mark is gay, she's apt to kill him. Or herself. Mark is scared to death she'll find out."

Carlos yawned. "She'll get over it. Besides, that one would never kill herself."

"Maybe she won't find out." She yawned, too. She was having trouble keeping her eyes open.

"Ha! It's hard to keep those things a secret."

"He promised me he'd tell her he had a job on the show and will leave it at that. He's not about to tell her . . ."

She woke with a start. Carlos was snoring next to her. Sitting up, she looked at her watch. Two-thirty. Her skirt was a mess. She tried to smooth it. She took her jacket and coat from the chair where she'd tossed them, picked up her purse, stuck her feet in her shoes. At least the nightmare hadn't come.

She gave Carlos a gentle kiss. "Good night, doll."

He murmured, "Love ya," and rolled over.

Turning out the lights, Wetzon stepped into the hallway and closed the door, arranging the do-not-disturb sign on the doorknob. The hallway was empty. No one around at all. How different it was now. The Theatre she'd been part of had been so sexual. Not sexy, but sexual. Everybody was doing it. And when they weren't doing it, or planning to do it, they were thinking about doing it. The fire escapes in the tacky hotels had been gridlocked after rehearsals or performances. Partners changed frequently. Married in New York meant single on the road. It was as if creativity made everyone horny.

By comparison, Wall Street, where money and power were the sex, where people were horny for the next deal, next conquest, not the next body, had seemed dull to her when she'd changed careers.

Now, however, the road was tame. Circumspect. AIDS had made everyone fearful. Spontaneity was abandoned. Even safe sex wasn't safe anymore. She walked down the hall to her room.

Where had she put her key? She searched her pockets, then her bag. There it was at the bottom of her purse, under her makeup pouch. She put it in the lock and turned it, opening the door.

The light from the hallway streaked into the dark room. Hadn't she left all the lights on? God, had the Ritz taken to turning off lights on a timer or something?

She closed the door and groped on the wall for the light switch. Then stopped still. There was something soft on the floor. . . . She searched for the doorknob. Near the second bed there was a faint movement, a shift of the shadows.

She froze. Someone was in the room with her.

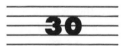
Although overwined and sleep-befuddled, Wetzon threw open the door to the hall and stepped out, flipping on the overhead light as she did so. "Gotcha," she said softly. *Like papa bear,* she thought, *let's see who's been sleeping in my bed.*

"Ow! For pitysakes!"

Wetzon jumped back into the room and slammed the door. Smith, in a white silk nightgown, was sitting up on the second bed, rubbing her eyes.

"Smith! Goddammit. What are you doing here? And in my bed!" She noticed at once that all of her things were now lumped on the bed she had intended to use to lay out her clothes.

"I can't believe you woke me out of a sound sleep just to ask me that," Smith said querulously, hand protecting her eyes. "Turn off that light."

Wetzon switched on the lamp on the chest of drawers, taking in the fact that Smith had spread her accessories out on the top of the bureau. She flicked off the overhead light. "How, may I be so bold as to ask, did you think I was going to get into bed?" She began sorting out her clothes from the pile on the bed, feeling Smith's eyes boring into her, sizing up her humor, which was getting worse by the second. There were no hangers left for Wetzon's clothing. "Shit, fire, and corruption!" She kicked the closet door shut.

"Sweetie pie, really. I thought you were out for the night."

"And whom would I be out with, pray tell?"

Smith shrugged her fabulous shoulders delicately. "Well, there are a few people connected with the show who are not queer. One or two. For example, a technical person who is rather attractive and who appears to be crazy about you. . . ." She had that smug look on her face that made Wetzon crazy.

"What are you talking about, Smith?"

"Walt." There was that smug look again.

"Walt? Walt Greenow? How the hell did you meet him?" It was astonishing how quickly Smith had made herself at home in Wetzon's theatrical world as well as Wetzon's room at the Ritz. "Crazy about me? Read my lips. Walt Greenow is *not* crazy about me. I ran into him last Saturday for the first time in over ten years."

"You never know how to accept a compliment." Smith's tone had changed slightly from sugar-coated wheedling to a plaintive whine.

"Give me a goddam break, will you?" Wetzon rummaged in her suitcase for the extra-large T-shirt. "What are you doing here anyway?"

"I thought we should be together at this time."

Wetzon stared at her partner. Had she found out about Mark? No, she couldn't have. She'd be a basket case if that had happened. "Oh, yeah?"

"Besides, my room at the Four Seasons was a disaster."

"Disaster, darling? You don't know from disaster," Wetzon said, and regretted it immediately. But Smith took no notice.

"It was the size of a broom closet."

"How tragic."

"There's an AMA convention in town and not another decent room anywhere."

"So lucky me, I have a roommate." Wetzon picked up her coat, which she'd dropped on a chair. "Dammit, why didn't you leave me any hangers?" She dropped her coat back on the chair. It was no use. She undressed and put on the T-shirt, then switched on the night table light.

"We can get more from housekeeping tomorrow. Don't be so disagreeable. It'll be such fun. You and me together."

Wetzon twirled a circle with her index finger. "Whoopie." She went into the bathroom. Her creams and lotions were stacked on top of the toilet tank, while Smith had spread out everywhere else. She removed her makeup with an oily pad and scrubbed her face, applying moisturizer generously. A deep frown seemed carved into her forehead and the ends of her lips were turned downward. She gave her reflection an insincere smile, and thought: *To hell with you, goody two-shoes.* To the tune in her head of "Officer Krupke," from *West Side Story,* she methodically transferred Smith's myriad cosmetics and lotions to the top of the toilet tank and put her own back where they'd been.

All except for her eyeliner, which plopped into the open toilet. *"Shit!"* Bad deeds were always punished—at least hers were.

"What are you doing in there, sweetie pie?" The lovely thread of uncertainty in Smith's voice made Wetzon smile even as she fished her eyeliner out of the toilet and dropped it in the wastebasket. Humming, she washed her hands, dosed them with cream, and returned to the bedroom.

"I suppose you talked your way into my room." She switched off the light on the bureau.

"It's what I do best, sugar."

"Have you spoken to Mark?" She pulled back the covers and slipped into bed. God, she was tired.

"Yes, and do you know what my clever baby has gone and done? I'm just so proud of him."

"No. What?" She pushed aside the second pillow and laid the first one flat, then nestled down into it.

"He talked his way into a job on *Hotshot* while he's in Boston."

"Good heavens. He is certainly his mother's son." Wetzon closed her eyes and found she couldn't open them. "Turn off the light, will you, Smith? I'm dead." She could feel herself drifting off.

"Sweetie pie, no!"

Wetzon's body gave a violent jerk, waking her. "Dammit, Smith!"

"You woke me up, so now you have to stay awake and talk to me."

"About what?" She reached out and turned off the light.

Smith turned it on again.

Opening one eye, Wetzon saw Smith was still sitting up. "Christalmighty, do you want me to read you a bedtime story?"

"You are an absolute poop. Very well. You may turn off the light, and I'll just sit here in the dark."

"I give up!" Wetzon sat up and thumped her pillows. "All right. You have your wish. I am now awake. Talk to me."

"Weeeelll. Let me see . . . I had a lovely dinner with Joel at Joseph's."

"Just you two? Not the twin?"

"Oh, no. Audrey, too. It's so lovely to see sister and brother so close."

"Oh, yes, lovely." Wetzon's eyes were closing again.

"She sticks to him like Velcro."

"So I've heard. Could we turn out that light? It's hurting my eyes."

"You'll fall asleep."

"No, I promise." She grinned at Smith. "Not until you give me permission."

"Very funny," Smith said, but she reached over and snapped off the light.

A radiant kaleidoscope of rainbow colors dazzled Wetzon's eyes. She snuggled down under the covers fervently wishing she'd stayed the night with Carlos. "Carlos and I had dinner with Twoey and Sunny Browning."

"Twoey and Sunny Browning," Smith repeated in an annoyed voice.

"Yes, they seem quite taken with each other."

"Humpf! It just goes to show you that I was right about him. He's a wuss."

"You're wrong, Smith. You wouldn't know a nice guy if you fell over him, but I'm too tired to argue . . ."

"Wetzon, don't you dare fall asleep." Smith was standing over her, shaking her.

"Go away."

"I have more to tell—"

"Talk fast," Wetzon mumbled.

Smith got back into her bed. "Audrey Cassidy's charming, all things considered. I never thought I'd say that about one of them."

"Them?" A muffled horn sounded from the street.

"You know. Dykes."

"The correct word, Smith, is lesbians."

"Whatever. Mort joined us for a drink, and he and Joel got into a discussion about how much they could give Gideon if he comes in and doctors the show. Mort would have to give up some of his percentage as a director, and your friend Carlos, even more as choreographer."

"I don't want to hear this—"

"It's just like the Street, sweetie pie. To get the deal done successfully, everyone must compromise."

"Is that it? Can I sleep now?"

"No. There's more. The best is yet to come. Mort started talking about missing Dilla—it was very moving, I must say—and how her assistant was a loser, not up to the job as production stage manager."

"Yeah, Phil. He's in trouble, I think." Her eyes were seamed closed. "Is that it?" she murmured, beginning to drift.

"Wait. Now it gets better."

"Hurry up, Smith."

"So they're talking about Dilla and what do you know, Audrey looks really strange. Her face gets very red, and she says she'll be right back. Mort and Joel don't even notice. They're so involved in who would give up what.

And by the way, sugar, I think it's really very odd that Joel represents Mort, Gideon, and Carlos. Isn't that a conflict?"

"Ethics from you, Smith? What is the world coming to?" She laughed and found she was wide awake. "It happens all the time in show biz."

"Frankly, sweetie pie, it would seem to me that from the creative person's point of view, he'd be better off represented by someone with no other interest in anyone else in *Hotshot*. Well, you know what I mean. Maybe even someone like me." She fell silent.

"Smith, are you sleeping?"

"Huh? Uh? Oh. No. Well, maybe."

"Then, would you please finish your Audrey story?"

"Oh. Didn't I tell you?"

"No, you didn't. Don't you *dare* go to sleep until you've told me."

"Oh, all right. Audrey went off to the ladies' and I followed. When I got there, she was sniveling into a handful of tissues, poor dear."

"About what?"

"I *told* you—"

"*No—you—didn't.*" Wetzon had the powerful urge to get out of bed and strangle Smith.

Smith's contented smile was palpable even in the darkness. "Well, it seems that Audrey Cassidy was the secret investor and what's more, Dilla was dumping that Orkin woman for Audrey."

Dilla and Audrey? What had Susan known? If Susan had wanted to stop Dilla from leaving, wasn't it logical to start with Audrey?

Logical? Murder? What was she thinking? Wetzon closed her eyes and listened to Smith's even breathing intersected from time to time with a gentle snore. Trust Smith to drop a bombshell on her when Wetzon was so weary she could scarcely keep her eyes open. Now Smith was sleeping like a baby, and Wetzon's brain was on overdrive.

Well, that piece of the puzzle certainly explained Audrey's odd behavior on the plane. Did Susan have an alibi? What if she'd met Dilla at the theatre that night after everyone had gone, and Dilla had told her she was going off with Audrey?

Would Susan have taken the ring before killing Dilla? After? No. She pushed that thought away. It was like people being interviewed after a neighbor commits a gory murder and everyone saying, "He was such a soft-spoken, gentle person. He could never have done that." Weren't most murders done in the heat of passion? Violence against a victim well known to the murderer, usually a relative?

At five o'clock, with Smith still sleeping the sleep of the innocent—well, that was a misnomer of the first order—Wetzon got out of bed and took a hot shower. Her body was a mass of knots; she needed a good sweaty workout. Maybe Carlos would work the company before rehearsals and she could join in. Dipping her head, she blow-dried her hair, shaping it with her fingers, then tossing it back into place. Wetzon's wild abandoned hairdo, that's what it was.

Without resorting to light, she pulled on stretch jeans, a black silk turtle-neck, an oversize red cotton knit sweater, and saggy socks. Smith slept on undisturbed. The courtesy terry robe lay at the foot of Smith's bed.

Bitch, Wetzon thought. On an evil impulse she went back and grabbed the robe, hanging it in the back of the closet.

There was no place to go at five-thirty and nothing to do. The Ritz coffee shop, where she loved to breakfast, wouldn't open until seven, probably. She had the new Frances Fyfield paperback to read, but if she put on the light, Smith would have a hissy fit. I'm a prisoner in my own room, she thought, feeling sorry for herself. She crawled back into bed and closed her eyes.

When she opened them again, her first thought was that it was raining. A loud thump came from somewhere above. Every light was on. Smith's bed was empty, and the bathroom door was wide open. Billows of scented steam filled the room. The sound of the shower accounted for what she had thought was rain. Abruptly, the shower stopped. Wetzon dozed off again.

"How long are you going to lie there?" Smith demanded.

Wetzon opened one eye. Smith was wearing a slim, almost ankle-length charcoal skirt and low black boots. A vivid fuchsia cashmere showed under a slightly lighter gray blazer. Chic was an understatement.

Wetzon yanked the covers over her head. "What time is it?" she grumbled.

"Time to eat. I'm starving. Come on, let's go." Smith pulled the covers off Wetzon. "You're dressed already!"

Wetzon sat up. "After you dropped your *bon mot* about Dilla and Audrey, I couldn't sleep. You certainly didn't have that trouble." Another loud *thump* came from the ceiling, making them both look up.

"Theatricals misbehaving." Smith yawned, patting her mouth. "Put on some makeup and let's go downstairs for blueberry muffins."

After the minor accident when she stuck the mascara brush into her eye, and had to wash up sooty tears from her cheeks, Wetzon forsook anything more complicated beyond combing her hair and putting on lipstick.

In the hallway the thumping sounded overhead again. As they passed Carlos's room on the way to the elevator, Wetzon saw that the maid was making it up, which meant that he was either having breakfast in the coffee shop or more likely was in the midst of one of Mort's endless creative staff meetings.

The elevator doors opened. A room service cart, loaded with stainless-steel–covered serving plates, took up most of the space. "Going up," said the waiter, an elderly man with pale blue eyes in a cream of wheat face. "One more floor."

"Come on." Smith pushed Wetzon on ahead of her. "We'll go for a ride."

This is totally out of character, Wetzon thought suspiciously, crammed up against the cart.

When the doors opened, Smith and Wetzon stepped out, and the waiter pushed the cart slowly down the hall away from them. The rumble of angry male voices came from somewhere on the floor. Pungent cigar tainted the air.

"Someone's having a feast," Smith said. "And a fight."

"And a cigar," Wetzon said. "Coffee. Quickly." She tried to catch the closing elevator doors, but was too late. And when she turned around, Smith wasn't even there. Where had she gotten to?

She trailed back down the hall and caught sight of Smith following the room service cart, chatting up the bewildered waiter. The same male rumble was coming from behind the double doors where the cart stopped. Several voices, all raised. Was that Carlos? Uh oh.

"Just take Arlington," the waiter said patiently to Smith. He knocked on the door. "Room service."

With her hand behind her, Smith was making sweeping motions. What the hell did she want Wetzon to do? Oh, maybe see if there was a name on the check. It was propped up on edge between an empty goblet and a sweating stainless-steel pitcher of cold orange juice.

As Wetzon tried to take a casual peek at it, someone inside began fumbling with the door. The voices grew louder. Now she recognized Mort's as well. In the confusion, Wetzon snatched the check. It was made out to Mort Hornberg. She placed it back on the table, mumbling, "I think you dropped this—"

A furious howl interrupted her, followed hard by a heart-stopping crash, shouting, then an ominous thump, thump, thump . . .

The waiter pushed the doors open, releasing cigar fumes. "Oh, excuse me." He looked frightened.

"Get out of here!" someone yelled.

"Mort, are you crazy? Let go of me!"

"Mort, let him *go!*" That sounded like Joel Kidde.

The waiter came stumbling out of the room. He stood in the corridor, confused about whether to run and get help or stay and get the check signed.

"Ow!" That was Carlos, and it was enough to make Wetzon push the waiter aside and rush into the room. No one was going to hurt her Carlos.

Before she saw anything, she felt the wind. It rushed like a hurricane through an open window, driving the draperies mad. The room was frigid. She looked around quickly, trying to process what was happening. Behind her, Smith screamed.

Then she saw Joel tugging Mort off someone—oh God, Carlos. Legs. That's all she saw of Carlos. The rest of him was dangling out the window, five floors above Newbury Street.

Wetzon would never fully remember how they rescued Carlos. What she would remember clearly were Smith's shrill shriek, Joel's desperate struggle with Mort, someone exhorting, "No, no!" and Carlos's kicking legs. And the intense cold. Some time later she would have a sneaking suspicion that it was Smith who gave Mort a hard whack on his previous wound, which made him release Carlos long enough for Wetzon to grab Carlos's waistband and pull him in. She had a vague memory of holding him wobbling in her arms and babbling, "Good shape, good shape."

She saw the blood rush from Carlos's face and he crumpled, sinking both of them to the carpet. Mort was stamping around the room howling, clutching the side of his head, shaking off Joel's feeble ministrations of "There, there, old chum."

"Closing the fucking window, someone!" Wetzon heard herself yell. She was hugging Carlos to her, his head on her breast.

"Birdie, you'll break my eardrum," he croaked. Color seeped back in his face.

Dimly, Wetzon heard someone hammering on the outside doors. No one in the room acknowledged it.

The window closed with a loud slam, and the curtains and draperies were drawn by someone with long, slim legs in Donna Karan hose. Smith.

"Well," Smith said, dusting off her hands, "show business is certainly entertaining." She strolled over to the doors. *"Com*ing," she called in a lilting voice, as if everything were perfectly fine and she were receiving guests.

Carlos struggled to his knees, shaking his head like a punchy boxer.

More hammering on the doors. "Is anything wrong in there?"

Somewhere close Wetzon heard another door shut. Joel had somehow succeeded in coaxing Mort, old chum, into the bedroom, old chum. Looking around, she saw they were in a large sitting room with an assortment of sofas and club chairs.

Smith righted a toppled side chair, straightened an end table. The frenzied knocking on the doors continued. Smith surveyed the room. When she opened the double doors, Wetzon and Carlos were standing, and the room looked undisturbed. "Yes?" Smith inquired, all innocence.

Hotel security—no doubt about it. A burly chested man with dyspeptic eyes peered at them suspiciously. He wore a brown suit and to the unenlighted might have looked like a businessman. To Wetzon he looked like a cop. Sort of an Irish Detective Morgan Bernstein. "We had a report of a disturbance . . ."

A strange low sob filtered in from the bedroom.

Smith's laugh tinkled. Bells, bells, bells, Wetzon thought. "Oh no, Mr. . . . ?" Smith paused and fluttered her lashes. What made her think anything that obvious would distract?

"Dolan," Hotel Security said, utterly captivated.

"Well, Mr. Dolan, we were just acting out a little scene." She swept her arm toward Carlos and Wetzon. "Weren't we, sweet things?"

"Right," Wetzon agreed. She gave Carlos a gentle hip nudge.

"Oh, right." His voice papery-thin, he was eyeing Smith warily.

"Thank you so much for checking, *dear* Mr. Dolan. You don't know how *incredibly* secure you make me feel here at the Ritz." Smith flashed one of her sultry smiles at Dolan. The poor man had a stunned look on his face when she closed the door on it.

The sobbing grew louder. Smith flicked her eyes toward the bedroom. "I hate to hear a grown man cry," she said.

"What's the Barracuda up to?" Carlos hissed at Wetzon. "No good, that's for sure."

"She did help save you, you know," Wetzon whispered in his ear.

"Well then, she must have had an ulterior motive."

"I did actually," Smith said with tremendous good humor. "But a little gratitude might be nice." She inspected her manicure. "I was only protecting my investment."

"You mean *our* investment."

"Whatever." Smith frowned. "What is going on in there?" She pointed to the closed bedroom door.

"That's Mort having a breakdown," Carlos said. "And a soupçon of gratitude from me to you, old dear." He bowed deeply.

Smith slit her eyes at him, as if trying to see if he was mocking her, then clearly decided he wasn't because she treated him to one of her medium-warm smiles. Wetzon wasn't so sure. She caught Carlos's hand. "Let's get out of here. I need coffee desperately."

Arm in trembling arm, they walked down the hallway to the elevator, following Smith, who was pressing the down button impatiently. Dolan was nowhere in sight.

Carlos cleared his throat gently, as if speech was painful. "I've got to get over to the theatre." His hands fidgeted at his bare wrist—where was the Panthere? He still appeared shaken, the skin on his face taut across his cheekbones. A pulse trembled in his eyelid.

"Shouldn't you eat something?" She was worried about him.

"Had coffee before Mort got crazy."

"That's not breakfast. Your adrenaline's been pumping. You have to feed it."

"Oh, Birdie." He hugged her and planted a kiss on her forehead. "Don't frown so. We don't want lines, do we?"

The elevator stopped. A luggage cart loaded with three fat suitcases, a bellhop on one side and a young couple holding hands on the other, left them a small space in the center of the car. The elevator sank to the lobby, its occupants mute, each undoubtedly wrapped in his or her own thoughts.

The moderately crowded coffee shop was really a slightly less formal dining room, set up for breakfast with linen tablecloths. Bright sunlight streamed through the windows facing Newbury Street. At a table for four, Twoey sat *tête-à-tête* with Sunny Browning.

"Humpf," Smith said. She fluttered her fingers at Twoey, who didn't see her.

"Lucky us," Wetzon said to Carlos out of the corner of her mouth. They were being seated at the table next to Sunny and Twoey, who were heads together, studying some kind of diagram Sunny was drawing on a piece of hotel stationery.

"The pie gets sliced up like so until payoff," Sunny was saying. "And after payoff," she drew another circle, "like so."

"*Ahem,*" Smith said.

"Xenie!" Twoey jumped to his feet, his face a splendid coral.

Smith bestowed her sweetest smile on him. "Twoey, sugarplum, it's so good to see you." She pulled out a chair and sat down. "Thanks awfully, I'd love to join you."

Sunny's face froze in startle position. Wetzon turned her back to hide her laugh. Smith was about to poison the well. Wetzon sat next to Carlos, both as far away from the other table as possible.

"Well, good, darling," Carlos murmured, patting her thigh. "Now the Barracuda's back in character. For a minute there I hardly knew her."

"Do you want to tell me what happened in Mort's room?"

"All in good time, pet." With unsteady hands, he opened the *Globe* he'd picked up as they crossed the lobby. "Charming." Folding the paper open to the entertainment section, he handed it to her.

The first thing Wetzon saw was a two column picture of Mort in his tweedy cap. The headline read:

MORT HORNBERG
ONE-MAN BAND

The article went on for several paragraphs describing how Mort had single-handedly put *Hotshot* together. Only in the final paragraph were the others—Carlos, Aline, and Sam—mentioned.

She handed the newspaper back to Carlos. "How generous of Mort to include you all. *Noblesse oblige.*"

"Yes, isn't he a prince?" He was rereading the article as if he found it hard to believe.

"No, you are, my love." She took the newspaper from him and dumped it on the floor under the table.

They ordered large orange juices, a pot of coffee, and a basket of muffins.

"The strain of the tryout getting too much for the great impresario?" Wetzon asked, after the waitress left.

"Huh?" He looked at her, then took her hand. "I'm sorry, Birdie. I was just wondering if any of this was worth it anymore."

"I think not, but I'm not hooked into it, dearie. The Theatre is no longer my life. Besides, you know full well that when *Hotshot* arrives in New York and Frank Rich gives it a marvelous review and you're a big hit, love will conquer all. Everyone will forget all this."

"How right you are, but a short while ago my whole life flashed before me, and truth to tell, it shook me up."

"But Carlos, that's Mort. You never have to work with him again. In fact, you can join a long line of people who say they're never going to work with him again. Some in this very city working on this very show. Bet on it. There are some nice people left in the Theatre."

"Sure." He grinned at her, all bright-eyed and bushy-tailed again. "I can think of one or two immediately."

When their breakfast arrived, they dug in, ravenous; dancers were always hungry.

"You knew Mort was crazy. He's always been crazy." Wetzon poured her army of vitamin pills onto the linen tablecloth and began swallowing them, one at a time.

"God, Birdie, do you think they really help?" He was staring at her column of pills. "Maybe I should start."

"Keeps me straight."

"Well, forget it then." He buttered a blueberry muffin lavishly. "Speaking of *that*, trying to keep up the pretense that he's a breeder is what makes Mort so crazy. Someone ought to out him!"

Wetzon choked on her last pill. "You wouldn't . . ."

Carlos spread his palm on his breast and said angelically, "Not me, darling. Not *ever.*"

Smith laughed, drawing their attention back to the next table. Sunny had a forced smile on her face. Twoey was beaming, and good old reliable Smith was being as lovable as only Smith knew how.

"Poor slob," Carlos said.

"Enough of that. Now tell me what happened upstairs."

"Not terribly interesting." He took a swallow of coffee.

"Tell." The finger she pointed at him was stern.

"Oooo, scary."

Wetzon scowled.

"Okay. Mort said he might want to bring Gideon in to do some doctoring. We had a little discussion on how and where to trim our percentages to make room for him."

"Just as I thought. And Joel, who represents all three of you, was acting as mediator, right?"

Carlos nodded.

"Smith thinks it's a conflict of interest that Joel should represent all three of you in this situation."

Carlos raised an elegant eyebrow. "I hate it when the Barracuda is right."

"She's very smart about business things."

"Well, Joel—who's definitely in the process of selling me out—let Mort do most of the talking. Mort said he felt that the biggest cut should come from my share because I was only the choreographer and everyone knew choreographers contribute the smallest amount to book."

"Yeah, like Fosse, and Bennett and Robbins." Wetzon was incensed.

"And don't forget Gower."

"How could I? What did you say?"

"I told Mort I didn't mind if Gideon were really going to contribute something and everyone coughed up a small percentage, but no way was it going to be just me."

"And then?"

"He said he was surrounded by ingrates who wouldn't have careers in the Theatre if it weren't for him."

"He didn't!"

"Oh, my, yes, he did."

"He's starting to believe his press clippings."

"I told him the very same thing, and he went crazy, jumping around like old Rumplemortskin, and throwing punches. That's when I said I'd rather close down the show than be the only one to give up percentages."

Wetzon took a sharp breath. "God!"

"Not true, darling, but he made me mad as hell. Who the fuck does he think he is, Hal Prince? I was just as involved as he was from the very beginning. In fact, I *brought* him the idea. The show is almost all music and dance. Christ!" Carlos's palm smacked the table; coffee splashed from cups to saucers.

"Who opened that window? It was like Mount Everest in there."

"Joel was smoking a cigar," Carlos said. "I opened it to clear the air." His lips formed a skeleton smile. "Next time Mort tries something like that—"

"Next time? Carlos, this is crazy."

"Next time," Carlos reiterated. His eyes were stony. "I'll kill him."

CHAPTER

"What do you think?"

Smith, in a pale gray, man-tailored Calvin Klein suit, was doing model turns in front of the three-way mirror.

"Great, Smith." What was she doing here anyway? For that matter, what was she doing in Boston?

"You're not paying any attention!" Smith said heatedly. "In fact, you're a real downer today."

"What do you expect? Mort tries to shove Carlos out a window at the Ritz-Carlton and you take me shopping." Wetzon tore off the skirt she'd managed to pull on over her leggings.

Smith patted her flat tummy. "I'm taking this. It'll be perfect for the spring." She peeled off the jacket and hung it on the hanger.

Wetzon took the spot in front of the mirrors Smith had temporarily vacated. "I think these mirrors are a cheat. They're designed to make us look thin."

"If I'd known you'd be such a crab, I wouldn't have invited you along. Mort was just a bit nervous. Don't take it all so seriously."

"Excuse me?" Seething, Wetzon was certain steam came from every visible orafice. "I don't think we're on the same wavelength here." Bonding with Smith was really grating on her nerves. Get out of here before you blow it, she ordered herself.

"Where are you going?"

"I'll be at the cosmetic counter downstairs buying a new eyeliner." *Because my other one dropped in the toilet when I moved your stuff.*

Wetzon closed the fitting room door. She would have liked to raise her chin to the ceiling and howl, but she didn't have the nerve to do it in Bonwit's. Muttering to herself, she headed down the stairs (she never rode when she could walk) to the main floor.

Admit it, show business was depressing her. It wasn't just Mort, it was everything. The cold, damp theatre, the endless tech and dress, everyone back stabbing and bickering, vying for center stage. It was vicious. And the idea that talent can be so easily replaced.

At least Wall Street didn't even pretend to lay claim to your heart and soul and wring it every which way. She didn't like the unmistakable feeling of dread, evil, and imminent disaster that had settled over her since Dilla's murder. And it wasn't just the shock of Mark's confession, or even of Mort's attempt to push Carlos out a window.

What she would really like to do was keep walking—out the door of Bonwit's, get in a cab, get on the shuttle, and go home. A subtle longing for the security she felt when she was with Alton ambushed her on the stairs. "Good God!" she said aloud, stopping short. A saleswoman wearing a blue nametag looked a question at her. Wetzon smiled and shook her head. "Just thinking out loud." She continued down the stairs to the ground floor. Security? Alton meant security. That's what it was, but was that enough?

Two women dressed like dancers in leggings and saggy socks were standing, backs to Wetzon, in front of the Lancôme counter. Or rather, Wetzon saw as she drew closer, a woman and a teenage girl. Wetzon parked herself next to the teenager and waited for the clerk to finish demonstrating the powdery slate eyeliner, just the one Wetzon wanted. The young girl looked vaguely familiar.

Suddenly the mother looked up. "Leslie!" she shrieked. The woman scooted around her daughter, making for Wetzon.

"Mel! I can't believe it!" Then they were hugging each other, stepping back and inspecting and then hugging again. "Melanie Banks, you look wonderful!"

"It's Melanie Alexander now. How long has it been?"

"Fifteen at least." Wetzon's eyes welled up.

Mel, recovering, pulled the teenager over. "This is my daughter, Sarah Ann. Leslie—" She looked at Wetzon's unadorned left hand—"Wetzon. Leslie and I were in a couple of shows together."

"And some classes and even one Millikin show. Pleased to meet another dancer," Wetzon said, grinning at the pretty teenager. "When I saw the two of you standing at the counter, I thought, dancers." Mel's red hair was faded a bit from the fiery color it had been, but her daughter's was vivid, surrounding a face so young, so fresh. "Are you still dancing?" She remembered Mel had married a law student, Kevin something or other. He was going to Fordham then.

"Yes, sort of. Wait till Kevin hears." Mel hugged Wetzon again. "Are you in Carlos's show? We're coming to the preview tonight."

The clerk cleared her throat.

"Oh, excuse me," Mel said. "We'll take the gray." She searched in her pockets and produced a charge card.

"You can get one for me, too, please," Wetzon told the saleswoman. Turning back to Mel, she continued, "I'm not in the Theatre anymore. I've been a headhunter on Wall Street for . . . almost ten years."

"Mom, I'm going to look at the earrings," Sarah Ann announced.

"Okay. Kevin's with O'Donnell, Bullard and Kalin, and I've got a dance studio."

"You're kidding!"

Melanie beamed. "Ballet, jazz, tap—you know, the works. Everything for the budding young thing to carry to Broadway." She signed the slip and took the small bag from the saleswoman. "Only there's no Broadway anymore."

"Tell me about it. Ho-hum revivals or one English circus after the other, all flash, lots of fog, and nothing underneath. Like a helicopter on the stage." Wetzon handed over her American Express card. "I came up to see *Hotshot,* which, by the way, is an original. Carlos's work is just terrific."

"What are you doing this afternoon?"

"I don't know. Watch rehearsals, maybe. They're tedious if you're not involved, and everyone's nerves are frazzled."

"Why not come and take a class with me? I've got dance aerobics starting at three." Mel dug in her shoulder bag and came up with a card. "It's not far —just a way down Newbury Street, across from Spenser's."

"I—"

"Chicken?"

"No. And I could use the workout."

Mel glanced at Wetzon's leggings and pink Reeboks. "You wouldn't even have to change. How about a coffee now?"

"Can't. I'm waiting for my partner, who's upstairs buying out all the Calvin Kleins."

"Okay, then . . . Sarah Ann? Let's go." Mel waved to her daughter and pointed to the entrance. "Wasn't it awful about Dilla?"

"Awful."

"And to think, I used to envy her. Everything that woman did, even the nasty stuff, came out to her benefit."

Wetzon signed the credit slip and refused the bag, dropping the narrow box into her purse. "Until last week."

"I remember in *See Saw*—were you in *See Saw* with me?"

Wetzon shook her head. "No. Carlos and I were still in *Pippin.*"

"Well, then you might not remember this. Dilla came in one day—she was dance captain—wearing a fabulous mink, down to her ankles."

"Who could forget it? The rest of us were all barely surviving on our chorus minimums. Was she going with Joel Kidde then?"

"Ma—"

"One minute, Sarah Ann. No, that was later. Listen, you knew—we all knew—she was gay. Remember when she got promoted out of the chorus on *CoCo?* No, you weren't on *CoCo,* were you?" She didn't wait for Wetzon to respond, grinning suddenly. "You know, I haven't dished with anybody about those days in years."

"So who gave her the coat?" Smith was getting off the elevator carrying a bulging clothing bag.

"You know—what's his face—that big-shot general manager. The one they all deferred to."

A little light flickered on in Wetzon's brain. "Lenny something?"

"Yeah. What a memory. Lenny Kaufer."

C H A P T E R

Wetzon counted fourteen on the line at the Colonial box office, and four were reading Mort's interview in the *Globe*. Not bad, considering the show hadn't opened yet. But how often did Boston get Broadway tryouts anymore? Probably not too often. These days many producers didn't want to risk the costs of an out-of-town tryout. Instead, they held weeks of previews in New York, for which they now sold tickets at full price, and everyone from the theatre community savaged them. But then, perhaps the producers had brought it on themselves by charging full price in New York while the show was still in the worked-on stage.

A sharp Boston wind sweeping across the Common rattled the lobby doors. Wetzon shivered and kept her coat buttoned.

Smith's nose was red; her eyes teared. "You have checked with the office, haven't you, sweetie pie? After all, it is Friday and we're playing hookey."

"When would I have done that? We've been practically joined at the hip since you moved yourself in with me."

Smith's lower lip reassembled itself into a pout.

Temper, temper, Wetzon warned herself. *Remember she's your roommate for another two nights.* She forced herself to smile at her partner. The problem was, while she and Smith managed to work exceptionally well together in spite of their differences, the extracurricular Smith drove Wetzon crazy. Wetzon craved her privacy. If it weren't for Carlos, she would have been on the first shuttle flight out of Boston this morning. "There's a phone near the stage door. I'll call B.B. and see that no catastrophe has befallen us." But she had lost Smith, who was now intent on some event on the street. Christ, she had the attention span of a four-year-old.

Through the etched glass panel Wetzon saw that a silver limousine had pulled up in front of the theatre. Joel Kidde and Gideon Winkler were getting out.

"There's Joel." Smith fluttered her fingers, beaming. "And Gideon." She was definitely on the make.

"Smith, how is dear Dickie Hartmann?" Wetzon said. "It's a shame he can't be here for the opening."

"Who?"

That was perfect. Joel Kidde was another one of those powerful attractive men, but Richard Hartmann had fewer scruples even than agents. It wouldn't be wise to underestimate him. If Hartmann wanted Smith, he would have her.

A year ago, after the shooting, Wetzon had put the evidence that would get Hartmann disbarred in a sealed envelope addressed to Assistant D.A. Marissa Peiser. Marking it "to be opened in the event of my death," she'd left it in her safe deposit box. It was time she dealt with it and put it behind her, as she was trying to deal with the recurring dream.

She opened the door to the inner lobby and entered another world entirely. Here chaos reigned supreme. The energy was electric. Assistants and technicians were everywhere, working at top speed. Behind the last row of seats was the sound console with mixing boards. A technician in earphones with a mouthpiece was talking and gesturing to someone on the lighting monitor backstage. He was probably the master electrician who was always on the producer's payroll and traveled with the show.

In the old days before computers, union electricians, carpenters, and propmen were older, having worked their way up from grips, but the man in the earphones was in his twenties and had hair down to his shoulders. It had probably been difficult for the last generation of stagehands to adjust to the new generation of computers.

Carlos was on stage demonstrating a change in one of the dance numbers. He looked steady and sure. Bless him, she thought. She could not think of her life without Carlos.

"I love this part of it, don't you?" Sunny was standing beside her, holding a clipboard jammed with papers. Today she was wearing brown jodhpurs, boots, a Ralph Lauren blue-and-green flannel shirt, and a perfume Wetzon recognized, one she'd once worn. Replique. A slouchy tan leather hat covered her blond hair.

Where had she tied her horse, Wetzon was tempted to ask her, but she said instead, "I do, too." Wetzon could taste the excitement. Tonight, she knew from experience, almost everything would work. Most of the kinks on the technical side would dissolve. And shining through would come the production, for better or for worse. It was like the birthing process.

"I heard what happened this morning," Sunny said in a low voice, adjusting her hat backward with the tip of her finger. "Mort can get a little excitable—"

"That's the mother of all understatements."

"What I'm saying is, don't blow it out of proportion. You and Carlos are close. You can help us bring the show through this. And we all know it's the production that really counts. When a show is a smash, everyone forgets these petty little differences."

"Petty little differences, huh? I know. But Mort is certifiable. He ought to be locked up."

"You don't understand, Leslie. Mort's got his hands full with Sam. He's locked himself in his room and he's refusing to rewrite 'Who's That Killer?' Sam *knows* Joclyn can't hit an A flat. Besides, the melody is a real steal from Marvin Hamlisch. If we open with it, Hamlisch's lawyer will sue us up the wazoo. And he'd be right. And now Aline's carrying on because she says Mort is destroying her precious book."

"Book? This is not a book show—or am I missing something?" Christ, Mort was strolling up the aisle with Mark and they were holding hands, and not like father and son. Wetzon went into gear, moving forward, careful not to trip over the cables that snaked across the floor from the computer board in the center of the house. "Mark!" She waved at them, trying to catch their attention, but Mort had stopped to communicate something to JoJo, who was sitting center orchestra with his arm around Poppy's shoulders. In that instant Wetzon knew JoJo and Poppy were lovers. She filed that away, returning to the problem at hand. "Mark—" Mort did not relinquish Mark's hand.

"What's up?" Sunny had followed her. Behind them, Wetzon heard Smith's brittle laugh.

"We've got to warn Mark his mother's in the theatre," she said.

"Who's Mark?"

"Sorry. Smitty."

"Oh? What's Smitty's mother doing here?" Sunny looked confused.

"His mother is my partner, Xenia Smith, and Mark—Smitty—is barely seventeen." She tried to get around Mort. "Mark!" Dammit, short of shouting . . .

"Does Mort know?" Sunny plucked at Wetzon's coat, holding her back.

The hell with it. "Mark, *heads up!*" Everything around them stopped, conversation and activity. All eyes were on Wetzon.

Mark finally looked up, having had a sixth sense that his mother was there, or maybe, he'd actually heard Wetzon's warning. Pulling his hand away from Mort's, Mark shoved it in his pocket. It all happened so fast that even Mort looked puzzled, so perhaps Smith hadn't seen. And even if she had, it was not such a big deal. It could have been entirely innocent. Sure.

"Isn't this amazing?" Smith gushed, coming up behind them. There followed one of those so-called pregnant moments. Then Smith said in a strangled voice, "Baby?"

Wetzon sharp-eyed her partner. Smith's face registered nothing at all.

"Mom." Mark stepped around Wetzon to greet his mother. He was half a head taller than Smith already and still growing.

"Smitty," Mort called proprietarily. Maybe Carlos hadn't told him of Mark's connection to Smith.

"Mom, I'm working. I can't talk now."

"I'll see you later, babycakes," Smith said, her voice catching on babycakes. She seemed to be searching his face. "Joel and I are going to Gloucester for the afternoon. . . ."

"What a great idea," Wetzon said, with more enthusiasm than she felt. Smith was definitely rattled. "It is a good idea, isn't it, Mark?" She placed herself between Mark and Mort Hornberg in the center of the orchestra with JoJo and Poppy. Mort motioned to Mark, calling again, "Smitty."

"Smitty?" Smith blinked, as if there was a cinder in her eye.

"They've nicknamed Mark, Smitty," Wetzon said. Blocking Mort, who was sliding out of the row toward them, she said through her teeth, "My partner is Smitty's mother. So watch yourself." She controlled the urge to smack him, as Smith had done, on his wound. Instead, she took his good arm, turned him around and steered him firmly toward the orchestra pit. Maybe with a little luck she could push him into it.

"I didn't know he had a mother, for Chrissakes." Mort yanked his arm away from her. "Let go."

"Spare me, Mort." When she sneaked a look, Smith had gone and Smitty was standing in the aisle as if his limbs had rusted and needed oiling. Poppy, the opportunist, rose from where she was sitting with JoJo, but her husband was too fast for her. Darting around Wetzon, Mort reclaimed Smitty.

"Damn!" Wetzon punched the palm of her hand and her shoulder bag slipped into the crook of her elbow. Wasn't opening a new show problem enough without all this added sexual intrigue?

"Sit yourself down and relax, girl." A cool, smooth hand touched hers. "Nothing you do is going to change anything."

"Fran, do you see what's going on?" What a question. She knew from experience that Fran missed nothing.

"I have eyes." He rubbed his swollen knuckles on the hand clutching the death's head cane. "And I've been a manager for almost fifty years. Best to stay out of it."

"He's so young, Fran, and Mort is such a—" She stopped. It served no purpose to go on about it. He didn't understand, but that was all right. He was a different generation.

"Dilla's the one who brought him in for Mort."

"That's so ugly—even for Dilla. I don't think anyone knew how young he is."

Fran's look was kindly in spite of the cold blue of his eyes. He squeezed her hand. "Let nature take its course."

"I guess you've seen it all over these years." Maybe this was a good time to sound him out about Lenny Kaufer. She sat down in the aisle seat in front of him. "I'll bet you have stories to tell."

JoJo slid out of the center row and moved down the aisle toward the stage. He gave her a knowing glance. Now what was that about?

"Yeh." Fran winked at her. "But I'm not talking. I want to go out with my boots on."

"How did you get started in this business, Fran?" She unbuttoned her coat.

The old man grunted. "My Uncle Bert was in the business. House manager at the Palace. He knew everybody. Everybody. You had to have a connection in those days."

"I don't think it's changed any. Who did you start with?"

"The best," he said. "Lenny Kaufer."

She willed herself to sound casual. "Lenny Kaufer? He's a legend."

"Nobody like him. Lenny trained me."

"That must have been an incredible experience, Fran. I always heard that nothing happened at any box office anywhere without Lenny Kaufer knowing about it and sanctioning it."

"He was the best—"

"Who was? Move it, Leslie." Aline sat herself down, squeezing into the aisle seat, hardly giving Wetzon a chance to slide over one. She wrapped her cashmere cloak around her. Her wrist was in a cast.

Fran closed up. Wetzon felt it. Damn Aline. On the other hand, maybe she could get them *both* started and shake out something interesting. After all, Aline had been around almost as long as Fran.

"So?" Aline said. Her pug face was layered with pancake, the blue eyeliner smeared. A ring of mascara crawled from the puffy bags under her eyes.

"Oh, Fran was reminiscing about the old days—with Lenny Kaufer."

Fran's swollen hand stiffened on the cane.

"Lenny Kaufer," Aline mused. "What a classy guy."

"Yeah," Fran agreed, loosening up some.

"And what a power. He controlled the ice on every show for years."

"What are you talking about, Aline?" Leaning on his cane, Fran heaved himself to his feet. Wetzon thought she heard him say, "Stupid bitch," but Aline obviously didn't.

"Come off it, Fran. They didn't call him the Iceman for nothing."

"Gossip like that," Fran said, caressing the head of his cane, "is not good for your health."

"Can you believe that?"

Aline scrunched her nose and poked her thumb over her shoulder as Fran's massive silhouette lumbered up the aisle. She was wearing a different pair of glasses today, one hundred percent retro. Rhinestones decorated the wing-tipped corners. "Acting as if he's Mr. Clean. Everyone knows he inherited the Icecapade from Lenny."

"Really?"

Aline nodded her head emphatically. Rhinestones glinted. "Why do you think the old fart is still hanging in there? He doesn't want to let go."

"I always thought Fran loved the business; that's why he's still around."

"Oh, I suppose we all love the business; otherwise we'd be"—her eyes flicked over Wetzon—"working on Wall Street."

Was that meant to be snide? Wetzon wondered. She was about to respond in kind when Aline added, "Take it from me, Fran is socking the money away."

"A little like having an annuity?" Wetzon asked, keeping her spikes in neutral.

"More like running a racket." She readjusted her cloak and glared at Wetzon as if Wetzon was in it with Fran.

"How'd you hurt your hand?"

"Oh, this?" Aline held out her arm, studying the cast as if she'd just seen it for the first time. "You know, aging bones, accident in the home. I flung out my hand to make a point and collided with an open door."

"Aline, is there a Mrs. Lenny Kaufer?"

"Yes. Celia. But she didn't last long after Lenny died. She never opened her mouth, not even then, when she could have. You know, she was one of those walk-three-paces-behind-your-man sort." Aline craned her fat neck. "Where is that boy? I'm starving."

Laughter came from the stage, and the cast applauded. Carlos danced into the wings, then reappeared in the orchestra, where Mort was standing. The one pass door from the stage to the orchestra was on house left. Wetzon's hands grasped the arms of her seat, but Carlos and Mort exchanged a few words, then threw their arms around one another.

"What did I tell you?" Sunny called. She was sitting across the aisle behind Twoey, her hand resting ever so lightly on his shoulder.

"I concede, Sunny." Wetzon turned her attention back to Aline. "So I guess Lenny Kaufer left his family pretty well fixed."

Aline's immense bosom trembled as if something were inside rattling the fleshy cage to get out. "Well, now, that's quite another story—Oh, *there* you are, ducky." Aline's assistant, Edward Gray, had made his appearance carrying a fat plastic shopping bag. All kinds of lovely junk food smells emanated from the bag.

Wetzon's stomach growled. Definitely time for lunch. Memories of the road came hurtling back from some deep recess, how everything was measured by meal breaks. Rehearsal, meal break, rehearsal . . .

"Birdie! Wanna have lunch?" An entirely recovered Carlos bounded up, exuding energy.

"I have to call the office first, but yes."

"And here I thought you were all mine." He skimmed his forehead with the heel of his hand. "Aline, darling." Bending, he and Aline exchanged cheek kisses.

"I do have a business to run." Wetzon rose. The Theatre was like quicksand, sucking her back, almost making her forget she was part of the dynamic (she yawned) headhunting team of Smith and Wetzon.

Carlos did a deep *plié*. "Have you seen Sam? There's an itty-bitty change I need—"

Aline shook her head. "I suppose you saw the *Globe*."

"How could I miss it? Birdie, I'll meet you at Remington's in fifteen minutes. Don't be late." Off he went to confer with JoJo.

When Wetzon turned back to Aline, Aline and Edward were feeding each other french fries. A burger dripping melted yellow cheddar sat in an open plastic container, precarious on the arm of Aline's seat. Entirely engrossed in Edward and her food, Aline didn't even look up when Wetzon said, "See ya later."

There was always a telephone near the stage door. She came up through the pass door into the wings. Across the stage someone snapped, "I'm tired of taking the heat for you." Kay's voice, tough and uncompromising. "Get your fucking act together."

Who was she talking to?

The stage was raked on a steep angle and dotted with myriad marks. God, she'd hated dancing on a rake like that. Injuries galore. She hoped dancers were getting hazard pay for that now; they certainly hadn't in her time. Wetzon slipped around the back near the redbrick rear wall. How many times had she done this when she was a dancer?

The cue board and monitors were stage left and she could just make out Kay and Phil. Poor Phil. Too much, too soon. He was clearly out of his depth in *Hotshot.* Kay's assistant, Nomi, was standing at Kay's elbow. Two against one. Maybe she should . . . No, she thought. Stay out of it. It's between them.

Just off the stage were the star dressing rooms, two or three depending on the stars, because one could be used as a suite—for someone the caliber of Liza Minnelli. Since there were no real stars in *Hotshot,* the dressing rooms had been assigned by raffle. Three downstairs, the rest upstairs.

A pair of actors, laughing, intense, came down the stairs where the chorus dressing rooms Wetzon knew well were like maids' rooms in old mansions: rabbit warrens. They brushed past her with distracted apologies, and she followed them to the stage door. Something in the air coming in from the alley, an odd pungency, vaguely gamy, made her nose tickle. She squelched a sneeze.

The ancient call-board was a thicket of personal messages, phone numbers and advertisements, the grubby menus of several local restaurants. Sitting on a pillow in a thrift-shop swivel chair was a stubby woman in gray cords and gray oxfords with gum soles. Her stiff orange hair protruded like an unkempt hedge over the tabloid she was reading. *The Improper Bostonian.* Wetzon had never heard of it.

An actress was baby talking on the only phone near the outside door.

"Excuse me, is there another phone backstage that I can use?"

The orange-haired woman looked up from her paper. She had a mole on her chin that sported two stiff black hairs. "The men's smoker—Go back and make a right—"

At that moment the actress hung up and dashed out the stage door. The phone began to ring.

"Aw, for Chrissakes," the stage door person growled from behind her paper. "Damn gypsies."

The phone continued to ring. Wetzon picked it up. "Yes?"

"Please deposit another seventy-five cents," a digital voice intoned.

"I haven't made a call—" Wetzon looked at the stage door person. There was no movement behind the newspaper.

"Please deposit another seventy-five cents," the operator repeated.

"Look, here," Wetzon said. "I have to make a call to New York. The party that owes you seventy-five cents has left the building. I would appreciate it if you would clear the line so that I can make my call." She hung up and waited. The phone was mum. Her nose tickled again and she sniffed. Sour apples.

She picked up the phone, put a coin in and dialed "O" and her office number. When the operator came on, Wetzon said, "Collect, please." She sneezed.

Walt Greenow in a plaid flannel shirt came in from the alley with one of the theatre stagehands. Both carried cables and boxed equipment. "Hey, Leslie," Walt said. They squeezed by Wetzon and disappeared down the corridor. They seemed to have brought the fermenting smell in with them.

"Excuse me," she called to the orange-haired woman. "Isn't that a peculiar odor?"

Lowering her paper with deep reluctance, the woman gave a thunderous sniff. "Aw, for Chrissakes! They did it again." She rose and threw her paper on the chair. "Keep your eye on the door, wouldja?" She didn't wait for an answer.

The phone stopped ringing. "Smith and Wetzon," B.B. said.

"I have a collect call from Wetzon in Boston—" the operator began.

"Okay," B.B. said. "I'll accept."

"Hey, Birdie!" Phil Terrace materialized from the corridor. "Has anyone seen Mort?"

"Hi, B.B." Wetzon shook her head at Phil and he opened the stage door and went into the alley.

"What's that godawful smell?" Poppy Hornberg was carrying a piece of silvery fabric. "Leslie? Have you seen Mort?"

No one paid any attention to the fact that Wetzon was on the phone. "No, I haven't," she said. Poppy frowned and went back into the house.

"Wetzon—" B.B. said.

"Did Phil go out?" Fran Burke was standing at her elbow.

"Hold on, B.B." To Fran, she said, "Yes, about a minute ago."

Fran lumbered past her, pushed the stage door open with his cane, and called, "Phil?" There was no response, but Fran went out anyway, came back into the theatre, shaking his head. He looked furious. "If you see him, tell him I'm looking for him." He thumped back the way he'd come.

"B.B.? Are you still—" But her words were knocked out of her by someone, who flew by and out the stage door, slamming Wetzon hard against the wall. Her ankle gave a bad twist. "Yeow!" She dropped the phone.

"Hello? Wetzon? Wetzon?" She could barely hear B.B.'s voice as the earpiece swung back and forth, clunking against the wall.

She grabbed it and spoke into it. "B.B., I'm sorry. It's like Grand Central Station here. I'll call you later." She hung up the phone. Then she put her weight gingerly on her complaining ankle. You klutz, she thought. It didn't feel like a sprain, but she'd be wise to ice it, and quickly. Damnation! Everyone connected with this show was like the walking wounded. Wrist casts, banged heads, arms in slings, sprained ankles. All she'd wanted to do was make a simple phone call.

Who had bulldozed her? Where was he going in such a rush? Angry, she shouldered open the stage door and stepped outside. The snow was a blessing. She took a deep, cleansing breath, and saw Mark shivering against the brick wall of the theatre. His face was drawn, terrified. He seemed to be rubbing his hands in the snow.

Concerned, Wetzon reached out to him, but he backed away. "What's wrong? Are you sick?" Mark stumbled and she caught him. "You'd better come inside." He wasn't wearing a coat and his lips were blue.

Slinging Mark's unresisting arm over her shoulder, she half-supported him into the theatre and dropped him into Cerberus's empty chair, on top of the crumpled newspaper.

He clutched her hand desperately. "Don't leave me," he pleaded.

He seemed about to say more, and she said, "Not yet. Just breathe." Closing her eyes, bloody dots danced on her lids. Bloody dots and flashing lights. Her ankle throbbed.

She opened her eyes, still patting Mark's shuddering back. On the floor, snow and grit melted into a rusty soup. Mark jiggled restlessly, humming under his breath. Wetzon crossed one leg over the other. Her right boot had a ring of crusty reddish mud around the bottom, near the sole. And the sole of her left, when she checked, was laced with blood and melted snow.

It came to her slowly: Someone had tracked blood to the stage door where it had bled into the snow.

"Mark?" Wetzon's voice was hushed. "What's going on here?"

The braying of a wounded animal issued from somewhere in the depths of theatre. Wetzon jumped. Ahead of her, the shadowy corridor was a maze of unexpected turns. The cry came again. Now voices seemed to be responding.

"It's Mort—" Mark looked possessed; he was half-standing, about to take flight.

The stage door to Allen's Alley behind the theatre was half-open; voices were coming from the alley. Footsteps thumped down the hall, accompanied by the braying, and the orange-haired woman appeared, her face a ghastly green. "Call the cops," she gasped, swaying. "There's a stiff in the smoker."

Outside, the rumble of voices stopped. Phil Terrace burst through the door, brushing snow from his jacket. He took off his oversize cap and shook it out. His face was shiny, a kind of oily sheen mixed with melting snow, and his expression was expectant. "Leslie?"

He *knows*, Wetzon thought.

The doorkeeper was beginning to panic; her arms became uncoordinated wings. "It's Mr. Hornberg. I saw his cap. Call the cops. Someone bashed Mr. Hornberg's head in."

Speechless, Wetzon looked at Mark. *He knows, too;* she thought. She stumbled to the phone, her hands shaking, and dropped the receiver. "You do it, Phil. Call 911. Someone's murdered Mort."

Phil gaped at her. "Huh?"

What was he waiting for? "Call the police. You must—" Wetzon took a ragged breath and lunged for the dangling receiver.

Moving swiftly, Phil placed himself between her and the phone. Cerberus of the orange hair screamed, "Call the cops!"

"What are you doing, Phil?" Wetzon demanded. "Are you crazy? Get out of my way." Behind her, someone grabbed her shoulders. Her ankle protested.

Fran Burke was holding her. His wool coat glistened with unmelted snow. "Easy, girl." Where had he come from? She pushed back at him. "Get out of my way, Fran. Someone—Mort—has been murdered in the men's smoker. Ask her." Wetzon pointed to the orange-haired woman. The orange-haired woman burst into tears.

"What's all the screaming about?" Walt Greenow was standing in the corridor.

"Leslie claims someone offed Mort." The hysteria factor drove Phil's voice up an octave. He started laughing. "He's too mean to die."

"Call the police," the orange-haired woman sobbed. "Call an ambulance."

"Christ," Fran said. "How are we going to get the show open?"

Walt frowned. "I'm going to have a look. Maybe you made a mistake."

"I didn't make a mistake." Cerberus sat down in her chair, blubbering.

What had happened to Mark? Wetzon tried to free herself from Fran.

"Take it easy, girl. If Mort's dead, our moving faster isn't going to help. Maybe he's not dead."

"Oh." Maybe he wasn't. Fran was right.

Phil's laughter burbled. "Smoked in the men's smoker," he said.

The laughter unglued her. She thought: *Mort would die if he knew he'd come to his final rest in a toilet.*

"Everyone wait here," Walt ordered. He went off down the corridor.

"I didn't hear anything," Phil said. "No one can shoot off a gun in the theatre and keep it quiet."

"Weren't you outside?" Wetzon shook her head impatiently. "And anyway, how do you know it was a gun?"

He flushed. "I don't. I just assumed . . . That's what I would have used on him." He said it with a grisly pleasure.

"That's just wonderful, Phil. Why are we standing here as if we're waiting for the overture to start? Move away from the phone, Fran."

Phil was laughing again. "The men's smoker. What a way to go." Neither he nor Fran moved.

Wetzon leaned against the wall. Her eyes met those of the orange-haired woman. Something was going on here that didn't include them. Images flew past her: Mort ranting, stamping his feet, cruelly humiliating people. Where was Carlos? Oh, right. Waiting for her at Remington's.

Fran rubbed his nose. His leather gloves were dark with moisture. "Someone better find Sunny. We'll need a statement to the press."

"What kind of statement?" Sunny was looking from one to the other.

Twoey loomed up behind her. "Wetzon, you've got blood on your face." He would have come to her, but the small space was suddenly crowded with people.

Wetzon touched her cheek. How had she gotten blood on her face? Whom had she touched? Fran? . . . Mark. She stamped her foot, Mort-inspired, pleading with them. "What's the matter with all of you? Get out of my way." She tried to worm herself between Phil and Fran Burke.

Poppy came in from the alley, wearing a fur coat and combat boots, followed by Aline and Edward, and . . . Kay. . . .

"Wait until we know for sure," Fran said.

"Know what?" Poppy asked, brushing snow from her fur.

"Let's all go check it out," Phil suggested. He sounded as if he were inviting them to a picnic.

"You can't," Wetzon said. "You'll contaminate the crime scene."

Aline let her eyes roam their faces, as if making an assessment. "What crime?" she said cautiously.

"What is *she* talking about?" Poppy fixed Wetzon with a hostile stare.

Phil laughed maniacally.

"Let's be careful what we say," Fran said. "Poppy, you stay here."

"Not on your life," Poppy said.

It was like some goddam Charlie Chan movie from the 1940s, Wetzon thought, watching them all troop off.

Poppy's voice floated back, "What is it? You can tell me."

Wetzon jumped for the phone, punched in 911, and waited. No sound. She looked at the receiver in her hand, her eyes following the wire to its multicolored roots.

Someone had pulled it out of the box.

"He's gone. Dead!" Aline was the first to appear, then Kay Lewis, who looked, for once, disconcerted. Brushing her cape, agitated, Aline kept repeating, "So much blood."

"As in the Scottish Play," Wetzon murmured.

Kay said, more to herself than anyone, "I've been around so long I thought I'd seen everything."

Aline stared at her. "I'm going back to the hotel. Edward, please." She motioned to a rather chalk-faced Edward, and clutched her cape around her. Her wrist cast was blotched with blood.

"It would be better to stay until the police come. No one's even called them yet."

"Yes, they have."

"How could they—? Oh, no, not from the phone in the smoker?"

Aline nodded, shuddering.

"So stupid," Wetzon fumed, pacing the tiny space. "Who made the call?"

"Fran did."

"And I suppose everyone crowded into the smoker?"

Aline nodded again. "Come on, Edward." She held the door open.

The cold air felt good. As if nature brought reason to a murder scene. How absurd. The dank alley was suddenly bright with the rolling lights of a police car; snowflakes danced in the headlighted spots. Two uniformed police officers got out of the patrol car, slamming their doors. They stopped Aline and Edward and exchanged a few words. Aline shrugged, and the cops politely ushered them back to the theatre. The crackle of the police radio sullied the otherwise silent alley.

"Leslie—" Walt was standing behind her, very close. "Take this." He put something in her hand.

"What—?"

"Put it away. Don't ask any questions." He reeked of sweat.

"But Walt—" She put it in her purse.

"It was in his hand." Walt faded back and was gone.

Snow fell like talcum, and she thought again of Carlos sitting in Remington's waiting for her. She looked at her watch. Not even one yet. The object Walt had slipped her floated from her subconscious. She hadn't even had to look at it to know what it was. Carlos's beloved Panthere watch from Cartier's.

Another squad car skidded to a stop in the alley and this one slammed with a dull crunch into the right fender of the first. "Shit!" someone spat as the driver side door opened.

Could Carlos . . . ? No way! Wetzon moved farther from the door. No. Mort was eminently killable. He'd alienated everyone—or almost everyone.

Twoey was at the stage door waiting, and he took immediate charge, introducing himself as the producer. The producer? With Mort out of the way, Twoey had given himself a promotion. *Stop it, Wetzon.*

The all-too-familiar business of herding those present together to take statements began. Twoey was everywhere, introducing them to the police, soothing the weeping widow, getting them all seated in the front orchestra, near the stage. But no one was able to stay seated, jumping up and down like Mexican beans. Mark had reappeared but he was avoiding Wetzon, wouldn't even meet her eyes.

Sunny was in a trance, paler than usual. Edward patted Aline's good hand continuously, patting and patting. She jerked it away. "Don't do that. You're giving me *agita.*"

The house lights came on; a bare bulb worklight was lowered from the flies. Walt Greenow advanced stage front and whispered something to Twoey.

An oversize man in a black raincoat circumnavigated the rake and stepped to the edge of the stage. He looked up at the grids containing almost a thousand dimmers and nearly as many lights, then out at the small, nervous group in the orchestra. "I'm Detective Willis Madigan, BPD."

Poppy's voice rose in a howl.

Wetzon came down to the apron. "Detective Madigan, please can you send for a doctor for Mrs. Hornberg?"

"Try to stay calm, everyone. We're going to get your statements as quickly as possible, then we'll let you go. I'll be back to talk with you individually as soon as I can." Madigan didn't say anything about a doctor.

Aline rose from her seat abruptly, stepped into the aisle and fainted dead away. Edward groaned and covered his face. He made no move to help Aline.

"Mark, get some water," Wetzon said. Mark looked like death walking, but he obeyed. Kneeling in the aisle, Wetzon tried to coax Aline into a sitting position. "Would someone help me?" No one moved. What a lot they were, she thought angrily. Narcissists. All wrapped up in themselves.

Walt stood over her; Twoey knelt beside her.

Someone laughed, high and hysterical. Sunny?

They propped the unconscious woman up. "Aline, can you hear me? Get your head between your knees." *Between your fat, dimpled knees,* Wetzon thought. *Lord, Wetzon, why does your fertile brain make nasty jokes at a time like this?*

Mark returned with water in a paper cup, and Aline's eyes fluttered open. From her vantage point on the floor, Wetzon saw the knees of Mark's jeans were smudged with that funny deep rust color of dried blood.

A uniformed officer with scruffy brown hair and a notepad introduced himself as Officer Bryant. He invited Nomi, the lighting assistant, to come with him to the back of the orchestra; another officer took Walt Greenow into one of the stage dressing rooms. JoJo and Mark were designated next.

Conspicuously missing and probably at Remington's were Peg Button, Carlos, half of the cast members, and possibly Sam Meidner, if indeed he'd been lured from his hotel room.

Phil moved over two seats to sit next to Wetzon. Had he pulled the phone cord from the wall? "What do you think is going to happen?" he asked.

"I don't know, Phil."

Fran sat behind them, breathing hard. "We'll get a new director. Carlos, or maybe Gideon Winkler." He didn't sound unhappy.

"What the fuck is going on here?"

There was a dead silence. Everyone's eyes were on the stage. Phil jumped out of his seat; Fran lay a hand on his arm, pulling him back.

The worklight caught in the eyes of the man, blinding him to his audience, but unmistakably framing him against the backdrop.

Poppy Hornberg emitted a bone-chilling, paralyzing wail.

CHAPTER

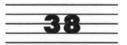

"Who are you?" Detective Willis Madigan emerged, a huge shade, from the wings.

"Who the fuck are you and what are you doing on my set?" Mort Hornberg was standing on the stage, alive and well and breathing fire. And just behind him, Carlos, his hand shading his eyes, peered into the orchestra, where everyone was on his feet, even Aline.

A violent shiver shook Wetzon. Then who—Who?

After the long moment of shocked silence, everyone began talking at once in a kind of hysteria of relief.

"Mort! Thank God." Sunny's voice broke. She clung to Twoey, who stared up at Mort, showing no emotion at all.

Shrieking, "My darling, you're alive!" Poppy made the stage through the pass door and embraced Mort as a lover might. Mort looked flabbergasted.

Stepping around the happy couple, Carlos came to the apron, knelt and peered into the house. "Birdie? Is that you? What's this all about?"

She waved at him, but couldn't be sure he saw her.

Madigan's roar rose above the babble. "If you're Mort Hornberg, who is the dead man in the smoker?"

"Dead man?" Mort said.

"In the smoker?" Carlos stood up slowly.

Aline said, "Oh, my God, then—?"

"Who is—?"

Fran bowed his head, his jowls creased with pain. Only he had remained seated when everyone else had jumped up. Had he known all along the dead man wasn't Mort?

"Everyone please be quiet!" Madigan ordered, raising his voice over the hubbub. "Mr. Hornberg, there's been a homicide in the men's smoker. We presumed it was you." He looked out into the orchestra, then down at his notepad. "Miss . . . ah . . . Watson, would you please come up here."

"Why would anyone think it was me?" Mort's face was blotched with outrage.

Wetzon rose. It seemed she was going to be the next to be interviewed.

Twoey caught her hand and squeezed it. "Do you want me to come with you?" he asked.

She shook her head, then stood on tiptoes and whispered in his ear, "Could you have brought the show in?"

His face broke into a wide grin. "With a little help from my friends." He nodded at Sunny.

"Wait a minute, wait one minute." Mort stamped his foot and pushed Poppy away from him. "What's this going to do to the performance tonight?"

"Mort, please, there's someone lying dead in the smoker." Poppy clung to him. "We all thought it was *you.*"

Madigan cleared his throat. "Okay, if the dead man isn't Mort Hornberg, then who is he?"

"I can answer that question for you, Willis." A short man in an Irish knit rainhat and a brown L.L. Bean stormcoat took center stage.

B movie all the way, Wetzon thought, as she came up on stage. Even to exit and entrance lines. Actually, the whole scene since Mort's miraculous resurrection was being performed like a play within a play, with everyone acting his part to the hilt. The cast was presently doing *Murder in the Men's Smoker* and was pretty much the same group that had performed so valiantly in *Dilla's Death.*

Except for . . .

It was Sam Meidner lying in his own blood in the men's smoker.

In the same instant Madigan read from the ID in the wallet: "Samuel Meidner."

The gasp from the onlookers was so in unison it might have been choreographed. It was part of the performance.

"I take it you all know this man?" Madigan looked from one to the other for verification.

Edward tittered.

Mort said, "You don't mean to tell me that it's Sam you took for me?"

"We all did," Twoey said.

"He was wearing your hat," Poppy said.

"I'm wearing my hat. What's got into all of you?" Mort was furious with them. "We'll take another half hour and then get back to work. We have a performance tonight."

"You mean we're going on?" Phil spoke for everyone.

"Of course, unless the representative from the Boston Police Department sees fit to close us down. Does he?"

Madigan shrugged. "It's your choice. But the men's smoker is off limits. I'm sealing it, and I'm going to post a man at the door to see it stays that way."

"We can't do a performance without a working men's room, Mort," Sunny Browning objected. "And how will it look, I mean, doing a performance with Sam—?"

"Isn't there act-of-God insurance for something like this?" Twoey asked.

Mort looked at Twoey scornfully. "No one—and I mean *no one*—closes down my show."

"If I can break in here, I want my officers to get everyone's statement. Including yours, Mr. Hornberg. In fact, we'd be happy to take yours right now."

"Who would have wanted to kill poor old Sam?" Carlos said, *sotto voce,* moving into the wings with Wetzon. "He was a harmless old—"

"If we all mistook him for Mort, then the murderer may have, too. Which would give almost everyone here a motive. I'm glad you were in Remington's where everybody could see you."

His eyes slipped away from her and out into the orchestra of the theatre. Wetzon's eyes followed. Smitty. Wetzon caught an exchange between the boy and Carlos that she didn't understand and would have questioned had not one of the uniforms tapped her on the shoulder. With his head he motioned her toward one of the dressing rooms.

The room she entered was freshly painted an off white. Stage makeup, some in an open blue metal toolbox, the rest lying willy-nilly about the dressing table, was the center of attraction in the narrow room. Tucked into the frame of the bulb-studded mirror were photographs. A box of tissues, a dingy bra, and an open package of Fig Newtons fought for space with the jars, tubes, and brushes, tools of the trade.

Under the dressing table were a crumpled pair of lacy black tights and two pairs of tap shoes.

Wetzon sat on the bench in front of the dressing table. Greasepaint—although it was no longer really greasepaint—had a certain resiny odor. A whitish powder lay like pseudosnow on the base of a black porcelain lamp, its shade ecru with age. Wetzon stared into the mirror. Her face was smudged red, like the smudges on Mark's jeans, as if she'd put on her blusher in the dark.

The cop taking her statement was the one with the scruffy hair, who'd come on stage with Madigan. Officer Bryant. After she answered the name, address and occupation questions, Bryant asked, "How did you get blood on your face and coat?"

She looked down at her coat. Matted fur, dried sticky. Had she gotten it from Mark? "I don't know. There was blood mixed with snow on the floor near the stagedoor, but how did it get on my coat?" And what was the blood doing near the door? Sam was lying dead in the smoker. Touching the stiff fur of her coat, she said, "We don't know that this is Sam's blood."

"But we can find out." Bryant proceded to take some scrapings from the matted fur and store them in a glassine bag.

She was thinking disconcertedly that they would do the same thing with Mark's jeans when Bryant snapped his book closed and told her not to leave town without letting them know.

"I'm going back to New York on Sunday. Is that going to be a problem? I have a business to run."

Bryant frowned. "I'll mention it to Madigan."

Wetzon made her way across the stage to the pass door. Carlos was sitting orchestra left, giving a statement to one of the other officers, and motioned her over.

"Can we try again? Remington's—in ten minutes?" He looked at the cop. "How much longer?"

"Ten minutes is okay."

Wetzon continued up the aisle, heading for the ladies' lounge. She had to clean the blood off. In the last row Phil sat with a woman in her forties, maybe late forties, large round glasses and brown, shoulder-length hair held in place by a red velvet headband. She wore a black cloth coat. They were having a heated argument in whispers so that all Wetzon could hear was the searing sibilance, like a snake hissing, which Phil broke off the minute he caught sight of her.

"Hi, Phil."

"Mom, this is Leslie Wetzon. She's a friend of Carlos Prince."

The woman smiled, exposing enormous teeth and a lot of gum, and offered her hand. "Pleased to meet you."

"The same here," Wetzon said, trying not to stare.

Phil's mother was wearing a ring with a huge yellow diamond. She was also the woman Wetzon had seen in the lobby of Susan Orkin's building, the woman Susan had refused to see.

CHAPTER

"Don't hang up, goddammit!" It was Mort yelling. "Susan!"

Nudging the door gently with her toe, Wetzon peered into the ladies' lounge. Its baroque and rococo carvings and murals seemed a more apt backdrop to murder than the hunting lodge severity of the men's smoker.

Mort banged the phone box with his fist. "Shit!" The tickle in Wetzon's nose became a sneeze, and Mort spun around and clapped his hands. "Just the person I wanted to see. Leslie, come in here. When are you going back?"

"Probably Sunday morning . . . the Boston PD willing." The lounge, too, had an odd odor, this one, like citronella. It must be the cleanser they used. She sneezed again and blew her nose.

Mort's face was a garden of yellow and purple bruises; his breath was sour milk. "You wouldn't consider going back tomorrow?"

"Before the opening? Why would I do that? I came up for the opening. Besides, they might not let me leave."

"What do you mean they might not let you leave?"

"Excuse me? Sam's been murdered—or had you forgotten?"

"Darling, that's why I need the favor. For the good of the show. Carlos— *all* of us—need you to do something." Mort reached out, ignoring her flinch, and took a lock of her hair. He rolled it over his fingers. "We *need* you, Leslie." He was playing her for all he was worth. "And, trust me," he continued, his voice husky. "I can get you out of Boston."

"And if I say no is ya gonna try to strangle me and trow me out a winder?"

Mort looked wounded. "Come on, Leslie. I had a bad reaction to the

medication. It happens. All I'm trying to do is get this show on. And everyone keeps getting in my face."

"May I quote you?"

He grabbed her arms and shook her, hard. "Why do you keep twisting
everything I say?"

She snapped, "Let go of me," and brought her heel down on his toes in
their soft Bally boots.

"Oh, Christ, oh Christ!" He let her go and hopped around clutching his
foot.

Wetzon watched him, then heard herself say: "My mission would
be . . . ?" What was she saying?

Mort stopped in midhop. His face lit up. "You've got to bring Susan up
here. For the opening. If you go back tomorrow morning, you can do it. We
need her here."

"Susan? Susan Orkin? Why?"

"To tell the truth, I'm not sorry to lose Sam—of course I never would
have wanted it that way—but it's a lucky break for the show. Nelson is a real
talent; he'll take care of any new music we need, and Susan's written more
than half the lyrics already—She hung up on me just now." He shuffled his
feet and put his hands in his pockets. "She blames me for Dilla. Christ, I
didn't kill Dilla. I wouldn't have. I needed her. Look at the loser I've got to
work with in her place." Removing his cap, he ran a comb through his
paucity of hair. "Maybe someone will do me the kindness of relieving me of
Phil." He took a small mouth spray from his pocket and sprayed his mouth.
Eureka! The citronella-like smell.

"Starring in *Henry Two,* Mort? If so, you're playing to the wrong audience. Tell me, did you stay on in the theatre with Dilla the night she was
murdered—after everyone left?"

"Leslie! How can you ask me something like that?" Funny how Mort was
beginning to sound like Smith. Did she attract people like that? And he'd
answered her question with a question.

Wetzon sighed. She was about to be a schmuck. "What makes you think I
would be able to convince Susan to come back?"

"Carlos told me you and Susan were college buddies. He thought maybe
you could be helpful."

Carlos! The rat. "Carlos listens fast."

"Leslie, will you try? Just *try.*" Crocodile tears welled up in Mort's eyes.
"I'll be eternally grateful. I'll *owe* you."

"You would? I'd like to collect on that right now."

"What do you want?" Mort slipped that everyone-takes-advantage-of-me look on his face.

"I want you to keep your bloody hands off Smitty."

"What?"

"You heard me, Mort."

"How dare you make judgments about me? Who do you think you are?" He splayed his hand at her as if he were casting an evil spell.

"I've known Smitty since he was a child, and I know you've made that boy a lot of promises."

"Listen, you self-righteous bitch, who are you to sit and judge me? You've never been married. I bet you've never even had a decent relationship with anyone. You sit over there on Wall Street and make money on sleaze and dirt. You think you're fucking Joan of Arc? You know what happened to *her,* don't you, bitch?"

Wetzon turned her back on him and walked into the bathroom. She looked at her face in the mirror. Dried blood did not become her. Wetting a paper towel, she dabbed gently at the smudges. Mort's threat rang in her ears. He'd stopped screaming "bitch," but she could see him out of the corner of her eye raging, stamping around the lounge.

In truth, she would give just about anything to get out of Boston. The old joke danced through her brain—*who do I have to fuck to get off this show?*—and she laughed.

She went to the door and leaned against the door frame. Mort, eyes bulging with rage, stopped and looked at her. "If you'll make me that promise, I'll go in and see Susan tomorrow," she told him.

"That's easy enough to promise. The kid's been getting a little tiresome anyway. Every time I turn around, he's there underfoot." He had sheepish, shitkicker written all over him. And the storm was over.

"Just remember, you'll have to clear it with Madigan."

She left him in the lounge, admiring his own image in the mirror. But he had drawn blood. Was there some truth in what he'd said? Was she self-righteous? Had she never had a decent relationship?

In the back of the orchestra, Detective Madigan was talking to two men, one carrying a medical bag and the other loaded down with cameras. Since they had already taken her statement, she ambled down the aisle. She could now try calling her office. Madigan beckoned to her.

"Oh, Miss. One moment, please."

Damn. She retraced her steps.

Madigan was concluding his conversation. "Take a seat. Be right with you."

She sighed. Write this day off. She envied Smith lunching in Gloucester, blissfully unaware of Sam's murder. She did not sit down.

"Now then, just a few more questions." Madigan had draped his coat over the back of the seat. He was looking through some notes, grunting. "You were the first person Juliette Keogh told about finding the body?"

Juliette Keogh? Wouldn't you just know that the orange-haired fashion-plate would have a name like Juliette? "Right." She shifted from one leg to the other.

"Take a seat," he said again. This time it was an order.

She sat on the edge of a seat, ready to fly.

"She said you were on the phone near the stage door."

"I was trying to talk to my office, but there was so much traffic back and forth and out the door, not to mention everyone talking to me, I finally gave up. I think that was before she . . . um . . . Juliette . . . went to check on the funny smell."

"I want to know everyone who came in or went out." Madigan had a small white scar in the middle of his left eyebrow, and his hair parted around it.

Her hand touched her own scar as if to see if it was still there. "Everyone? God, it was a regular army of people." She thought for a moment. "Fran Burke, Phil Terrace, Poppy Hornberg, Walt Greenow, and a stagehand. One of the cast—Nancy, I think—was on the phone before I was. Almost everyone passed through. Except Mort and Carlos." Madigan reached out and fingered the matted fur of her coat. "Do you think one of them might have brushed up against me and got blood on my coat?"

"We'll know after the lab takes a look at what Bryant picked off." He looked down at his notes. "Anyone else?"

Mark. She sighed. There was no avoiding it. "Mark Smith. The one they call Smitty."

"Are you an athlete? Do you lift weights, work out, play ball?"

"I take dance classes. Do you want to feel my muscles?" She gave him a stern look. "I didn't kill Sam, Detective. I had neither motive nor means. And I'm five feet two inches tall and weigh ninety-six pounds. If I wanted to kill someone, I would use something that evened out my height and weight, like a car."

He gave her a quick quarter-smile. Not much, just enough to acknowledge the logic of what she'd said.

Something began to tickle her memory. The men's smoker . . . She had played the Colonial. . . . Then it hit her. "There are two ways to get to the smoker," she said. "One is from the stage; the other is through the lobby.

Did you know that? The murderer could have come and gone through the lobby."

Madigan nodded. "It's possible. Let's talk about what happened after Juliette Keogh spread the alarm—"

"Almost everyone turned up. Again, except for Mort and Carlos. And Sam, of course. Juliette thought it was Mort. Hell, we *all* thought it was Mort. The hat, you know, and Sam and Mort looked somewhat alike, and yet not. Juliette and I wanted to call the police, but they all wanted to see for themselves. It was a little sick. I guess they must have felt it was too good to be true."

Madigan gave her a quizzical look. "I hear Mr. Hornberg's not a very likable fellow. I understand he's been pretty rotten to everyone on this show."

"He's an *artiste,*" she said. "Because he's so talented, everyone still lets him get away with being an *enfant terrible.*"

"And you are not connected to the production?"

"No. I'm a headhunter. I move live bodies around Wall Street. But I used to be a dancer. I'm here as a friend of the choreographer, Carlos Prince."

"Oh, yes. The one Mr. Hornberg tried to throw out the window this morning. He certainly had a good motive for wanting to see Hornberg dead."

"No, he didn't. Carlos wants *Hotshot* to be a hit. He wouldn't have killed Mort, at least not before the New York opening." She smiled grimly at her joke.

"So that's the way it works?"

"Yup. Maybe you should look and see who wanted to get rid of Sam."

"Maybe." Madigan kept his shrewd eyes on her face. What did he expect of her? "Who disconnected the phone?"

"I don't know. Everyone was crowded into that space. You might try fingerprints. . . ."

"Thank you for the suggestion." Madigan's voice was solemn. "Do you own a gun, Ms. Wetzon?"

"No! Was Sam shot?"

"What makes you ask? Did you hear a gunshot?"

"No. You asked me if I owned a gun. Come to think of it, someone may have mentioned it."

"We have to wait for the coroner's report, but it looks like the back of his head was crushed by the usual blunt instrument." He sounded discouraged. "Any ideas?"

"I suggest you call Detective Morgan Bernstein in New York, Midtown North, and get the report on Dilla Crosby's murder."

"And who," Madigan said with extreme patience, "is Dilla Crosby?"

"Don't tell me no one mentioned that Dilla Crosby, the production stage manager, was murdered a week ago just before the show left New York?"

"I'm not telling you." He sat down behind her, barely fitting his backside into the seat. His thighs were like two overstuffed blue serge bolsters. "And do you think the two killings are connected?"

"That's not for me to say." Was he playing games with her? "I didn't know either of them that well." She turned her back to him and watched the uniformed cops. Having finished their interviews, they stood on stage looking around, like actors without their next lines.

"All right." Madigan rose, and searched his pockets. He came up with a bent and none too clean business card and handed it to her. "You think of anything else, call me. If I'm not there, leave a message and I'll get back to you."

"I have to go back to New York tomorrow for the day . . ." He was frowning at her. "But I'll be here for the opening tomorrow night. If there's going to be an opening."

"Where are you staying?"

"At the Ritz."

She felt his eyes on her as she walked to the pass door. Did he think she was involved? He gave even less away than Silvestri did. Silvestri. He would have a fit about this. As if it were her fault.

"Awful business, isn't it?" Kay came out of the wings, Nomi following. "Poor Sam never hurt a fly. Someone was obviously after Mort." They stopped in front of the lighting monitor.

"Obviously."

When Wetzon got back to the stage door, a repairman was fixing the phone wires while Juliette Keogh told him about the murder in amazing detail.

"Oh, yeah?" the repairman kept saying. And, "No kidding?"

Wetzon waited impatiently for him to finish, gather up his tools and leave, but he was in no hurry. This was probably his last job of the day.

"The wife, huh?" the repairman said to Juliette-Cerberus, as Wetzon finally got to use the phone. When the operator intercepted, she said, "Collect. For anyone." She looked down at the concrete floor. Someone had washed up the blood.

"Good afternoon, Smith and Wetzon." B.B. sounded frazzled.

She waited for him to accept the charges. "Hi, B.B. What's happening?"

"Oh, great, Wetzon. I guess you got my message." Relief flooded across the telephone lines.

"No, I didn't. I'm at the theatre. What's up?"

"Lois Danzigger accepted the offer from Paine Webber."

"That's super. Congratulations. When does she start?"

"Two weeks from Monday."

"Nice going, B.B. Be sure to walk her through the routine of Xeroxing, etc. Anything else?"

The only message that sounded pressing was from Artie Agron, and the number he'd left was his home number, which she knew from the 201 area code. Tearing a pink memo page from her Filofax, she jotted it down. "I'll call him. Leave the rest for me on Monday. What about Smith's messages?"

"Richard Hartmann."

"Did you tell him Smith was at the Four Seasons?"

"Yes. Shouldn't I have?"

"Call him back and tell him she's at the Ritz."

"He's coming up to Boston."

"Is he indeed?" She thought, *deeee-lish.* Hartmann v. Kidde. Sparks for sure.

"The other line is ringing. Can you hold?"

"Yup. But make it quick." She waited, tapping her foot. Cerberus had lost her audience. Now she was up to her nose in the Boston *Herald,* which Wetzon noticed had a big photo of Mort, facing out.

B.B. said, "Are you still there, Wetzon?"

"Yeah. Anything else?" JoJo passed through with Joclyn Taylor, his hand resting on her ass. He was talking about her top note, but his tone and approach were seductive. The stage door opened, sending in a draft of raw cold, and the pair vanished into the alley behind the theatre.

"Yes. Max took a call from a Detective Bernstein this morning. Bernstein wanted to know where you were. I called him back and told him you're at the Ritz and he said he'd tried you there and left word, but if I hear from you, you should call him right away, and—"

Her feet did an impatient time step. "Spill it, B.B. I'm running late."

"You shouldn't talk to any reporters."

C H A P T E R

"Thanks for siccing Mort on me, old chum," Wetzon said, seating herself at Carlos's table. A double martini sat untouched in front of him.

He grinned at her, a shadow grin. "I thought you wanted to help, dear heart."

"I do. And I'm doing it for you, not for him. If it weren't for you I wouldn't even be here. I *hate* this." Her vehemence surprised her.

"I'm sorry, Birdie."

"It's okay. I think Susan is having a breakdown. She thinks she's next on the killer's hit parade. I don't know if she'd chance coming up here where she's certain the murderer is. I'll call her and see if we can have lunch, but honestly, Carlos."

"I'll have a mushroom cheeseburger with the works, fries, everything," he told the waiter. "What about you, Birdie?"

She looked at the menu. "This is Friday, isn't it?"

The waiter nodded.

"New England clam chowder. And a vodka martini straight up, very dry." She needed something a whole lot stronger than beer.

"I know, Birdie. Mort is a major shit, and I know we both have the sneaking suspicion that poor old Sam didn't get his head smashed because he's poor old Sam."

"Probably." She smiled one of Smith's smug smiles and knew it. "Mort and I did a little old-fashioned trading. Sort of *quid pro quo.*" She sat back and folded her hands on the table like a schoolgirl. At the bar JoJo was running his fingers up Joclyn's spine and Joclyn was looking as if she liked it.

But Joclyn was an actress and knew which side of her bread had the butter. One did not turn down the overtures of the musical director. So much for show business.

Carlos said, "Old-fashioned trading? Now I wonder what that would be."

"I asked him to keep his paws off Smitty."

"And he agreed?" Carlos sounded surprised.

"Yup. But not before he called me a self-righteous bitch who's never had a decent relationship with anyone."

Carlos gave her a searching look, then he took her hand. "And you believe him?"

She shook her head and pulled her hand from his. "Don't want to talk about it."

"Please don't take it to heart, Birdie. It's just Mort's lousy way of keeping you off-balance."

She pressed her lips together and nodded. "Yeah. I'm really proud of myself."

Carlos went off to the men's room and Wetzon found her eyes drifting back to JoJo and Joclyn again. JoJo had his hand up under Joclyn's sweater.

Well, was Wall Street so different? Only last year a major firm had what insiders dubbed the Case of the Loose Weenies. Sexual harassment of a female broker by a regional manager, no less. No one was surprised because said manager had been accused often enough for his firm to have bought off reasonably several previous accusers, but this time the woman wouldn't accept the generous sum offered. It seemed she had the guy on tape making very graphic suggestions about what she could do for him and he for her. Faced with the facts, the perp was fired—but with one full year's severance. Tra-la.

"Listen, Wetzon," one of the managers had said. "If you want to get your weenie wet, there are better places to do it than in your own office."

Bless Anita Hill for raising everyone's consciousness, she thought. The head of the retail division of another major firm, who was fond of entering the branches under his jurisdiction and asking, "Is there anything worth fucking here?" was also history.

Carlos returned as their order arrived. Thick cheddar cheese melted over a fat burger.

"That's enough cholesterol for twenty people, and then some."

"Drink your martini, darling. Today, I'm not depriving myself of anything. Mort is insisting on playing the preview tonight. He says Sam would have wanted the show to go on."

"It's a moral dilemma."

"Just so, Birdie. And Mort has never been troubled by morals." He finished his martini and signaled for a refill. "What do you suppose we're going to do for a men's room?"

"Maybe they'll rent those portable potties."

"Classy, darling." He cut into the burger with a knife and fork and began eating. The waiter set another martini in front of him.

"You'll never guess who I ran into this morning. Melanie Banks." The chowder was abundant with clams and nicely spiced.

"No kidding?"

"She's married with a teenage daughter and has a dance studio. They'll be at the show tonight. Isn't that nice?"

Carlos crossed his eyes. "Lovely, darling."

"All right. I give up. Why don't you give me your theory about who killed Sam."

"I wanted Nelson to do the score from the beginning, but Mort said he'd never done a full Broadway score so we signed him on to do the dance music. I told Mort from the beginning Sam would be a problem."

"Are you blaming Sam for being murdered?"

"No, dear heart. Sam always comes apart under pressure. *Came* apart. You should have seen him on *Grayson's Daughters.* If it weren't for those sterling fellows, Kander and Ebb—they did me a big favor—we would have just folded."

"John Kander and Fred Ebb." Wetzon smiled. "The nicest guys in the business. They and very few others are the ones I miss." She spooned some soup into her mouth. "But wait. Are you saying *Mort* killed Sam?"

"No, I'm not. Are you kidding? Mort wouldn't get his hands dirty. He'd have someone else do it—if he wanted to get rid of Sam."

"I think we're going in the wrong direction. I think someone thought Sam was Mort and whacked him by mistake."

"Carlos!" Smitty had come into Remington's, wild-eyed and without a coat. He was wearing a clean pair of jeans.

Quiet, Wetzon told herself. You're not his mother. Besides, he's full grown.

Carlos waved to him and he rushed over to their table, flushed and agitated. "Mort wants to see you right away." His eyes devoured the food on the table.

"Have you eaten?" Okay, Wetzon couldn't help herself.

Mark shook his head.

"Then sit down and eat the other half of Carlos's burger. Carlos isn't going to finish it, are you, Carlos?" Without waiting for an answer, she took the remaining burger and put it on her bread plate.

"Thanks a heap, darling," Carlos drawled. "Okay, Smitty, sit yourself. What's with Mort?"

"The new lyrics for 'Who's That Killer?' just got here, Fed Ex'd from New York."

"A very fitting song title for this show, wouldn't you agree, dear heart?"

Smitty sat down and scarfed up the rest of the burger, what was left of the fries and Wetzon's roll, while Wetzon and Carlos exchanged amused glances.

"He's a growing boy," Wetzon murmured. She finished her martini, already feeling a warm glow.

Carlos raised a wicked eyebrow at Wetzon and paid the bill. "Let's go stage a new number." He looked over at JoJo and Joclyn, leaning into each other. "Come on, you two. You're being paged."

Outside, it was still snowing. The snow was beginning to pile up in little dry dunes. They ducked into the front of the theatre. Five people stood on line at the box office. Wait till the news got out about Sam. People would claw for tickets.

If anything, the preperformance chaos was worse, enhanced by the murder. Someone was calling cues sporadically on the speaker from backstage. Sounded like Phil. But nothing was happening. Two men with long hair were on the sound board—one working with dials, the other pacing back and forth. Kay was in the orchestra signaling—probably to Nomi in the mez, when suddenly there was light, full out.

"*Christ,* now the *fucking* lighting board's *frozen* with everything on at *full!*" As this signified a problem with the software, Kay didn't even try to stay calm.

"Where's Mort?" JoJo demanded, on their heels.

"If he were here, we'd hear him," Wetzon murmured. The light painted haunted faces all around.

"He's in the big dressing room." Smitty was all puffed up with the importance of his assignment.

"I think I'll go back to the hotel and make some calls," Wetzon said, feeling *de trop* in this tumult.

"Wait." Carlos took her hand. "Stay and listen to the number. You're my rabbit's foot."

"Charmed, I'm sure."

Carlos squeezed her hand, and they followed Smitty through the pass door, fording the fierce rake like mountain goats. Piano music came from one of the stage dressing rooms, up and syncopated.

"Hey, that sounds nice." Wetzon's feet twitched to dance.

Carlos greeted the actors who had assembled, waiting to be taught the new number. They had about four hours of work ahead if they were to put it in for tonight's performance.

When they came into the dressing room, Mort was giving himself a shot in the rump, while Nelson Koch, the dance music arranger, was playing the number, standing up, reading from sheet music on top of the piano. Mort pulled up his pants and tossed the hypodermic into the waste basket. "B twelve. Energy juice," he said defensively, catching Wetzon's eye.

Nelson played the number through while Smitty produced photocopied lyrics and passed them around. Everyone looked pleased. "Then we can use it to underscore later in the show and reprise it for the finale." A short, stubby man with a high forehead, Nelson seemed to acquire stature as he spoke.

"Perfection!" Carlos hooted.

"Let's go to work!" Mort said.

Now came the joy of hard work, sweat, and a sense that everything fit. Wetzon was envious. Everyone had forgotten her. She wandered toward the stage door, thinking that Nelson had just had the break of a lifetime.

Juliette was back in her chair. Now she was absorbed in the paperback of *Scruples Two.*

"The lyrics are gorgeous! Perfect! Susan, you've outdone yourself." Poppy, in a white mink coat down to her combat boots, crooned into the phone. "You should have seen them all." Pause, listening. "When are you coming up?" Long pause. "I wish you would." Poppy's eyes glanced over Wetzon.

"I'd like to talk to her," Wetzon said.

"Well, all right, Susan, if that's the way you feel, but you're wrong. The police told us that they found a derelict covered with Dilla's blood in the theatre sleeping off a big drunk. They think he bashed her head in and stole her purse."

"They do?" Wetzon said in a loud voice.

Poppy frowned. "Well, wait a minute. Someone wants to talk to you. No, don't hang up, it's not Mort. Lola, Carlos's friend." Poppy handed Wetzon the receiver, waiting for Wetzon to correct her, but Wetzon smiled sweetly at Poppy and took the phone.

"Susan?"

"Oh, Leslie. What was that crazy Poppy talking about Lola for?" Susan sounded different. Stronger? Well, certainly less fearful. "I'm not going to let them do this to me. That's why I wrote those letters. They won't come after me if they think we know who they are."

"They? Who's they, Susan? And what letters?"

"Listen, Leslie, I'm telling you, I know how to flush out the killer, and—"

"Good. Susan, I'm coming back to New York tomorrow for the day. Can we have lunch? You can tell me all about it."

"You've found something?"

"Maybe. Susan, did Poppy tell you Sam has been murdered? And it looks like the same way as Dilla."

"Sam? Sam Meidner? No! What's going on? Wait a minute, I'm going to see if I can get CNN."

"Susan? I'll talk to you tomorrow."

"I bet Poppy's still standing there."

"You got it. Susan, is everything else okay?"

"No one's tried to break in again, if that's what you mean."

"Good."

"But that doesn't mean I'm not taking this seriously, Leslie. Someone tried to get in here. They'll try again when the show gets back to town."

"I think it was probably just bad luck and coincidence. The break-in has nothing to do with Dilla's murder."

"Oh, Leslie, you're entirely too trusting."

"Unless, of course, you haven't told me everything. . . ."

Susan's voice changed. "Tomorrow. Twelve-thirty. St. Ambroeus."

Wetzon hung up the phone. It hadn't been her imagination. There was a piece of the puzzle missing and Susan was holding out. Well, she would find out tomorrow. Turning, she was surprised to see Poppy was waiting for her—expectantly—as if they were going to do something together. Her white mink reeked of violets.

"You're going back to the hotel?" Poppy had small, weasily eyes and an unabashed stare, a lantern jaw, and no lips, just two flat lines. Her red hair was a storm of unkempt curls.

"Yes."

"I'll go with you."

I don't need an escort, Wetzon thought, but she said, "Fine."

Allen's Alley—someone had told it her was named for the 1940s radio comedian Fred Allen—was deserted and a little eerie. The snow fell and the wind puffed it hither and yon.

"Let's get a cab," Poppy said.

"It's only a short way. But if you want a cab, don't let me stop you. I need the air." The outside elements were peaceful compared to the tempest inside the theatre. Wetzon started walking and Poppy followed her, complaining.

"Susan thinks she's got us in a bind over the score."

"Doesn't she?" Snowflakes clung to Wetzon's cheeks.

"Maybe. Maybe not. With Sam out of the way . . . and no more Dilla . . ."

Wetzon turned to stare at Poppy.

"Oh, you're surprised? Maybe you think I didn't know Dilla pimped for Mort, and maybe you think I didn't know he protected her—for some reason?" Poppy wasn't modulating her tones and she caught the attention of two snow-sliding college kids carrying Boston U bookbags. The Public Garden on their right looked like a fairyland in the snow.

"Please, Poppy. I really don't care." Wetzon's eyelashes were feathered with snow.

"I didn't kill her, but I'm glad she's dead."

Christalmighty, what had brought true confessions on? "Listen, Poppy, I don't want to hear any more. You can all kill each other, for all I care."

"How would you like to marry someone and then find out he's slept with the world—the *male* world?"

"Go away, Poppy." Wetzon was running now, slipping on the white carpet of snow. She could make out the Ritz ahead.

"I bet *you* don't think she deserved to die."

Wetzon skidded to a stop, turned to face Poppy, screaming, "No one does! *No one!*"

Poppy laughed at her. "A lot of people had good reasons to kill Dilla. I bet you don't know that while Lenny Kaufer was dying of cancer at University Hospital, surrounded by his loving family, Dilla was cleaning out his safe deposit box."

After all that, it was Poppy who broke off her one-way conversation. And Joel Kidde was to blame. He was standing at the entrance to the bar expectantly, as if he'd seen them coming and was waiting for them. Before Wetzon's eyes Poppy became all coy and girlish. The woman who had thought herself a widow only a few short hours ago now began fussing with Joel's lapels.

Wetzon rode the elevator up to her room rolling over in her head Poppy's vindictive words about Dilla. She would have liked to hear more, but it was just as well. There was enough time for a shower and a snooze, and maybe even a snack before the show.

Not until she put her key in the lock did she realize, dismayed, that Joel's being back probably meant that Smith was also. She opened the door tentatively.

Smith was in a frenzy, frantically laying out her tarot cards on the bed. She didn't even hear Wetzon come in and only looked up when Wetzon came to the foot of the bed. Smith's normally glowing olive skin had taken on a jaundiced cast.

"What's the matter?"

"You! You ask me what's the matter?" Smith shrieked. She gathered up her cards and threw them at Wetzon, who found herself in a tarot shower. Then Smith began to moan, hugging herself. "It's your fault," she cried, tearing at her hair, rocking back and forth. "My boy . . . my boy is . . . ruined."

It had gone too far now. Wetzon rushed to the bed and held her. "Please, Smith. It'll work itself out. You'll see."

"My boy is a . . ." She choked. "I can't believe he would do this to me." She began to sob, face pressed against Wetzon's fur coat.

Wetzon held her and stroked her hair. What could she say to make it better? "What did the cards say?"

"Nothing good." Smith fell dramatically back against the pillows, two of which Wetzon saw had come from Wetzon's bed.

"What?" Rising, Wetzon hung her coat over the back of a chair, flicking at the bloodstained sections. She might be able to blot the stains out because the coat was wet with melted snow. She got a towel and did what she could. It would have to go to the cleaners when she got home.

"That my baby has begun a long journey."

"So he has."

"It's this whole business with the Theatre. You always made it sound so glamorous." Smith was pointing an accusing finger at Wetzon.

"Not true." Wetzon shook the moisture from her coat and hung it back over the chair. She began to pick up the scattered cards. *"You* took him to all the hit shows. Being interested in the Theatre doesn't make someone gay, you know." She handed the cards back to Smith. The top card had two royals falling from a tower that had been struck by lightning. Smith took one look at this card, shrieked, fell back and put the pillows over her head. She lay there moaning.

"Smith—" Wetzon sat down on the side of the bed. "Your face will be a mess for tonight."

"Oh," came muffled from the pillows.

"Mark is very young. He may just be going through a phase—a crush— you know—"

Smith's head came out from under the pillows. "But with *men?* Oh, dear God, how can he do this to me?"

Wetzon took her hand. "Come on, get in the shower. You'll feel better. We'll ask room service to bring up a snack."

Finally, after much coaxing, Smith crawled out of bed and took over the bathroom.

Kicking off her wet boots, Wetzon curled up on her bed. "Nothing is forever," she said out loud, watching the blinking message light on the phone. She didn't want to know what her messages were; she didn't want any more problems, at least not tonight.

She picked up the phone and called housekeeping. She asked for more towels, more soap, and more hangers immediately. Her feet were cold, and when she inspected her ankle, it was slightly swollen and blue. Still holding the phone, she pulled the covers back and got under them. Then she dialed for her messages.

B.B. She wrote it down, and crossed it out.

Morgan Bernstein. Surprise. He left a number. She jotted it down.

Silvestri. Did the whole world know where she was, dammit? He, too, left a number.

New York *Newsday* had called. And Liz Smith. What was that about?

Channel 7 News.

The *Post.* What the hell was going on? Had they heard about Sam's murder and wanted information? But why call her? There were plenty of others who had more information.

The shower went on in the bathroom. Smith was going to have a bad time of it, but then, so was Mark. Well, Smith would just have to make the adjustment as other parents had before her. After all, she and Mark were not the queen of England and the prince of Wales.

Easy for you to say, Wetzon, she told herself. How would you like it if you found out your seventeen-year-old was gay? You, who have never had a decent relationship with anyone.

Rankled, she got out of bed, found the scrap of paper from her Filofax on which she'd written Artie Agron's New Jersey phone number, placed the call, got back into bed, and let the phone ring.

"Hello." A child's voice.

"Hello. Is your daddy there?"

"Daddy, it's for you."

"This is Artie."

"Daddy, who is it?"

"Robert, hang up the phone."

"Daddy—"

"Hang up! Mary!" There was a clatter sounding as if the receiver had been dropped. "Hello. Who is this?"

"Leslie Wetzon. I like your secretary."

Artie laughed. "Listen, I'm glad you called. You know I gave Terry a start date of four weeks from last Monday, but I think my manager is on to me. I don't want to get fired with my pants down."

"Are you telling me you haven't Xeroxed your books?" It never ceased to amaze Wetzon that even seasoned brokers like Artie, who were thinking about changing firms, would delay photocopying their accounts. Without copies of their clients' statements, it would be very difficult to get accounts transferred. A broker would have to resort to memory—an unreliable route —or worse, have to beg his clients for copies of their last statements. Clients get nervous if financial decisions don't run smoothly and many would opt to remain with the broker's previous firm. So both the manager at the new firm and the headhunter were constantly exhorting the broker to have his book copied.

Who actually "owned" these accounts was debatable. In recent years Merrill Lynch, by insisting that every broker hired sign a restrictive contract, had taken to hitting departing brokers and their new firms with restraining orders, which virtually put the broker out of business. Legally, it could be argued that in New York State one could not be prevented from earning a living. But the firms were reluctant to carry the expense of legal action, so a financial settlement was arranged: they "bought" the accounts from Merrill. It smelled a lot like blackmail to Wetzon, but there it was.

"I was going to do them a little at a time next week and the week after, but what if he fires me Monday? I'll be up shit creek."

"You bet you will." And I'll be out a really nice fee, Wetzon thought.

"I need someone to help me take everything out tomorrow so I can get copies made."

"Tomorrow's Saturday."

"I know. Mary has the kids. I can't find anyone I trust . . ."

"I'm in Boston, Artie."

"Shit! You're calling me from Boston?"

"Yes. But wait. . . . I have to come back to New York tomorrow for a lunch appointment. I could meet you somewhere in the morning, say around eleven."

"There's a copy place around the corner from my office, but it's closed on Saturday. Can you help me find one?"

"Sit tight. I'll get B.B., my associate, on it right now. Then we'll both meet you. . . . Where?"

"On the Madison Avenue side of the GM Building."

She hung up and caught B.B. at the office, giving him the assignment. "And when you find a place, call Artie. Do you have his home number?"

"Yes."

"I hope you don't have plans for tomorrow."

"Aw, Wetzon . . ."

"I'll give you ten percent of my share."

"How about twenty?"

"B.B.! Oh, all right. Fifteen."

"Deal."

"Good. I'll meet you at eleven in the Madison Avenue lobby of the GM Building, introduce you to Artie, hear what you're going to do and let you both go do it. This is not something I can get into. I know at least a dozen brokers in that office, plus the manager and assistant manager. If anyone should be there tomorrow, we're all dead."

When she hung up, Wetzon was wired. Artie was probably as sure as a placement could get, once he had his books copied. It meant he was committed to making the move. She looked at her watch. Five o'clock. "How are you doing in there?" she called out to Smith. Smith didn't respond, but a moment later the shower stopped.

The door opened and a turbaned and toweled figure came out of the perfumed fog and mist. "I'll never get over this," the figure said morosely.

"Yes, you will. You and Mark love each other."

"But I've had a thought."

"Yes?"

"Therapy, sugar. I should have thought of it right away. Mark will start therapy immediately. Dickie will know the right person."

"Dickie. Ah yes." Even Hartmann's name, uttered with such affection by Smith, gave Wetzon a chill. What if he was using Smith to keep track of Wetzon and the evidence she had that would destroy him? "By the way, *Dickie* phoned the office looking for you. I told B.B. to call him and tell him where you are."

"Oh, sweetie pie, you're such a dear." She was so delighted that Wetzon felt guilty.

"I have some lousy news, too."

Smith looked up while toweling her hair dry. "Nothing could be worse than—"

"Sam Meidner's been murdered. You missed all the excitement by going to Gloucester."

"We didn't go to Gloucester after all. I was too upset and Joel had to go to the theatre."

"He did?"

Smith frowned. "What does this mean for our investment?"

"Not to worry. The show does go on. It'll be a sellout in Boston."

"Good. Joel says Sam is a pathetic has-been and should never have been hired."

"God, Smith, the man is dead."

"Oh, puh-*lease.* Did you know him?"

"Yes. Slightly."

"Did he have an ungrateful child?"

"How would I know? Probably. Doesn't everyone?"

"Humpf."

"Smith, whoever killed Sam may have mistaken him for Mort. It means there's a killer loose in the company."

"Did you order anything?" Smith fluffed her hair without combing it.

"A club sandwich and some soup."

"Sounds wonderful. I'll be right out." Humming, she went back into the bathroom and closed the door. Her mood had changed entirely.

Wetzon lay under the covers. How about a smidgeon of strychnine in Smith's coffee? Or maybe she could push Smith out a window and blame it on Mort. Naa. It would be easier to get her out of the hotel room. Hartmann would have Wetzon's undying gratitude, at least for the moment. She moved the phone to her stomach, groped for the memo pad with Bernstein's phone number, found it, called it.

"Bernstein's wire. Gross speaking."

"Detective Gross, this is Leslie Wetzon. I believe Detective Bernstein is looking for me."

"He was, but he's gone home. It's Friday. You know, the Sabbath."

"Oh. Has something happened?"

"The story in the papers . . ."

Wetzon sat up. "You mean, the papers know about Sam Meidner already?"

"Sam Meidner? No. We just heard about him an hour ago."

"Listen, Renee, I've had four calls from journalists, including one from Liz Smith. What the hell is going on?"

"The media all got anonymous letters saying that Dilla Crosby's killer is someone with *Hotshot* and that you were hired to find him."

"Oh, God!"

"*Do* you know who did it, Ms. Wetzon?"

"No! How would I know?"

"The letters say you do."

C H A P T E R

"Listen, Les, this killer is emotional. Do you know what I'm saying? I don't want you standing in the wrong place, opening your big mouth and saying the wrong thing."

Why did Silvestri always set her up for a fight? Talk about saying the wrong thing . . . "Is that official?"

"Christ, Les, what does official have to do with this? You're a goddam sitting duck for a murderer."

"What are you talking about, Silvestri? I'm not the one who's going to be murdered up here. Mort is."

"Mort? Hornberg?"

"Yes."

"How do you know?"

"I keep my ears and eyes open and I make simple deductions. And there isn't anyone connected to the show who doesn't want to see Mort dead. And I mean that."

There was a moment of silence, then Silvestri said, "I've talked with Madigan, and I want you to get your ass back to New York, and fast. Do you hear me, Les?"

She slammed the phone down. She could hear him shouting at her as she replaced the receiver. Who did he think she was that he could order her around? Oh, sure. Just one more person she didn't have a decent relationship with. Thanks a heap, Mort.

The phone rang again, almost immediately, and she let it ring until Smith called, "Why are you letting the phone ring? Answer it."

Why was everybody telling her what to do? That's what happens when you're short, Wetzon thought, kicking the covers off and swinging her feet to the floor. She answered the phone and her tone was surly.

"Well, I see you're still sticking your nose where it doesn't belong." Dickie Hartmann was oozing smarmy.

"I'm sure I don't know what you're talking about," Wetzon responded, cold and icy as Boston Harbor in midwinter.

"Put my girl on and snap to it."

Wetzon stood up and aimed the receiver for the glass top of the night table. The explosive crack on contact was music to her ears. "Ooops," she said, listening to him curse. "Sorry," she added in a high soprano voice. "Yoo hoo, Smith. It's little Dickie Hartmann for you, and snap to it."

A vision in a white terry bathrobe tore out of the bathroom, all scowls for Wetzon, and grabbed the phone. "Sweetie—"

The bathroom floor was clogged with towels where Smith had dropped them; everything was covered with a fine layer of dew, including the single remaining unused towel. Wetzon peeled off her clothes and let the shower thump down on her shoulders and back. She was, if anything, almost relieved to be leaving Boston, getting out of Smith's magnetic field, even if for only a few hours. Unless Susan Orkin had something momentous to reveal, Wetzon could probably work her over, reason that the break-in attempt had been a fluke, and get her to come up on the three or four o'clock shuttle.

When Wetzon emerged from the bathroom, room service had been and gone. Smith was lying on the bed with her shoes on, sipping a glass of red wine and looking smug as a cat. She wore black velvet bell-bottoms and a glittery crimson sweater, all sequins, with a scooped neckline.

"So?" Wetzon's beer and a tall glass were resting on ice. She poured, tilting the glass as the foam rose.

"He's here. He's speaking tonight at the NRA dinner. He's filling in for Dan Quayle."

Wetzon picked up the blow dryer. "Why am I not surprised?"

"Oh, don't be such a tease. He got a mistrial. Isn't he the best?"

"A mistrial? Wouldn't you know. Another drug dealer saved, and more taxpayer money going for the new trial." She turned the hair dryer on high and hot, drowning out Smith's response, and shaped her hair with her hands. When she turned the dryer off, Smith just picked up the conversation where they'd left off.

"Anyway, sweetie pie, I'll see you at the theatre tonight, and you're welcome to come with us for a late supper."

"Why how nice of you to ask. Are you sure Dickie would want me?"

"Sugar, he was the one who suggested it."

"Indeed?"

"But I told him I was sure you'd made plans with your theatre friends." She said it as if Wetzon's theatre friends were a lower form of humanity.

"And so I shall. But thanks all the same."

Smith gathered up her handbag and her cloth coat, throwing a covetous —no doubt about it—look at Wetzon's fur. "See you later."

"Bye," Wetzon said, chortling. She wondered how long Smith would be able to resist mink.

After Smith left, Wetzon ate the club sandwich and finished the beer. She put on her makeup, thinking over the events of the past week.

Premonitions were weird. Yesterday, she herself had mistaken Sam for Mort in the theatre. Had Sam been murdered for himself or because someone thought he was Mort? Silvestri had said the killer was emotional. What exactly did that mean? If she could only have a conversation with Silvestri that did not break down because of the emotional subtext between them. . . .

What was Sam doing with Carlos's Panthere watch? If Walt Greenow was telling the truth about finding it in Sam's hand.

One of Madigan's crew had taken scrapings from everyone's shoes, bagging them for the lab people. But the crime scene had already been contaminated by the number of people who had gone to check on whether Mort was still alive.

Why hadn't they just called the police from the stage door phone? Who had suggested they make sure he was dead? Fran? Phil? Walt? She couldn't remember.

She put on a black silk turtleneck, a slim wool ankle-length skirt, and fastened her new Donna Karan belt with the gold metal disks. She still had a twenty-three inch waist and she was proud of it.

When she emptied her purse, there it was. Carlos's watch. Eighteen grandiose karats of gold. And encrusted with blood. Damn. She picked it up, rolled it back and forth in the palm of her hand, then called Carlos's room.

"Yo?"

"Are you receiving? I want to give you something."

"Birdie! I could use a neck massage."

"I'll be right over." She wiped the blood off as best she could, slipped the watch on her left wrist, put a comb, some tissues, ten dollars and her American Express card into a small clutch bag. After making sure she had her key, she folded her coat over her arm, closed the door and walked down the hall to Carlos's room.

"Ah, Birdie, my own true love." Carlos pulled her into the room. "This is truly a nightmare from beginning to end." He threw himself on the bed. "Who would want to kill Sam? He was such a nonentity."

"I don't think it's a question of who would kill Sam. It was Mort who was getting his head bashed in, not Sam."

"Jeeezus, Birdie!"

"Yeah, well, almost anyone here—and elsewhere—including thee and me, does not have Mort's well-being in mind."

Carlos rolled over on his stomach. "Do my neck."

She sat down beside him and massaged his neck, while he moaned. "Any tighter and you wouldn't be able to talk."

"Don't comment, just use those wonderful hands."

"What time is it?"

"Oooo ooow." Carlos moved his left wrist to where he could see it. "My watch. Jesus, I forgot to get it."

"Where'd you leave it?" Feeling slightly treacherous, she slid her nails down the back of his neck.

"It needed a new battery. Do that again."

Wetzon stopped what she was doing and slid the watch off her wrist, then dangled it next to Carlos's nose.

He reached up and grabbed it, stared at it, nodded, rolled over and sat up, strapping it to his wrist. "How come you have it? Gee, Birdie, that was awesome. I'm a new man." He grinned at her. "You ought to hire out as a sideline."

"Thanks. I'll consider it." She studied him, her face somber.

Carlos took her face in his hands. "What's up, pet? Is this getting to you?"

"Is it getting to you?"

He leaned over and kissed her forehead. "Not to worry. I'm a grown up person. I can handle it." He stood and did a quick soft shoe as best he could on the nappy carpet, spread out his arms and said, "Ta da."

"Walt found your watch in the men's smoker. Sam was clutching it."

He stared at her, frozen in his finale. "Ooops."

"Did you drop it, mayhap?"

"No." A worried frown settled over his face. "It needed a new battery. I asked . . ."

"Who?"

He didn't answer.

"Come on, Carlos. You have to tell me. Are you covering for someone?"

He sat down on the bed and rubbed his index finger on his teeth.

"Carlos! Who did you give it to?"

"I gave it to Smitty."

CHAPTER

It had stopped snowing. The Public Garden, the Ritz, and Newbury Street were a Charles Aubry albumen print. The city of Boston under snow had a magical nineteenth-century feel to it.

Carlos and Wetzon chitchatted in the cab, studiously avoiding the subject of Smitty, although Carlos worried the Panthere without looking at it, and Wetzon's sentences drifted off without endings.

At the Colonial, a line snaked out the door and down the sidewalk. A news van was parked in the no-parking zone in front of the theatre. Two reporters were working the ticket line. A photographer was shooting flashes. As their cab slowed, a woman with a camera ran over and called out to them, motioning for Carlos to roll down his window.

"Go around to the alley," Carlos told the driver.

"It'll be a full house tonight, even with the snow and the Porta Pottis," Wetzon said.

The woman with the camera followed them halfway down the block, then gave up and returned to the theatre.

Allen's Alley was blocked by a police car. A young officer got out of the car and waited for them.

"So much for keeping our tootsies dry." Carlos paid the driver and they edged past the police car. "Carlos Prince and Leslie Wetzon, choreographer and assistant."

The cop let them through.

"I see I've had a career change."

"Would that it were really so."

The stage door was propped open with a brick. A blunt object, Wetzon thought. Where had it come from?

A cadavorous man with rheumy eyes was Cerberus tonight. He had a spent butt clamped between thin yellowed lips; his smoke-edged voice seeping out around it. He was telling Walt Greenow how tough it had been to get in from Needham, what with the storm and all.

Wetzon stamped the snow from her suede pumps. They'd need an overhaul if they lasted till she made it back to New York. If *she* lasted to make it back to New York.

It was almost half hour and the exquisite fear of that first performance in front of an audience was a firm presence backstage. The sweet tension was intoxicating.

"Birdie, Fran has a ticket for you. You're sitting with me."

"I'm honored."

Carlos gave her a pulled punch in the jaw. "He's probably out front. I'm off to *merde* my gypsies."

"*Merde* to you, my love." She kissed him lightly on the lips.

Excitement, barely contained, was a palpable essence and technicians were scurrying back and forth testing lighting, sound, winches. Any minute now they would open the doors and let the civilians in.

"But if you change the palette, you'll *ruin* my clothes." Peg Button's angry voice rose over the buzz of an electric drill.

"Talk to Mort. I'm argued out," Kay replied.

On stage an electrician stood on a tall ladder changing a burnout on the third torm left.

A soft percussion loop followed by string instruments tuning up filtered through the house and show curtains and from under the stage floor, adding to the theme of buoyant apprehension.

Wetzon came down the steps and into the empty house. The wood plank and the computers were gone, as were the wires and cables that had made the aisles a lethal obstacle course. The first group of ticket holders were massed at each aisle entrance, eager for ushers to show them to their seats. The excited expectation that normally filled a theatre at the first public performance of a musical had been enhanced, no doubt, by the murder of the composer. This audience, at the very least, would not be demanding and judgmental. By just being there, they'd gotten their money's worth.

Bucking the flow of traffic, Wetzon worked her way up the side aisle. Boston theatregoers still dressed for theatre, which was more than you could say for the careless and inappropriate dress of many New Yorkers.

Three monitors clung to the edge of the mez, incongruously high-tech among the lavish carvings and gold leaf of the ninety-three-year-old theatre.

Adding to the incongruity were the three white Porta Pottis lined up like giant sentinals in the lobby near the ladies' lounge.

Fran Burke stood against the back wall near the sound booth talking to Sunny Browning. He was flexing his swollen hand on the head of a hospital-issue aluminum cane. When he caught sight of Wetzon, he signaled her over by tilting his head.

"Do you want me to talk to the kid?" Fran was saying as Wetzon reached them.

Sunny shook her head. "No, I guess it's better if I do it. I'll get Twoey. He's known him for years." She looked at Wetzon appraisingly. "I hear you are investigating Dilla's murder."

"Gossip travels fast. But honestly, I don't know any more than you do . . ."

"I wouldn't get involved if I were you, girl." Fran reached into one of his capacious pockets and brought out a collection of rubberbanded tickets with holes punched in them. Dead wood, they were called, because theatre passes had originally been made of wood. "I have a ticket for you." He shuffled through the pack and pulled one out and handed it to her. L102. "Carlos has 101."

"What happened to your beautiful cane?" Wetzon put the ticket in the pocket of her coat.

"This one's better for snow," Fran said offhandedly.

"Fran!" A young man appeared from the lobby. "Bill wants to know if you put three tickets away for Joel Kidde."

"Yeh. Excuse me, ladies." Fran took to movement slowly as if his joints had locked when he stood still for any length of time, which they probably did. Watching him, Wetzon thought: He's the grand old man of company managers. It made sense he would control the network of ice—if there really were one.

"Something up with Smitty?" Wetzon and Sunny were pressed against the wall by the entering crowd.

"Mort wants me to get rid of him."

"When?"

"Now. Tonight. I'll wait till after the performance, but what a shitty thing —not to let the kid stay for the opening."

"Real class, that Mort Hornberg." Wetzon felt a frisson of guilt as she moved toward the center aisle. This had been her doing, but why did Mort have to be so heavy-handed about it? He could have sent Smitty away after the opening.

The house lights dimmed slightly. Wetzon saw Smith with Joel Kidde take their seats down front. Audrey Cassidy and Gideon Winkler sat next to them. Gideon's golden hair hung loose to his shoulders. He was wearing his cape and could have been mistaken for a WASP vampire.

Wetzon was seated, one in from the aisle, and as the house lights dimmed, JoJo appeared on the podium, a fat penguin in his black tux. A tremor went through the audience, followed by a spattering of applause. JoJo raised his arms, pointed to the cymbalist. Wetzon's heart thudded. This was the birthing moment. The cymbals clashed and the overture—a rare event now in the modern musical, but one Wetzon loved—began, rich and complex, with marching brasses one moment blending to a haunting ballad on strings. The audience was elated.

Carlos slipped into the aisle seat beside her and squeezed her hand. His was dry and cold.

The house lights went out. The red velvet stage curtain rose like swag draperies, revealing a brightly painted scrim of a carnival scene, a shooting gallery, which as they watched, seemed to explode in a thousand lights like fireworks on the Fourth of July, and in its wake revealed the entire cast for the opening number.

Over the roar of the rapt audience, Wetzon said, "Amazing."

Carlos grinned at her, looking pleased.

The first act swept by as each number received an ovation, forcing JoJo to pause for the applause. Carlos began to squirm. Twice he jumped up and disappeared to the back lobby where Wetzon knew the creative staff congregated, pacing.

When the first-act curtain came down with an explosion of lights and a crescendo of cymbals, Wetzon was already out of her seat and up the aisle, listening. For as long as she had been in show business, everyone connected to a show, friends and family, was expected to mingle with the audience at intermission and pick up the flavor of the comments.

"Where did it happen?"

"I heard the orchestra pit."

"No, I think it was in a urinal."

"Can you imagine—"

"I heard he was a compulsive gambler, that it was a mob killing."

"Really? Didn't he get sued for support by an ex-lover or something?"

"They're all talking about the murder." Wetzon was irritated beyond words. "What are you hearing, Aline?"

"Same as you." Aline gave her a sideways look. "I hear you're a detective."

"Oh, please. I was doing someone a favor, is all. The show is wonderful." As she'd hoped, everything had fallen into its creative place, and the first act played, even if it was a trifle too long.

"It's working. But the first act's too long." Aline was wearing a red dress that was more fringe than dress. "Most of them only came because they like blood. Ghouls. You know, we had only half a house sold until word of Sam's murder got out."

"But it's going so well." Wetzon refused to let Aline's negativity get to her. Across the lobby she saw Twoey, his face glowing, talking to Smith and Joel.

"There's always the second act," Aline said glumly.

The house lights dimmed once more and JoJo was back on the podium.

Wetzon settled into her seat and Carlos was beside her as the curtain went up for the second act. "Did you see Mort? Is he pleased?"

"He's in the alley retching, darling."

"Oh, good."

In the middle of the opening number a lightning streak of blue light cut across the stage, followed immediately by yellow, red, then a circling kaleidescope of colored lights underscored by frantic whooshing. Primaries and secondaries gave way to each other in fractions of seconds, slicing the stage with color. A tremor, like an aftershock, rolled through the audience. Carlos groaned and rose from his seat. The orchestra squeaked to a halt, were admonished by JoJo to continue, and jerked forward.

Disconcerted cries came from various parts of the theatre. The actors could hardly be seen through the intensely swirling colored lights. Running footsteps thudded down the side aisle. Kay. Mort's voice. Muffled screams.

Carlos raced down to the orchestra pit and scooted across the theatre to the pass door, following Kay.

Without warning, all the lights went out. It was as if someone had pulled a giant plug, thrusting the entire theatre into darkness. The audience gasped. The orchestra stuttered, stopped, started. Had someone screamed?

A light. A bare white bulb worklight suddenly lit the stage.

"Ladies and gentlemen, may I have your attention please?"

Mort stood under the worklight. The beam elongated him grotesquely, playing ghoulish games with his face.

"Who's that?"

"Morton Hornberg. Can't you recognize him? His picture was in the paper this morning. . . ."

"He's older than I thought. . . ."

Mort said, "We're having a problem with one of our computers that regulates our lighting, but with your indulgence, we're going to continue the show with the worklight and hope that you'll let your imaginations do the rest. If anyone would prefer to come back for a later performance, stop at the box office on the way out. But I would ask you to stick around. There'll be some bumps, but you'll get a swell performance."

Mort got a round of applause. No one left. It was, Wetzon thought, as if they were hanging in to see blood.

In spite of Mort's promise, the second act was hairy. The company was rattled, and it was almost a relief when the curtain came down to a standing ovation. The audience had already begun to file out quickly in the semidarkness.

On stage, everyone looked stunned. The actors, still in costume, were milling around distractedly, clustering up near the lighting board.

Mort was screaming, "You goddamn idiot! You can't get anything right! It should have been you that got it, not Dilla."

Phil's face looked creased and ill. "Go fuck yourself, Mort."

"What did you say? What was that?"

"I said, fuck you. It should have been you that got it, not Sam."

"Get out of my theatre!" Mort was jumping up and down. "Get out of my theatre! I'll see you'll never work again."

Wetzon's eyes were drawn away from Phil, away from Mort to the empty rows of the theatre yawning back from the stage. Someone was standing in the dark, watching.

"Did you see her?" A woman's voice, close by.

"Poor Kay."

"Kay?" Wetzon said. "What happened to Kay?" She posed the question to JoJo, who had come up from the orchestra pit.

"Don't know. Joclyn, did something happen to Kay?"

Joclyn's face was a scourge of smeared makeup. "She came running up here to deal with the mess and smashed into Phil's stool near the stairs and took a header. Broke her ankle."

Straining her eyes to the rear of the stage, Wetzon caught a glimpse of Nomi kneeling over a stretcher.

"Hi ho, hi ho, it's off to Mass General we go," Gideon sang, grinning.

"So?" Mort demanded. "What do you think?" His hands were on his hips and he looked belligerent.

"Of course, it's salvagable. You'll need a new score. This one won't do at all."

Smith was nodding enthusiastically. Wetzon moved away. What the fuck did Smith know about it? In the wings Smitty stood, ashen faced, watching Mort. Like his shadow.

Someone was up on a ladder, trying the lights, while Walt was playing with the computer. Wetzon wandered over to watch, and as she watched, the computer flickered and came back on line.

"Got it!" Walt shouted, gathering a small crowd around him and the computer.

"Oh, shit," someone said.

"Look."

On the screen across the lighting plot was a white band on which were typed the words:

MURDER: THE MUSICAL.

CHAPTER

"I know it was someone's weird idea of humor . . . but—" With the tip of her finger Wetzon drew a *W* on the frosty glass. She twirled the glass and watched her initial moisturize and drip onto the linen tablecloth.

Carlos was on his second martini when their grilled tuna arrived. Tremont Street, outside Hamersley's Bistro, still had car traffic though it was moving slowly in the aftermath of the snowstorm. In his open kitchen Gordon Hamersley, wearing his ubiquitous Red Sox cap, was fielding the last of his entrées.

Gideon had stood on stage for an hour taking the show apart while Mort and Carlos steamed. "We absolutely must bring in Glenn Close. You can't do this type of material without a star. I know Glenn would love it."

"How the fuck do you know?" Mort demanded.

"Well . . ." Gideon tried to look modest but failed. "I took it on myself to call her during intermission. And we'll bring Guare in to come up with a little wit. This one has a lead ass."

"Over my dead body." Aline's face was livid. No doubt John Guare's days would be numbered if he turned up in Boston to work on the book.

Gideon smiled. "Darling, anything can be arranged."

"Wake me when it's over," Carlos announced, and whisked Wetzon away to Hamersley's, where he pleaded with Gordon to feed them even though it was late.

Now, an hour later, Wetzon looked across the table at Carlos. "You're getting very drunk."

"You bet your ass I am." He ordered up his third double martini.

"Tough about the show," the waiter said.

"Good news *do* travel fast." Carlos oozed frigid charm, but the waiter didn't get it.

"The lady sitting over there. She told me the first act was great, but too long. She told me to tell you to cut the number about revolvers."

Carlos saluted the white-haired lady, who beamed at him.

"Oh, Lord." Wetzon raised her eyes to the ceiling.

"I wish I were going with you tomorrow." Then softly, "Birdie, darling, stay in New York. Don't come back."

"Why?"

"I don't think it's safe. That stupid Susan may be able to write a wonderful lyric, but she didn't do you a favor with those anonymous letters. Oh, yes, I heard all about them. Needless to say, it's on everyone's lips. I think whoever killed Dilla also got Sam."

"Why do I not get my back up when you tell me to go home, but when Silvestri says it . . ."

"I take it the flatfoot ordered you home." He laughed.

"I hate a sloppy drunk."

"Don't worry about me. Arthur will be up tomorrow."

"What if I can't get Susan to come back?"

"Oh, dear heart, not to worry. We'll manage. You saw the first act. It's all there, no matter what Gideon says. And if it turns out he's going to reconceive the show, I'll be home in a New York minute."

The cabdriver who took them back to the Ritz recognized Carlos and told him that the lyrics were hard to understand. Get the actors to enunciate, he urged Carlos.

Everyone's a critic, Wetzon thought, as she paid the driver and pushed Carlos out of the cab because he was doubled over. "Nerves," she told the driver.

When she slammed the cab door she saw Carlos was tilting badly.

"Oh, Mr. Prince," the doorman said, following them into the hotel. "Excuse me for saying . . . I thought you might want to know—"

Carlos looked at him as if he had two heads, which, to Carlos's inebriated eyes, he probably did. "Speak up, my man."

The doorman touched his shiny black hat. "My cousin Sean saw your show tonight."

"Oh, goody. And what advice does Cousin Sean have for me?"

Wetzon gave Carlos a bit of elbow.

"He thinks you can make it better by switching the number you end the first act with to the opening of the second."

"Deliver me," Carlos groaned, and kept walking. "It's started, Birdie.

Every porter, cabdriver, waiter, and his cousins are going to give me notes on the show."

"Thank you very much and good night," Wetzon told the doorman, running to keep up with Carlos.

He rested his arm on her shoulder and leaned into her, spraying her with gin fumes. "Please take me away from all this."

They had the elevator to themselves, which was a good thing considering Carlos's condition. "If only I could. Funny, how I've never seen it before. You're all killing each other bit by bit. Every day a little death."

"Oh, pet, you're so clever. You and Sondheim."

They got off the elevator. Wetzon followed Carlos, who was doing drunken leaps down the corridor. At any moment, he would fall on his face. The door to Wetzon's room was standing open; Smith's makeup case and overnighter were in the hall.

"I have a fairy godmother after all," Wetzon murmured.

"Of course you do, dear heart, and her name is Carlos Prince."

"That does it. Go to your room."

"Come over and tuck me in, Birdie. There's a little something I need to talk about."

Wetzon stopped in front of her open door. Dick Hartmann was helping a radiant Smith on with her coat.

"Oh, here's Little Miss Wetzon," Hartmann said. The attorney had a focus problem with one eye, so you always felt he was talking to someone next to or behind you.

"Sweetie! I'm so glad to see you. I was just about to leave you a note."

"Oh, shucks, are you moving out, Smith?"

"Dickie has a suite at the Four Seasons."

"How lovely, *Dickie*. Smith, I'm going back tomorrow. Artie Agron's manager is on to him. B.B. and I are going to help him clear out and copy his books."

"Well, of course, business comes first. I hope you're not too disappointed."

"I'll live."

Smith pursed her lips. "My baby is on his way home."

"To New York?"

"Yes. Mort insisted on it, and rightfully so, I think. Don't you, sugar?" She looked at Hartmann, whose nod was imperceptible. "Mark didn't tell the truth about his age, and Mort was extremely concerned. Joel had his limo take Mark to Logan for the last shuttle." She sighed and fluffed her hair, stepping past Wetzon into the corridor. "Joel is such a dear."

"Yes, he is. And he's absolutely crazy about you." Hartmann flashed Wetzon a nasty look, which flew over her shoulder. "You should have seen him, Dickie. He couldn't do enough for Smith. 'Night, y'all." She closed the door, smiling, then surveyed the room. It looked as if a cyclone hit it. "But, sweetie pie," Wetzon said aloud, "it's all yours."

She gave her coat a shock by hanging it on a real hanger instead of over the back of the chair. Picking up all the towels, she piled them on what had been Smith's bed. The white terry robe she lay across hers. She had the overwhelming urge to lie down with it.

"Not tempted to do anything foolish, are we?"

She hadn't heard the key in the lock, and when she spun around, there was Hartmann standing near the door. He made a gun of his finger and thumb and cocked it at her. His floating eye was disconcerting, and she wanted to laugh at the melodrama, but she knew his connections were dangerous.

She gave him her most guileless smile. "You've heard of the To-Be-Opened-in-the-Event-of-My-Death letter, haven't you, dearie? Well, we have one."

His lean face froze. "You're out of your league," he said. The door closed behind him.

"Soon," she murmured. "Soon." She waited until she was sure Smith and Hartmann were gone, then stepped out in the hall. Pocketing her key, she made sure the door was locked, then walked over to Carlos's room and rapped on the door.

Carlos let her in, whispering, "I'm on with Mort." He looked pleased but lay a warning finger across his mouth.

Yawning, Wetzon sat on the edge of his bed.

"Sure, Mort. . . . No, you're right. . . . I know. Uh huh. Tighten the second act. Oh? Good. Yeah, see you tomorrow." He hung up and did a jeté. "Yeow!"

"What? What?"

"Mort threw Gideon out of the theatre and fired Joel. I'm going to fire Joel myself. For once, the Barracuda is absolutely right." He grinned at her, caught her up in his arms and waltzed her around the room. "My darling Birdie," he said, when he came to a stop. "So much joy. So much sorrow. Do you not think we live life full out?"

"In technicolor."

"Yeah, well. . . ." His mood deflated.

"Smith is moving into Hartmann's suite at the Four Seasons."

"Good for her. Better for you." Head inclined, he studied her.

She knew him so well, as if their nerve ends were connected. He was trying to get her to read his mind so he wouldn't have to tell her what he wanted to tell her. "Mort sent Smitty away. I guess he was keeping his promise to me. . . . Joel's limo took him out to the airport tonight."

"Away from all this. That's good." He sat down on the bed and looked at his watch, sighed, looked at Wetzon.

"I'm off, dearie." Wetzon opened the door.

"Wait, Birdie." He stood up, reached behind her and closed the door. "There's something I didn't tell you."

"Oh?"

"The night Dilla died . . . I told you Smitty came to me for help . . ."

"Yes?"

"He said he'd tried to break up a fight between two bums and one had cut the other with a broken bottle."

"Oh, God, Carlos." She leaned against the door.

"Well, he was some mess. His clothes were torn and he was covered with blood."

The explosion, when it came, did not bring with it the expected, now intimate smell of cordite. Oh, she was on to it, though. She knew its tricks. This time she wasn't going to let it run away with her. She would catch it, hold it, and make it go away for good.

But it fooled her.

She was outside her body, floating. The sky was ink-dark. Below her a car was traveling down Route 9 toward Claytonia, toward the farm, toward home.

No! She tried to cry out, break the dream. Instead, she spun ahead. A car was coming from the opposite direction at full speed. In the wrong lane.

"Daddy, watch it!" She was crying.

For a nine-second freeze frame, she saw the startled faces of her parents through the windshield glass.

The explosion brought with it a fierce yellow flame and then the suffocating odor of gasoline.

No! No! No!

She awoke uncovered, in a raging sweat, her arms over her eyes, rocking from side to side, shaking. The covers were on the floor. She pulled them up and hid under them, shivering. How could they die like that? She was only twenty. Didn't they know they were abandoning her when she most needed them?

Rolling over on her stomach, she buried her head in the pillow to stifle her sobs.

This is what a breakdown is like, she thought. You lose control. Her

parents had been dead almost twenty years, killed by a drunken driver in a
fiery crash only three miles from their home. Why now? In the depths of her
being she knew she had blocked it away, and kept it away. But not any more.

When the fear subsided, the pain—a dull, raw ache under her breasts—
remained. Was this what Sonya had referred to? Was this the other trauma
that had to be dealt with? It didn't take a shrink to translate the meaning of
her dream.

Wetzon dried her eyes on the pillowcase and groped for her watch, then
the light. She was in Boston at the Ritz. It was still as death. Her watch said
five o'clock. She was out of breath as if she'd tapped through the entire
"Mirror Number" from *Follies* without taking a breath.

The room pressed in on her. The ceiling seemed to inch down as in the
Wilkie Collins story about the traveler in the strange bed. When she got out
of bed, a cramp shot through her left calf, sending spasms of pain from calf
to foot to thigh.

What was happening to her? In agony, she hobbled to the bathtub and
ran the water icy cold, massaging her calf. *I've got to get out of here.* Thrusting
her foot into the cold water, groaning, she flexed and massaged the cramp
away. Her right ankle was black and blue and tender. She was falling apart.
Get dressed, pack up, and check out, Wetzon.

In less than an hour, she was showered, dressed, made up and packed.
She carried her own bag to the elevator. The hotel was just waking up. It was
Saturday, after a snowstorm. No rush to go anywhere.

When she got on the elevator, not expecting to see anyone she knew at
that hour—theatre people were not morning people as a rule—she plowed
into Joclyn, who was getting off.

"I'm sorry. I thought this was the lobby." The actress's face was streaked
with tears and mascara clung to the little creases under her eyes. Her flirta-
tion with JoJo didn't seem to be making her very happy. She turned away
from Wetzon.

"Joclyn, is there anything I can do?"

"You?" It was an accusation.

"Yes. I've been there, you know."

"Oh, have you really?"

Shut up, Wetzon, she thought. You're going to come out of this bruised.
"I mean, I'm a gypsy still."

Joclyn seemed to be giving that some thought. When the door opened to
the lobby, she walked out, then turned. "You're not one of us anymore.
You're one of them."

The words were a stinging slap. They rolled around in Wetzon's head as she waited for a cab. Joclyn was right about one thing. Wetzon was not a gypsy anymore. She was a neurotic woman, pushing forty, *who had never had a decent relationship with anyone.*

The author of those words was getting out of a cab in front of the hotel. "Leslie, darling!" Mort greeted her with a wet kiss. "You're off? Do well by us."

She got into his cab. "Where did you just come from?" she asked the driver.

"Logan."

"Logan?" What the hell had Mort been doing at the airport? "Well, that's where we're going."

The ticket clerk at the USAir shuttle counter was talking to a cohort who had just handed him a cardboard container of coffee. Because Wetzon was the only customer, he was taking his time. Why shouldn't he? After all, it was Wetzon who wanted to get out of town in a hurry. She would have sprouted wings and flown if she could.

When he finally concluded his conversation, the clerk smiled at Wetzon politely and took her credit card. The first flight was at six-thirty, he told her, and that had just left. She picked up her bag and followed the gate number directions to the security belt, placing her coat, bag, and purse on it, then passed through the entrance without a problem.

A tacky food service place—the airport equivalent of a greasy spoon—was just on her left. Wetzon ordered a small orange juice, decaf coffee, and a toasted English muffin; flicked a crumpled candy wrapper and assorted crumbs off the seat of a chair; and sat, careful not to touch the table, which was sticky enough to catch flies. The other tables were occupied by a workman in an airport uniform and two elderly women in polyester pantsuits and permed hair that had gone kinky.

Spreading two napkins on the table, she set up her breakfast, taking her vitamins from their tiny Ziploc bag. Her thoughts centered on herself. The dream had shaken her, driven all other thoughts away.

"Leslie, hi! Gosh, I was hoping to run into you."

Wetzon came jolting out of a near trance. Sunny Browning was standing over her smiling with all those long, white teeth. Would her next words be a neigh?

"Coffee, please," Sunny told the counterman. She had pulled out a chair and was sitting before Wetzon had a chance to say anything. "Well," Sunny said, "can you believe all this?"

Wetzon shook her head. "How come you're going back?"

"Things to do," Sunny said vaguely. She stood and took the coffee mug from the counterman and sat again. She was wearing the same outfit she'd worn on the plane trip up, black on black, sweater, jacket and boots, but instead of a skirt, black leather pants and a metal and leather chain belt. Her mane of streaked blond hair was caught under the collar of her coat. Before the shooting and her medically inspired haircut, Wetzon had loved the feel of her hair on the back of her neck in the winter. Sunny took a sip of coffee and left a lipstick ring on the cup. "Some odds and ends to tie up."

"Like?"

Sunny stared at her, green eyes from dead white skin, fingering the strands of pearls that fell to her waist. "So you *are* a spy—"

"A spy? Oh, please. Susan is an old friend. She's terrified that whoever killed Dilla is going to come after her."

Sunny snorted. "Isn't that a little ridiculous?"

"You think Dilla's murder was a once-only aberration?"

"I'm not saying that, Leslie. It just doesn't make sense to believe it's one of us."

"Then how do you explain Sam?" Sunny played with her pearls, not bothering to respond, and Wetzon added, "Susan thinks someone in the *Hotshot* company killed Dilla and she's probably right. She also thinks someone is stalking her."

"Stalking her? She's crazy." Sunny took a sip of coffee, her eyes on the counterman, then looked back at Wetzon. "You don't think it's me?"

"Is it?" Wetzon pushed her half-eaten muffin away and reached for her mug. Little globules of fat fought for space on the black surface of the coffee.

"God, Leslie, I've never seen this side of you."

"You've never seen *any* side of me, Sunny." She gave Sunny a cynical half-smile.

Sunny sipped her coffee, eyes downward. "Well, I couldn't care less about Susan."

"What about Dilla? Did you guys get along?" Wetzon was starting to feel perky again. There's nothing like a murder investigation to get the blood coursing through your veins, she thought.

Sunny pulled her hair out from her coat. "Sure. She was okay." She wasn't very enthusiastic.

"With Dilla out of the way, Mort will be more dependent on you."

"So? That isn't enough to kill over. And what about Sam? Why would I ever do that?"

"I think Sam died because he looked like Mort."

"Well, there you are. I don't want anything to happen to Mort." She grinned at Wetzon suddenly. "Yet. And you're right about one thing, Leslie. With Dilla gone, Mort will depend more and more on me to produce his shows. He has no choice. I'm going to take very good care of Mort."

"Okay. Do you have any theories about who would want to kill Mort?" Wetzon asked.

Sunny laughed. "How can you ask that with a straight face?"

Now Wetzon laughed, too. "Yeah. I guess the answer to that question is 'we all did.' "

"I love Mort," Sunny said, "but he's selfish, manipulative, egomaniacal, and not a little crazy."

"How about sadistic?"

"Well, that, too. He does seem to zero in on the very things that people don't want to face about themselves. He's very intuitive."

"He is indeed."

"But he's always sorry after one of his tantrums."

"And he never apologizes, does he? He always gets other people to do it. That way he never has to admit he's wrong."

Sunny looked at Wetzon thoughtfully. "You're right. One of the things I'm going to do in New York is get Phil to come back."

"You mean Phil's already left Boston?"

"No one seems to know where he is. They must have gone back last night."

"They?"

"Edna. His mother."

"I feel sorry for Phil," Wetzon said, standing. "He's young and eager. Mort has been pretty rough on him, and Mort usually likes young men."

"Leslie—"

"How do you know he'll come back?"

"He will. Phil knows that the play is the most important thing. He comes from a theatre family."

"You mean, his mother, the treasurer?"

"In a way. You remember Lenny Kaufer, don't you? Well, Phil is Lenny's grandson."

C H A P T E R

With an enormous sense of relief, Wetzon watched the city of Boston recede as the plane lifted off and climbed into the snow-clouded sky. Escape. Freedom. Whatever you called it, she felt she was home free.

In truth, nastiness and backstabbing were not confined to the theatre, but there was something about this small, glittering world that made it particularly poisonous. She had always carried a deep nostalgia for her life in the Theatre, but now she saw with awesome clarity that it was mean, meaner than Wall Street could ever be. The Theatre was a faithless mistress. She seduced your heart and soul, then made a beggar of you and gave nothing whatsoever in return, but only seemed to because it was all artiface. Maybe, somewhere deep inside, Wetzon had always thought she might go back. But there was nothing to go back to. The Theatre was her past. She would never —could never—go back.

"If Phil is Lenny Kaufer's grandson, then Edna Terrace must be—"

"Do you want a beverage?" The steward handed them small packages of salted nuts.

"I'm coffee'd out," Sunny said.

Wetzon declined as well.

"Edna Terrace?" Wetzon prompted. She broke open the bag of nuts with her teeth. Salt, sweet salt.

Sunny nodded. "Yeah, Edna's Lenny Kaufer's daughter. I never knew Lenny. He was gone before I got into the Theatre. But everyone knows about him. He's some sort of legend."

Sunny was looking at her expectantly, so Wetzon said, "I didn't know him. He didn't seem to ever work for any of the producers I worked for, like Papp or Hal Prince or Stu Ostrow. Women liked him and men liked him. Every show he managed paid back its investment. I think I'd already left the Theatre when he died. Edna and Phil must be fixed."

"I don't know. Edna always looks frayed and frumpy. She doesn't dress or act as if she has money. I heard the treasurers' union gave her a card without the usual apprenticeship, because of Lenny."

Wetzon considered the massive yellow gemstone Edna had been wearing when Phil introduced them. It didn't go with the picture everyone was drawing of her. "Did you get a look at that ring she was wearing?"

"Noooo. What about it?" Sunny was fiddling with some papers in her handbag and didn't look at Wetzon.

Wetzon had the distinct feeling Sunny was lying. You couldn't miss that ring. "It looked like the one you and Carlos described to me, the one Dilla was wearing."

Sunny smiled at her. "Oh, you must be mistaken, Leslie."

The plane climbed into another flight path above the clouds and dazzling sun streamed through the small window. The sky was a frosty blue.

"What's in all this for you, Sunny?" Wetzon demanded. It came out harsher than she'd meant it to.

But Sunny didn't take offense. "You mean, how long am I going to hang out in Mort's shadow?"

"Yes."

"I've been planning this for years, Leslie. I'm going to produce musicals with and without Mort. I've got two properties under option. *Hotshot* is the last show I work on as Mort's assistant."

"Oh, when did you tell Mort?"

"Leslie, I'm sure you know damn well I haven't told him anything. I don't need grief." She grinned at Wetzon. "I've already talked to Carlos about directing and choreographing one of the shows."

"You did? That devil didn't breath a word."

"I left the book with him. It's about relationships between the sexes." She crossed one leathered leg over the other and the leather squeaked. "I'll send you a copy. You might help convince him—"

"I'm happy for both of you if it works out, but Carlos doesn't listen to me."

"False modesty."

"Maybe. What about Mort? He's still got a lot to say."

"Leslie, wake up and smell the roses. Mort's old hat. If it weren't for

Carlos, there'd be no *Hotshot*. Frank Rich won't pull any punches. Mort will be lucky if he comes out of this alive, let alone with the reviews in his pocket. And the way he and Poppy live, they'll both end up in the Actors' Home in Englewood. Do you know she had a limo drive her back to New York last night after the preview so she could get her hair done for the opening?"

Wetzon giggled. She could think of no worse fate than to end up in the Actors' Home, having to listen to actors puffing up their careers. There was no retirement home for Wall Streeters. Too bad. Traders were infinitely more amusing than actors.

"The captain asks that you take your seats and fasten your seat belts. We are going into our landing pattern for LaGuardia and beginning our descent." The plane dipped and banked, immediately clogging Wetzon's ears. She opened her mouth and rotated her jaw, and then they were on the ground.

It had taken less than forty-five minutes. A line of travelers was waiting for the next shuttle to Boston. Her peripheral vision caught a figure going into the men's room. A slope of shoulder, the rolling gimp, something reminded her of Fran Burke. "Is Fran in New York?"

"Not that I know of."

Short of running into the men's room on a wild-goose chase, Wetzon chalked it up to the nervous aftermath of her dream. The individual had passed so quickly out of her line of sight, she wasn't sure she'd seen anything at all.

"Where are you headed?" Wetzon asked. They followed the signs that said *Ground Transportation.*

"Times Square. I've got an appointment with TDF about getting unsold *Hotshot* preview tickets to the TKTS booth. We'll give them some to sell but they're asking for more than we want to give them. You know how it is. Everything's a negotiation."

"Life is." Wetzon shifted her suitcase to her other hand. "I always thought the TKTS Booth was a rip-off."

"Why?"

"I'm convinced the producers overprice their tickets so they can cut them in half and sell them at the Booth. I bet if there were no discount Ticket Booth on Forty-seventh Street, ticket prices would drop by at least a third."

"You're not the first person to say that, but I'm not at all certain it's true."

"It's obscene to charge sixty-five dollars for anywhere in the orchestra or front mez. I wish, if you're going to produce, you would look into a new ticket pricing policy."

"I'll keep it in mind," Sunny said cheerfully. "So can I drop you?"

"No, thanks. I'm headed home."

"What flight are you taking back?"

Wetzon had no intention of returning. "I haven't decided. I want to talk to Susan first."

Cabs were lined up bumper to bumper at the cab stand. They separated with a wave.

It was a gray and overcast New York that Wetzon came home to, but there was no snow or rain. It looked as if it had rained hard overnight. The sides of the road and some of the dips were puddled.

She was afraid for Smitty. Smitty. The name he had given himself seemed more macho than Mark. He was trying so hard to be grown up. He'd found out somehow that Dilla was using him for her own purposes. But was that motive enough for killing her? Hell, Sunny Browning had more motive.

The cabdriver was Indian or Pakistani and knew what he was doing. He tore through Queens, only skidding once on the slippery steel patches of the Triborough Bridge. Except for the usual backup at the bridge tollgates, the road was clear. Even the FDR Drive, with its alternately closed lanes in constant repair, had moving traffic. To her left, the towers on Roosevelt Island looked like a cardboard mockup floating in the middle of the East River.

A gigantic moving van was parked in front of Wetzon's building, and a shouting argument was in progress among an ape-size truck driver, a tearful young woman with a baby hanging from a front satchel across her breast, and Roger Levine, the president of Wetzon's co-op board. It appeared that a new tenant wanted to move in, but because of the strike, it was not going to be allowed. Wetzon had forgotten entirely about the strike.

Jorge, the weekend doorman, in jeans and a heavy sweater, was standing out front carrying a placard that said 32B 32 J BUILDING WORKERS STRIKE. He seemed more interested in the argument than in picketing. He had waxed the ends of his mustache so they curled up stiffly like rat tails.

Using her outside door key, Wetzon let herself into the building. Grace Elman, a retired schoolteacher whose interest in the building bordered on obsession, was sitting at a small table in the lobby. A long white florist box lay on the floor at her feet. "Hello, Leslie." She looked at the suitcase. "I realize you're a very busy person, but I hope we can count on you to fill in on guard duty while the strike is on. The times available are posted in the elevator, and you can just sign up."

"I'll try, but my schedule is erratic. How are the negotiations going?"

"There are none. The negotiating committee for the union went off to

Florida for the weekend." Grace looked down at the box at her feet. "Oh, this just came for you."

Flowers. In a long, narrow box. Roses. Wake up and smell the roses, Sunny had said.

Wetzon picked up two days' accumulation of mail, which included a photocopied list of instructions on tenant services. Another list was posted on the wall near the elevator, and inside the elevator was a signup sheet for volunteers to cover the door and take out the garbage. With everyone working or having young children to care for, Wetzon figured they would end up having to hire a guard, at least for daytime. It seemed an illogical economy to have tenants do guard work.

Her apartment was sanctuary. It had felt her absence. She could tell. She'd been away a whole lifetime. It was so good to be home.

But it was after ten, and she'd have to get moving if she was going to meet B.B. and Artie Agron at eleven. She emptied her suitcase on the bed and hung up her clothes. The laundry went into the washing machine. She stared hard at the florist's box, almost hoping it would go away. Oh, hell. She opened the box. An abundance of roses, long-stemmed and deep red. The card said, *I love coming home to you.*

Wetzon's stomach did a forward roll. Alton did all the right things, the things any woman would give her right ovary for. He was easy to be with. He was attractive. He had plenty of money. He made decisions quickly. He loved her. And he was good in bed. Not in order of importance, she thought. She put the roses in a vase, picked up the phone and called him, knowing his machine would answer. She left word that the flowers were beautiful and she would call him later, that she was back in the city possibly only for the day. She wasn't at all sure she was ready to see him tonight.

The one thing she wanted—had—to do before she got going was call Smitty. She picked out Smith's number and listened to the phone ring. Smith refused to buy an answering machine. She was probably the last hold-out in Manhattan.

There was a click, then an exasperated, "Mom, stop calling me!"

"Mark, it's me, Wetzon."

"Oh, God, Wetzon. I didn't mean it." Mark sounded desperate. "Mom's called me eight times already this morning."

"Well, she's worried about you."

"I guess." Sullen and spoiled, which he was. "Only she made Mort send me away."

"No, Mark, I did."

"You? Wetzon, I thought you were my friend."

"I am." It was all she could do to keep from calling him sweetie or baby. "Mark, you were a sweet package sold to Mort by Dilla for certain favors."

"Dilla told me. She laughed at me when I told her I loved Mort and he loved me and he was going to do all these things for me."

"Honey, Mort has been making and breaking those promises to young men for years."

He snuffled into the phone. "I asked him after you told me that on Thursday night, and he laughed. He said I was a nuisance and was getting in his face all the time."

"Mark, let's have dinner tonight, what do you say?" *Oh, God, Mark has a motive for both murders.*

"How could he do that to me? I loved him. I'd do anything for him."

"Mark, honey, this is all part of growing up, I'm afraid. How about if I pick you up around six and we can go some place fun? I don't want you to be alone."

"No, please, Wetzon. Don't you see? They set me up." His tense voice came to her dead and flat across the phone lines. "And they're not going to get away with it."

Doom. Gloom. Rain. A slippery glaze underfoot. Icy fingers playing on her soul strings. Her dream about her parents' death had wiped her away.

Wetzon stood under her awning waiting with little patience for an empty cab to cruise by. The damp chill seeped through her black wool leggings. There were plenty of unlicensed cabs—known in the city as gypsies—but she'd never felt comfortable getting into one of these because they had no insurance and you had to negotiate your fare.

What was Mark up to? She felt a terrible responsibility for him, and she was afraid. People had killed for less.

But there were other suspects certainly. Perhaps even Mort himself. Phil. Aline with her wrist cast. Fran Burke. What about his fancy cane? A blunt object. But Fran had no motive that Wetzon could see. Unless Mort was asking for a share of the ice.

Two people had been killed with what appeared to be the same, or similar, blunt instrument, and yet no one seemed to have any idea what the murder weapon was.

A cab was coming slowly down Eighty-sixth Street with its roof light on. She left the cover of the awning and rushed into the street, waving. He stopped for her. "Fifth and Fifty-eighth. The General Motors Building," Wetzon told the cab driver. *Clean your mind and focus on Artie and the job at hand.*

She had left a message on Sonya's answering machine asking with some urgency for a session today or tomorrow. "My dream took a nasty turn," was what she said.

They took the Eighty-sixth Street transverse. The park was raw, trees bereft of leaves, brown, flattened winter grass—deserted but for the few obsessive joggers who run through snow, sleet, hail, and dark of night.

Closing her eyes, she thought: Why can't I accept that Alton loves me and can give me a good life? *Because,* a voice responded, *you've never had a decent relationship with any man.* That's not true. *Okay, name one,* the voice said.

Name one? Sure. Um. There was . . . Well, what about Carlos?

Give me a break, the voice said.

The driver made a left onto Fifty-eighth Street and pulled up to the curb. She gave him seven dollars, got out and opened her umbrella. It was Saturday and no one had yet strewn around those little white beads that melt ice. The steps were slick.

Probably one of the ugliest buildings in New York, the GM Building was built with a sort of basement plaza—a basement plaza?—where the architect had placed shops, which could scarcely be seen and were therefore often unleased. Still, the building had a Fifth Avenue address, and F.A.O. Schwarz on the ground floor, and it was directly across from the east entrance to Central Park and in the heart of the upscale shopping district —Bergdorf's, Bloomie's, Tiffany's—and surrounded by posh hotels like the Pierre, the Plaza and the Sherry Netherland. So it was unlikely that its owners had ever been in financial trouble as so many other Manhattan real estate owners had during the worst of the recession.

Wetzon walked through the lobby to the Madison Avenue side of the building, and there was B.B. in clean and pressed jeans, a red-and-white ski jacket with a lift ticket still hanging from the zipper head, and white joggers, standing near the elevators. He was reading *Institutional Investor.* Wetzon laughed. If they were really hiding their identity, he would have given them away with his choice of reading material.

"You're a walking advertisement," she said, sidling up to him.

"Oh, Wetzon." He blushed and dropped the magazine as if she'd caught him grazing through a porno magazine. "I . . . um."

What was up with him, Wetzon wondered. He looked guilty as hell about something. If she didn't know better, she'd be adding him to her list of suspects in Dilla's and Sam's murders.

But this was no time for probing questions. Her heart wasn't in it, and Artie Agron, a small, wiry man in gray sweats, a Mets cap over his frizzy hair, was coming into the lobby from Madison carrying an enormous briefcase. He hadn't shaved and looked so disreputable that a guard asked him for his

ID. God, Wetzon thought, these guys don't know anything about clandestine.

"I don't know what bug they got up their ass," he grumbled to Wetzon, shaking hands. "I come in here every day."

"But not unshaven and wearing a baseball cap, I'm sure. Artie, this is my associate, B.B., short for Bailey Balaban."

"You related to the supermarket guy? He's my client."

"No." B.B. shook his hand. "I found a copy place on Lexington that'll take care of everything. We just have to get it over to them."

"Okay, here's the story." In spite of the fact that they were in a no-smoking area, Artie lit a cigarette, keeping his back to the guard. "Me and Balaban go up to the office. Wetzon, you wait down here so Balaban can slip some stuff to you and come back up and get more. If no one's up there, we can move faster." He got on the elevator with the lighted cigarette. If he didn't follow the rules on small things, what did he do on big things, Wetzon thought, watching B.B. follow him. She waited near the window looking out on Madison. Umbrella fought umbrella for a slice of sidewalk space; someone was sure to get a spoke in the eye. Rain never stopped shoppers. B.B. and Artie emerged from an elevator.

"There's two rookies up there, but they're so busy trying to keep up with the paperwork—" Artie was carrying his briefcase, bulging open, and B.B. followed with two shopping bags and a stuffed New York Athletic Club gym bag over his shoulder. It had to be B.B.'s. Wetzon didn't think they'd let Artie within ten feet of the NYAC.

"Three, maybe four trips, Wetzon," B.B. told her.

She walked with them to the street. The rain slanted down. "Do you want me to hang around?" He'd needed the security of her presence until he had his book. Now he wouldn't need her anymore.

"Naa. We're okay, right, kid?"

B.B. nodded, then hung back slightly. "Wetzon, can I talk to you about something?"

"Now?"

"Oh, no, I mean Monday."

"Smith will be back Monday."

"No, not Smith. You. Privately." He was very earnest.

"You coming, kid?" Artie was getting restless, and wet. He hadn't bothered with an umbrella.

"Sure, B.B. Go on now. We can have a drink after work Monday if you want." She patted his arm. Was she getting maternal, or what?

"Thanks, Wetzon."

Something was definitely up with him. She wondered if Harold, their ex-associate, had lured B.B. away to work with him and Tom Keegen. Smith would be wild.

Remember, Wetzon told herself, nothing is ever final. Except death. She opened her umbrella and threaded her way up Madison, finally leaving the crowds behind her around Seventieth Street. The shops all had sale signs in their windows, but Wetzon, although she stopped to look, wasn't really seeing anything but her reflection.

She was convinced that Susan would come to Boston if Mort were willing to change the billing. Bill her as lyricist. Who would complain? Sam's agent or lawyer? Sam was dead. It was in the agent's or lawyer's best interest to get the show open.

St. Ambroeus was the perfect place for an elegant brunch or lunch on the East Side, and as usual, it was crowded. It seemed as if everyone in New York had had the same idea. Wetzon was a little early. Maybe she should call Susan and head her off. She left word with the maître d' that if Ms. Orkin should appear, Ms. Wetzon would be right back.

There was a phone on the street. She'd passed it on the way.

The rain had become a soggy mist. Her hair curled wispy and annoying around her cheeks and forehead. She pushed it away. It was time, she thought, to begin putting it up again in the old, comfortable dancer's knot. She popped a quarter in the slot and called Susan, checking the number first in her Filofax.

"Hello. I'm unable to come to the phone right now. Please leave me a message after the tone."

She must be on her way. Wetzon went back to St. Ambroeus, squeezing by two well-dressed, very proper senior citizens with four boys of various ages from about four to eleven or twelve, all in dark blue suits, white shirts, and blue-and-red striped ties. Grandparents and their perfect little grandsons.

"Did Ms. Orkin arrive?" she asked the maître d'.

"No."

Fifteen minutes became a half hour. She was hungry and tired. She tried again. "You're sure you didn't seat Ms. Orkin?"

"Yes."

Behind the baked goods counter filled with croissants and lovely pastries, a striking young woman with long brown hair had looked up when Wetzon mentioned Susan's name. "Ms. Orkin comes in for chocolate croissants every morning."

Wetzon smiled. "A girl after my own heart."

The salesgirl looked confused.

"Forget it," Wetzon said. "Did she say anything about lunch?"

"She didn't come in this morning. Did you try calling her? Maybe she was delayed."

Wetzon nodded. What the hell, she would try again. She went back out on the street and called Susan's number. The line was busy. She'd been held up, that was obvious. Probably by Mort calling from Boston. Moisture formed on Wetzon's face. Lovely for the skin, she thought. The temperature had warmed perceptibly. She was only a few blocks from Susan's. Who needed a fancy lunch? She'd do her mission for Morton, tell Susan that looking for Dilla's murderer among the vampires was hopeless, and be off.

Just ahead of her a black nanny, her white uniform showing under her navy coat, pushed a child in a stroller, plastic-encased like a closet bag.

When Wetzon turned on Eightieth Street, she had to sidestep twenty or more noisy, hyper youngsters emerging from a yellow school bus with New Jersey plates. A teacher and what looked like two harried mothers were trying to herd them into a line. Sheep dogs would have done it better.

She gave them a wide berth and arrived at Susan's building about the same time a short, gray-haired black woman in a storm coat came from the opposite direction, pulling a sniffing and cavorting Izz, on the leash. There were four pickets in front of the building. The strikers all looked wet and surly. When Izz caught sight of Wetzon, she yelped, broke away from the elderly woman and leaped at Wetzon, landing wet paws and all on the fur coat. "Hi, Izz."

"Oh, oh, I'm sorry, Miss." The woman tried to recapture Izz. "She was overnight at the vet, so she's a little wild."

"It's okay. I'm a friend of Ms. Orkin." Wetzon snuggled the damp little dog. "What was wrong with her? She looks okay to me."

"Upset stomach or something. Ms. Orkin's not home. I'm Rhoda, her housekeeper."

"Are you sure? I just tried her and the line was busy. We're supposed to have lunch."

"I don't know. Maybe she changed her plans, . . . Miss—"

"Ms. Wetzon."

"Isabella, you behave now. If you'll take her up with you, Miss Wetzon, I'll go on and do my marketing. I'll just go in with you and tell them it's okay."

The guard near the door was a short, swarthy fire hydrant, in a dark green uniform. His hair was slicked back and shiny.

"This lady's okay, you hear? She's going up to Ms. Orkin's," the house-keeper told him.

The little dog licked Wetzon's face and wriggled. Wetzon set her down on the floor of the elevator and tried to capture her leash as the car rose, but when the elevator door opened, Izz escaped. She didn't go far. She came to a sudden stop at the door to Susan's apartment; her ears flattened.

"Susan?" Wetzon rang the bell tentatively. Izz had her nose up against the door, whining. She rang again. No sound came from the apartment. Izz began to scratch frantically at the door. Wetzon rang the doorbell once more. She could hear it ringing in the apartment.

She stepped back and looked at Izz. The dog collar. What had Susan said? *The dog collar has a little inside pocket for my house key.* Wetzon stooped and undid the little dog's collar. There was the pocket. And there was the key. She slipped it into the lock and opened the door.

With a low growl, Izz sprang into the apartment. Wetzon followed, stepping into a black pit and right off the edge of the world.

CHAPTER

48

Something wet and slimy touched her, clawed at her. She tried to push it away but couldn't move. It dug its wet nose into her neck. Wetzon groaned and rolled over. She was wrapped up like a mummy. In a patchwork quilt. Where was she?

She wriggled and managed to free an arm. Izz pounced on it, licking. She remembered now. Someone must have thrown the quilt over her, and she had fallen and passed out. Nope. A small pang on the right side of her forehead gave the lie to that scenario.

She was suddenly conscious that she was lying on a bed of nails. The dog began to tug at the quilt, growling, as if trying to free her. "Oh, Izz. Stop." She tried to get out of the tangle, but her hands weren't helping her because she couldn't stop them from shaking.

Her eyes burned. Pizza breath was searing her lashes. With a great effort, she sat up. The little dog crawled into her lap, cowering.

"*Suntze ti!* A light went on, blinding her. "Miss? Miss? Are you all right?"

She peered up at him from under the quilt. "Who are you?"

"*Sto mu gromova!*" He stepped back and something crunched underfoot. "I'm the super here. Tony Novakovich." He was a tall man with a slight stoop and spoke in Balkan-accented English, except for his exclamations, which were in a totally foreign language. "*Suntze ti!* What goes on here?"

Wetzon looked around. Broken china, crockery, books, clothing lay everywhere. Everything in sight trashed. "What—?"

"In my building! But do not worry. The police are coming."

"Oh, God," Wetzon groaned.

"The guy downstairs called them already. He said it sounded like some-one was being killed up here."

"Yeah, me." But she was very much alive. She touched her head gingerly. A bump was rising on her forehead. "Where's Susan? Ms. Orkin?" Near the door was what was left of a Louis Vuitton suitcase, sliced open, its contents scattered on the floor. So Susan *was* planning to come to Boston.

But where was she now? The sour taste of dread rose in Wetzon's throat. She plucked at the blanket, set the quivering dog on the floor amid the shards of china, the detritus of a life, and stood. The floor tilted. She grabbed the super's corduroy-clad arm to steady herself. Izz began circling the refuse on the floor, whining. "I'm worried about Susan, Mr. Nova—"

"*Do Djavola!* I do not know how they get in," Novakovich was saying, his hands in constant motion. "This is a secure building."

"Maybe Susan let them in." She released his arm and stood without tipping.

"I do not think so, Miss. She is a pretty smart lady. Now, the other one—rest her soul—Miss Crosby—she has—had—some strange friends."

Where was Susan? Wetzon shed the quilt and began to pick her way around, careful to nudge objects aside with the side of her boot and not step on them. Had whoever had done this found what he was looking for? God, was this what Susan had been so terrified of?

She could hear Novakovich talking on the intercom, telling the security guard to send up the cops when they got there.

The living room was even worse than the foyer. Sofa cushions were sliced through; tiny feathers floated on the air and spilled over the coffee table and rugs. The piano had been brutalized. Izz stayed close to her ankles, sniffing. Cassettes and CDs, some in, some out of their jackets, lay crushed on the floor near what was left of an expensive sound system. Dull ashy light bled through vertical blinds.

A wide hall led to the bedroom wing. All along the hall photographs clung precariously to the walls as if a tornado had blown through. Several had crashed to the floor, their glass shattered. Wetzon picked one up. An unsmiling Michael Bennett wearing a black T-shirt under a dinner jacket and a radiant Dilla Crosby, her boobs spilling out of her low-cut gold lamé sheath.

Wetzon set the photo on the floor against the wall. Every day a little death, she thought.

The master bedroom was a garden room, or had been. A forest of plants were upended in their dirt on the cream carpet. The mattress was on the floor, sliced up like the sofa in the living room. No bed cover. It had been used to smother Wetzon. Closets yawned, their contents tossed. An eerie silence pervaded the room except for the panting dog and the *drip, drip, drip* of a faucet.

"Susan?" Wetzon stood listening.

Izz scampered into the bathroom and Wetzon followed. A wet towel lay crumpled on the checkerboard tiled floor amid bottles of makeup, jars of face cream, cold medications and aspirin. The open medicine cabinet's mirror was a spiderweb of splinters. She held her breath and pulled back the shower curtain, half-expecting to see Susan lying there, hacked by Norman Bates. But the tub was empty. The clear plastic liner was wet and one of the faucets was dripping. She ran her fingers lightly along the white tile. Wet. Had Susan been in the shower when she heard a burglar?

How had he gotten in? Wetzon went back down the hall and checked the second bedroom. It was set up as an office. Drawers were thrown open and shelves were emptied. Papers and books were strewn about. More dirt on the dark wood floor. An abundant grape ivy lay stunned, its roots exposed.

And in the center of the room was an old Shaker rocker; propped up on its seat, like a nasty joke, was the skull of the steer that had hung in the foyer. A painted pine cradle lay seemingly undisturbed near the desk.

She met Novakovich in the hall coming out of the master bedroom. "What a mess. The cops are on their way. What am I gonna say to my board?" Wetzon followed him into the foyer and watched him open the door. "No sign of Mrs. Orkin?"

"No." Fear curled round in her breast, tightening. "Something terrible has happened to her."

The super shook his head. "She went out of town. She told me she was going."

"Maybe, but I don't think so. Her suitcase is over there." Izz rubbed against her leg, tail between legs, ears flattened. "What about the kitchen? Did you look?"

"Yeah. It is as bad as everywhere else—"

"Isn't there a service door in the kitchen?" Wetzon was already through the kitchen door. More trashing here. The little dog whined and ran to the service door. "This door—did you open it?"

"*Do Djavola!* Excuse me, Miss. I keep telling them keep it locked. They never listen."

Izz thrust her nose in the tiny space between the door and the jam and pushed, whining, growing more and more agitated. Novakovich kneed the door open, careful not to touch anything. But Wetzon remembered he'd already touched the front door and the intercom.

A gleaming black garbage can stood right outside the door, its cover a foot away. Newspapers and magazines were stacked separately on the floor. New York was deep into recycling.

Wetzon stepped out on a battleship-painted landing right behind Izz, who had started trembling and whining again at the edge of the stairs. She looked down.

"Bozhe moy! Bozhe moy!" Novakovich wailed.

A lime green towel streamed like bunting over three of the stairs.

And on the landing below Susan lay on her back, naked, smiling up at them through a curtain of blood.

C H A P T E R

"I'm a hayseed, my hair is seaweed, and my ears are made of leather and . . ."
A child's voice drifted up from somewhere below.

Novakovich crossed himself. *"Bozhe moy! Bozhe moy!"*

Wetzon crept down the stairs, hugging the side wall. Spots of white plaster flaked through chipped gray paint. Susan looked so tiny, like a child. A gory-headed child. Maybe . . . there'd just been the flicker of movement in her hair. Dear God! A fat black waterbug crawled out from under Susan's blood-matted hair. Wetzon's scream caught in her throat.

Her foot touched the lime green towel, and she bent to pick it up. It was damp.

"And your ears are made of leather and they flop in rainy weather . . ." a woman's voice sang.

The throaty, rich chuckle of the child rose and surrounded Wetzon, floated up past her. Then, *"Again, mommy, again!"*

Wetzon shook the towel out and covered Susan's body. There was no doubt she was dead.

A frightened shriek came from above. "Mercy, Lord! Mercy!"

Startled, Wetzon looked up. Rhoda. She had forgotten about Susan's housekeeper.

Novakovich, equally unsettled, muttered again, *"Do Djavola!"*

Wetzon ran up the stairs, but Novakovich had successfully blocked Rhoda from the landing. "There's been a terrible accident," he said gruffly guiding her back into the kitchen.

Resisting, Rhoda demanded, "Where's Miss Susan?"

"Susan must have surprised a burglar. She fell down the stairs." Putting her arm around the woman, Wetzon guided her away from the service door.

"Lord, Lord," Rhoda cried.

Novakovich muttered, "I gotta get the cops." He crossed himself again.

"I thought you said the guy downstairs had called them."

"Yeah, but he called about a fight. This is different."

"Mercy, mercy." Dazed, Rhoda was looking around at the mess, still clutching the plastic D'Agostino grocery bag in one hand and a worn black leather purse in the other. "I have to go to her. She's a good girl. She doesn't deserve no more trouble." She tried to press past Wetzon to the service door.

"Rhoda, please. Mr. Novakovich is going to take care of everything."

"But Miss Susan—" The old woman's eyes were cloudy. Cataracts? Wetzon hadn't noticed it earlier.

"Susan is dead, Rhoda."

"Lord, rest her soul," Rhoda whimpered. Wetzon put her arm around the bony shoulders and walked her back to the front door.

"What a thing to happen in my building, with my men on strike." Novakovich motioned to them. "Come with me. You cannot stay here."

"But my groceries. I have to put them away," Rhoda protested.

Novakovich shook his head. "We gotta to leave everything exactly like we found it, like I see on the TV; otherwise we could mess up evidence."

He had touched things. She had covered Susan with the towel, Wetzon thought, bewildered. The evidence was already messed up.

"Sweet Jesus, take her home," Rhoda muttered. Tears crept down her cheeks, pausing in each ridged wrinkle and working their way downward.

"Don't say nothing about it if someone gets on the elevator. I do not want my people to panic. We have good security here normally—but you know these temporary guards, they do not have relations with people in the building so what do they care—" Novakovich was talking to the air. Neither Wetzon nor Rhoda was listening.

The elevator stopped on five and a tall, dark-haired woman in a ranch mink got on. She was carrying a Brunschweig and Fils shopping bag crammed with fabric swatches and samples. And she picked up on Rhoda's tears at once, but Wetzon wagered she wouldn't ask, not in front of a stranger. Upper-class New Yorkers made a fetish of not showing their curiosity, but Wetzon could feel it radiating from the woman.

"Mrs. Engelbrecht."

"Tony?" That's all she said, and when Tony didn't respond, the dark-haired woman just nodded. In the lobby she picked up a bundle of mail and left the building.

Wetzon got Rhoda seated on the sofa in the back of the lobby, away from the line of traffic to and from the elevator. The housekeeper was still clutching her grocery bag and her purse. "We can't leave her alone up there," Rhoda said. "Someone's got to sit with her."

"No. It's all right." Wetzon patted her hand. "There's nothing we can do for her now." She was thinking that some evil energy had been let loose, that what had been unleashed by Dilla's murder had gone on to infect everyone. Was it something that Dilla had incited? Well, of course it had to be. Damn! The pieces would start fitting together like a picture puzzle and then one piece wouldn't fit. Something . . .

Tony was talking on the phone somewhere out of sight. He reappeared. "I better tell them not to open their back doors." He disappeared again.

"Izz!" Rhoda jumped to her feet. "Where's that little dog?"

Wetzon hit her forehead. Godalmighty, she was losing it. They'd left Izz upstairs. Where had she disappeared to? *Please,* Wetzon thought, *not near Susan. Please make her not be near Susan.* "You stay here. I'll go up and get her. I think I know where she is." In her mind's eye she saw Izz sitting next to Susan's body. A Maltese honor guard.

Riding up in the elevator she felt an unspeakable anguish. She saw moviola images from years gone by: a young Susan Cohen hunched over the table, one leg double-crossed over the other, calling out, "Fourth for bridge," as Wetzon came back to the dorm from a class. Susan and Wetzon sitting on the grass on the ag farm, studying, but not . . . Wetzon confiding problems with a boyfriend whose name she no longer remembered, and Susan saying, "They're not worth it. We really don't need them to be happy." Had Susan been trying to tell her she was gay and had Wetzon been too thick —too naive—to pick up on it?

She had not taken Susan's terror seriously. Perhaps the killer was not a burglar, but Susan's stalker. Perhaps it had something to do with Dilla's murder.

Wetzon shivered. Why hadn't he—or she—killed Wetzon, then?

Novakovich had left the door to Susan's apartment ajar, and Wetzon slipped through. The very ferocity of the trashing frightened her. Almost as if it were . . . intentional. Wasn't that the word Silvestri had used? No. He had said *personal.* What had the killer been looking for? And had he—or she —found it?

She called, "Izz?"

The apartment was deathly quiet. It gathered her into its cocoon of turmoil. On the street below a horn sounded, far away, and then a siren. Wetzon closed her eyes. Her lips were dry and chapped. *Talk to me. Tell me what happened.* Blue Canton, pieces of it, were underfoot. They crunched when she walked on them like the gravel driveway leading to her childhood home.

"Izz?" She walked through the kitchen onto the back landing, past the open garbage can. Did one ever get used to the smell of death? She would have to ask Silvestri.

Susan was a small bulge under a lime green towel, and Izz was not there.

Wetzon came back into the apartment and walked down the hall past the study, to the bedroom. No Izz. Where could she be? The study. Had she seen a slight movement when she'd passed?

If Susan had worked there, Izz would have stayed with her. "Izz!"

The old painted pine cradle was rocking, a hair's-breadth, making hardly any sound on the wooden floor. No human hand in sight.

Wetzon eased forward. The cradle rocked.

The licorice eyes were dull with fear. They admonished her. "Izz. Come on out of there. Come on, baby." Wetzon got down on her knees. The little dog bared her teeth. Wetzon opened her palm and held it out to the dog. Izz sniffed cautiously, then licked Wetzon's palm.

Wetzon lifted her from the cradle. Papers were strewn over the floor, pieces of poetry, lyrics maybe. A desk diary. Tucking the dog under one arm, she flipped through the pages of the diary, looking for the past two weeks. She saw her name in Susan's clear, almost childish hand. And each day, other names. Turning over one more page, she saw that day's date. She saw her name and one other. She closed the date book and buried it under the other papers.

The other name in Susan's diary was Smitty.

C H A P T E R

Two uniformed cops got off the elevator with Novakovich. Izz, in Wetzon's arms, bared her teeth and trembled.

"This way. I'll show you. This way. I made sure nobody touched anything. I know what to do." Novakovich was flushed, swollen with the importance of his new role, and the rank odor of nervous sweat formed a shield around him. Who wanted to get too close? He led them through the kitchen to the back service door.

"Jeeze, what a mess." This came from the second cop, a tall Hispanic, with the inverted triangle build of an Olympic swimmer. His badge said *Colon*. "You sure nobody touched anything?" He looked at Wetzon.

"N-n-no, n-n-no, I s-saw to it. Don't worry." Novakovich was so nervous, he was stammering.

"I put a towel over her," Wetzon said. Now she had the attention of both cops. "It was lying on the steps as if she'd dropped it, the towel, I mean." She thought: I'm amazingly calm.

"Who are you?" Colon demanded. He had his little pad in his hand.

"I'm Leslie Wetzon, a friend of Susan's. Susan Orkin. We had a lunch appointment, and when she didn't show, I came over—"

The other cop, whose tag said *Better*, was black and square jawed. A pencil-thin mustache clung to his upper lip. He had short legs and a stocky upper body, like a weight lifter. He was gay. Wetzon sensed it rather than saw it. He made a note in his little black book and asked her to spell her name. *Good, better, best,* danced through her mind.

"You shouldn't have touched anything," Colon said.

"I t-told her not to," Novakovich said. "D-Didn't I tell you that?"

"I know, but she was naked and I—well—I just couldn't leave her lying there like that."

"But you didn't move anything?"

"No. That's all I did. I didn't even touch her. I didn't even see if she was still alive. I knew she was dead."

"We'd better get someone out here," Colon said.

"Let's have a look first, Norman." Better nudged the back door open with his foot, and Colon and Novakovich followed him.

Wetzon stayed where she was. She'd seen enough. Izz whimpered and licked her hand with a dry tongue, and Wetzon hugged her, burying her face in the soft fur, as Susan had a scant week earlier.

Novakovich pushed past her and stood leaning, panting, his palms on the wall near the elevator, head down. His face was the color of paper, hands grimy, the nails uneven, one grossly discolored. The crusty scab of a half-healed cut ran jagged across the back of his left hand. Sweat beaded the nape of his bent neck.

"All right." Colon's manner was brisk. "Let's get down to the lobby. I want a statement from both of you. Mr. Nova—"

"Novakovich." He raised his head and wiped the sweat on his face with his forearm.

"Please see that no one in the building goes out on that landing," Colon told him. "We're going to block it off now."

"How'm I gonna do that?" The smell of him was corrupting, especially in the closed elevator. "I got a strike going on."

"Use your intercom. No one will be allowed in or out of this building unless you can identify them."

A small pain, like a bruise, began to throb behind Wetzon's ear, joining the throb from the bump on her forehead. "Are you from the Nineteenth?" she asked.

"Yes," Better said.

"Please tell Ed O'Melvany—"

"You know O'Melvany?"

Wetzon nodded. She was breathing through her mouth so she wouldn't have to smell Novakovich's fear.

In the lobby, Colon looked around, then led them to where Rhoda was sitting on the sofa, her head bowed, mumbling. She held a small black Bible to her breast. The uniformed security guard watched their procession, openly curious.

"Ma'am, would you kindly—"

"She's Susan's housekeeper, Rhoda. I don't know her last name," Wetzon said. "I guess you'll want to talk to her."

Colon looked carefully at Rhoda. "Yes. Was she in the apartment when it happened?"

"No. I met her on the street. She'd picked up Izz—Susan's dog—" Wetzon said, nodding to the dog in her arms, "—at the vet's and gave her to me to bring up to Susan while she did the marketing."

Colon turned his back while he and Better had a brief conference. Better took out his radio from his back pocket. He was already talking into it as he walked up the steps to the street, and an EMS siren made its presence known with its urgent *waaa-waaa-waaa-waaa.*

"And Mr. N—" Colon didn't even attempt it this time. "I want everyone who comes in identified. No deliveries till the detectives get here."

"Everybody must sign in anyway—because of the strike."

"Good. I think we'd better have a look at the sign-ins for the last two days."

"The mountain," Rhoda muttered.

Better came through carrying a couple of sawhorse barricades and a roll of yellow crime-scene tape, walking straight to the elevator. Two EMS attendants followed him.

Novakovich wrung his hands. *"Do Djavola!* What if there's a fire? The fire department will fine me because the back stairs are blocked." He was standing in the middle of the lobby howling.

Funny what you zero in on, Wetzon thought, feeling oddly detached.

"Do you hear me, Lord?" Rhoda said.

"Mr. Novakovich," Wetzon called, "let the police handle it and it'll be over faster." She seemed to know just the right thing to say.

"Thank you, Ms.—" Colon gave her a tiny, careful smile.

"Wetzon."

"I'd like to get a short statement from you, er, Rhoda, if you'll come with me."

Rhoda cringed, fear in her eyes. "Be with me, Lord."

"It's okay, Rhoda," Wetzon assured her. "You'll be wanting to go home. This will get you there faster." There. She'd done it again.

"I just want to ask you a few questions and the detectives will be here any minute. Then we'll send you home in a car."

Colon helped the frightened woman up and took her, still hanging on to her purse and her bag of groceries with one hand and her Bible with the other, to what Wetzon figured must be the mail or package room. They were probably going to use it for the command post as soon as the detectives arrived. Novakovich was standing near the guard talking to a woman in a mink-lined raincoat over sweats, with twins in a double stroller, their eyes round with excitement over the blue uniforms of New York's Finest. One was trying to wriggle out of his seat belt and had almost done it.

"An accident, Mrs. Murphy. You do not have to worry. It is not on your side of the building." The super shuffled through the papers on the marble-topped table and pulled two sheets. "Start a new sign-in," he told the guard, then walked Mrs. Murphy to the elevator, continuing to assure her that everything was fine in such a nervous, almost frantic manner that Mrs. Murphy's face had taken on an uneasy expression. Or maybe it was just his pungent odor. She made a distinct effort to get between him and her twins to block out his agitation. "Kevin, stay right where you are," she admonished the child, who had at last managed to climb out of the stroller.

It was only when Colon came out of the mail room and approached Novakovich that the super paused and drew back. Mrs. Murphy gave the stroller a brisk push onto the elevator and followed. The door closed. Colon began to talk to the super, gesturing with his notebook.

In Wetzon's arms Izz finally heaved a sigh and stopped trembling. Susan had written Smitty's name in her date book. Did that mean he'd been here? She didn't know what to make of it. Mark—as Smitty—had become as devious as Smith, in his own way. Had he murdered Susan? Had he clobbered her—Wetzon—his friend? Was he capable of murder?

Sure, we all are. Would he have done it? Wetzon couldn't bring herself to think so.

She had not torn the page from the date book and she could have. Tamper with evidence? She couldn't do it. Not so fast, Wetzon, she chided herself. Hadn't she tampered with evidence by returning Carlos's watch, which Walt *said* he'd found in Sam's hand. What if Walt had killed Sam and planted the watch? No. Then there would be no reason to smuggle it to her. He would have left it there to be found. And the watch had blood on it.

What Walt had done was wrong. And she had compounded that wrong because she wanted to protect Carlos. But it was a bad decision and she knew it. She had too much respect for law enforcement. With Susan's date book, she'd managed to obfuscate, make it a little harder to find. But they would find it. She was merely buying time.

Colon had finished with the super and was coming back to Wetzon when two more uniformed cops came in the front door, then behind them, detectives. No O'Melvany. Izz began trembling again. Wetzon stood and took a few steps across the marble floor. O'Melvany wasn't there. Panic began to flutter in her breast.

"What's going on?" one of the uniforms asked.

"Don't you know? We've got a DCDS," Colon said. "A Susan Orkin. What are you guys here for?"

"Christ," the other said. "We've got a page of complaints from her, about her. Last night she calls us after midnight to get some crazy woman out of her apartment, and this morning her downstairs neighbor calls and says it sounded like someone was being killed up there."

C H A P T E R

"Not you again." Eddie O'Melvany looked grim. "I couldn't believe it when Better called it in." Izz bared her teeth when O'Melvany reached out and patted her head. He had arrived on the scene only minutes after the others.

Wetzon put her hand over her eyes, bit her lower lip, but couldn't keep the tears from coming. "I'm sorry," she said. It was maddening, *maddening* not to be able to control her emotions.

In the continuing moviola of her mind, quicksilver pictures spun by, things she hadn't remembered. Susan running down George Street, the cuffs of her flannel PJs hanging from under her jeans, late for an eight o'clock class in English Comp. Susan admonishing her for not picketing Rutgers administration to protest some long-forgotten infringement of free speech.

"I'm sorry." More tears. Izz sat up and licked Wetzon's chin, sopping up the tears.

O'Melvany handed her a linen handkerchief and waited for her to dry her eyes and blow her nose. He took a roll of tropical Life Savers from his pocket, popped one in his mouth, then held the roll out to her. When she shook her head, he put it back in his pocket. "This your dog?"

"No. Susan's."

"I'm going up to have a look. When I get back, you can fill me in."

"Okay." She dried her eyes again. His handkerchief was real linen and had his initials on one corner, white on white. Her mascara had come off all over it.

He started for the elevator, where a technician carrying a load of camera paraphernalia slung over his shoulder was waiting, then stopped, turned back to her. "I left a message downtown for Silvestri."

If Wetzon were a witch, O'Melvany would have been promptly reduced to ashes, Sonya or not. This would only increase Silvestri's macho sense that he was always bailing her out of trouble when she could damn well bail herself out—if everybody would just leave her alone.

What the hell was she going to do about Mark? And who was the woman Susan had called the police to throw out? The police would know that.

A parade of Crime Scene Unit detectives and technicians began filing in, mixing with the curious tenants who were hanging around. Novakovich was huddled with one whose demeanor told Wetzon that in spite of the runner's garb, he was probably the president of the co-op board and most likely a lawyer. New York was rancid with lawyers, and they clustered with their like on co-op boards all over the city.

Izz jumped off Wetzon's lap and began making little circles. Uh-oh, what had she done with the leash? Too late. Izz was squatting, and the muted colors of the patterned carpet beneath her were slowly darkening.

Rhoda appeared again, escorted by a uniformed cop, no longer carrying the groceries, just her Bible and her purse. Her face was gray. Izz came to life and danced around the old woman. "You, girl," Rhoda said, pointing a knobby finger at the dog, who shot up and licked it, "you behave yourself now." Her teary eyes met Wetzon's. "God rest their souls, they spoiled her. Imagine putting all that love on an animal when there are so many children—" She shrugged. "I got me a ride home." She nodded to the uniform.

"What about Izz?"

"Oh, you'll have to take her, Miss. They don't let dogs in my project."

Izz was looking up at them, tilting her head from one to the other, as if she knew they were talking about her.

"I don't even have any dog food. I wasn't going home . . ." Oh, shit, Wetzon thought.

"She eats the dried stuff. There's a big bag upstairs. Ask them officers to give it to you."

Izz made a half-hearted attempt to follow Rhoda, stopped, looked back at Wetzon. She seemed to decide that Wetzon was the more perfect patsy.

The lobby was suddenly full of people. Cops. Tenants. Guns. All closing in on her.

Wetzon couldn't breathe. She tore off her beret and stuffed it in her pocket. Her heart pounded with an urgency that scared her. Air. She had to get air. She picked up Izz and threaded her way out to the street. No one stopped her. A uniform was stationed in front of the building, impassively watching the crowd of onlookers that had gathered. Subdued strikers with their placards were exchanging information with some of the people watching the activity.

Two blue-and-whites, their colored lights rolling, were among the cars double-parked, and there were a lot of those because Saturday was still an alternate-side parking day. Dispatchers' disembodied voices crackled over police radios.

"I'm a hayseed, my hair is seaweed, and my ears are made of leather and they flop in rainy weather . . ." She was lined up with four other freshman, each with a giant-size name tag hanging from her neck. They were being ordered to sing. "I'm a hayseed, my hair is seaweed . . ."

The girl next to her hissed, "This is so stupid." Her name tag said Susan Cohen.

"Sing," the sophomore commanded. Susan Cohen and Leslie Wetzon grinned at each other and shrugged, and they sang, "I'm a hayseed, my hair is seaweed, and my ears are made of leather and they . . ."

Wetzon stood on the sidewalk, gulping big chunks of moist air into her lungs. Izz began to squirm, and Wetzon set her down in the gutter between a white Acura and a black BMW. Her knees trembled violently. She sat down on the edge of the sidewalk, huddled in the narrow space between the two cars, shivering, pulling her fur coat around her. Near her boots a condom nestled next to a penny—head up for good luck—and a child's grimy white sock. Izz tried to climb into her lap, but Wetzon was hugging her knees.

If she made herself small enough, maybe she wouldn't die.

Somewhere in the logical half of her brain, Wetzon knew she was having a panic attack, but it was a downhill roller coaster ride. She couldn't stop it.

Get out of here, a voice urged. *Run! Run for your life!*

She caught Izz up in her arms and stood, balancing herself for the moment against the Acura, then walked out into the street away from Susan's building.

When she got to Fifth Avenue, she began to run.

CHAPTER

Wetzon came out of Central Park near the Museum of Natural History with no memory of how she'd gotten there. Central Park West was being repaved and only a single lane was open either way. She knew impatient drivers waiting their turn for the single lane had to be leaning on their horns, but her heart was pounding in her ears, blocking everything else out.

A voice screeched at her, "Whatsamatter, you deaf?"

She stopped. An old woman in a brown stormcoat that had seen better days said, "You better leash your dog, lady, or he's going to get run over."

Dog? She looked down and there was Izz trotting along beside her. They crossed Central Park West together, Wetzon wheezing badly, unable to get air, intent for the Beresford.

Alton was back. Alton wouldn't let her die.

"Good afternoon, Miss." A doorman she didn't recognize was on the door, but he must have recognized her because he added, "Mr. Pinkus got in a couple of hours ago."

Alton was waiting for her, saying her name, standing in his open door in blue jeans and a soft white buttoned-down shirt. She fell into his arms with a certainty that he would take care of everything. "Leslie, what is it?" Concern softened his voice as he stroked her hair and kissed her forehead.

"Oh, God—Can't breathe." She propelled herself out of his arms, panicked. He had a fire going in the fireplace. She dropped to her knees, gasping. "I'm going to die . . . Oh, God." Her head sank to the carpet.

Alton lifted her, put his arm around her shoulders. "Breathe into this—" He held a paper bag to her lips. Izz whimpered.

She pushed the bag away. "Can't, can't—"

"Leslie, listen to me. You are not going to die. You're hyperventilating. Breathe into the bag. It will help, I promise you."

Don't fight it, she told herself, obeying. Her asthmatic wheezing began to subside. She felt the tension draining from her body and she leaned back into him, intensely aware of his cleanshaven cheek, the fragrance of his aftershave, his damp hair. And his desire.

The fire snapped and stuttered. She had stopped shivering and her coat lay on the floor near them. Izz had made herself cozy on it.

Alton was sitting on the floor holding her, his back against a club chair. "I guess you really missed me."

She touched his face. "It's been a bad week."

"Do you want to tell me about it?" He caught her hand and held it.

"I wouldn't even know where to start. . . ."

"Start with your friend here." He nodded at Izz. Izz's shiny black nose twitched.

"That's Izz. She belongs—*belonged*—to my friend Susan Orkin."

"Gary's ex-wife?"

"God, Alton, do you know everybody in the world?"

"Probably." He grinned down at her.

He was such a lovely man. She looked around the elegant room. For months now, she'd spent almost every weekend here, but it wasn't her. It was Alton. Older. Reserved. Well-balanced. And settled. None of which she was. Could she live here? She didn't think so. She would always feel like a guest. "Oh, Alton, I don't know."

"What don't you know?" He cupped her face in his hands and kissed her.

The ringing woke them. Izz jumped up, dancing around, barking. They were curled up against each other on the floor under a soft woolen throw.

"Don't answer it," Wetzon murmured.

"It's not the phone. It's the intercom," he said, kissing her ear. He got up and went into the kitchen. "Yes?" He had the lean tight buns and the legs of a runner.

She closed her eyes. She wasn't going to die. At least not yet. "Tell whoever it is to go away," she said.

"Come back in half an hour." Alton snapped off the intercom.

Wetzon sat up. "Tell *who* to come back?" He was putting on his jeans, zipping his fly. "Alton!"

"Your friend Silvestri."

"Why didn't you tell him to go away?" She didn't even try to keep the wail out of her voice.

"He says you left the scene of a crime—"

The fire had subsided to embers. Wetzon shivered. "Alton, I'm sorry—"

"You'd better tell me what's going on." He sat down on the sofa, picked his shirt up from the floor and put it on.

Wetzon wrapped herself in the throw and sat down next to him. "A week ago Susan Orkin's lover, Dilla Crosby, was beaten to death just before the gypsy runthrough. She was the production stage manager on *Hotshot,* Carlos's show."

"What does this murder have to do with you?"

"I was there."

"Of course, you were." He took her hands in both of his, warming them. His eyes told her he loved her. She had never felt so secure.

"It wasn't just me. A group of us found her. I knew Susan at college, but I didn't know she was Susan Orkin until she called me. She told me she was afraid someone would kill her, too."

"And you said you'd help her."

"Oh, Alton, I was just going to keep my eyes and ears open in Boston. That's all. She was so frightened, but she wouldn't ask the police for help."

"So you agreed."

"Yes. Then Susan thought she could flush out the murderer by sending anonymous letters to the media saying that I was investigating the murder and that I had uncovered new information."

"I'm not liking what I'm hearing. How much more is there?"

"Sam Meidner was murdered in Boston yesterday."

"I saw the papers. I didn't know it had anything to do with you. Is there anything else?"

She nodded. There was a lump in her throat she couldn't seem to swallow. "Susan is dead. She fell down her service stairs trying to get away from a burglar. I found her. That's why I have Izz. I was scared and I ran away."

He put his arms around her, and she buried her face in his shirt, knowing that what was left of her makeup would smudge off on him. "I'll never let anything happen to you," Alton said. "Ever. You're very precious to me."

Izz sat up, ears alert. The doorbell rang. She leapt off the sofa, barking, and ran to the door.

"Dammit. It's not a half hour yet, is it?"

He shook his head, stood. Wetzon began to gather up her clothing scattered on the floor, when suddenly Alton swooped down on her, picked her up, and carried her into the bedroom. He set her on the bed. "Get dressed. I'll hold him off."

The doorbell rang again. Izz's barking grew shrill.

The silk paisley robe she'd given Alton for Christmas lay on the bed. She dropped the throw and put on Alton's robe. A suitcase was open on the bench at the foot of the bed, partially unpacked. Alton dug around in it looking for something, found it, and slipped it into the pocket of the robe, giving her hipbone a brief fondle.

"What's this?" Her hand found the pocket.

The doorbell rang again with an impatience that could only be Silvestri.

"Souvenir of Caracas." He left her, heading for the front door.

It was a tiny red silk purse with an envelope flap held by a snap. She opened the snap. A zipper closure, which she unzipped.

Silvestri's voice froze her. It rose over Alton's. Izz continued to bark. Wetzon reached into the little purse and pulled out a ring. Three flashy emeralds set deep in a yellow gold band. She slipped it on her ring finger and held it up.

But she wasn't really seeing it. She was seeing the other ring, the one with the big yellow diamond that Edna Terrace was wearing in Boston. The one that was strikingly similar to Dilla's missing ring. How could she have been so stupid? The ring was the MacGuffin.

Silvestri was leaning against the arched doorway between Alton's foyer and living room, glowering. The little dog was sniffing his Nikes and wagging her tail. The more he glowered, the more she wagged. Alton was building up the fire. His feet were bare.

So were Wetzon's. Alton's robe came to her ankles. She had washed the smeared makeup from her face and combed her hair. The ring remained on her finger.

Izz saw her first, ran to her, jumped at her with happy little leaps.

Straightening, Alton replaced the poker, his eyes on her face. "Shall I leave you two alone?"

"Yes," Silvestri said.

"No." Wetzon sat on the sofa, and Izz jumped on her lap. "This is strictly business. It is, isn't it, Silvestri?"

She felt he wanted to strangle her, could almost feel his hands on her throat. She didn't like the mixture of power and joy that suffused her. *Would the real Leslie Wetzon stand up?* What had become of her? She'd been replaced by this mean, manipulating bitch. Oh yes, one who had never had a real relationship with anyone. How could she ever condemn Smith?

"Leslie?" Alton was looking at her.

"It's okay, Alton. You can leave us. But only if you stop scowling at me, Silvestri, and sit down."

Alton made a point of touching her, her cheek, the top of her head, before he left the room. Like, *this is mine, Silvestri. Keep off the grass.*

Silvestri sank into one of the club chairs, and Izz promptly deserted

Wetzon for him. She'd adopted him, it seemed, and he looked nonplussed with the small dog in his lap.

"I know I shouldn't have left," she said, watching him try to escape Izz's wet kisses. "She's fallen for you, Silvestri." For a brief moment she saw in his eyes a terrible loneliness that shook her. Her eyes dropped to the ring. *What am I doing?*

"So that's how it is," he said.

"Yes." She thought: *Tell me you love me, Silvestri. Put up a fight for me. Tell me we can be together forever and I'll take the ring off.*

But he said, after a long pause, "Fair enough." He was massaging the back of the dog's ears and Izz was limp with love. "Fair enough," he repeated. "You left a crime scene."

"I had an anxiety attack. O'Melvany talked to me. I had to get out of there."

Silvestri took his notepad from his inside pocket and adjusted his shoulder holster. "Why don't you give me everything from the time you left for Boston till you found Susan Orkin's body." His manner was formal, his tone cold-to-neutral. She'd lost him.

She gave Silvestri a succinct account of her activity, leaving out Carlos's watch at Sam's murder scene and Mark's peculiar behavior. Neither did she mention Susan's date book. They would find it soon enough.

"This is what I know. Dilla may have been leaving Susan for Audrey Cassidy."

"Who's that?"

"The columnist. Audrey has a movie and theatre gossip column in the *Spectator.* I don't think Mort Hornberg killed Dilla because it looked like the same kind of M.O. and the murderer must have mistaken Sam for Mort."

"Maybe Hornberg wanted to get rid of Meidner, too."

"Mort's a bully and a coward. When he kills people he does it verbally. He's no murderer. He's more likely to be the one who gets murdered." She picked at a loose thread on the silken cuff. "He's been truly vicious to everyone, me included."

"Oh?" She'd managed to stir his interest again.

"Yes. He told me I was incapable of having a real relationship with anyone."

"Did he now?" He didn't look at her. "You came back for what reason?"

"You ordered me to come back—or have you forgotten?"

"Get off my case, Les."

Nausea hit her. She fought it. "Silvestri, I'm sorry. I didn't mean—"

"Yeah, sure, Les. Let's get on with this. It's getting late."

She felt her heart harden. "Mort asked me to bring Susan back to Boston tonight. She was doctoring the lyrics and with Sam gone, Mort wanted her there for touchups. And I had to come in anyway to help a broker move."

"Anything else you want to add?"

"Silvestri, did anyone find a small chamois bag with—" She paused, "—jewelry, diamonds, and stuff, a lot of it, in it at Susan's?"

"Not as far as I know, but they're still combing through everything. It could turn up. What about it?"

"I saw it last week. Izz kept bringing me things from another room while Susan was helping Dilla's family pack Dilla's things. Susan was upset that Izz had brought me the bag. She put it under the sink in the kitchen."

"I'll check it out." He set Izz on the floor and rose. "From here on, you'll be dealing with Bernstein."

Her cheeks burned as if he'd hit her. It took her a minute to recover. "The burglar may have been looking for the jewelry. I told you Susan was afraid of someone. She must have come out of the shower and surprised the thief, and then fallen down the stairs trying to get away." Wetzon picked up her coat and followed Silvestri to the door. His shoulders sagged and her palms itched to touch him.

"You think it was an accident?" He was looking down at her bare feet, and she knew he knew she was naked under the robe.

"Wasn't it?" She hung her coat up in the hall closet. "Did you have a coat?"

"No." He adjusted his jacket over the gun. "The M.E. says she didn't try to stop her fall. Which means she was either dead or unconscious before she hit the ground."

CHAPTER

Wetzon towel-dried her hair and ran a comb through it. Steam from the shower had fogged up the mirror. And worry about Mark had fogged up her brain. She wiped the steam from the glass with the corner of her towel.

The woman in the mirror was gaunt, her gray eyes huge. When the steam obscured her image, she didn't invite it back with the towel.

Instead, she went into the bedroom and pulled on the black wool leggings she kept with other clothes in one of Alton's dresser drawers, and one of his white T's. She topped it with his pale blue V-necked cashmere that, on her, came to mid-thigh. In the bathroom she opened the window to let the steam diffuse, hung up the towels, and finally got on the scale. Ninety-three pounds, and clothed, too. No wonder she felt so fragile. She'd dropped three pounds. Worry, stress, always did that to her.

Determined to eat her way back—a delicious thought—she began foraging for food. Alton's housekeeper had restocked the refrigerator so there was fresh orange juice. She poured herself a tall glassful. Sipping, she looked down at Eighty-first Street from the kitchen window.

The streetlights had little misty haloes and the Hayden Planetarium across the street was an enchanted fortress rising out of the mist. No one below carried an open umbrella, but the sidewalks looked wet. Alton had taken Izz out to get her a leash and dog food at the pet shop over on Amsterdam. Dinner would be Chinese takeout.

Back in the bedroom she made herself a nest on the carpet with the phone she'd plucked from the night table and her Filofax. Pen at the ready, she called her answering machine. The cluster of gems on her ring finger cued her that her life had taken an unexpected turn. She closed her eyes to it.

The first recorded message was a breather who panted into the phone, then hung up. Damn. Was she going to have to worry about whether it was a wrong number or directed at her? She waited for the second beep. More breathing. "Get a life, dammit," she muttered.

As she spoke the panting stopped, and a third message came on. "Wetzon, I'm sorry. I didn't mean it. Oh, God, I'm sorry." Mark disconnected in the middle of an hysterical sob.

Stunned, she listened to the rest of her messages through a jungle of conflicting emotions. Three hangups. Probably Silvestri looking for her until he figured out where she was.

Beep. "Hi, Wetzon. B.B. here. It's four o'clock and we've finished. He's a weird guy. See you Monday . . . um, and don't forget I want to talk to you privately."

Beep. "It is two o'clock Saturday afternoon. I can see you on Sunday at four, Leslie. No need to call back if this is okay." Sonya's warm empathy flooded the tape.

Beep. "Birdie!" Carlos sounded upset. "Mort just told me about Susan. Where the hell are you? Are you all right? I had a really strange message from Smitty. Listen, I don't want to talk to a tape. Leave a number where I can call you tonight after the reviews come in. . . . Whoever said this was fun?"

There were no other messages. Wetzon called the Ritz and left her name and Alton's phone number for Carlos.

Taking a fortifying swig of orange juice—it needed alcohol—she dialed Smith's home number. The phone rang again and again. No answer. Had Mark gone back to school? Or would he have gone to Boston? She hung up, rose, set the glass down on the dresser next to the photograph of Alton *en famille* in ski clothes on the slopes of Aspen. Holding on to the bedroom door, she did some stretches and releves.

She poured a dollop of vodka into the half-empty orange juice glass and topped it liberally with juice. Returning to her spot on the bedroom floor, she pointed the remote at the TV. The six o'clock news came on. The television reporter, a blond woman by the name of Mimi Tucker, was announcing Susan's death. Ms. Tucker, wearing a shiny red raincoat and matching red kissy-lips, stood in front of Susan's building. The camera swept the crowd, picking up the strikers, who waggled their signs as if on cue. Police moved about behind the reporter, including one man who had the words *Crime Scene Unit* on the back of his dark blue jacket.

"The nude body of poet Susan Orkin was found on the back stairwell of her Upper East Side cooperative apartment early this afternoon by superintendent Tony Novakovich and a friend of Ms. Orkin who became concerned when the poet did not keep a luncheon appointment. We'll have an exclusive interview with Mr. Novakovich later in the program."

The camera quickly panned the street and the police barricades, then came back to Mimi.

"Ms. Orkin's apartment had been ransacked and police have labeled her death as suspicious. Ms. Orkin was at one time married to prominent New York Congressman Gary Orkin. The marriage of five years ended in divorce. Police have asked anyone who may have information about Ms. Orkin's death to please contact them at this number . . ."

When Alton returned with a jubilant Izz, who came flying at her as if they'd been parted for weeks, Wetzon turned off the set. "I'm potted," she informed them. Izz now wore a red collar with little rhinestones. Wetzon looked up at Alton. "Alton, rhinestones? I can't believe you bought her a collar with rhinestones. Not you."

"Her name is Isabella, isn't it? They didn't have diamonds." He helped her up. "Come on. Dinner's getting cold." He led her into the kitchen, where he set out a feast of food. She was suddenly starving.

A lumpy, red plaid dog pillow lay under the window. On the floor near the sink was a white-and-blue bowl that said *dog,* and it was full of dried dog food. Izz was sniffing at it disdainfully.

"How did you know how much to give her?"

"You think I'm a novice at this?"

"You're not?" She refilled her orange juice and gave herself another splash of vodka.

"We always had dogs. Tessa even bred dachschunds for awhile."

Wetzon still got a funny quiver when Alton mentioned Tessa. He and Tessa had been high-school sweethearts and her death five years ago had devastated him. He'd retired prematurely, looking for something new to capture his imagination. The memoir he'd written of his years as a union organizer and national labor leader had been incredibly successful and was still in print. Wetzon had met him two years ago when he was serving on the board of Luwisher Brothers. Alton and Twoey's father had been friends.

"I always liked dachschunds, especially the wiry-haired ones." Wetzon looked down at Izz, who was circling the food. "Whatever am I going to do with a dog?"

"We'll manage." He was pouring hot-and-sour soup, thick with strips of bean curd and bamboo shoots, into bowls.

She held up her left hand and looked at the ring. "It's beautiful. Do you really think we'll be okay?"

"I know we will. Eat up. You seem awfully thin to me."

"So do you." He didn't respond, but he looked pleased. He'd been trying to get his weight down.

When they finished the soup, he set the bowls in the sink and began dividing up shrimp fried rice, moo shu pork, steamed dumplings and eggplant with garlic sauce. "What about your kids?" she asked.

He laughed, looking boyish. "They're hardly kids. They have their own lives now. This is my life." He laid out a pancake on his plate, spread it with hoisin sauce and the moo shu mixture, rolled it up and handed it to her.

"And my life."

"Ours."

"You take such good care of me." She made fast work of the roll, watched him make one for himself.

"It'll be good. You'll see. We'll travel—"

"What about my business?"

"I wouldn't want you to change anything, Leslie."

She touched his knee under the table with her bare foot and he caught it and held it. "You are a lovely man, Alton."

"Sandra's having a dinner party next month. Everyone will be there. We'll let them know then, shall we?"

"Okay." She felt as if she were on a train hurtling downhill toward—

"You don't look okay."

"It's not us. I'm worried about Mark, Smith's boy. Well, I guess he's not really a boy anymore. He's come out—said he's gay—and rechristened himself Smitty. And that's just the good part. He may be involved in these murders. . . ."

"How do you know he's gay?"

"He told me. He's not hiding it."

"Does Xenia know?"

She nodded.

"The poor kid."

"Smith thinks it's a virus. She's going to put him in therapy."

Alton smiled and shook his head. "A strange lady, your partner. What makes you think he's involved . . . in these murders?"

She sighed. "Take my word for it. By the way, Twoey is having a wonderful time."

"Twoey?"

"Oh, my God, Alton. You don't know. You were away when everything happened. Twoey's one of the producers of *Hotshot* now. Mort needed money and Twoey wanted to get his feet wet, so I brought them together. It's trial by fire, but he's enjoying it."

"He always wanted to be in the Theatre, to produce plays. He went to Wall Street because of his father. I could have gotten him into ATPAM years ago, but his father would not have been happy about it."

"ATPAM? The press agents and managers union?"

"Yes. I knew one of the top men there. We'd worked on some mediation panels with Ted Kheel."

Wetzon set her fork down. She was feeling whoozy. Had Alton just said he knew somebody at ATPAM? "Who was it you knew?"

"He's dead now. He died a couple of years before Tessa." Alton's eyes grew distant.

Wetzon waited. Patience was not one of her strong suites. Anyway, she knew the answer to her question. Alton's contact at ATPAM had been Lenny Kaufer.

"Tell me about Lenny Kaufer. He's all mixed up in this." They'd finished the moo shu and the dumplings and only a few green peppers which neither of them ate, remained on the plates. Izz was curled up under the table, her head on Wetzon's bare foot.

"Leslie, the man's been dead for at least eight years."

"Humor me." She wrinkled her nose at him, playing cute. That would never do.

But Alton said, "How can I resist you? Lenny and I were on a couple of mediation panels. I didn't know him socially."

"He was up to his ass in ice, I've been told."

"Ah, Leslie, you do have a way with words. What's ice?"

"Skimming, graft, bribes, theatre stuff. I vaguely remember reading in *Variety* that when the Shuberts automated their box offices, they announced an end to graft."

"I wouldn't know about that. Lenny was a nice enough guy. Played a mean game of poker."

"I'm certain Dilla's murder and everything that came after has something to do with him."

"He's been dead for years. How can it?"

"Alton, I saw a bag of jewelry—diamonds, gold, the real thing—the first time I went to see Susan. Izz kept bringing me presents while Susan was helping Dilla's family pack up her stuff. One of the things she brought me was a bag of jewelry. Lenny/Celia was embroidered on the inside lining. Susan was upset I'd seen it."

Alton frowned. "I seem to remember that Kaufer's wife was named Celia."

"Exactly. And several people described a gorgeous and somewhat unusual ring Dilla had been flashing around the week before she was murdered. Which, it seems, was not on her finger when they took her body away."

Alton cleared the plates from the table, scraped the peppers into the garbage and stacked the dishwasher. "Are you saying that someone killed Dilla Crosby for the ring?" He sounded doubtful.

"Seems crazy, doesn't it?" She rubbed her eyes. "It's just that when Phil Terrace introduced me to his mother in Boston, she was wearing a ring that looked just like the one they said Dilla had been wearing." Bemused, she held up her hand and admired Alton's gift.

"Slow down. Who is Phil Terrace?" Alton poured himself two fingers of Glenfiddich and leaned back against the sink.

She loved the smoky fumes of the single-malt scotch. There was something sensuous about it. "Phil Terrace is Lenny Kaufer's grandson. He was assistant stage manager on *Hotshot*. He took over as stage manager after Dilla was killed. Phil's mother is the treasurer at the Imperial Theatre, where the show is opening."

"Coincidence?"

"Maybe. Maybe. Dilla was Lenny Kaufer's mistress. He gave her a mink coat."

"Then he could have given his wife and his mistress the same jewelry. It's been known to happen."

Wetzon put her finger to her nose and looked at him cross-eyed. "Now why didn't I think of that. It's so logical."

"You would have eventually, but two heads are always better than one." He smiled down at her. His feeling for her was so intense, it upset her. She withdrew, not really aware she had done so until he snapped his fingers. "Hey, where did you go?"

"Oh. I was thinking that you're such a nurturer, and I love you for it. You make me feel cared for and protected. We don't *have* to get married."

He set his drink down and crouched beside her so they were eye to eye. "Leslie, I don't want you just for weekends. I want you every day for the rest of my life."

"Alton—" She touched his cheek and was afraid. Had Mort been right, then? Was she—

"Leslie, tell me what you're thinking."

"Mort Hornberg told me I was incapable of having a real relationship with anyone." Had she accepted Alton's ring to contradict Mort?

"That's ridiculous." He stood and pulled her to her feet, dislodging the dozing Izz. "And you believed him?"

"Thirty-nine years of living proof, Alton. I'm not able to commit to anyone."

"Until now." He said it firmly.

"Until now." She repeated it in a quavering voice. "Alton, do you think there's something wrong that we don't fight?"

"Fight? What do we have to fight about? Let's go to bed."

So there, Silvestri, she thought, but she got no further because the phone began to ring. "It's Carlos!" She spun away from Alton, racing for the bedroom. "Hello?" She sat down on the bed, then jumped up, sat down again.

"Magic time, Birdie!" He was shrieking; she had to hold the phone away from her ear. "Birdie, you would not have believed it! Everything, and I mean *everything,* worked. Listen to this from the *Globe:* 'The production team of Morton Hornberg, Carlos Prince, and the late Sam Meidner have reinvented the musical.' "

"Wow!"

"The tip of the iceberg, m'dear. From the *Herald* we have: 'What can be more American than the gun and what can be more American than the American musical theatre? In *Hotshot: The Musical* we have the felicitous marriage of the two.' "

"Oh, Carlos, I'm so happy for you."

"Wait, darling, it's not over. Try this on: 'This show's brilliance is stagger-ing; its humor, demented; its music and dancing, radiant; its cast, stellar. There's nothing to compare it to. It breaks its own ground and takes no prisoners.' "

She heard the rumble of voices in the background. "I couldn't be happier for you all. *Us* all. Who's there with you?"

Alton lay down beside her and she rumpled his hair and grinned at him, mouthing, *It's a smash.*

"Arthur, darling, and—wait—one more: 'Wit and wonderment took over the stage of the Colonial Theatre tonight.' So what do you think? Personally, I think I'm the second luckiest man in the world."

"The *second* luckiest? Okay, I bite. Who's the first?"

"Andrew Lloyd Webber, darling."

"Very funny. Tell the truth, were there no quibbles?"

"I was saving it. The best. 'One has to question the motivation for a show like this that goes all out to celebrate the symbol of violence in America.' Is that good enough for you? I think we can handle it."

"Well, after all, it is Boston. Carlos, is Twoey excited?"

"Beside himself."

"Twoey is beside himself, Alton."

"Wait a minute, Birdie. There's someone here who wants to talk to you." She heard muffled voices.

"I guess Twoey wants to talk, Alton."

"Hello? Wctzon?"

Good grief. "Mark! I've been so worried about you."

"Wetzon, I'm sorry. You've got to believe I didn't mean it."

Wetzon's excitement chilled. "Mark, what are you saying?"

"Just tell me you're okay." His voice broke.

"Listen to me, Mark. I'm okay. Were you up at Susan's this morning?" She looked at Alton. He held out his hand, and she switched the phone to her other ear and snuggled up next to him, inhaling his Glenfiddich aura.

"Leslie." The serious, cautious tones of Arthur Margolies, Esq., Carlos's lover, came across the wire.

"Arthur, thank God, a sensible person. What is this about? What's wrong with Mark?"

"Leslie, what Smitty—er, Mark—is trying to say is that he was at Susan Orkin's apartment when you got there and—"

"Oh, Arthur, no!" She buried her face against Alton's chest.

"I'm bringing him home with me tomorrow after we talk to the police here in Boston. He's trying to tell you he was sorry he hurt you. He was frightened and ran away."

"Hurt me? I don't understand."

"It was Mark who attacked you this morning at Susan's apartment."

C H A P T E R

"So what do you think?" Wetzon was hunched up on Sonya's couch. She had just finished describing the horrific alteration in her dream pattern.

Sonya studied her gravely. "I think you've lost too much weight."

"I know." She gave Sonya a wan smile. "Think of the fun I'll have eating my way back. I'm really worried about Mark—"

"Mark Smith has a mother and he has friends. You throw yourself into other people's problems as a substitution for dealing with your own."

"What problems?"

"Oh, Leslie."

Wetzon bit her lip. "Mort Hornberg told me I was incapable of having a real relationship with anyone. Do you think that's true?"

"Why are you taking what he said as gospel?"

"Maybe because I have this gut feeling he hit on the truth about me."

"If you can't make a commitment to yourself, how can you commit to a relationship?"

Wetzon turned the emerald ring on her finger around and around. "Alton is a wonderful man. He'll take care of me. I'll never have to worry about anything."

"Is that what you want?"

"Sometimes I get so tired of coping."

"Are you angry with your parents for dying?"

"No, of course not," Wetzon snapped. "It was an accident. It wouldn't be reasonable to blame them, would it?" She watched her hands tremble. Stop it, she ordered.

"Reason has nothing to do with it. The child Leslie was abandoned."

"I wasn't a child."

"You were child of your mother, child of your father. It's okay to be angry."

"I'm not angry. Why do you keep harping on that?"

"Leslie, why do you suppose your subconscious linked your own brush with death from the explosion of a gun and the car crash that killed your parents? It's time to heal the past and move on. Look at it, and then let it go, Leslie. Old wounds fester if you don't deal with them."

Wetzon stared at Sonya and felt the first tears sting her eyes. She grabbed a handful of yellow tissues from the box on the coffee table. "They left me alone and I was so . . ."

"I know. It's all right to be scared. Soothe the child. Tell her it will be okay, that you love her."

Wetzon sobbed into the tissues, unable to speak. Sonya left the room and returned with a glass of water, which she handed Wetzon. Gradually, the sobs subsided. Wetzon felt drained but strangely at peace. The release was a narcotic.

Sonya smiled at her. "Let it out, Leslie, this is just the beginning. Next Thursday? Six o'clock?"

Nodding, Wetzon took out her Filofax and wrote down the appointment. "Thanks, Sonya." She put on her coat and beret.

"While you have your book out, do you have some time for me on the afternoon of April first? It's a Thursday."

Wetzon flipped over the pages. "April first?" The page was blank. "I'm okay. What time?"

"Save me the afternoon." She was very solemn.

"The afternoon? The whole afternoon?"

"Yes. I'll tell you more about it closer to the date."

"Okay." She wrote *HOLD—Sonya* in the April first rectangle and dropped her Filofax into her purse. At the door she said more to herself than to Sonya, "I've got Susan's dog. I haven't had a dog since I was a kid."

"You don't have to keep it," Sonya said.

"Oh, but I do," Wetzon said slowly. "I think I need her as much as she needs me."

"Unconditional love."

Unconditional love. Wetzon turned the words over in her head as she walked back to the Beresford. The weather system had shifted again, and a wall of arctic air had invaded the city from Canada. The chill felt good. She was intensely aware of herself, every muscle, vein, and nerve end, her heart-beat, the breath going through her lungs.

The sharp change in temperature had caught most people in their rain-coats, but not Wetzon. Above her, navy-edged clouds driven by gusts of cold wind scudded across the darkening sky.

She crossed over to Amsterdam on Seventy-ninth Street and walked east. Carlos was okay. She didn't have to worry about him. And she, Leslie Wetzon, headhunter extraordinaire, and sometime detective, would marry Alton Pinkus, the perfect man, and live happily ever after. Of course she would.

And what about Mark, she asked herself as she put her key into the lock. Izz was barking her little head off on the other side of the door. Mark couldn't have murdered anyone. And that was that. Any evidence that he did had to be circumstantial.

"I'm in the kitchen," Alton called.

She hung up her coat, dropped her hat and bag on the hall table. In the kitchen she gave him a kiss on the cheek.

She sniffed. "Smells great, whatever it is."

"Steamed mussels; pasta with tomato, basil, and fennel sausage; Eli's sourdough; and Greenberg's brownies. I'm going to enjoy fattening you up."

A tiny buzz started in her brain. Was he trying to take over her life? "I'm okay the way I am."

She saw him assessing the damage and assessed it with him.

"Leslie—"

"No, it's okay. My fault."

"Tough session?"

"Tough enough." Did he want her to tell him about it? How could she say that she still hadn't come to terms with her parents' fiery death after so many years? That she felt she would always be abandoned by anyone she loved? That was it, wasn't it? And then all at once she was telling him and he was holding her against him, stroking her hair.

"I will never, ever, leave you. You know that, don't you?"

She knew that, but he was almost twenty years older than she was. It was inevitable that he would abandon her. She pushed the thought away, but it was still with her, lurking, as she and Izz walked back to her apartment that evening, over Alton's objections.

He'd said, "I'd feel better if you stayed here."

And she'd answered, "Not yet. Besides, Izz should get used to my place."

The union pickets had called it a day at sundown, obviously, because they weren't around. No one was on guard duty inside and the outside door was locked. She took her keys out and let herself in. Next to the elevator was a notice that no packages would be accepted for delivery until the strike was over.

Well, fine. She wasn't expecting any.

While she was taking her mail out of the box and collecting the Sunday *Times,* left during the strike in a tall stack in the lobby with everyone else's, someone rang the outside bell. Izz ran for the door territorially, barking.

"Izz, you are such a yenta." Wetzon looked around the corner. A tall man in a buttoned-up rawhide coat stood there, motioning for her to let him in. She'd never seen him before. Shaking her head at him, she got on the elevator. She heard him banging on the iron grillwork over the door but paid no attention. She was not about to be a statistic.

Her home was an oasis. When she entered it and closed the door, she could block the world out. Here she was truly safe.

She changed into her terry robe, while Izz inspected the apartment. "I'm thirsty," she told the dog, "how about you?" She filled a bowl with water and set it on the floor, wondering if she was going to be one of those old ladies who talk to their pets. Taking a beer from the fridge, she poured it into a glass, watching the head rise, pouring more.

The mail was mostly junk. A preferred customer sale notice from Saks. Two banks were trying to sell her Visa cards, offering outrageous credit lines. And a notice that a package was being held for her at the post office. Now what could that be?

The phone rang. She stared at it, listening to Izz's little nails clicking on her hardwood floors as the dog roamed the apartment. *Oh, hell.* She heaved herself up and grabbed the phone on the fifth ring. Too late. "Hi, hold on," Wetzon said. "The message has to run through." Damn. Her answering machine was blinking eight, counting this one, messages.

"Leslie." Alton sounded relieved.

"I'm okay, Alton." Don't hover, she thought.

"A Detective Bernstein just called. He's looking for you. He'd like you to call him."

"I haven't checked my messages yet." She wrote down Bernstein's number as Alton gave it to her. "I'll call him."

But she didn't. She took a shower, sipping her beer while the hot water massaged her body. Her head was pounding.

Sometime later when she was laying her clothes out for the morning, she saw that she'd gotten another call; now there were nine messages. *To hell with all of them.*

She got into bed next to Izz, who, being a dog of superior intelligence, had taken stock of her new home and chosen where she would sleep. The paper on which Wetzon had written Bernstein's phone number crackled in the pocket of her robe. She pulled it out. A 718 area code, which meant Bronx, Queens, or Brooklyn. She guessed Brooklyn, where there were many communities of Orthodox Jews.

Bernstein answered on the first ring. His voice was neutral.

"Leslie Wetzon. I hear you're looking for me."

"Yeah." Bernstein cleared his throat. "O'Melvany filled me in on the Orkin murder. And I've talked with your boyfriend."

"My boyfriend?" It was odd to hear Alton called her *boyfriend.*

"Yeah—I mean—ex." He gave what seemed a little embarrassed laugh. "We got a profile to work with now. Looks like both murders were probably done by the same perp."

"What about Sam Meidner?" *Silvestri, you're my ex now.*

"We don't have enough information about that one yet."

"Can you tell me the profile?"

"The murderer battered their faces in and inflicted little damage elsewhere. None of the victims were sexually assaulted or mutilated, but the murderer knew them and they knew the murderer. Each killing was personal."

She thought: *I don't need a criminal profile to tell me that.*

"The murderer is a young white male, probably in his twenties, who's been deprived of a strong father figure."

Her heart sank. Izz opened her jet eyes and stared at her. "Anything else?" Wetzon said it with as much enthusiasm as she could muster.

"Yeah. We figure the killer's real confused about his sexual orientation."

C H A P T E R

"So listen to this, Wetzon." Gordon Prell was steaming across the phone wires at her. She shifted the phone to her shoulder and flipped through her messages. There was no sign of Smith, and there'd been no answer at her apartment last night.

Wetzon had not been able to bring herself to listen to her messages. Not last night, not this morning. All she could think about was that Silvestri's profile of the murderer fit Mark to a tee. And Silvestri had to know it.

"Are you listening, Wetzon?"

"Yes, Gordon." She mouthed thanks to Max who'd just handed her Gordon Prell's suspect sheet. Gross production in 1992: eight hundred thou. Nice.

"I'm getting zero'd on the deals here. That's not what they promised when I came over."

"You're not getting anything at all?" She found that hard to believe.

"Well, I'm getting some, but not what I used to get. So I says to Beverly—she's Alan's assistant—how come I'm not getting a piece of this, and she says no deals are coming down this week and she has no allocation, and I happen to know for a fact that's not true."

"How do you know?" She looked at Susan's photograph on the lower left of the front page of the *Times* and felt her heart catch in her throat. The headline said:

MYSTERIOUS FALL KILLS POET

Trust the *Times* to be conservative.

"Because that putz Ray flaunted it at me. Well, maybe he didn't, but his girl told my girl."

Nice going, Gordon, she thought. Make the *girl* headhunter feel good. She considered hanging up, but instead switched ears and opened the newspaper to the rest of Susan's obit. What a whore you are, Wetzon, she told herself. "Gordon, talk to Alan."

"You haven't heard the rest of it. I've got this gorgeous ashtray on my desk from the Petrified Forest, and when I told Ray he's nothing but a dickhead, he peed in my ashtray."

"He what?"

"You heard me, Wetzon. So I went into Alan's office and let him have it, and you know what Alan said?"

"I can hardly wait to hear. . . ."

"He has the nerve to say to me, 'Well, Ray is number two in the office. He can pee in your ashtray. When you get to be number two, you can pee in his."

Wetzon clapped her hand over her mouth to cover her laugh, then pulled herself together. "Gee Gordon, that's awful. So I suppose you want to talk to a couple of other firms."

"No, I don't. Management at all these firms are nothing but flaming assholes. Why should I trade one asshole for another? Not on your life. *I'm* going to be number two." He hung up in her ear.

"Oh, God," she said aloud. "Only a masochist would put up with this." She was weary to the bone, having slept in fits and starts all night. But no dreams, good or otherwise. At six Izz had awakened her and Wetzon had stuck her bare feet into her boots and thrown her fur coat over her flannel nightshirt, stuffing her pockets with paper towels and a plastic bag. Then she and Izz stood in the gutter in front of the building shivering, looking at one another, until Izz finally began to circle.

A door slammed and Wetzon started. She'd dozed off. It was ten o'clock, and here was Smith coming through the door wrapped in mink, charcoal smudges under her eyes. Wetzon didn't have the heart to tease her. Smith looked whipped.

Throwing herself into her chair, Smith said morosely, "We're going to make a lot of money." She slipped out of her coat. "It's really cold. I'm glad I didn't give my mink away in a mad impetuous gesture." Silently, she dared Wetzon to say something. "You don't look any better than I do."

"The years are just dancing away with us."

"Oh, please." But Smith smiled a minuscule smile.

"How's Mark?"

Smith bowed her head. "He's insisting we call him Smitty."

"Fine with me. How's Smitty?"

"That Arthur Margolies person is very nice, and Ma—*Smitty* can't seem to warm up to Dickie, God only knows why."

"God and Wetzon."

Smith gave her a searing look. "Please, no jokes. I can't handle it. This is all extremely traumatic for me. Can you believe the police suspect my baby . . ." She stopped and called out, "Coffee, Max sweetie. Please hurry." Staring at Wetzon, she said, "Where was I? Oh, I can't even say it, it's so awful. If it weren't for Dickie, I would have had a breakdown."

Max opened the door and handed each a fragrant mug of coffee. "There, there, dear." He gave Smith a sympathetic pat on the shoulder and left.

"It's so ridiculous. He seems so angry with me," Smith said. "What have I done? Oh, my God." She began to cry.

Wetzon rushed to her and held her. "It'll be okay. You'll see. Our Smitty is not a murderer."

Smith sniffled. "Since you got us into this, we're going to have to put our minds to finding the real one."

"Excuse me? *I* got us into this?"

"And the cards are so confusing. I can't read what they're saying. Wands and swords. Wands?"

"Wait a minute. By wand, do you mean a stick?"

"Maybe."

Wetzon thought: *The murder weapon. Fran Burke's cane.*

"What am I ever going to do? I don't know how I'll live through this. . . ."

"Smith, any evidence they have is circumstantial, and he's come forward of his own volition and talked to the police in Boston and here."

"That's true." She dried her eyes and blew her nose.

"A lot of people had motive and opportunity, not just Smitty."

"Yes, yes, you're right. I know my baby didn't do it." She pulled her mirror from a drawer and looked at herself, frowning. "But he's changed so, I hardly know him. How can he be one of those . . ." Searching the pockets of her mink, she found what she was looking for—her Vuarnets—and put on the dark glasses. "He's going into therapy, starting today. Maybe it's a vitamin deficiency."

"Smith, please, being gay is not a disease."

"We'll see."

"Is he going back to school?"

"Not yet. I don't think it matters anymore. He's had early admission at Harvard. All he has to do is take his finals in May. I'd like to keep him with me until he goes to college. A lot of things can happen in six months." She took off her dark glasses and stared in the mirror again. "I look like Dracula's mother." Her eyes settled on Wetzon's left hand, didn't register, then did. "What's that?" she shrieked. "Why didn't you tell me? Let me see."

Wetzon held her hand out to Smith. "I guess I said yes."

"Oh, for pitysakes. You *guess?* Show a little excitement." She held Wetzon's fingers on her palm and studied the ring. All she needed was a jeweler's glass to check the stone.

"Whoopie." Wetzon twirled her finger in the air.

A knock sounded on the door.

"Come," Smith commanded.

The door swung open and Max blinked at them. "The market is up forty-five in heavy trading. No one wants to talk."

"Keep trying, dear Max. Someone will," Smith said. "Close the door behind you." She smiled at him.

"How about lunch?"

"You know you'll have to supervise them better. Can you imagine? No one wants to talk." Smith caught Max's inflection exactly. "Lunch? Oh, sweetie pie, I can't today. I'm getting a manicure, pedicure, and a facial. Then Enzo is going to trim me." She ran a hand through her curls. "In fact—" she looked at her watch, "I'd better get moving." Standing, she got back into her coat. "Anything I should know about?"

"You might check your messages."

"Oh." She fanned through the pink slips and dropped them in her waste-basket. "Nothing." She grinned at Wetzon.

"Very funny. Kidder is supposed to be on the block again and Sandy Weill is eyeing it, and there's a rumor that Lehman is going to be a leveraged buy-out."

"Tell me something new. Sandy Weill is a bottom feeder. He's not going to pay top dollar for Kidder and GE is not going to sell Kidder at a bargain price. It's all about testosterone."

"Thank you, Louis Rukeyser."

But Smith was already out the door.

Wetzon spent the rest of the morning touching base with her regulars, listening for any signs of "the itch," as she called it. But the trading was hot and the only itchy-sounding broker asked her to call him next week. What to do? She read through Susan's obit again.

Hungry, she opened the door and remembered she had promised B.B. some time. She'd take him to lunch. "B.B., come on and get a bite to eat with me. Max can hold the fort, can't you, Max?"

Max nodded. Into the phone he said, "Tell me, Joe, what is your product mix? Uh huh. And your assets under management? Well, that's very good."

The phone rang, and B.B. grabbed it as they were putting on their coats. "Smith and Wetzon. Hold on. I'll see if I can catch her." He pressed down his hold button.

"Who is it?"

"Detective O'Melvany."

"I'd better take it." She went back to her desk, picked up the phone. "Leslie Wetzon."

"Ed O'Melvany, Leslie. We have some crime scene photos of Susan Orkin's place. Can you come have a look at them? You might pick up something we didn't."

Well, if that wasn't flattering . . . "How about three-thirty this afternoon?"

"Deal. We're on Sixty-seventh Street, between Lex and Third. Ask for me."

Wetzon and B.B. walked up to La Cucina in the Pan Am Building, where you could get a fairly decent sandwich on a French roll and salad already made up, packaged in plastic. The Pan Am Building was now the Met Life Building, but it would take a generation—at least—for New Yorkers to adapt to the name change.

A cold wind had blown away the rain clouds and cool northern sunlight bathed the city. The president was speaking at a U.J.A. luncheon and police had erected barricades along Forty-sixth Street and up Park Avenue to the Waldorf. The streets were teeming with cops, especially around the hotel.

"So what's up, B.B.?" Traffic was sparce because lurid warnings of gridlock had been broadcast on the media. "The tuna niçoise is very good."

B.B. was silent as they chose their sandwiches and helped themselves to coffee. Wetzon paid the cashier and they sat down at one of the tables. He hung up his navy duffle and dug into his salad and sandwich as if he hadn't eaten in a week. Working on her own sandwich, she knew he would tell her soon enough what was on his mind, but she wasn't so sure she was going to like it. It was as if he had something to confess. Of course, he was going to tell her he was the murderer. Didn't he fit the profile? Didn't half of America?

Finally, B.B. looked directly at her, then blurted out: "I'm leaving."

C H A P T E R

58

Wetzon sighed. "When?" Good thing he was telling her and not Smith. Smith would have torn him limb from limb.

"In the spring. The end of April."

"Why?" She'd lost her appetite. The thought of training someone new was anathema to her right now.

"Wendy and I are getting married."

"B.B., you're so young." Why did this young kid have no problem making a commitment?

"I'm twenty-five now, Wetzon," B.B. said, as if twenty-five were ancient. "Wendy's father and grandfather are vintners. We're moving to Oregon, and I'm going into the family business."

He was so earnest and ingenuous. "Well," she said, "that's wonderful. We'll be sorry to lose you."

"Wetzon, I hope you're not mad at me." There was nothing left of his lunch but a curly carrot strip and some bread crumbs lying soggy in salad dressing.

"I'm not. You have to move on with your life."

"Smith will be mad—"

"I'll take care of Smith." She patted his hand. "Go on back to the office. We can talk more about it tomorrow."

She drank her coffee and watched B.B. gather up his empty containers and throw them away. He was a clean-cut, decent young man, and he was passing out of their lives. Oh, yes, Smith would be furious. They had been months finding Max after hiring people who either didn't show up, didn't last, or couldn't handle either Smith or telephone sales technique. Or both. Training someone new always cut into earnings because of the time and supervision it took. That responsibility would fall on Wetzon. One more problem.

Onward and upward, she thought, rising. She tossed her plastic container and coffee cup into the trash basket and walked through Grand Central Station to the Lexington Avenue subway. The lunch crowd mixed with travelers who came in via train from Westchester and Connecticut. Fast-food shops emitted pizza, popcorn, and hotdog odors, and the sun was a radiant stream through the glorious skylight way above.

She got on the Lexington local and sat, her thoughts roiling. Moments later, a derelict in jaggedly torn jeans—the real thing—and a filthy nylon jacket sat down next to her. Grime had settled into his pores unchallenged. He was munching M&M's from a cellophane bag one at a time. She shrank away, thinking she ought to get up.

"Want some?" He thrust the package at her, smiling, showing a double-toothed gap.

"Huh?"

His foxy eyes stared at her.

"No, thank you." She rose and moved away from him, but he kept grinning at her and holding out the bag. Why did she feel so guilty about hurting his feelings? Flushing, she looked out at the dark tunnel with its flashing red lights. She had lost her sense of humor.

She got off at the Sixty-eighth Street stop, near Hunter College and the massive, redbrick Seventh Armory, home, the sign said, of the Second Brigade, 42nd Infantry Division. The Nineteenth Precinct was on a mostly residential block. The building, one of the old stone precinct houses that can still be found here and there around the city, had been recently cleaned and renovated. The renovation was obviously done in 1991, for just under each hanging lamp on either side of the door was a plaque, 1887 on the left, and 1991 on the right.

She climbed the outer stairs wondering at the baby blue painted window and door trim. All that was missing were the quaint window boxes overflowing with pansies.

Inside, the building was colder than it was on the street. A woman with clipped white hair and a wide, makeup-free face was sitting huddled in a blue overcoat at a metal desk, a large sign-in book open in front of her. To her right was a red-and-white Coke container with a straw coming through its cover. The sign on her desk said: *All visitors must sign in.*

"I have an appointment with Detective O'Melvany."

"Name?"

"Leslie Wetzon."

"Sign in. Down there. Turn right. Use the stairs. Elevator doesn't work. Detectives are on two." She was a woman of few words.

Two husky young men in sweats, carrying duffel bags, were coming down the stairs. They gave her the once-over, and she smiled. It gave her a lift, and hell, she had to admit she had a thing for cops.

The squadroom looked the same as any squadroom. Detectives at desks, on phones, standing around drinking coffee, working on reports. On the walls were cluttered bulletin boards and cardboard notices. An elderly couple, clinging to one another, were being comforted by a woman detective. The same battered old typewriters were scattered about the room. What, no computers?

O'Melvany met her halfway and brought her into his office. He was very friendly, took her coat, got her seated in one of the metal chairs with the fake leather seats, and offered her a Diet Coke, which she refused. A stack of folders and a cassette machine were on his desk. Behind the desk was a large bulletin board. A map of the precinct was pinned on it. He said, "I'd offer you coffee, but it's really poisonous."

She shook her head. "Was Susan murdered?"

O'Melvany turned the machine on and emptied the butt-filled ashtray into a wastebasket before replying. "Looks that way," he told her. "She didn't try to stop the fall. No bruises on her hands. She was dead or unconscious when she went down those stairs. Her head looked like the Crosby woman. He hit her square in front."

"He?"

"Generally speaking."

"Still no murder weapon?"

"A pipe maybe."

"Or a cane?"

"Maybe."

"Death by blunt instrument unknown." Wetzon closed her eyes and pressed her hand over her mouth. *I can't stand this,* she thought.

"You okay?"

She nodded.

"You don't look it." When she opened her eyes, he was standing over her, oddly concerned, as if he knew her better than he did. It was confusing.

"I am," she assured him. "Let's get on with it."

"Are you up to giving us a statement?" He sat down on the edge of his desk, one big foot on the floor.

"Isn't that why I'm here?"

"Okay, walk me through."

"Susan and I were supposed to have lunch Saturday, but . . . she was afraid of someone. She has been since Dilla was killed. Susan thought she was going to be next."

"Why would she think that?"

"She wouldn't tell me. I think she knew, though. She said someone was stalking her, that someone had tried to break into her apartment. When she didn't show up, I called the apartment and got a busy signal. I thought she was at home so I went on over."

"How did you get in?"

"I met her housekeeper, Rhoda, downstairs with Izz, Susan's dog. The dog recognized me, so I offered to take her up with me while Rhoda did the marketing."

"Was the door to the apartment closed?"

"It was locked. Izz had the house key hidden in her collar. I knew that from my first visit."

This piece of information didn't seem to surprise him. "So you unlocked the door. Then what?"

"I don't remember. I woke up wrapped in a quilt with the dog licking my hand and the super standing over me. I have a bump on my head, here." She touched her forehead. "So I guess I either got hit or fell." *Smitty, oh, Smitty.*

"What did you do when you came to?"

"The super and I looked around. The place was ransacked and trashed. We found Susan on the landing. That's it."

"Who is Smitty?"

Had he read her mind? She gave him a hard look. "Are you trying to trip me up?"

O'Melvany grinned and rubbed his mustache. "Just checking. We found Ms. Orkin's date book and his name was in it. We know Smitty is Mark Smith."

"Mark Smith did not kill Susan."

"His fingerprints were on the service door."

"Oh, God. Eddie . . . Detective O'Melvany—"

"Eddie is fine."

"Eddie, this has nothing to do with Smitty, believe me. Who was the woman Susan had to call the police to get rid of Friday night?"

"Let's have a look at the pictures first." He reached behind him and picked up the folder.

"Do I have to look at Susan?"

"If you can." He handed her the folder.

She clenched her jaw and skimmed through the photos of the murder scene. It was far worse than she remembered. The tuna niçoise lay like mortar in her stomach. She moved on to the photos of the apartment, slipping one behind the other as she went along. Wait a minute. She pulled the last one back. "What's this?" She handed it to O'Melvany.

He glanced at the photo. "The garbage pail outside Ms. Orkin's door."

"Look at this." She pointed to something near the empty pail. "It looks like a headband."

"It is. Must have been Ms. Orkin's."

"A headband. Susan didn't wear a headband. Besides, she'd just come out of the shower." Wetzon stared at the photo. A headband. Who wore a headband that she knew? Someone did. Sunny? "The woman who came to see her Friday night. Who was it?"

O'Melvany put the photographs back in the folder, all except the last one. "Someone by the name of Edna Terrace."

C H A P T E R

The guard on the door at the post office told her it was just six o'clock, which meant she was too late; the post office was closed. Damnation! She'd have to pick up the package tomorrow morning before work. Wetzon stood for a moment in front of the building, thinking. Across the street three men argued in Spanish over the domino game they'd set up on a folding table on the sidewalk. Didn't Phil Terrace also fit the police profile? Maybe he and his mother were a murderous duo? Ma Terrace and son.

She walked over to Broadway. Zabar's now had refrigerated cases offering scores of small containers of prepared foods . . . just right for singles. She wandered around the store; with no appetite, nothing was tempting. The cheese counter was approachable, though. She took a number. Forty-nine. The counter above the shelves said thirty-eight. Did she want cheese? Maybe a chunk of Rocquefort, some niçoise olives and a semolina bread.

"Leslie!"

Startled, she dropped the slip with her cheese number. "Arthur! When did you get back?" Arthur Margolies, Carlos's lover, dapper in his blue pinstripe suit and Burberry raincoat, gave her a peck on both cheeks. He was carrying a wire basket full of coffee, brie, boxes of pasta, a bottle of extra virgin olive oil.

"Last night." He looked exhausted and had pouches under his eyes to prove it.

"How bad is it for Mark?" Wetzon demanded without preamble.

He looked around. "Bad. Do you want to get a bite of dinner? Poiret?"

"Why not?" Suddenly she didn't feel much like being alone. She waited while he paid for his purchases. It struck her that Arthur to Carlos was a lot like Alton to Wetzon. Someone steady and reliable.

When they were settled in at a corner table at the restaurant, Wetzon said, "The police asked me to look at photos of the murder scene this afternoon." She looked up at the waiter. "I'll have the green salad and the roast chicken, well done. And a glass of dry red."

"Make that two," Arthur said. "But with a glass of chardonnay here." After the waiter left, he asked, "For what purpose?"

"To see if I could spot something they didn't. You know, what's-wrong-with-this-picture. And I did." A busboy arrived with baguettes and butter. Wetzon broke off pieces of the roll and slathered them with butter.

"Oh?"

"Yes." She held up her hand, chewing, swallowing. "A headband that I'm sure did not belong to either Susan or Dilla."

"Who then?" Arthur's eyes found her ring. "Something new?"

"Phil Terrace's mother wears a headband and Susan had to call the police Saturday night to get her out of the apartment." She rolled the ring around her finger. "And yes, this is new. It's from Alton."

Arthur had such empathetic eyes, was such a kind man, that Wetzon was sure he could see right into her soul. "This is serious, then?"

She nodded. "Am I making the right decision, Arthur?"

"Only you know that, Leslie."

Their drinks arrived and neither spoke again until the waiter had left.

"I feel . . . I don't know . . . trapped? I keep thinking I'll be forty on my next birthday and shouldn't I stop playing . . . ?"

Arthur smiled and raised his wineglass to her.

"Go ahead and smile, Arthur. Carlos would have hooted. I feel as if I'm supposed to settle down with a solid citizen." She touched glasses with him.

"Alton Pinkus is very much that."

"Oh, what the hell." Grinning at him, she took a swallow. "I'll be a little married. Like everybody else." She waited for the familiar tingle of the alcohol in her bloodstream. It was taking its own sweet time. "Arthur, what about the Panthere? Did Carlos tell you?"

"That Walter Greenow found his watch in Sam Meidner's hand and slipped it to you. Carlos had given it to Smitty for a new battery."

"Yes. How did Smitty explain that?" Their salads arrived, a mound of mixed greens with thin slices of tomato. The waiter ground fresh pepper over the mounds.

"Smitty said he'd had the battery put in, which was true, and somehow lost the watch in the theatre."

They sat in companionable silence for a few minutes, picking at their salads. "Arthur, is it possible that Sam swiped the watch from Smitty?"

"Why would he do that?"

"Sam's had a klepto problem for years. Carlos knows about it. Ask him. Sam could have appropriated the watch . . ."

"Could be. Sam Meidner was attacked from behind. The two women got it in the face."

"What does that mean?"

"I don't know. Maybe that we have two murderers."

"Oh, God." She stopped while the waiter cleared their salad plates and served the chicken, a small, crisply roasted bird surrounded by tiny vegetables. "Arthur, Smitty didn't do it. It's all circumstantial, right?"

He avoided her eyes. "Eat up, Leslie," he said.

"Oh, Arthur." A chill ran through her. "But Susan was afraid of someone. She said someone had tried to break into the apartment after Dilla was murdered. She wouldn't have been afraid of Smitty."

"Let me tell you about the show." Arthur patted her hand. "Our Carlos has exceeded himself. The numbers are a joy, truly unique. I think he's well on his way to directing on his own now." There was immense pride and love emanating from him as he spoke about Carlos. Carlos was so lucky to have him.

"He always said he was happy as a clam as a choreographer without the responsibility of pulling a whole show together on his own."

"Well, we all grow up, don't we?"

"I guess we do. Some of us kicking and screaming all the way. Arthur, may I talk to you as my lawyer?"

"Of course."

"A year ago, after Brian Middleton was murdered, I found some brokerage statements that indicated Richard Hartmann was laundering money. Brian had been Hartmann's FC—financial consultant. Isn't it a crock? The firms think *stockbroker* sounds crass so they change the name to *financial consultant* to change public perception."

Arthur set his fork down and took a sip of wine. "Go on."

"I warned Smith not to get involved with Hartmann, but she didn't listen to me—she never does—and she told him—"

"About the statements?" His calm demeanor was shaken.

She nodded. "Hartmann threatened me—"

"Oh, Leslie—"

"Smith is fragile—Don't look at me like that, Arthur. Take my word for it, she is. She was into a major affair with Hartmann. I thought if I told the authorities, she would go to pieces. And I have to admit, he frightened me."

"You should be frightened. He's no one to play cat-and-mouse with. What did you do with the material?"

"It's in my safe deposit box in an envelope with a letter detailing what I found. I marked the envelope: to be delivered to the attorney general in the event of my death." A tiny bell went off in her head. *Safe deposit box.*

". . . for me to deal with."

"I'm sorry, Arthur, I lost you. Are you saying you'll help me?" Hadn't Poppy Hornberg said something about a safe deposit box?

"Yes. Leslie, I want you to get that envelope to me as soon as possible."

"There's an A.D.A. I met who prosecuted the Middleton case. Her name is Marissa Peiser. She's really terrific. Maybe you can get it to her."

"He's a dangerous man." He didn't have to tell her whom he was talking about.

"I know. He threatened me again last week in Boston." The waiter was hovering. "Just decaf please, black."

"Regular," Arthur said.

"I'm getting my life in order, and I don't want this hanging over me anymore."

"I can send a messenger for it tomorrow."

"To the office. I'll stop at the bank on my way in."

When they came out of the restaurant, the night was a gemstone. Clear, cool, dry. The sky was a deep midnight blue cavern. Lights from the restaurants and buildings up and down Columbus gave the street a bustling, open-twenty-four-hours look. A riot of jungle sounds complete with chirping erupted from a small white van parked too close to the corner. Some new kind of car alarm.

Down the block in front of Wetzon's building the rolling lights of a police car were flashing red and white.

"Arthur, what do you suppose—?" She hurried forward.

The police car was double-parked in front of the building. No one was in it. She fumbled with her key until Arthur took it from her shaking fingers. Inside the lobby, nothing seemed out of the ordinary. No tenant on guard duty sat at the reception table. Wetzon pressed the elevator button.

Two uniformed cops, a man and a woman, stepped out of the elevator.

"Officers, what is the problem?" Arthur asked.

"You live here?" the woman asked.

"No, Ms. Wetzon does."

The man took out his pad and looked at it. "You're Miss Leslie Wetzon? Twelve-D?"

"Yes."

"Looks like someone attempted to gain entrance to your apartment."

It was true, and not a little terrifying: Twelve-B's housekeeper had opened the back door to put out the trash and surprised a person in a ski mask trying to jimmy open Wetzon's door. The resourceful woman had slammed her door and called 911.

Wetzon found Izz trembling under the bed. Except for a deep gouge in her door and some scratches in the paint around the lock plates, there was nothing else to indicate the break-in. But the fact was, someone had used a crowbar between the door and the jamb.

In the kitchen, Izz's bowl of water was upended, and the floor was dotted with clumps of dried food, now more like soggy Cheerios. "You're as bad as Smith," she told the dog, wiping up the bits of food with a paper towel. Izz couldn't care less. Her tail up, she was enthralled with Arthur, sniffing his shoes, the cuffs of his trousers.

"You can't stay here alone." Arthur bent and patted Izz on the head absentmindedly. "I didn't know you had a dog."

"She was Susan's." Wetzon scooped up a squirming Izz. "And I'll be fine, Arthur. He won't be back. It's too open here, and everyone in this building minds everyone else's business. And a good thing, for me, they do."

Arthur frowned. "Isn't this what you told me happened to Susan Orkin before—"

"Yes, but—" The stern look on his face stopped her. "How about if I take a cab over to Alton's?" She crossed her fingers under Izz's warm little belly.

"I don't believe you."

"Arthur, you are getting more and more like Carlos every day. I promise I'll put a chair up against this door and the service door. Okay?"

"What good will that do?"

"Please, Arthur."

"You'll notify Detective Bernstein about this right away?"

"Yes, I will. Scout's honor."

After literally pushing him out of the apartment, she did as she'd promised. She left word for Bernstein. There were now twelve messages on her answering machine, nine of which were those she hadn't checked yesterday. Sighing, she played them back.

Two calls from Carlos, three hangups, Sonya's call, two calls from Smith and one from Alton. All Saturday. That was nine. Between Sunday and today three more had come in. Two were hangups. The third was from Alton. He wanted her to join him and Senator Moynihan for dinner at the River Café. His disappointment at not reaching her was apparent.

She left word on his answering machine that she was very tired, was going to sleep early, and would phone him in the morning.

For the first time in months she slept straight through, waking with her alarm at six-thirty. She got up and tilted the blinds open. The world outside was dark taupe, the roofs of the brownstones barely discernable. On the other hand, she reminded herself, each day was beginning to lengthen as March approached. And springtime in New York was always a festival of colors, odors and sensations. When it wasn't raining.

Izz yawned and snuggled down in the afghan.

"What do you say, Izz? Do you want to go out or are you just possibly paper trained?" That was a thought. Wetzon padded down the hall, unlocked the door and brought the *Times* and the *Journal* in before she remembered the attempted break-in. Not smart, she told herself, opening the door like that.

Pulling the sports pages, she laid them out on the bathroom floor. "Oh, Izz, come have a look at what the Knicks are doing."

The dog sauntered into the room and sniffed at the paper. Wetzon got in the shower. When she came out Izz had inaugurated the *Times*. "Well, thank you, Isabella. You are my kind of pooch." She rolled up the newspaper, checked the back landing through her peephole, then put the soiled paper out with the garbage.

She had a meeting at nine-fifteen with Tom Greenberg. He'd asked her to come to his office, assuring her that no one knew her there and that it didn't matter anyway even if someone did. She wasn't so sure.

After orange juice and her vitamins, she put up coffee and let it drip through while she did twenty minutes of yoga, moving to the barre, and finishing with a headstand. It was wonderful what a night's sleep could do.

On a day like today, she felt she had put bad dreams behind her forever. And the break-in? It could have been just what it was, having nothing to do with anything. Who was she kidding? In her bones she felt that it might have more to do with Richard Hartmann than Susan and Dilla. Once Arthur had the papers, she wouldn't have to think about it again.

The ring was an unfamiliar weight on her finger. But maybe it was providing some kind of ephemeral stability, as if click, click, click, everything was falling into place.

She picked up the envelope from her safe deposit box at Citibank and walked to the post office, where she had to take a number and wait. When her number flashed overhead, she presented the package slip and was handed a thick padded envelope marked *Books*.

It was getting late. She shoved the padded envelope into her briefcase with the envelope for Arthur and flagged a cab heading down Columbus.

White, Mooney's branch office in midtown was on the fourth floor at 650 Fifth Avenue. The receptionist, a young black woman with straight brown hair and purple lipstick, sat behind a glass enclosure breaking off pieces of a doughnut that lay on a greasy napkin. "Yes?" She had a powdered sugar mustache.

"Mr. Greenberg. I have a nine-fifteen appointment."

"Your name is?"

"Mrs. Brenda Goldstein."

The receptionist pressed several buttons and said, "Tom? There's a Mrs. Brenda Goldstein here for you." She looked at Wetzon and hung up the phone. "Through that door and walk straight down and make a right. He's the third office after you make the turn." She went back to her doughnut.

Everything in the branch was in various shades of brown. Desks were cordovan, partitions beige, carpeting sable tweed. The doors to the offices were open and she caught glimpses of brokers at precariously stacked desks talking on phones, peering into computer screens. A nameplate was posted on the glass wall next to the door of each private office. Most of the names were those of people with whom she had talked over the years but never met.

The boardroom, where the smaller, often younger, producers sat, was more of the same. Each broker had his own beige cubicle, an L-shaped brown desk, a brown chair, and paper by the gross. Two young men were standing talking over their beige partitions, drinking coffee. It was hard to know if they were exchanging gossip or ideas. The Street was a hearty mix of both. A few, men and women, were on the phones. Once again she was struck by the similarities between the Wall Street boardroom and the police squadroom.

She turned the corner, counted three offices and stopped in front of the one that said *Tom Greenberg* on the glass. Greenberg was on the phone. He pointed to the chair in front of his desk.

"We got out on the blip. Yeah. Forty and a half. I dunno. Let's sit with it a few days. I think we're ripe for a correction."

Wetzon took a seat thinking he looked a bit like a wharf rat: weasily eyes, short dark Fuller Brush hair. The rat was stuffed into a gray pinstripe, the jacket of which hung over the back of his chair while he sat in his crisp white shirtsleeves. Smoke spiraled up from somewhere behind piles of papers and black ringed-binders. He was a veritable tinderbox. Greenberg had told her he was forty-five. He looked every bit of it.

"Wetzon," he'd said, when she called him two weeks earlier and invited him for a drink. "I've been at six firms in twenty years. I'll go anywhere for a check."

His production was half a mil; otherwise, she wouldn't have bothered.

Greenberg banged down his phone. "Brenda Goldstein, huh?" His nails were bitten to the quick.

"Well, I didn't think it would be professional to flaunt Smith and Wetzon at a firm we pull brokers from. May I close the door?"

"Naa. What do I care?"

"I'd feel more comfortable with it closed."

"So close it."

She got up and closed the door, sat again. "Aren't you worried that your manager will find out you're looking? He'll be all over you and your accounts before you came back from your first interview." It was almost impossible to keep any secrets on the Street, and with brokers moving from firm to firm like nomads, a prospect was sure to be recognized. Word would travel back to his branch like brushfire.

"Hell, no. I don't worry about that. All I have to do is turn Gloria loose on them."

"Who's Gloria?"

"My wife. If I'm lucky I go home and Gloria has a headache. They all know I'm afraid of Gloria, and if *I'm* afraid of her, *they* better be. You know, all Jewish men are afraid of their wives."

"They are?" His windows faced out on Fifth Avenue. She could see the uptown side of St. Patrick's Cathedral from where she was sitting.

"Listen, my father was afraid of *his* wife and his father was afraid of *his* wife. Whole generations of wimps." He scowled at her and puffed on his cigarette. "So whaddaya got for me, Wetzon?"

White, Mooney—Greenberg's firm—and Bliss Norderman—Wetzon's

client firm—were in the midst of a major feud. Each was offering huge up-front bonuses to the other's brokers. Just last week the entire Bloomfield Hills office of Bliss Norderman, including the manager, had walked across the street and opened an office for White, Mooney. When she left Green-berg thirty minutes later, Wetzon had his okay to set him up with Bliss, Norderman. Bliss was paying headhunters a bounty, an incentive over the regular fee, to steal White, Mooney brokers away for them.

When she got to the office it was after ten. Arthur's messenger waited in their tiny reception area. Wetzon hung up her coat and pulled the manilla envelope from her briefcase, borrowed Max's pen and addressed it to Ar-thur. She handed it to the messenger. Waving to a pale and curiously agi-tated B.B., who had come to the doorway of his cubicle, she asked Max, "Smith in yet?"

"She came in about ten minutes ago."

That explained B.B.'s condition. "Thanks." She gave Max's shoulder a squeeze and opened her door. These days, she was never quite certain what she would find, but what she saw next was clearly a surprise.

Smith had recaptured her aura. The suit she'd bought in Boston could have been designed just for her. She had a new shorter haircut and huge Donna Karan gold earrings were clipped to each earlobe.

"Tomorrow at four will be fine," she was saying into the phone in her clipped business-development voice. "I think you'll find our firm quite re-sponsive to your needs. Both I and my partner, Leslie Wetzon, have experi-ence with firms undergoing restructuring." She hung up and made a big checkmark on her calendar.

"We do?"

"Just remember, sweetie pie, that the primary object of our business is to get the money from their pockets and into ours."

"How could I forget?" Wetzon took the padded envelope she'd picked up that morning at the post office from her briefcase.

"What's that?" Smith rose and rotated her shoulders. She looked very pleased with herself.

"I don't know. It came in the mail. I don't remember sending for a book." She pulled the staples out with her letter opener, and peered inside. Something wrapped in bubble packing.

Removing it, she tore the scotch tape away from the packing. "Good grief!" She dropped it on the desk as if it were on fire and reached for the phone. Should she call O'Melvany or Bernstein?

"Let's see."

"Don't, Smith—"

Too late. "You are a wonder, sweetie pie. I've *totally* misjudged you." Onto the suspect sheets on Wetzon's desk, Smith emptied the glittering contents of the chamois pouch Izz had presented to Wetzon in Susan's kitchen a little over a week before.

C H A P T E R

"I think the mother did it." Smith flashed Bernstein one of her sugar-sweet smiles. "Mothers will kill for their children."

"What mother?" Bernstein was practically drooling over Smith.

"She means Edna Terrace," Wetzon said. "The treasurer at the Imperial. Phil's mother. When I was a dancer, we all knew that the treasurers kept billy clubs under their windows."

"Jeez," Gross said. "Did you see this?" She was holding up a star-shaped pin made entirely of diamonds.

"Just write it down, Gross, and give the ladies a receipt. We're not shopping, for Chrissakes—pardon my French."

"And what about that disgusting old man with the heavy cane?" Smith demanded.

"Huh?"

"She means Fran Burke."

"I would appreciate it if you would stop translating for me, sweetie pie," Smith said, tartly. "This nice gentleman understands me completely, don't you, Detective—ah—Bernson?"

"That's Bern*stein,* Smith." Wetzon smiled an apology at Bernstein.

"Yeah, well, maybe." Bernstein was oblivious. "But your kid is still a suspect. I'm going up to Boston to talk to them up there."

"They'll be back in two and a half weeks." Wetzon handed Gross a huge ruby ring that had rolled behind her coffee mug.

"I wanna get this closed before Purim, right, Gross?"

Smith rolled her eyes at Wetzon and mouthed, *Purim? Give me a break.*

"Sure, Morg." Gross had slipped a diamond bracelet on her wrist. She was wearing a red skirt that strained at the waistline, and wrinkled black hose. "Not bad, huh Morg?"

This time Wetzon rolled her eyes at Smith.

"The receipt, Gross." Bernstein headed for the door.

Gross sighed and took off the glittering bracelet. She signed her name at the bottom of the list of jewelry and handed Wetzon the receipt on a creased piece of paper. There was writing on the back. Wetzon turned it over. "Wait. Where did this come from?"

"What is it?" Bernstein came back into the room.

"It's a letter from Susan Orkin."

"Where'd it come from? Gross?"

Gross shook her head.

"Maybe it was in the bag with the jewelry," Smith suggested, too sweetly, from Wetzon's point of view. "Any . . . one can see it's been folded like a letter. What does it say?"

" 'Dear Leslie,' " Wetzon read aloud. " 'If something should happen to me, you'll know what to do with this.' " It was signed "S." Her eyes misted. "I'll know? How would I know?"

"I still would like to know where it came from. I suppose it could have been folded up inside and come out when we emptied the bag. I'll take this, if you don't mind." Bernstein relieved her of the letter and ran his eyes over it.

"Why should I mind? You're taking the jewelry. We'll need another receipt."

"Easy come, easy go." Smith shrugged. "Who gets it after you're finished with it?"

"Oh, for godsakes, Smith—" Wetzon gave Gross a sheet of blank paper, and Gross began recopying the inventory list from the back of Susan's letter.

"Well, sugar, someone had to ask. You never would."

"It's part of the estate, I should think. Whoever inherits. Did Susan leave a will, Detective?"

"The detectives from the One Nine went over the apartment. No will turned up."

"How about a safe deposit key? I guess not, huh? The apartment was such a god-awful mess." Taking the newly signed receipt from Gross, Wetzon folded it and put it in her Filofax.

"Gimme the bag, Gross. I wanna have another look at it." Wetzon cleared some space on her desk and Bernstein emptied the dazzling contents of the pouch once again. The phones were quiet. The room was so still, Wetzon could hear everyone breathing. Bernstein turned the pouch inside out. "What's this?" he said. He was pointing to the embroidery on the inside lining. *Lenny/Celia.*

"Jeeze," Gross said. "I didn't see that."

"Gross, you wouldn't see your foot if it was nailed to your nose."

Smith made a coughing sound behind her hand, which Wetzon tried to ignore, with only moderate success.

"Who are they?" Bernstein demanded. "What do they have to do with Orkin and Crosby?"

"I'm not sure," Wetzon said. "I think they're Lenny and Celia Kaufer. Lenny Kaufer was the most important general manager on Broadway for over thirty years. Celia was his wife. Dilla Crosby was his mistress. He was also Edna Terrace's father and Phil Terrace's grandfather." She could see the little register in Bernstein's mind tallying up the information. Bernstein and Gross were like two refugees from a 1940s B movie.

As if to reinforce her thought, Bernstein said, "Come on, Gross. We have work to do." He handed Gross the pouch and watched as she turned it right side out and replaced the jewelry, fingering each glittering piece lovingly.

Bernstein was halfway into the reception area oozing impatience. "Shake a leg, Gross. We don't have all day."

Max's eyes were spheres. He was pretending to make notes on a suspect sheet in front of him. When the phone rang and he had to answer, he was distracted. "Smith and Wetzon, good morning. I mean, good afternoon. Who's calling please? Hold on." He pointed the receiver at her. "For you, Wetzon."

"One second, Max." She accompanied Bernstein to the door. "Edna Terrace is in New York, but her son Phil is in Boston with *Hotshot.* Although, I guess, he might have been in New York when Susan was murdered because he and Mort Hornberg had a big fight and Mort threw him off the show. And Poppy Hornberg was in New York, too. She came down to get her hair done."

"You wanna work for me, Ms. Wetzon? Maybe Gross would like to trade places. Gross, you listening? You could maybe learn something here." Bernstein was giving Wetzon a very friendly smile.

Well, well, well, she thought. "I'm flattered, Detective." Gross was just getting it and she wasn't liking it. "But I'm sure Detective Gross knows a lot more than I do." Wetzon walked them out, trying to smother a laugh. "Who is holding, Max?" She was laughing out loud as she passed his desk.

"Barney Beck."

"Hi, Barney." Smith was hunched over her desk working on something.

"Wetzon, I made Steve Zuckerman an offer this morning. No upfront. A guarantee of four a month versus a fifty percent payout for six months. Then a flat fifty-five percent for the next six months with a lookback of ten percent if he comes in with the same numbers after a year."

"A generous offer, Barney." She was taking careful notes on the offer. What was heard and what was said didn't always jibe.

"See that he takes it, Wetzon."

She hung up the phone. Steve would take it, of that she was fairly certain. "Barney has an offer out to Steve Zuckerman," she said to Smith's back. "What are you doing?"

"Shshsh," Smith said. She was staring at her Tarot cards, which were laid out on her desk in a Celtic Cross. "Come here!" She gathered them up abruptly and thrust them at Wetzon. "Shuffle."

"Your wish is my command, O great Oracle of Delphi." She stood next to Smith and shuffled the cards.

"You never take the Tarot seriously—and you of all people should. It never lies. Keep shuffling." She shook a finger at Wetzon. "You could maybe learn something here." The last was said in an uncanny imitation of Bernstein.

"Give me a break, Smith." But Wetzon had to smile.

"Now hand them to me." Smith held the cards against her breast and closed her eyes, then opened her eyes and laid the cards out in another Celtic Cross, slowly, sighing, groaning. Finally, she exclaimed, "Look!"

"I'm looking. What am I suppose to be seeing?"

"This is your reading I'm doing. See, two kings."

"All right. Two kings . . ."

"The King of Cups. This is Alton Pinkus. He's covering you, but the King of Swords is in your future. I don't know why I bother trying to help you get your life together. You never listen to me."

"Wait a minute." Wetzon was staring at the King of Swords. She knew who that was. Silvestri. "You mean—"

"Dick Tracy. It dismays me that you're letting Alton Pinkus slip through your little fingers."

"I'm not. Honest. Silvestri is gone for good."

"That's not what I see here," Smith insisted. "And here's something else. The Knight of Pentacles. A message about money."

"That's Barney Beck hiring Steve Zuckerman."

"No!" Smith shook her head. "Something else. See this? Your home and how you relate to others. Death. And the Tower is governing your deepest emotions."

"That sounds too ominous for me." Wetzon turned away. Smith was depressing her.

"And the Wheel of Fortune is the resolution!" Smith was excited. "You must watch what you do and who you're with. You shouldn't be alone. Move in with Alton, why don't you?" Smith's hands shook as she gathered up the cards.

"Oh, really, Smith." Sitting at her desk, Wetzon saw that two of the phone lines were lit.

"One more thing." Smith shuffled the deck and fanned the cards face down across her desk. When the phone rang on the third line and Wetzon reached for it, Smith said, "Let Max get it, sweetie pie." She rubbed her hands together vigorously, and held them over the cards as if warming them, then began selecting cards with little hesitation from the long line.

Wetzon waited. Now Smith was laying out the cards she'd selected, murmuring ominously. No one got the phone. "I'm taking it, Smith. The guys are busy." Smith didn't respond. Wetzon said, "Smith and Wetzon."

"Hang up the phone," Smith said, without looking up from the cards.

"Ms. Leslie Wetzon, please."

"Smith and Wetzon." When Max's voice overlaid the caller's voice, Wetzon quietly hung up. The caller had a vaguely English accent.

"What's the problem, Smith?"

Smith collected the cards and faced her. "What secret are you keeping from me?"

"Secret? *Moi?* I don't know what you're talking about."

"Sweetie, don't pretend you don't know what I'm talking about. Is it something to do with Ma—Smitty? Please tell me. The cards connect it to a young person."

"It's got nothing to do with Smitty." What was Smith talking about? The watch perhaps? No. When the realization struck Wetzon, she thought, Smith is amazing. It had to be B.B.'s resignation she saw in the cards. Wetzon had to find a time to tell her when B.B. wasn't around. Smith would kill him.

At that fortunate moment, Max's knock interrupted Smith's interrogation. He opened the door tentatively.

"Oh, do come, Max, for pitysakes."

Thank you, Max, Wetzon thought fervently.

"A man by the name of Bryan Kendall is on the phone for you, Wetzon."

"Bryan Kendall?" She'd never heard of him. "What firm is he with?"

"I don't know." The phone rang and Max went to get it, closing the door.

"They never learn," Smith said. "Did we get this week's *Wall Street Letter?*"

Wetzon handed her the outrageously priced ten-page newsletter that carried the inside dope on what was happening on the Street. She pressed the blinking button. "Leslie Wetzon."

"Ms. Wetzon, my name is Bryan Kendall. I'm with the law firm of Kendall and Slotkin. I would like to arrange a meeting with you in my office."

"Why? What is this about?" *Now what?*

"Susan Orkin was a friend and a client."

Her tone softened. "I'm sorry about Susan. She was my friend as well." What would Susan's lawyer have to discuss with her?

"It concerns Susan's will. Ms. Wetzon, Susan made you her principal beneficiary."

CHAPTER

"I don't understand," Wetzon said for the third time in less than an hour. A full week had passed and she was sitting opposite Bryan Kendall, Esquire, in his law office on Park Avenue. A cup of black coffee sat in front of her, untouched. Also untouched was the legal envelope Kendall had handed her.

Kendall, a dignified man with gray hair in marcel waves, was in his late fifties. His hand sculpted miles of tiny metal chips into a tower over a magnet base. "What don't you understand?" In person, the English accent was more pronounced.

"Until a few weeks ago, Susan and I hadn't seen each other since college."

"No matter. She asked me to prepare a new will after Dilla died. She signed it the day before her own death." He took a document from a neat folder on his desk.

"You're telling me that Susan has no relatives?"

"That's correct."

"Mr. Kendall, Susan was terrified that something would happen to her. Do you know what she was afraid of?"

"No, I don't."

"Oh, God, what does this all mean to me?"

"The will has gone to probate. Susan designated me as her executor. There are two other beneficiaries. Susan left ten thousand dollars to Rhoda Rockefeller."

"Rhoda Rockefeller? You mean her housekeeper? Her last name is Rockefeller?"

He nodded. He had a nice twinkle in his eye. In that instant Wetzon decided she liked Bryan Kendall.

"And she left twenty-five thousand dollars to the Actors' Fund."

"That's very generous. What am I supposed to do now?"

"The estate owns the apartment and it will be sold. The money, after closing costs and taxes, will then go to the beneficiary. You. There are some minor debts—"

"But wasn't the apartment mortgaged?"

Kendall shook his head. "They paid cash for the apartment."

"Cash? For an apartment in that building? Where would they get all that cash?"

"They used their savings. Susan and Dilla each owned other apartments, and they sold them when they moved in together. Actually, the apartment was always in Susan's name."

"Excuse me, Mr. Kendall, what kind of numbers are we talking about here?"

"Please call me Bryan. We're going to be speaking and meeting with some frequency. I believe we can probably see eight or nine hundred thousand in the market today, maybe more."

"Oh, God . . ."

"And Susan had an account with Merrill Lynch, as well as life insurance."

"I feel awful about this. I don't want her money. I don't need it. How would it be if, when the apartment is sold, I donate it to a couple of AIDS groups and the Meals on Wheels program?"

"It's yours to do as you wish."

"I think Susan would approve. Is that it?"

He leafed through the will. "The dog, Isabella. She would like you to take her."

Wetzon smiled. "I already have."

"Good. There's also a car, a Jaguar. It's in a garage on Lexington."

"God, a car." It was mind-boggling.

"Then one final thing. The copyrights on her poetry and lyrics will be transferred to you as her heir. I would suggest that you keep them. It won't amount to a lot of money. I knew Susan very well. Her writing was the driving force in her life."

"Okay. Thank you." They rose at the same time and shook hands. "Arthur Margolies is my lawyer."

"I know him."

"He's out of town until Monday. . . ." She was in shock.

More than two weeks after Dilla Crosby's murder, the police seemed to be no closer to the murderer or even the murder weapon. The *Times* gave the investigation sporadic to no coverage, but the *News* and the *Post* and even *New York Newsday* managed to come up continuously with screaming headlines.

Smitty had not been arrested. He was living at home with Smith and seeing a therapist. His mother had bounced back with incredible resilience.

Edna Terrace had not been arrested either, but her photograph had appeared in all of the newspapers, her face obscured by a raincoat.

Hotshot: The Musical was finishing up its last week in Boston, sold out to the rafters, irony of irony. Smith was right. They would make a lot of money. That is, their pension would. All that remained before opening night in New York was the week of previews.

According to Carlos's daily phone reports from Boston, once Mort had let up on him, Phil Terrace had blossomed into an excellent stage manager, and no one on the show had come to blows. Such it is when a show is a hit. In fact, at the beginning of the second week in Boston, Mort and Poppy had gone to Sarasota, where they had a house, leaving the show in Carlos's hands.

Wetzon walked over to Madison. Every cab was occupied. It had rained every day since March had dribbled in. Two weeks of dampness, soggy shoes, torn umbrellas, mud on raincoats, and mildew. Every face she passed had that bleak pinched look that came from the absence of sunlight. She kept walking. On the corner of Fifty-seventh and Fifth a food wagon stood under a dripping umbrella. The vendor was selling pretzels that had to be spongy with moisture. In a doorway, a Senegalese vendor held up silk scarves with the Hermes signature in the center, most likely knockoffs. Two female tourists were feeling the merchandise and exclaiming in Italian.

She caught a No. 7 bus up Amsterdam. The bus was crowded. Wet umbrellas sprinkled those seated; everyone was irritable. The smell of wet wool was oppressive. Wetzon, jammed between chunky, sweating men and their attaches and umbrellas, studied her ring.

Tonight was Sandra Semple's big dinner party, where Alton was going to announce their engagement. Why wasn't she more elated?

When she got off the bus, she was thinking, I could call and tell him I'm not feeling well. All the way up in the elevator, she combed her brain for a reasonable excuse for not going. It was an exercise in futility.

Izz's enthusiasm, on the other hand, more than made up for what Wetzon lacked. Sensing Wetzon was going out, she followed her from room to room, not letting her out of sight. Izz stood on her hind legs with her paws on the rim of the tub while Wetzon showered. "It's okay, you dumb bunny," Wetzon assured her. "You're going with me." Izz blinked and stretched her tongue to catch the droplets of water that sprayed her.

What did it all mean, Wetzon thought, as she blow-dried her hair. With her free hand she pulled her hair back from her face. Not quite long enough. It might be ages before she had the length for her topknot again. In the bedroom she took her black spandex jersey from the dry cleaner's bag and stepped into it, pulling it on and slipping her arms into the sleeves. It wasn't even snug. She *had* lost a lot of weight.

She sat down on the bed and Izz joined her. Bernstein's card was next to the phone; so was O'Melvany's. She was collecting detectives' cards, or so it seemed. She called O'Melvany because Susan had been murdered in the Nineteenth Precinct.

"O'Melvany."

"Hi, um,"—she never knew what to call him—"this is Leslie Wetzon. Is this a bad time?"

"You got me on my way out. What do you have?"

"I thought you should know that I had a call from a lawyer named Bryan Kendall of Kendall and Slotkin. He told me I am Susan Orkin's chief beneficiary."

O'Melvany whistled through his teeth. "How much are we talking about?"

"The apartment, some stocks and bonds, a car, her copyrights, whatever the safe deposit box yields and maybe some insurance. You might want to call Mr. Kendall." She gave him the phone number. "I suppose that gives me a motive."

"If you knew about it before."

"I didn't. And I don't want the money. It's blood money. I hate it." Her voice cracked; she swallowed hard.

"Take it easy." He sounded concerned. "Maybe you should talk to Sonya."

"It's okay. I'm okay. I saw Sonya yesterday. Thanks. Is there anything new? I didn't see anything in the papers about the bag of jewelry."

"You won't. We're keeping it to ourselves for the time being."

After she hung up, she finished dressing and put her makeup on more carefully than usual. This was a special occasion. She attached the leash to Izz's rhinestone collar. They were holding back on the bag of jewels. Why?

The phone rang as she was belting her raincoat. Izz began barking, running to the door and back.

"Forget it, dog." She answered the phone.

"Birdie, darling!"

"Carlos! God, it's good to hear your voice. When are you coming home?"

"Tomorrow, and I can't wait."

"Me, too."

"How's the show?"

"Great. Mort went off to Florida."

"I heard. Do the police have anything new on Sam's murder?"

"Listen, dear heart, the cops have been hanging out here since Sam got it. They know the show by heart. One paunchy detective even did the opening number for me after the Wednesday matinee.

Wetzon giggled. Izz pulled on her leash. "How was he?"

"Are you kidding?"

"I've got to go, doll. Tonight is Sandra Semple's dinner party and Alton's making the grand announcement."

"Are you excited?"

"Truth?"

"Of course."

"I'm scared."

"La di dah, darling. You'll be 'Sadie, Sadie, Married Lady' before the summer solstice."

"Oh, please. May I hang up now? I'll see you Sunday. Arthur invited me to dinner."

"Good. I just have one more thing on my little mind. . . ."

"Yes?"

His voice sobered. "I had a drink with Fran Burke tonight."

"What kind of cane was he using?"

"Gray metal or aluminum, or something. Can I finish here before you take over?"

"But of course."

"He gave me a weird message for you. I don't know what it means, and I'm not crazy about delivering it, but he said you'd understand."

"Talk fast. I'm going to be late."

"Fran said to tell you that you should return what doesn't belong to you."

Wetzon's hands were freezing. A tiny pulse throbbed in her throat.

"You look beautiful, Leslie." Alton took her hand and kissed her clammy palm. "Stop worrying. They'll all love you." They got off the elevator and walked down the hall to the last apartment, where Alton rang the bell.

She wanted to tell him she didn't care whether they loved her or not, but she didn't say it. She dreaded this night. After tonight her commitment to Alton would be formalized.

Sandra Semple opened the door and flung herself at Alton. "Dad!" She was wearing almond silk brocade pants, a black body suit cut to her cleavage, and an almond and black brocade vest. It was her own design and Wetzon had seen it on a model in *Mirabella.* "Come in. Come in." She kissed the air next to Wetzon's cheek. "Hello, Leslie."

A maid in a blue uniform with white trim took Wetzon's raincoat, and she found herself standing alone; Sandra had moved Alton on into the living room with dispatch. Wetzon could hear the enthusiastic greetings all the way out to the foyer.

This was the third time Wetzon had been here and she'd never felt comfortable. Sandra never quite looked her in the eye. Alton's daughter obviously didn't approve of her. Maybe she should just take her coat back and slip away.

"I thought I'd lost you." Alton loomed up in front of her. "Come on, I want you to meet some people who are dear to me." His hand settled possessively on the back of her neck. Like a yoke, she thought.

The living room was a blur of faces. She recognized Janet Barnes,

Twoey's mother, and good vibes, Laura Lee Day, who was chatting with an attractive man in a navy blazer.

"This is Adam, my older son, and Jill, his wife." A big man, like his father, Adam was heavier by some fifteen or twenty pounds. He looked more like the photo of Tessa than his father. Adam, she knew, was a reporter for the *Washington Post,* and Jill, a short woman with frizzy red-blond hair, was a free-lance writer whose articles appeared in magazines. Her wide blue eyes settled on Wetzon's ring, and she nudged her husband.

"And this is Lawrence." Alton moved Wetzon to face his youngest child, a twenty-five-year-old edition of his father. Lawrence was in the University of Iowa writer's program. He shook her hand and Alton moved her on to others, cousins, long-time family friends.

"Isn't sex lovely," Laura Lee whispered as their cheeks touched.

"What kind of thing is that to say?" Wetzon flushed. How could Laura Lee know that Wetzon and Alton had made love before they came downtown?

"Darlin', you have that blurry-edged look about you that only comes after good sex."

Wetzon laughed. "Oh, Laura Lee, you are blessed."

"I'd like you to meet Paul D'Amico. Paul, this is my friend, Leslie Wetzon."

"Leslie." Paul D'Amico shook her hand and smiled at her with incredible green eyes.

"Alton, this is my friend Laura Lee Day, and this is Paul D'Amico." While Alton and Paul shook hands, Wetzon mumbled to Laura Lee, "Who is he?"

"Dinner, everyone," Sandra announced, standing in the archway to the dining room.

Laura Lee whispered, "Tell you later."

Sandra seated Alton at the head of the table and herself to his right, Jill to his left. Wetzon was seated between Adam and Lawrence. She was a fish out of water.

The only person she didn't remember meeting was a dark-haired woman who sat across from her. Several times Wetzon looked up from her plate and found the woman studying her. With nervous fingers she found her wineglass and sipped.

Sitting between Alton's two sons, Wetzon was tongue-tied. The first course was a mushroom risotto. She managed to swallow a small amount of the congealing mixture on her plate until the main course was served, a gallantine of chicken with miniature steamed vegetables, followed by a salad and three little balls of fruit sorbets and rolled crisp almond cookies. Conversation roamed from local politics to the arts, to economics and finance. By the time coffee arrived, Wetzon knew she'd had too much wine.

The dark-haired woman was still staring at her.

"Ahem." Sandra stood, smiling and happy. "We have a thrilling family announcement to make."

Oh, God, Wetzon thought. Thrilling? What was so thrilling? An irresistable urge to slip under the table seized her. Still, Sandra seemed happy about it. Wetzon closed her eyes. *Here it comes.*

Beside her, Adam suddenly rose. Wetzon opened her eyes. "Jill and I are going to have a baby," he said. "Congratulations, Dad, you're going to be a grandfather."

Alton looked dumfounded. Wetzon felt his eyes on her. Sweat rolled down her back, settling in the band of her pantyhose. He seemed to be asking her approval as the dinner guests watched. But what did Adam's baby really have to do with her? She had to do something, so she smiled at him, and Alton beamed.

Everyone at the table began asking questions about the baby, and Wetzon thought, *maybe he won't say anything about us.* Then she prayed he wouldn't.

Sandra began pouring the champagne, which the maid had set out in two standing ice buckets. Watching her glass fill, Wetzon knew she wouldn't reach for it. Champagne did not agree with her, and anyway, she didn't feel like celebrating. She looked at her watch. Ten o'clock. This was the longest evening she'd ever spent.

Alton got to his feet. "I have some news myself," he said. "Come over here next to me, Leslie." A murmur ran around the room as Wetzon rose and joined him. "You all know my friend, Leslie Wetzon." There was his hand again on the back of her neck. "Well, Leslie's made me very happy by consenting to be my wife."

The shocked silence that followed was broken at last by Laura Lee. "Well now, best wishes and much happiness to you both," she exclaimed.

The rest joined in, but Wetzon knew it was half-hearted. Alton didn't seem to notice. He tilted her chin and kissed her, and over his shoulder Wetzon caught Sandra's undisguised disapproval.

Wetzon looked desperately for Laura Lee. But Laura Lee had moved her seat to talk with Janet Barnes. The maid began to clear the table. Sandra suggested that everyone adjourn to the living room, where coffee would be served.

It was the perfect time for Wetzon to escape, and she did.

Distinctly light-headed, she went upstairs, used the bathroom, combed her hair, stalling. She wandered into the library, a room of soft green carpeting, high ceilings, wood paneling. There was even a rolling ladder to reach the upper shelves of the bookcases.

On a table were assorted family photographs in simple silver frames. Tessa, Alton, and their children at different ages. Tessa and a younger version of the dark-haired woman who had stared at Wetzon all evening. Wetzon picked up the photograph.

"Tessa and her little sister," a voice at Wetzon's elbow informed her. "Lydia Davidoff."

Startled, Wetzon dropped the photograph. Lydia picked it up and looked at it a long time, then set it back on the table.

"I'm sorry," Wetzon stammered, guilty, not knowing why.

"What would a girl like you want with Alton?" Lydia said. "He has to be at least thirty years older than you."

"I'm thirty-nine."

"Even so." Lydia wandered around the room straightening things that didn't seem to need straightening.

"He's a wonderful man." Why was she defending herself?

Lydia stopped and faced her. "A girl like you can get men her own age."

"Excuse me?"

"You don't fit with us. We're a very close family."

It came to her all at once. "You're in love with him."

Lydia's dark eyes filled with tears.

Oh, God, Wetzon thought.

"Wetzon darlin', I wondered where you'd gotten to." Laura Lee blew into the library like a crisp March wind.

Lydia turned away and left the room.

"Oh, God," Wetzon said aloud this time, sinking into a chair, her head in her hands. "That was Sandra's mother's sister. I mean, Alton's sister-in-law. She's in love with Alton. I feel awful."

"Oh, darlin', in the love-and-marriage game there is always someone who loses and someone who wins. And it's the winner who is sometimes the loser, if you catch my drift."

"I do."

"Well then, come on back to the fray."

"Not until you tell me who that gorgeous man is."

"You mean Paul?"

"I do."

"Promise not to tell."

"Who would I tell?"

"Well, darlin'," Laura Lee steered her out of the library. "He's a Jesuit."

"Laura Lee! A priest?"

"Isn't that delicious? You can't imagine what it does for makin' love."

It was after midnight when Alton and Wetzon got back to his apartment. Alton was jubilant; Wetzon subdued. Izz greeted them, ran around the living room, jumped on the sofa and settled in.

"You're tired," Alton said. "It was a strain, I know."

"Yes and yes." She smiled at him. "Congratulations, granddad."

"Does it bother you?"

"No."

He put his arms around her. "I love you very much. How about June?"

She buried her face in his shirt. "Who's June?"

He laughed. "Our wedding."

"Oh. June's fine."

"You could be a little more enthusiastic."

". . . I talked to Lydia."

"Oh, for Chrissakes, what did she say? Leslie, Lydia's a nut case."

"She's in love with you, Alton."

"I'm not in love with her."

"Were you ever involved with her?"

"Oh, Leslie. It was nothing. It meant nothing. It was something that happened after Tessa died. I was lonely and she was there." He was very upset.

She stroked his back and said, "It's okay, Alton. Really. It doesn't matter."

"What did she say to you?"

"It's not important." She pulled away from him and went into the bedroom, sat on the bed and slipped off her shoes.

"It is. She obviously upset you."

She lay back and stared at the ceiling. "She said I wouldn't fit with your family."

Alton lay down beside her and held her. "Damn that woman," he whispered into her hair. She turned to him. "Oh, baby," he said.

Sometime later, when she was washing her makeup off her face, Alton came and watched her. "Hi," she said, catching him in the mirror.

"Hi, yourself. Is everything okay?"

She dried her face with the towel and patted in moisturizer. "Sure."

When they got back into bed, she told him about Susan's will. "I'm going to give most of it away," she said.

"Whatever you want to do is fine with me. I can take care of you."

She hated that expression. "I can take care of myself. I've got a good business."

"Sure you have." He said it too quickly.

"The police are holding on to the bag of jewelry, not saying anything to the press or anyone."

"What bag of jewelry?"

"The bag I told you about that I saw in Susan's apartment. It had Lenny/Celia embroidered on the inside. You remember." He seemed not to have heard her. "Alton?"

"I'm sorry. I just remembered something about Lenny Kaufer's funeral. It was really weird, now that I think of it. Celia Kaufer stood up and made a plea for money."

"A collection? At the funeral? I thought Lenny Kaufer was a wealthy man."

"I suppose he was."

"And his wife had to beg for money at his funeral? That doesn't play." But as she said it, it began to make sense. Lenny Kaufer had to be rolling in *cash,* and where was the logical place to store it?

The missing piece of the puzzle was what Poppy Hornberg had told her. Lenny Kaufer had stored his fortune in his safe deposit box.

It came again when she least expected it. The blinding flame, the searing heat, the burning stench of cordite. Intolerable! She forced herself awake.

Darkness smothered her. Alton mumbled in his sleep, moved his arm, releasing her. At the foot of the bed a pale lump sat up. Two eyes glinted at her.

She eased herself out of bed. Alton's robe was hanging from a hook in the bathroom. She slipped it on and wandered into the living room, closely followed by Izz. Chilled, Wetzon settled herself on the sofa with the throw across her feet. Izz curled up on her feet.

The dream had been less vivid and shorter, and she'd been able to remove herself from it. What time was it? It was too dark to see the hands on her watch. And what difference did it make anyway? The real question was what was she doing here.

That line from *Fiddler on the Roof*—or something like it—kept knocking on her subconscious. What was it? Something Tevye says about a fish and a bird may fall in love, but where would they make a life together?

She loved Alton. How could she not? But he was at least two generations ahead of her. He was about to become a grandfather. She didn't want to live his life, and that, she was certain, would be how they would live. The amazing disappearance of Leslie Wetzon, she thought. She had seen it happen last night.

Alton had wooed and won the fair maiden because she'd let him. She'd been vulnerable. She'd accepted his enveloping love, leaned on his strength, because with him she'd felt safe. But in her heart she knew that she could never sign on with him for life. Final solutions were not in the game plan for her.

Izz stirred, watchful. Wetzon swung her feet to the floor, dislodging the dog, and padded over to the window. Fog shrouded the museum and the park. The lights of the crosstown bus pierced the haze, stopping with a diesel wheeze below her.

She found her purse on the table in the foyer and pulled out her pen and Filofax, tearing a pink page from it.

"What to say, Izz?" The dog cocked her head. At the kitchen counter, pen in hand, for a long time Wetzon stared down at the pink paper. Finally, she wrote:

Dearest Alton, I'm so terribly sorry.

There was nothing else to say.

The ring came off her finger easily, as if it were never meant to be there. She folded the ring into the note, wrote *Alton* on the small square, and propped it against the coffee machine.

In the bedroom she dressed quickly. Alton lay on his back, his hair rumpled, his face young in sleep. She would never know anyone like him again.

You're running away, the little voice said.

I know. If I stay, he'll talk me out of it.

Leashing Izz, who thought it was an adventure, and it was, Wetzon belted her raincoat and had just opened the outside door when she remembered Alton's keys. No use holding onto them. It would mean she wanted to come back. She slipped the two keys from her key ring and set them in front of the pink paper square.

The Sunday *Times* lay on Alton's door mat. She stepped over it, closing the door behind her.

Coward, the voice scolded. *You just let the best thing that ever happened to you slip through your fingers.*

The best, she agreed, stepping on the elevator, *but not for me.*

She passed through the lobby where a uniformed guard dozed in a chair. He opened his eyes as she and Izz flew by—because by this time she was running. In the morning he might think he'd dreamed it all.

Eastward, over Central Park, the sky was streaked with a pale glow. The fog was beginning to lift. Sidewalks were devoid of people, streets of cars. She could feel her city breathing.

Under her feet, the sidewalk tensed and she heard the muffled rumble of the IND express as it thundered past the Eighty-first Street station to Columbus Circle.

For several minutes she was the only person in the world.

And then the wail of a siren rose from somewhere across the Park. A yellow cab whizzed up Central Park West. Izz began to tug on her leash, and Wetzon walked west.

Columbus Avenue was still asleep. Stores were gated; fat green garbage bags sat in front of buildings waiting for the sanitation trucks.

A Con Edison excavation was in progress on the corner of Eighty-sixth Street. The faint smell of gas hovered over the area where a pit had been dug into the asphalt, and a van with blinking warning lights watched over men in yellow hard hats down in the hole. Another Con Ed worker stood watch above them. The sharp screech of a drill shattered the predawn quiet. When Wetzon and Izz passed, she saw the Con Ed man on the street wore small gold hoops in his ears.

She met no one in her lobby or on the elevator. Leaving a trail of clothing and leash, she crawled into bed. The last thing she remembered was Izz nuzzling the small of her back. And then she slept.

Her awakening came as from a long illness. Slowly. She was herself again, her own person. Izz licked her face and jumped off the bed, dancing, demanding to be fed. She fed Izz and made coffee, savoring each motion as she made it. The sun filled her kitchen with riches of light. As she showered, the song from *New Girl in Town* played over and over in her head until she finally sang "It's Good to Be Alive." And it was, it was.

She was working intently at her barre to the Brandenberg Concertos when her doorbell rang. Izz began barking. "Yes?" She looked through the peephole.

"Leslie, please let me in."

She closed her eyes, opened them. "Okay." Rolling her towel around the back of her neck, she opened the door. "Who let you up?" Alton followed her into the apartment and she closed the door.

"Your super. He recognized me." He bent down to pat Izz, who was making a fool of herself over him. He wore jeans, a blue shirt, a navy blazer. Dried blood marked a shaving nick on his chin.

Be strong, she thought.

"Leslie, I—" He reached for her and she backed away. He seemed an alien presence in her apartment, taking over her space.

"No, please, Alton. It's not going to do any good." She felt her lip tremble.

"I thought you loved me."

"I do. I always will."

Seeing the dent in her door, he said, "What happened to your lock?"

"Someone tried to break in Monday night."

"Monday night? Why didn't you tell me?" He was looking around, moving from the foyer into the living room.

"Because you would have pressured me to move in with you, and I can't do that."

"I didn't know," he said, as if to himself, taking in the quilts, the wall of books, the barre with its mirrored backdrop. "May I?" He pointed to the hallway.

She shrugged, watching him as he went down the hall and into her bedroom. A half dozen pliés at the barre kept her from thinking too much. He came back slowly. "Your apartment . . . I didn't understand . . . I—" He seemed to be searching for the right words. "It . . . you have . . . a very distinct voice."

She faced him, holding on to the barre, feeling the hard wood pressing against her spine. "I know. This is my home. This is who I am, Alton. Don't you think it's strange that you never once asked to see it?"

He looked devastated. "Leslie, I've assumed too much. Let me make it right. We don't have to marry right away."

"Oh, Alton, it's all wrong. It will never work." She folded her arms across her breast.

He came close and held her. She didn't move. Heart thumping, she felt the physical pull between them. "We'll make it work," he said. "I'll make it work."

Slipping away, she said, "I need some space, Alton. I don't want to be a trophy. I'm not sure I'd be happy in your world." She smiled a wry smile. "Come on, you don't really see me as Mrs. Alton Pinkus, do you?"

"I did. I also see you as Leslie Wetzon-Pinkus. I want you with me and I want you to be happy." His hands hung at his side, awkwardly.

"Alton, you are a dear, wonderful man, but I can't be with anybody. I've met you at the wrong time in my life. I feel trapped. I wanted to run away, which I did. I'm so sorry for leading you on. I'm sorry for everything."

"I'll give you space, baby, if that's what you need, but I will *not* give you up. I love you. You're my Leslie. I'm good for you and you're good for me."

"Alton, please, you're making it so hard for me."

"Is it Silvestri? Is that what it's about?"

"There's no one else. I'm really not your Leslie. I'm not anyone's Leslie."

Why didn't he see that and just go? Standing at her door, she couldn't hold back the tears.

"You are, but I'm willing to give you all the time you need. You'll see." He kissed away the tears. "I once told you I'm a patient man. I am."

Her phone began to ring. She opened the door. "Good-bye, Alton."

"For now maybe, Leslie. I'll call you."

She closed the door on him with a surge of guilt. She knew—had he stayed or had the phone not interrupted them—she might have caved in.

The phone stopped ringing when her answering machine picked up, clicking in. She recognized Arthur's voice immediately. "Leslie, I'm afraid—"

She grabbed the phone. "Arthur?"

"Leslie. Good, I'm glad you're home. Please, if you can come with me—"

"Where?"

"I've just had a call from the D.A.'s office. They've issued a warrant for Mark Smith's arrest."

CHAPTER

"He doesn't want me with him!" Smith was lying on her bed sobbing. Her world had truly come to an end.

"Ma, please understand." Smitty stood in the doorway, his eyes pleading with Wetzon. "I didn't kill anybody. Wetzon, please make her understand. I have to do this myself." He looked so like his mother, the deep hazel eyes, the olive coloring, the thick dark curls. "Ma, it doesn't mean I don't love you."

Arthur cleared his throat. "We have to get going."

"Go ahead." Wetzon walked them to the door. "We'll be okay."

"Leslie, unless they've come up with something new, they can't hold him," Arthur assured her.

She closed the door, sighing. From the bedroom she could hear Smith's anguished sobs. She sat on the bed and stroked Smith's tangled curls. "He's grown up, you know. He wants to handle his problems himself. You should be proud of him. He's a wonderful kid."

Smith rolled over on her back, her face puffy, the skin around her eyes, red. Wetzon handed her a tissue. "I know. I am proud of him. There's an ice pack in the freezer. I must look like hell." Smith was wearing purple pin-stripe trousers and a man-tailored white-on-white shirt with long sleeves. And she wasn't even wrinkled.

When Wetzon got back with the ice pack, Smith was sitting up and shuffling her Tarot deck. She stopped to press the coldpack gently against her face, then thrust it back at Wetzon. "This is very important."

"Oh, sure."

Smith reacted only with a raise of eyebrow as she laid out the cards using the Queen of Wands as her center.

As she returned the ice pack to the freezer, Wetzon could hear Smith murmuring to herself. She was still murmuring when Wetzon returned. "My baby is in trouble." Her eyes glistened. "But he did not kill anyone."

"I could have told you that without the cards."

"Very funny."

"According to the police, Dilla's and Susan's murders were crimes of passion."

Smith looked aghast. "You mean *rape?*" She gathered up the cards.

"Not that kind of passion. There are other kinds, you know. Anger, love, hate, jealousy, revenge . . ."

"Revenge? For what?"

"If you promise not to go crazy, I'll tell you what I think."

"Do you mean to tell me you know who did it?"

"I don't know for sure, but I think you were right about Edna Terrace."

"Who?"

"Oh, for godsakes, Smith, you said you thought the mother did it. Don't you remember, when Bernstein came to the office for the jewelry?"

"I forgot her name."

"Phil Terrace's mother. Read my lips."

Smith wrinkled her forehead. "I have no idea what you're talking about."

"The stage manager. Phil Terrace. He took over after Dilla was murdered. I can't believe you didn't meet him."

"I probably did. You can see how he's made a lasting impression on me."

"He's sort of chunky, short, balding, and tentative."

"How quaint." Smith yawned. "What makes you think I'd remember anyone like that?" She thrust her feet into her sandals and stood. "Wait a minute. Not the one who sweats?"

"Bingo."

"Ah, people who sweat when it's not hot are always the guilty ones. I knew if we put our minds to it we'd figure it out." She was heading for the kitchen. "I need some coffee."

Wetzon followed her. "You're saying *Phil* did it? Why?" She watched Smith fill her coffeemaker with water and the filter with coffee. The heady aroma of roasted hazelnuts filled the kitchen. "I hope that's decaf."

"It is. Tell me why you think it's what's-her-face."

"Edna? Okay, treasurers used to keep a club in the box office in case they were held up. The police didn't find one."

They listened to the coffeemaker *whoosh*. Then Smith said, "That's a little farfetched."

"And sweating isn't? There's more. Edna has been wearing a ring that looks an awful lot like the description of a ring Dilla wore the week she was murdered—"

"You mean she bashed Dilla Crosby for a ring?" Incredulous, Smith poured coffee into cups, and Wetzon carried them into the dining room, leaving Smith in the kitchen.

Wetzon raised her voice. "Listen to me, Smith. I've got it all worked out." She sat down at the table and took a handful of caramel popcorn from the huge bowl Smith set between them. "Once upon a time—"

"Oh for pitysakes." Smith gave an exaggerated groan, but Wetzon could see she had lightened up considerably.

"Once upon a time on Broadway there was a very successful general manager. You might say he was the king of general managers—This is good popcorn."

"Will you please get on with your story."

"Anyway, the king's name was Lenny Kaufer. He had a wife named Celia, and a daughter—Are you following me?"

Smith nodded, eyes to ceiling.

"A daughter named Edna. Princess Edna."

"Aha. Edna Terrace."

"I think she's got it," Wetzon said to the ceiling. "Lenny Kaufer was like the godfather, the king of ice. That's money skimmed from gross box office receipts, kickbacks, ticket scalping. Ticket sales weren't computerized then. They say it doesn't go on any more, but a couple of years ago a general manager on a hit show was fired because there was money not accounted for in ticket sales."

"I get it. Now will you get to the point." Smith was daintily eating one kernel at a time.

"The king had a mistress, a young chorus dancer."

"My Lord, not you!"

"Smith, give me a break. There must have been five hundred dancers auditioning for shows at the time. I was only one of them. Dilla Crosby was his mistress."

"Dilla Crosby? But she's a-a-she's a-" Smith choked on the word—"she's *gay.*"

Wetzon hid a smile. Ah, she thought, the education of Xenia Smith. Smith might just come out of this a better person. "Well, I guess Dilla was either bisexual or maybe, as people often said, just plain rotten and calculating. Anyway, the king gave her a gorgeous mink coat and a red Corvette, among other things."

Smith punched air with her right fist. "Yes!"

So much for Wetzon's daydream of a new Smith. "Thank you very much. So King Lenny was stashing cash and stuff away for years in his mega safe deposit box."

Smith smiled. She always smiled when she heard about money, or schemes to get same. "Go on."

"Then the king got sick—cancer—and it was bad. While he was in the hospital dying, with his loving family around him, someone with a key to his safe deposit box signed in as his wife, Celia, and cleaned everything out. And when the box was opened after he died, it was empty. I heard that story from Poppy Hornberg."

"Very ingenious."

"No. Very larcenous. At the king's funeral Celia Kaufer made a tearful appeal for the money. I heard that from Alton. I guess they weren't destitute, but they had an expensive life style that they could no longer support."

"Of course, it was never returned."

"Of course. This is like putting a picture puzzle together. Not all the pieces fit the first time around. Fran Burke was Lenny Kaufer's protégé. I think he's been sort of godfathering Phil."

"That old coot might have killed Dilla to avenge his mentor."

"True. When I first visited Susan, Dilla's mother and sister and brother-in-law were there packing her things. Susan's dog Izz—by the way—I have a foster dog now. A Maltese."

"You? A dog? How does Alton feel about that?"

"It's of no consequence."

"Wait a minute, where's your ring?"

"I've broken it off with Alton, Smith."

"I can't believe even you would do anything so stupid."

Offended, Wetzon said, "Well, I guess I did, and it's not up for discussion. Do you want to hear the rest?"

"Get to the end, please."

"You know you have the attention span of a duck? Remember the embroidery inside the pouch of jewelry that Susan sent me? It said *Lenny/Celia.* Everyone on *Hotshot* saw Dilla wearing that ring the whole week before she was murdered, but she wasn't wearing it when we found her. And when I met Edna Terrace, she was wearing a ring just like the one Carlos and Sunny described."

"So we're back where we started. Who would kill for a ring? Was it worth a couple of mil? If it was, I could see killing."

"Oh, shut up, Smith. If Dilla cleaned out Lenny's safe deposit box, she was killed for *revenge.* I bet Dilla thought by giving Phil a job, she could make up for what she had done. On the other hand, when the police drew up the profile of Dilla's murderer, they said it was a young man with no strong male role model, which is why Smitty—"

A tear rolled down Smith's cheek. "But sweetie, isn't Phil Terrace a young man? Does he have a father? It's so unfair."

"I don't know."

"Well, the police are not always right. I met that Fran Burke. That old man should be sent to the glue factory."

"Fran controls the ice now. If that ring belonged to Celia Kaufer, both Fran and Edna would have recognized it immediately. Maybe Dilla thought enough time had passed so that she could wear it."

"Then she was a fool."

"Fran hated Mort for how he was treating Phil. His eyes aren't so good. He could have mistaken Sam for Mort in the men's smoker. His cane is a blunt, cylindrical object."

"Yes," Smith said, excitement in her voice. "And he'd have nothing to lose."

"What makes you say that?"

Smith clasped her hands together under her chin. "Walter Greenow told me this is Fran's last show. He's dying of liver cancer."

CHAPTER

Wetzon outlined her lips with the lip pencil, then filled them in with a brush. Her hand trembled. Openings always made her nervous.

Almost two weeks had passed. *Hotshot: The Musical* had come in from Boston and played a week of totally sold-out previews. Ticket scalpers were lined up before the box office opened each morning. People were behaving as if it were the Second Coming.

Alex Witchel's wonderful interview with Carlos had appeared in last Sunday's *Times,* and Mort would be on the cover of *Time* next week.

Smitty had been indicted for homicide—Susan's—by a grand jury and was out on bail, but Arthur still felt the case would never go to trial. No hard evidence had come to light, only Susan's note in her date book and Smitty's thumbprint on the service door. And still no murder weapon.

"So what do you think, Izz?" Oh, dear, she was going to have to watch herself. Izz lay on Wetzon's bed watching Oprah, seemingly mesmerized by the timbre of Oprah's voice.

Alton phoned every day. Wetzon wavered each time she heard his voice. His steadying presence in her life was beginning to fade. Stepping into her standby basic black wool and spandex jersey, she pulled it up over her hips and stuck her arms in the sleeves. Yet she had to admit she liked the adventure of living alone again, the stir of anticipation about the new and unexpected.

Opening night curtain was six-fifteen. Early, so the critics could write their reviews and deliver them on the eleven o'clock news, as well as meet deadlines on the few daily newspapers left. She remembered the days when there were seven.

She put a coat of clear polish over her pink nails and fluttering her fingers, lay down on her bed waiting for the polish to dry. It was a good excuse for Izz to shimmy over and crawl up on Wetzon's belly to stare at her. "Don't look at me, watch Oprah." Oprah's subject was the joy of May/December marriages. Pointing the remote at the screen, Wetzon zapped her. Enough of that.

The phone rang. She jostled Izz aside and answered it, careful to protect her polish.

"Leslie? This is Sonya."

Wetzon had rescheduled her Thursday session with Sonya because of the opening. "Hi, Sonya. You didn't forget that the opening is tonight, did you?"

"No. I wanted to tell you why I asked you to hold April first for me. It's . . . well, Eddie and I are getting married."

Sonya and Eddie. . . . "You mean O'Melvany?" Wetzon felt a rush of . . . what? Envy?

"Yes. Are you surprised?"

"I shouldn't be. I knew that you guys were seeing each other, but getting married . . ."

"We both want it to be official, and we'd like you to stand up for us because you introduced us."

"Me? Gosh, Sonya, I'd be honored."

"We're going to meet at the Municipal Building at One Centre Street. One o'clock on April first. Can you do it?"

"Yes, of course. Sonya, best wishes and all that."

"Thank you, Leslie. You can't imagine how happy I am."

Try me, Wetzon thought. *Just try me.*

When her downstairs buzzer sounded, she draped her black cashmere shawl around her and left, much to Izz's distress.

In her lobby a nervous panther named Carlos was pacing. "Come on, come on, Birdie, we'll be late."

"Where's Arthur?"

"In the cab. Let's go." He hustled her into the cab next to Arthur.

"What's with your friend?" she asked, and they both laughed. Carlos ignored them.

The theatre marquee was a rainbow of brilliant hues. Barricades had been set up to keep oglers and photographers back. Celebrities always requested tickets for openings of shows that were going to be hits so that their photographs would be in the next morning papers. There would be plenty of stars out tonight. A mounted policeman sat high on his observation tower talking to a man in an ill-fitting tux and a yarmulke. Bernstein. All dressed up for the opening. Why was he here? Wetzon tried to get his attention but the crowd was thickening.

"Let's get a drink," Arthur suggested, and they headed over to Sardi's.

Spring had arrived three days earlier and not a minute too soon, either. She had not had her terrifying dream since the night she'd left Alton. Don't look for solutions, Sonya had said, and she was trying not to.

They had a quick drink at the bar and then came back to the theatre and took their seats. Around them sat Cher with a dark-haired young man, Mary Tyler Moore, Mike Nichols, and Diane Sawyer. Julie Andrews was two rows away. Sunny Browning had whispered to Wetzon in the lobby that she had placed Wetzon and Arthur next to the MacBeths, otherwise known as Frank Rich and his wife, Alex Witchel. Wetzon was aware from experience that you took care what you said on opening night because you never knew who was sitting next to you or in front of you. Or, for that matter, behind you.

It was dressed-to-kill night. Smith wore a black off-one-shoulder long narrow sheath with a slit to the thigh, and a huge lemony taffeta shawl. She clung exquisitely to Joel Kidde's arm. Behind her was Smitty, looking the handsome boy-man in black tie.

Wetzon's eyes traveled up to the mez, dreading the vision of Dilla's broken body. Just before the houselights began to dim, she caught another glimpse of Bernstein. Then the house went dark and JoJo appeared in black tie and tails. He waited for the applause to die down, then he raised his baton. The overture began.

The show sailed from number to number with at least three showstoppers in the first act. The fancy-dressed audience, which included investors and cast family members among the celebrities, seemed to be having a grand time.

During intermission, Wetzon ran into a radiant Poppy Hornberg in the ladies' room, her face pink and blooming, probably because of her recent stay in Florida. "Isn't it wonderful?" Poppy gushed. She seemed less acerbic, even mellow, and it was flattering.

"You look lovely, Poppy. A hit musical in the family agrees with you."

"Oh, it's not that—some part of it maybe—but I'm—" Poppy lowered her voice, but excitement raised it again. "I'm pregnant."

Good grief, Wetzon thought. Sonya was getting married. Poppy Hornberg was pregnant. What was happening? "I'm so happy for you and Mort. When?"

"We've been trying for years, Leslie. Can you imagine? The end of November."

Back in her seat as the second act curtain went up, Wetzon was distracted. She watched from a far planet until the finale, "Merrily, the M.16," brought the entire audience, except the critics, to their feet. The MacBeths left the theatre, and the ovations continued through the bows. Then JoJo reprised "M.16" as the audience exited.

"Well," Arthur said, with a broad smile, "shall we go backstage?"

"Of course."

They waited until the audience filed out, and went up on stage through the pass door. Well-wishers surged around the creators.

"Congratulations, Mort," Wetzon said. He was beaming in his ruffled shirt and Armani tux.

"Bless you, darling," he said, kissing her, shaking hands with Arthur. "It was wonderful, wasn't it? Quite my best work."

"I meant the baby," Wetzon said, intentionally wicked.

He actually turned red. "Yes, it's swell, isn't it?"

She moved on, and her place was filled by Carol Burnett, wearing the exact same dress as Smith, but with a coral shawl. Arthur had slipped away. Where was he? Twoey and Sunny were talking with Smith and Janet Barnes, Twoey's mother. Alton had left that morning for California, or he would most certainly have been there. The crowd swelled and Wetzon suddenly found herself in the wings, pushed up against the stage manager's desk. She caught sight of Phil briefly—wearing his baseball cap on backward, his face glowing—and she waved to him. Now, she stepped back and bumped something propped up under the desk. Whatever it was was wrapped in a blue canvas fencing bag. It toppled over. She bent to pick it up, grasping it through the canvas. It wasn't a foil; it was a baseball bat.

She straightened, smoothing her dress. Phil was into the Broadway Show League, wasn't he? She recalled the conversation in the Polish Tea Room the day *Hotshot* left town. There was nothing wrong with his being on the baseball team. On the other hand, the bat was a cylindrical-shaped object. And Phil was, as Smith had pointed out, a young man with, perhaps, some gender confusion and no strong father influence.

Bernstein was here somewhere. She could mention it to him.

A voice said, "Is there a problem, girl?"

Wetzon jumped. "Oh, God, Fran, you startled me. I was thinking about . . . Carlos. I haven't been able to get to him."

"Well, come with me," Fran said, taking a firm grip on her elbow. His cane, a metal one, hung loosely on his arm.

"What happened to your beautiful antique cane?"

"It was wormy and starting coming apart, so I put it away." His blue eyes were calculating, as if trying to read her. "I told you to leave it be, girl. You should have listened to me."

Across the crowded stage she saw Arthur and waved frantically. But he didn't see her. The din of voices, all talking at once, was deafening. She tried to pull her elbow from Fran's grasp. Couldn't. He had a powerful grip for an old man who was supposedly dying of cancer. "Let me go, please, Fran." But he was propelling her inexorably away from Carlos.

CHAPTER

Wetzon pulled back and kicked Fran in the instep, hard. He gasped in pain, releasing her. Without a look back, she plunged through the crowd to Carlos.

"Birdie, dear heart!" Carlos had spotted her pawing her way through the noisy crowd. Everyone and his cousin from every area of show business was here tonight, it seemed, because a hit was in the offing. You wouldn't find most of these people at the opening of a bomb. They couldn't even give those tickets away. Of course, there were always some who would come to take pleasure in a competitor's failure. But not tonight.

"Carlos! It was wonderful!" She threw her arms around his neck, smiling all the time, and whispered in his ear, "I think I've found the murder weapon. Phil's bat." If she could swipe that bat, the forensic people would be able to check whether there was any blood on it. . . .

"What? I can't hear you, darling. Tell me at Sardi's. Paul, Joanne, bless you for coming—"

Well, Wetzon thought, superceded by the ravishing Paul Newman. Joanne Woodward, wearing little makeup, still looked at least a decade younger than she had to be.

After Paul and Joanne moved on to congratulate Mort, Wetzon tried once more to tell Carlos.

"Carlos, Phil's bat. Can you get it out of the theatre tonight or hide it somewhere until I can find Bernstein?" Where was he anyway? She would do it herself except she couldn't now in front of everyone, and it would look suspicious if she stayed in the theatre after everyone left. Unless she could hide herself somewhere.

Carlos was looking at her as if she'd lost her mind. He said, "It's baseball season, Birdie."

"I'm serious, Carlos. It could be the murder weapon."

He winked at her. "Maybe I'll humor you just this once." Damn. He wasn't even taking her seriously.

"Wetzon!" Twoey grabbed her from behind and lifted her off the ground. He was glowing.

"I guess you're having a good time." She threw him a grin.

"The best. And I have you to thank. I *owe* you. Come on to Sardi's."

She looked pointedly at Carlos. "Don't *nag,*" he said, making his mouth a kiss.

Sardi's, which sat smack in the middle of the Theatre District on Forty-fourth Street between Broadway and Eighth, was the most convenient place for an opening night party and there was a certain history involved. For more years than most could remember Sardi's had been the most popular Broadway restaurant among show people, not so much for the food, but because Vincent Sardi made theatre people on every level feel welcome. He actually gave discounts to actors and their families, particularly during holidays when actors had to play both a matinee and an evening performance. Everywhere over the banquettes around the room were caricatures of present and laterday Broadway names. It was a hallowed tradition for opening night parties to be set there.

Tonight, Mort had taken over the entire restaurant to celebrate his latest soon-to-be (the critical approval hadn't come in yet so it was not official) smash hit musical. Move over *Phantom,* Wetzon thought.

Wetzon looked around for Bernstein. Maybe no one had bothered telling him there was a party after the show. She smiled. Mort would hate to pay for someone who wore a cheap tux and a yarmulke.

Applause started near the entrance as Mort entered, and she joined in half-heartedly.

"How do you think we'll do with the New York critics?" Twoey asked.

Wetzon saw Mary Cullin, Mort's long-time press agent, draw him aside for a whispered conference. Had the reviews begun to come in so early? She knew a private phone line had been set up so that Mary could get her call from someone at the *Times* the minute Frank Rich turned in his copy. "Great," she told Twoey. "With a few possible minor reservations about the subject matter."

"We can handle that. Can't we, Sunny?" Sunny Browning was wearing black, too. But, then, New York women always opted for black. It was their color.

"This will be a word-of-mouth hit," Sunny said, smiling. "I don't think the *Times* will matter. There was a line at the box office when it opened this morning. Edna told me we wrapped over a hundred thousand in advance sales before lunch."

"Was Edna wearing Dilla's ring, Sunny?"

Sunny's smile faded. "Leave it be, Leslie. This is a celebration."

Twocy was looking at them, confused by their intensity.

"You and Fran. What's the matter with all of you? That damn ring may have been the catalyst for three murders, Sunny."

They stepped back as Cher squeezed by, followed by Phil Donahue and Marlo Thomas. Joel Grey gave Wetzon a high five and a "long time no see, Leslie."

Sunny moved away and started talking to Mort. Twoey looked down at Wetzon. "Hey, congratulations! Where's the happy bridegroom?"

"If you mean Alton, we're giving it a rest."

"What? Come outside for a minute. I can't hear you over the noise." He guided her past a portly gentleman who was blocking the doorway talking to someone outside.

"Move one way or the other," a harassed man at the door said. It was his job to check invitations and names against the party list.

Out on the street behind police barricades the autograph seekers, the oglers and the media people swarmed. Flashbulbs popped. Stretch and normal limos were double-parked, clogging Forty-fourth Street. The sky above the neon marquees was a strange sulfery gray. Cold gusts of wind swept through Shubert Alley, tussling hair, swirling dirt into miniature cyclones. Wetzon's shawl offered little warmth.

"Twoey," she said, "it's not going to happen with me and Alton."

His face became serious. "You're making a mistake."

"Well, then I'm going to have to live with it." She felt herself getting angry. But Twoey was not to blame. She knew he cared for her. Her anger dissipated.

They went back inside and Wetzon found Arthur at the bar getting himself a scotch. "Beer for me," she said.

Aline's arrival on Edward's arm brought another wave of applause. They were followed by JoJo and his wife, a fat mama type with cascading jet black hair and the shadow of a mustache. JoJo always fooled around with someone in the company and he always came back to his wife.

Smith and Joel Kidde. She was fluttering her eyelashes at him. Did men still fall for that shit, Wetzon wondered. Joel had that proprietary male hand on Smith's bare neck. Bye-Bye Hartmann, Wetzon hummed to the tune of "Bye-Bye Blackbird." Joel was just another sleaze and not much better than Hartmann, but at least he would probably not end up in jail.

"Arthur, did you talk to Marissa Peiser?" she asked over the babble.

"Yes. They're going to present the Hartmann case to a Grand Jury. It's not going to be easy, I'm afraid, to keep you out of it, but she's going to try."

"And Smitty?"

"I'm confident that will never go to trial. Where do you suppose Carlos is?"

"I was wondering that myself." A germ of worry had begun to unsettle her mind.

"A martini, extra dry," Aline said. She edged herself toward Wetzon.

"Congratulations, Aline. You've got a sure smash."

"Yes." Aline's dress was a black curtain of bugle beads, and she wore a heavy gold cuff on the wrist where the cast had been.

"Have you seen Carlos?"

"No." She took a greedy swallow of her martini and looked at Wetzon with a touch of animosity. "You thin girls . . ."

"Aline, did you see the ring Edna Terrace is wearing?"

Eyes flat as Tiddley Winks stared back at Wetzon. "Leave it be, Leslie."

If she'd been Smith, she would have said, *Oh, for pitysakes.* "I'll see you later," she told Aline.

"I'll see if I can find Carlos," Arthur said, leaving her at the bar.

No one, Wetzon was thinking, including Carlos, wanted to make waves. Who were they protecting? Phil? The show? The thing to do was go back to the theatre. Strange that the only person here tonight she could trust on this was Smith, and that only because of Smitty.

She saw Sunny huddling with Mort, Kay Lewis in black silk pants and jacket, one of those Velcro casts on her bum ankle, and Nomi in a tuxedo pantsuit. Mary Cullin appeared behind Mort and ushered him into another room. The others followed. The *New York Times* had come in.

No Carlos, no Fran Burke, no Edna, no Phil. She began to sweat. Fran had seen her with the canvas bag. Find Bernstein, that was the ticket. Let him handle it. She made her way slowly upstairs, searching for Bernstein or Carlos. The only thing that remained was for her to go back to the theatre. Down the stairs, she scooted past the bar and out on the icy street. She'd left her shawl somewhere, or maybe Twoey had checked it.

Down Forty-fourth Street toward Eighth Avenue, she could see the lights of the glowing marquees of the Broadhurst, where Chita Rivera was starring in *Kiss of the Spider Woman,* and the Majestic, still the home of *Phantom.* At the St. James the marquee for the Who's *Tommy* was in bright yellows.

The wind was vicious. She stepped back in the doorway of the restaurant, hugging herself, and was bumped from behind by someone coming out. "Smith!"

"Where are you going?" It was an accusation. Smith was holding a drink. In her black velvet Carolina Herrara, she was half-naked, wearing flimsy satin sandals.

"Oh, for godsakes, Smith, go back inside. You'll freeze like that." Wetzon moved out of the way and the wind caught her hair and stood it on end.

Smith stepped out anyway, shivering. "Tell me where you're going."

"Okay. I think I saw the murder weapon at the theatre—out in the open, come to think of it, like *The Purloined Letter.*"

Smith threw the drink into the gutter, but the wind caught the glass, lifting it in a wicked gust, and dashed it to smithereens against the scene shots of *Crazy for You* in the Plexiglass display windows of the Shubert Theatre, across the street. Hands on Wetzon's shoulders, Smith insisted, "What are you saying?"

"The murder weapon has to be Phil Terrace's baseball bat. Carlos was supposed to smuggle it out or hide it somewhere in the theatre, but he's not here. I'm afraid something's happened to him."

"Let's go," Smith said, starting across the street.

"No. Go back to the party. See if you can find Bernstein."

Smith hesitated. Her gold and crystal earrings bobbed in the swirling gusts. "All right, but if you're not back in twenty minutes, I'm coming after you."

Nodding, Wetzon raced across the street into Shubert Alley. "Find Bernstein," she called back to Smith.

The wind whipped through Shubert Alley, riffling Playbills, scattering litter, pommeling her. She stopped at the Booth Theatre to catch her breath and then went on. Scaffolding on the construction across the way creaked and tilted ominously.

The marquee of the Imperial was brilliantly lit. *Hotshot: The Musical* spelled out in thousands of lightbulbs. Wetzon banged on the lobby doors, but the lobby was dark and the doors were locked. Pausing only a second, she ran through the alley to the parking lot, the shortcut to the stage door.

Eerie shadows leaned into her. A street sign—no parking—ripped somehow from its concrete bed, caught in the swirling wind, flew by a few feet from her and smashed into the brick side of the theatre. The wind scooped her up off her feet, screaming, and threw her at the stage door. She slumped to the ground and took stock of the physical damage. Torn hose, sleeve ripped at the shoulder, shoes a yard or so away, at least one of them anyway. She picked herself up and tugged at the stage door. "Damnation!" she screamed. The wind whipped the word from her lips.

A devilish swirl gathered up her shoes before she could get to them. She ran after them—Ferragamos did not come cheap—then gave it up.

When she turned back to the stage door, it was standing open.

C H A P T E R

Nothing lit the backstage entrance. Wetzon groped her way in, leaving the door as it was to let in a faint gleam of light from the parking lot. The door had probably been open all the time.

She stood in the darkness. It was hopeless. What was she to do? Take a breath, she told herself. She did, and yoo-hooed as if she were paying a social call, "Carlos? Are you here?" Her voice fell on dead air. She inched forward, touching the wall. She had done *Fiddler on the Roof* in this theatre. She ought to remember the basic layout.

The stage doorman's desk came up and bumped her. So far, so good. Now all she needed was a flashlight. Experience told her there would be one in the desk or on a hook nearby. She found it hanging from a hook on the side wall next to the desk.

Her feet were freezing on the stone floor. She should have gone back for her shoes. Too late now. She turned on the flashlight; its beam flickered. Dying batteries, damn it. She swept the light around, saw nothing, moved through the corridor into the wings. From there onto the stage. Even in the wan beam she could see the blue canvas case was gone. But where could Carlos be? Not wanting to think about what could have happened, she trained the light down on the orchestra pit and into the house. Standing on the stage of an empty theatre was creepy. She felt as if hidden eyes were watching at her.

"Carlos?" She crossed the stage to the stairway leading to the dressing rooms. She'd have to go up. Maybe Smith had found Bernstein and they were already on their way.

She put her foot on the first step and flashed the light upward. Nothing. "Carlos? Alley alley oxenfree!"

A low moan sent a shiver up her spine. "Carlos?" Where had the sound come from? Not up—down below. But the orchestra pit had been empty.

The costume room. Blast. That was a death trap, a maze. Another soft groan brought her down the stairs to the basement and into the costume room. She panned the dying beam around. Costumes on racks. Cluttered shelves, cartons of fabric scraps, a sewing machine, a dressmaker's dummy. The smell of fabric chemicals. And something else. The distinctive, sweet smell of blood. Someone groaned again close by; slowly, she turned.

The beam of light caught a movement on the floor near one of the costume racks. She scrambled over. Carlos lay on the floor. A nasty gash just above his right eye dripped blood. "Carlos!" She dropped to her knees and the flashlight slipped out of her hands and rolled away. "What have I done?" She lifted his head to her lap and almost immediately felt the blood seeping through her dress.

"Birdie—" He caught her hand feebly. "Get out of here. *Now.*"

"I'm not going to leave you. Who did this? Was it about the bat?" He didn't respond. "Don't die, Carlos. Please don't die." She fumbled for his pulse. Damn it, where was Bernstein?

In the darkness she groped among the costumes above her for something soft to put under Carlos's head. Crawling toward the weak beam of the flashlight, her hands came on a pair of shoes. It took less than a New York minute for her to grasp that someone was wearing them. And that someone had picked up the flashlight.

The light slammed into her eyes, blinding her. "Girl, what are you doing here?" Fran poked her shoulder hard with his cane. A ball of pain shot down her arm. "Didn't I tell you to leave it be?" He sounded furious.

"Fran, please don't hurt me. Carlos is lying over there bleeding. Can you help me get him out of here?"

"Fran?" A woman's voice, saturated in fear, called down the stairs. "Are you down there?"

"Yeah, Edna."

"Is Phil with you?"

"No. He's probably at Sardi's." Fran reached down roughly and pulled Wetzon to her feet. "Get out of here, now."

"But Carlos—"

"I'll see to Carlos."

Trust a murderer, she thought. No way. She'd go up the stairs and his accomplice would whack her with the bat. "Let me help you, please."

He grunted something which she took for acquiescence.

They couldn't lift Carlos's dead weight between them.

"Go get an ambulance," Fran said. His voice had grown weak. She felt his body shudder. The flashlight fell first, then the cane. Finally, Fran. Crashing, like the felling of a great oak.

"Fran, my God, what's wrong?"

He groaned. A fetid odor drove away the sweet smell of blood. Wetzon's stomach heaved. "Girl," Fran rasped, "tell them . . . tell . . . it was me. Lenny . . . my friend . . . dying . . ." His voice faded so she could hardly hear.

"Fran?" She put her ear close to his lips. His chest heaved and twitched.

"The car . . . Bitch had to have . . . tell them I did it. . . . She was something . . . felt she was doing you while she . . . stood there talking to you." He broke off, coughing, and couldn't catch his breath.

Wetzon raised her head and touched Carlos's wrist. Still a pulse there, thank God. "Fran?" He was still wheezing.

Fran caught his breath and began again. "She took it all . . . the key did it . . . nothing left in the box . . ." He grabbed Wetzon's hand in an iron grip. "Tell . . . I did it. . . ."

When he was silent, Wetzon tried to free her hand, but he wouldn't let go. His tortured breathing chilled her. "Fran? Can you hear me? Let me get an ambulance."

"Bum actor . . . left Edna and the kid . . ." A cough rumbled in his throat again, and his voice grew weaker. ". . . always said she didn't take . . . the box . . . believed her, and then . . . wore Celia's ring . . ."

"Fran, why did you kill Sam?" Fran didn't respond. His breathing came in short gasps. Maybe he was dying.

Carlos groaned. "Birdie?"

"Carlos, do you think you can stand?"

"Fran, where are you? What's going on down there?" Edna again.

Wetzon called, "Edna, get an ambulance! Fran is very sick." She heard a scream, followed by running footsteps.

Carlos groped for her, got to his knees. "Shit! I've got one major headache."

"What happened?"

"I don't know. I got the goddam bat and came down here to hide it." She could feel him fumbling around the floor. "Where is it?"

"Fran must have conked you." She picked up the flashlight and spun the beam in circles. "I don't see the bat."

"Fran? Jeesus, Birdie, not Fran."

"I'm afraid so. He confessed." She helped Carlos up and with her arm around his waist, his arm over her shoulder, they climbed the stairs awkwardly as she played the light on each step.

"I don't believe this. Christ, the reviews—did they come in?"

"You would think of reviews at a time like this."

"Birdie, if Fran confessed and only you heard him, is that good enough?"

"I don't know. He's not dead yet, but I think he's dying."

"Yeah, the Big C. of the liver."

When they got upstairs, there was no sign of Edna. "She's getting an ambulance, I hope," Wetzon said.

The shrieking whine of the wind jolted drafts of frigid air through the theatre and tore at the sides of the house. "What's going on out there?"

"It's like a hurricane. Do you want to wait here?"

"Not on your life." They made their way through the stage door and out into the alley, where the wind hammered them, lifted and ripped at their clothing. "If we can get to Shubert Alley, I can leave you near the Booth and get help."

They staggered like two drunks, buffeted by surly gusts of wind, clinging to each other. Oddly, the theatre area had cleared and there was practically no traffic. At the entrance to Shubert Alley, a tall black figure appeared to be waving and screaming at them, but they couldn't hear. They could hardly see for all the debris flying around them.

As they came closer, Wetzon cried, "It's Smith," but the wind ate her words. What was Smith doing jumping around like a crazy person? She was running toward them. As they reached Shubert Alley, she pounced on them, knocking them over. As she fell Wetzon saw something pass within an inch of her head. "What the—Smith, are you crazy?"

Carlos screamed. Wetzon turned and saw Phil, bat raised over his head. Above them the windows of the building seemed to be undulating. The scaffolding was gone. With a mighty boom the windows exploded. Glass shards showered on everyone below. Wetzon covered her head with her hands as great glass panels began to tear off the building. Captured by the fury of the wind, they were buffetted like bits of paper.

Edna came running from Forty-fifth Street. Wetzon saw Phil with his bat raised again, saw the look of astonishment on his face as a saber of glass touched his neck, separating head from body as neatly as the guillotine.

Phil's body, bat in hand, lingered suspended for a moment, then crashed. "Dear God," Wetzon cried. "Dear God."

The wind bounced and tossed Phil's head like a football, and dropped it on the street in front of the souvenir shop. Edna's screams mingled with the wail of the wind and the sounds of sirens. She bent over the head of her son as if she would pick it up. Wetzon jumped to her feet, unaware of the glass cutting her soles. "Edna, no, you mustn't. Come away." Edna's mouth was frozen in a scream.

An ambulance pulled into Shubert Alley, followed by two police cars. Bernstein in his tacky tux and his yarmulke. Slowly and methodically, barricades were put up, closing Forty-fourth and Forty-fifth Street. The wind, as if it knew, began to die down.

Dawn found Wetzon, Carlos, and Smith in an outpatient room at Roosevelt Hospital, drinking coffee with an antsy Bernstein. Carlos's head was bandaged, one eye partially covered. Wetzon's feet were bandaged and in blue hospital booties. A three-inch cut on Smith's shoulder had been sewn and bound in a dressing. They were shell-shocked.

"We got the whole story from Edna Terrace," Bernstein said, pacing. "How her mother died not long after her father. Phil heard stories about Dilla Crosby all his life. When Edna recognized the ring Dilla was wearing as her mother's, he decided to right the wrong and get it back."

"But why kill Sam?" Wetzon asked, even though she thought she knew. She set the coffee container down on the floor. Her whole body ached.

"He mistook him for Mort Hornberg."

Wetzon nodded.

"Christalmighty," Carlos said. "That poor bastard. What a way to go, mistaken for Mort."

"And I guess Phil killed Susan because he wanted the jewelry and the money."

"Yeah. Edna went to see Susan Orkin and begged for it. She was afraid her kid would kill again. And Orkin called the police to get Edna out of there. That did it."

"But why didn't Edna turn Phil in?" Wetzon asked. "She could have saved two lives."

"She's a mother," Smith said softly.

"I'm going to send you people home in one of my cars," Bernstein said. He picked up Wetzon's untouched coffee and drank it. "We're going to have to slip you out the side entrance; the front is crawling with reporters."

"Has anyone seen the *Times?*" Carlos asked plaintively.

"Oh, I forgot. There are some people here to see you." Bernstein opened the door and Arthur and Smitty were there.

"Well?" Carlos demanded.

"Frank Rich approved. 'Superb, albeit somewhat overproduced, which is Mort Hornberg's signature.' I think that's the gist of what he said."

"Ma. I'm so glad you're okay." Smitty hugged his mother. "Can you believe it? Phil did it. He was so nice to me."

Arthur touched Carlos's face gently. "I thought I'd lost you."

"Not by a long shot, darling." Carlos was grinning diabolically. "Birdie, come here, you." They opened their arms and gathered her in.

C H A P T E R

"I thought I'd remind you that I'm not coming into today," Wetzon said into the phone. She looked at her watch. "I'm going to Sonya and Eddie's wedding—"

Izz sat up, watching her.

"I remembered, sweetie pie." Smith sounded calm, even happy. "Smitty and I are having lunch and we're going to the zoo."

"How's it going with him and with you?"

"Fine, just fine, sugar. You see, I've discovered something over these few weeks."

Good God, maybe it *was* the new Smith. Wetzon put her feet into her new patent leather Ferragamos. Her soles were still tender and lightly bandaged. "What have you discovered, if I may ask?" One of these days she was going to have to bite the bullet and tell Smith that B.B. was leaving them.

"Actually, it was something Carlos said to me when we were at Roosevelt Hospital."

"And what was that?" She kissed Izz's wet black nose.

"He said gay men love their mothers best."

"Well, I'm very happy to hear that, Smith." Wetzon hung up laughing. Carlos was too much. And Smith would always be Smith.

Intending to wear her black suit, she changed her mind when she opened her closet. From the back she pulled out her red Gloria Sachs suit, which she'd paid only one hundred fifty dollars for because it had lost its buttons.

She'd marched herself to Tender Buttons and bought antique Victorian glass buttons and made the suit hers.

Dressed, she studied herself in the mirror. The red suit suffused her face with color. The skirt came almost to her ankles. Perfect. Long was back. The jacket was meant to stay buttoned, so no need to wear a blouse underneath.

Izz whined and hung her head.

"You are so spoiled." Wetzon shook her finger at the little dog and Izz licked it lovingly. "I'll be back. I promise."

In honor of April Fool's Day and Sonya's wedding, Wetzon treated herself to a cab downtown. Spring was here. The magnolia and dogwood trees blossomed along streets and in parks. Everything, everywhere, was abudding. Breathing in the balmy air, Wetzon thought, *God is in his heaven and all's right in the world.*

And she was foot-loose and fancy-free, in her red suit and going to Sonya's wedding.

Alton had finally stopped calling her every day. Six months, she'd asked him for. She needed six months to sort everything out, and he'd reluctantly agreed.

The cabdriver's name was Mohammad. He was bronze-skinned and wore an embroidered pillbox on his head. There were a lot of Mohammads driving cabs now in New York. "That's a nice dress," he said, eyeing her in the rear-view mirror as they rode down the FDR Drive.

"Thank you. I'm going to a friend's wedding."

He stopped across from the Municipal Building with its majestic columns and the U.S. and New York flags waving languidly in the soft spring breeze. "Maybe your friend is Muslim," he said.

"I don't think so." She handed him twenty-five dollars and told him to keep the change.

He handed her a pamphlet. "Maybe your friend would like to read this, or maybe it is for you."

It was an introduction to the Koran. She thanked him profusely and got out of the cab, making sure Mohammed was out of sight before she dumped the pamphlet in the trash basket.

The sun was overhead now, beaming down on the traffic gridlock in front of the massive building. Office workers sat in the park across the way eating their lunches amid the emissions from thousands of cars.

Wetzon felt a strong sense of history when she entered the old building and followed the signs in English and Spanish to the Marriage Chapel, across the floor of tiny tiles and up a circuitous marble staircase. She was walking in the footsteps of so many who had gone before.

It was exactly one o'clock when she opened the door to Room 257, the Marriage Chapel waiting room. At first all she saw was a garden of wedding dresses, most of them white, but one was yellow, and another ecru. The faces of the people sitting in auditorium rows were New York: white, black, yellow, red and brown.

"Leslie!" Sonya sat in the second row wearing a mauve silk shantung suit. In her hand was a nosegay of pink and white roses. She looked luminous. O'Melvany wore a white rose on his lapel and he looked nervous in his dark blue suit. He stood as Wetzon approached.

"Paredes party," the clerk, a weary-looking woman with mousy hair, called. A group rose, four adults and two little girls. The women and the girls carried fat bouquets of flowers, the men wore boutonnieres. The long train of the wedding gown was held barely above the floor by the little girls. They were directed into a room behind the clerk.

"You guys look great," Wetzon said, touching their hands.

"We're so glad you could come," Sonya said, kissing her.

O'Melvany looked at his watch and back at the door. He was really nervous.

"I'm so glad you asked me. Do you want me to hold the ring, Eddie?"

"Uh . . . excuse me a minute." O'Melvany left the room.

"I guess he's nervous." Wetzon grinned at Sonya. "I guess this is harder on them than us." *Speak for yourself,* she thought.

The Paredes party burst excitedly into the room, heading for the door, just as O'Melvany returned.

"O'Melvany party," the clerk said in a bored voice.

Sonya and Wetzon rose. Eddie was threading his way through the boisterous Paredes celebrants. "Let's go on in," Sonya said, taking Wetzon's arm. "Eddie will find us."

The Marriage Chapel was a triangular-shaped room with white moiré wallpaper and blue carpeting. Not much to look at. The service would be performed on a one-step-up platform. A middle-aged man whose back hair was combed forward over his baldness motioned them in. He was probably a justice of the peace or something like that. He greeted Sonya with, "You're the bride?" When she nodded, he said, "If you will stand here." He looked beyond them to the doorway. "Which is the groom?"

Which is the groom? Wetzon turned. She saw O'Melvany first. Her heart thudded. Silvestri was right behind O'Melvany. A much thinner Silvestri, also in a dark blue suit.

O'Melvany stood next to Sonya and took her hand. Silvestri stopped just inside the doorway. He looked as if he'd been punched.

"Come in, young man," the justice said. "Do you have the ring?"

Silvestri patted his pocket automatically, but his eyes never left Wetzon. He stood next to O'Melvany, and the service began.

Wetzon felt faint. They had been set up.

"Do you . . ." filtered through her consciousness. And "Will you . . ." She wasn't handling this well at all. "Yes, I will," someone said. She saw Silvestri's hand shake as he handed O'Melvany the ring. O'Melvany slipped it on Sonya's finger. Silvestri was standing only two people away and she could feel his pain as if it were her own. It *was* her own.

". . . husband and wife," the justice said.

O'Melvany was kissing Sonya, Sonya was kissing Silvestri, O'Melvany kissed Wetzon.

On the street in front of the building, O'Melvany said, "Come on, you two, we have plans for a little trip."

"I don't—" Wetzon said.

"No, I—" Silvestri said.

"We won't take no for an answer. This is our day." O'Melvany hailed a cab and helped Wetzon and Sonya in, got in himself and closed the door. Silvestri sat in the front with the driver.

Wetzon watched the back of his stiff neck turn red and wanted to touch him, but was glad for the protective glass between them.

"Leslie," Sonya whispered.

"I'll never forgive you for this," Wetzon responded.

"Oh, come off it, you two," O'Melvany said. "Take us to the ferry," he told the driver.

Sonya smiled and held O'Melvany's hand.

"The ferry? The Staten Island Ferry?" Wetzon hadn't been on the ferry since her first year in New York.

The Staten Island Ferry terminal lay at the foot of Broadway below Battery Park. The ferry was just loading when they got there. People streamed onto the boat, whose name was *AL. AL*, Wetzon thought. A ferry named AL? And then she saw that the life preservers were all marked *American Legion.*

She walked out on the front deck. The metal awning overhead held more life preservers. A warm breeze ruffled her hair as a lover might. She bit her lip to hold back the tears. How had she ever thought she could live without him? The realization made her numb.

The sky was an ingenuous blue with little white clouds. Essence of salt water and seaweed brought memories of the Jersey shore where she'd grown up. Below her the water was flecked with foam. Manhattan receded slowly. To her right, the Stature of Liberty stood majestic in New York Harbor. The ferry's engine hummed as the boat swept across the river. Tourists called out to one another and took pictures; a child in a stroller cried.

"Are you all right?" Sonya asked.

"Not really, but I'll manage."

"I'm sorry. Eddie thought . . . I thought—" Sonya looked sad.

"S'okay. This is your day. Be happy."

Eddie kissed her on the forehead and they left, holding hands.

After a while she walked inside. An old Greek shoeshine man with an ancient kit was singsonging, "Shine 'em, shine 'em."

She took the center staircase up to the bridge deck and went outside. There were fewer people here. She leaned against the railing staring down into the churning water. Somewhere below someone played a guitar and sang a Beatles song. She thought, *I'm going to die,* and clutched the wire of the railing.

"Where's your ring?" His shoulder touched hers.

She didn't look at him. She couldn't. "I gave it back."

"Why?" He slipped his hand under the jacket of her suit and the skin on her bare back tingled. She felt herself melting into him.

"Oh, God, Silvestri, what are you doing to me?"

"I love you, Les."

She let that settle on her for a while. His hand burned her skin. When they made the turnaround on Staten Island, he paid her fare, not letting go of her hand. Ahead of them, Sonya turned and smiled.

They faced Manhattan together on the bridge deck. Lower Manhattan sat in miniature on the platter of landfill, skimming the Bay.

" 'We were very tired, we were very merry . . .' " Wetzon's eyes teared and she let them.

" '—we had gone back and forth all night on the ferry . . .' " Silvestri finished the Millay quote for her and looked pleased with himself.

"What's going to happen to us, Silvestri?" She looked up at him as the ferry nudged into the slip. His eyes were a brilliant turquoise. She raised her face to his, and he kissed her.

The ferry quavered for a moment before it rested.

"No promises, Les. Let's just play it one day at a time."

She pushed him away and stood facing him, hands on hips. "Godammit, Silvestri. I bet you think you're the love of my life."

He brushed the strands of hair from her eyes. His laugh was pure joy. "Yup," he said.